Ravi's world has shattered. Cayenne's dark secrets have finally come to light, and a mysterious enemy threatens to dismantle The Trust from within. Haunted by betrayal, Ravi must confront the demons of his past while battling for the future of The Trust, the fate of the world, and his own heart. But can something so broken ever truly be mended?

BUILT FROM ASHES

ASHES

TRUST TRILOGY, BOOK THREE

FOX BECKMAN

A NineStar Press Publication
www.ninestarpress.com

Built from Ashes

First Edition, April 2024

ISBN: 978-1-64890-756-2

Also available in eBook, ISBN: 978-1-64890-755-5

CONTENT WARNING:
This book contains sexually explicit content, which may only be suitable for mature readers. Depictions of guns, stalking, emotional abuse, graphic violence, and death.

Chapter One

"I DO NOT like this," Val mutters for the third time, her voice low.

"Me neither," Ravi sighs, his eye not wavering from the scope. The rifle is a cool, sturdy presence under his hands. Something he can rely on. Rare as it is for him to roll out his sniper skillset on hunts, he's strangely nostalgic for his time in Israel. The simplicity of training and nothing else. Being so worn out each day he could slip into a deep, dreamless slumber.

Val rumbles a little under her breath like a building storm. Normally the angel is perfectly content to spend any time with Ravi in companionable silence—one of his favorite things about her—but he agrees the situation is less than ideal.

The pair perch on the second story of an abandoned big-box department store, a building slated for demolition in two months' time. Scouting hours ahead of the rendezvous, they'd found this vantage point hidden by a defunct escalator with a clean line of sight down to the meeting place. The perfect position to keep an eagle eye on the proceedings.

It's harder than Ravi expected it would be, staying on the sidelines while Harry and Nate are up close and personal with so many potential enemies. Even with Harry's Chosen invulnerability and her recent training regimen, she's still not ready for this kind of threat on her own. But as the most personable members of the team, she and Nate are the best options. One peek at Val's eyes and it's obvious she's not entirely human, and if this information broker is as savvy as Nate's vampire contact claims he is, the team can't afford to take chances.

Through the scope Ravi watches the broker, a gentleman of Filipino descent approaching middle age and fighting it tooth and claw. Clothes too flashy, recent hair plugs, rings on every finger. The man gesticulates through a joke, and Harry throws her head back to laugh with him. Nate joins in, grinning wide. He's leaned up against the broker's desk, dragged into the middle of the dead mall in a parody of legitimate office space. Several men surround the trio, big slabs of hired muscle in identical plain gray suits and sunglasses.

The broker's laughter fades as he eyes Harry with speculation. He falls silent, tapping a finger on the desk, one of his rings glimmering.

Something's off; the guy has twigged. Ravi lines up a shot, breaths slow and measured. Kneeling beside him, Val glances at him and tenses. Her massive maul materializes into her hands.

Nate throws a nervous glance up at their sniper nest and thumbs his nose.

That's the signal. In the space between seconds, Val disappears from Ravi's side, a faint rush of displaced air the only sign she had ever been there.

Two of the goons are lined up right next to each other.

Perfect.

Ravi exhales and squeezes the trigger.

The first goon's head shatters. Gray clay shards rain down as the golem collapses to the ground, limbs cracking sharply on impact. The angle on the second guard isn't quite as clean, and the round exits through the cheek instead of dead center. That would have done the job on something with a brain, but the magical paper within the golem's skull is a much trickier target.

However, Val appears in the next instant, and her maul finishes what Ravi's bullet started, smashing the golem straight down to the chest like a pottery vase. Nate has already jumped out of range of the other goons, making way for the many blades of Harry's urumi to snake out and take off a golem's hand in two clean slices.

The broker swears and kicks away from the desk, twisting one of his rings. A shield of thickened air swirls in a wide arc in front of him, some sort of protection enchantment. His eyes dart from the trajectory of Ravi's unexpected bullet to the ash-haired Amazon who teleported in front of him wielding a two-handed hammer as long as he is tall.

Having calmly locked another round into place, Ravi slides back the bolt and focuses on Harry's one-handed foe. The shot clips a neat hole through the golem's sunglasses, and the back of its bald head shatters. It drops like a puppet with its strings cut. Ravi tries not to smirk.

Two golems flank Val and close in, grappling with the haft of her maul, attempting to pull it from her grasp. She reels them both in and slams her forehead into one. The golem staggers, a wide crack splintering its face. Val grins and rams her fist into the crack. When she pulls it out, she's gripping a long strip of paper. The golem falls lifelessly at her feet, and she turns her attention to the next.

Meanwhile, Harry holds her own, dodging a punch from a big clay fist and keeping her distance. All her dedicated training shows. She yanks one to the ground with the urumi and crunches her boot down on its head.

Nate sidles back into view, having taken care of the most important part of the plan, and slipped away to message Constance as soon as the fight started. To Ravi's consternation, Nate has a piece of scavenged rebar he obviously intends to use as an improvised weapon. That hadn't been part of the plan. The professor dives in behind an enemy wheeling on Val and takes a baseball-like swing, cracking the golem across the back of the neck. Chips of clay go flying. The golem spins around and swipes at Nate. He ducks out of the way, but just barely.

Always diving into danger, this guy. Ravi shifts position, sliding back the bolt and taking careful aim as the golem rears a fist back, Nate perfectly positioned to take the full brunt of the hit.

Blinking through the shattered pieces of clay, Nate tosses Ravi a grateful salute with a cheerful grin, as the headless body falls at his feet. Ravi shakes his head while racking in another shell.

The information broker looks to have had enough, deciding that it's well worth abandoning his bodyguards to make a getaway. Keeping his magical shield in front of him, he starts backing away toward the exit.

An animal growl rises, loud enough that Ravi can hear it up on the second floor even over the scuffle of battle and the crash of breaking clay. The broker startles and begins to turn around when a huge brindled wolf tackles him from behind.

He hits the concrete with a yelp, his magical shield dissolving. Gently but firmly, the wolf sets white fangs against the back of his neck. The broker's hands twitch, slyly trying to activate another magic ring, until Ravi's next shot digs up a chunk of the floor next to his head. After a muffled curse the man spreads his hands out on the ground, wide and harmless.

The team smashes through the remaining golem bodyguards in short order. Ravi makes his way down the escalator with his rifle slung over his back. There are only a couple of enemies left near the perimeter. He puts on two knuckledusters, recent acquisitions to his arsenal, one shining silver and one dark iron. A pair of efficient combo hooks take care of the last two golems. Ravi brushes clay dust off his lapels and joins the team, slipping the knuckles back into the specialized pocket on his shoulder holster opposite his 9mm.

Still wolf-bound, the broker lays belly down. Val crouches to pluck the rings off his unresisting fingers.

"You shall get these back if you cooperate," she says

serenely. "This is not a theft."

"Constance gets a look at them first," Ravi insists. "Any darker enchantments are forfeit."

The broker's Savannah accent is thin and quavering. "Take whatever you want, just maybe get this wolf off me?"

Harry sits on the edge of the man's desk, urumi draped casually across her knees. "Mr. Guinto. Calvin. Cal. Can I call you Cal? Look, like we said before you got all Mister Veiled Threats, we only want some info. We're even willing to pay for it. And the only thing we ask in return is a little discretion."

The broker laughs weakly. "Hey, I am the *soul* of discretion. You don't get to live as long as I do in this line of work without knowing when to keep secrets."

"And when to spill them," Ravi counters, crossing his arms.

"Haha, yes, exactly." Calvin swallows. "So, get this wolf off me, and we can talk."

Harry nods at the wolf. "What do you think, doll? This is your show."

The wolf releases the broker's neck from her jaws. He flips onto his back and starts scooting away, only gaining a few inches before the wolf suddenly becomes a smiling, braided brunette in a brightly patterned bohemian dress straddling his lap.

With a concerned tut, Constance pats the man's cheek. "Terribly sorry about that, my good fellow. I did not draw blood, did I?"

"Uh… I'm fine?"

Constance helps him up and guides him back to his chair, sweeping away a clay foot to clear a space for him to sit. "I am quite sorry about all this fuss, good sir. You see, I have been seeking information on a particular demon for quite some time, but to no avail. Perhaps you can help me? I'd be most grateful."

Nate chuckles, leaning in toward Ravi. "You know what they say about sticks and carrots," he mutters, pitching his voice low for Ravi's ears alone.

Placing the idiom takes Ravi a second, but when he does, he huffs in amusement. Constance is all carrot. Or more accurately, a stick cunningly carved and painted to look like a carrot.

Calvin Guinto sits back at his desk, gathering his dignity around him. He adjusts his clothing and folds his hands, frowning briefly at his bare fingers. He aims up a tight, nervous smile. "Happy to help, folks." Harry still perches on his desk, and he eyes her with new appreciation. "So, you *are* the Chosen, huh? Rumor has it there's another one running around now. You're paler than I expected. Normally you're supposed to all be a little more, uh, *tanned*." He jerks a thumb toward Ravi, as if he's a perfect melanistic example.

"Not here for me, Cal." Harry pushes to her feet, coiled urumi shrinking down into a silvery coin she slips into her pocket.

"Right! So, wolf lady, tell me about this demon."

As if gathering her thoughts, Constance presses her palms together in front of her lips and closes her eyes. When she speaks, it's with a lyrical rhythm, as if telling a fairy tale.

"Long ago, there was a wicked man who summoned a demon to serve his whims. Of course, things didn't go as this man had planned, and the cunning demon did slay him as soon as it learned how best to trick him.

"This demon was then set free in the world, to hunt as it pleased. It took the form of a comely fellow, to lure its victims, and set about wreaking much mayhem and havoc in subtle, nefarious ways. Never outright, but in secret, causing chaos from the shadows. And all the while, he would kill folk, horrifically, supping upon youth and innocence as if it were a fine wine.

"I hunted him for many a moon. A slippery quarry, aye, but Constance Shaw can be slippery too." Constance favors the broker with a wink. "We played quite a game of cat and mouse until I enlisted the help of the very best of my many cousins. Able was a fine and virtuous man, well-versed with the blade. Together we cornered the demon, had him trapped and desperate as a fox beset by hounds."

Her face falling with sorrow, Constance pulls a thick plait over her shoulder and strokes it. "But cunning and vile this demon was, and aye, ruthless. Once I beheld my bloodied cousin fallen before me, I...I cast a banishment that went awry, and *perhaps* sundered time just a *little.* And that demon is here, now, in this city, killing again."

Ravi knows the look in her eyes well: guilt. Guilt in knowing you've unleashed something you can't take back. Set something terrible in motion despite your best intentions.

Yeah, he knows that look.

Calvin sits back and puffs out his cheeks. "Wow, good story. Okay, that's something to go on. Uh...when did this happen?"

"In the year of our Lord 1215," Constance says.

He stares at her.

Nate makes a sympathetic noise in his throat. "Yeah, she's from medieval times. We know it's a lot."

"Please, I'm an info broker in the occult black market. I've seen way weirder shit. It's just... That *exact* year—1215?"

"Aye."

The broker leans as far back in his chair as he can

manage. "Fuck me *running*. You're talking about Hartnell?"

It's as if Constance has grabbed a live wire. Her cheeks redden, and even her hair seems to frizzle slightly. "Aye! Know ye the churl's name?"

"This… You can't… Are you all fucking with me right now?" The broker glances around in disbelief.

Palms flat on the desk, Constance leans forward with an intensity she rarely shows. "You know of him? Speak, man."

"Know of him? *Know of him*? Know the Heart's Last Knell? A fucking *Demon Prince?* That's the guy we're talking about?"

Everyone exchanges blank looks.

"He's the what now?" asks Harry.

Calvin throws up his hands. "Are you kidding me? Hartnell the Lost Prince? Who without warning or reason abandoned his entire underworld demesne, leaving all that power unclaimed and sparking a full-blown war in the hells?"

"There has long been a war in Hell," Val says dismissively, which is certainly news to Ravi.

"There *has*?" Nate asks, bewildered.

Val's shoulders twitch in what might be a stoic shrug. "Demons are avaricious, power-hungry things. Beings of chaos that war amongst themselves as readily as they seek to cause devastation in this plane."

"Okay, sure, but geez, Val," Harry says, ruffling her dark hair. "A massive war in Hell seems like a pretty big deal. Why didn't you ever mention it?"

"Nobody asked."

"Val, buddy, we are going to have a chat about you *volunteering* information."

The best way Ravi's found to communicate with Val is to ask her a direct question. "How long has there been a war in the hells?"

"Eight hundred and one years."

"So…since 1215."

Constance takes a step back. "I can'st… I cannot have banished a demon *prince*. Such a thing is well beyond my ken."

"Apparently not." Calvin looks Constance up and down as if hugely impressed.

"Tell us how to kill it," Ravi barks.

"Right, right. Well, there's the normal anti-demon stuff, to smoke them out of disguise. Holy water makes 'em sizzle a bit but not much more, and they don't like prayer, though your mileage may vary depending on the demon. I'm sure y'all know there's like a zillion different types of demons. Some you can kill with mundane means. But the usual way folks deal with them is making an old-fashioned demon trap with salt and blood to summon and banish them back to the hells. I'm sure the sorceress supreme here knows how."

Nate holds up a finger with a polite cough. "Slight divergence, but is it capital-h Hell, or the hells, plural? Which is correct?"

Harry snorts. "Writing a paper, Doc?"

"*Duh*, Harry, of course I am, are you kidding? I'm going to write a *textbook* with all the stuff I've learned kicking with you guys."

"Both are correct," Calvin says. "It's semantics. A religious distinction."

"We call it Naraka," Ravi offers with a shrug. "Different hells that wicked souls are temporarily sent to before punarjanma. Rebirth."

Val states, "No one human belief is a full and accurate portrayal of the overlapping and interwoven tapestry of the nature of the unseen universe. There. That is volunteered information."

"Thanks, Val," Harry says dryly.

Calvin shakes his head. "But look, demon princes are tough. They're not run-of-the-mill imps and devils and such. They're smarter, powerful, harder to take down. The princes of hell all have their own weaknesses that they keep secret, even from each other. That might be a way to go, if I may offer a helpful suggestion. Might be able to enlist another demon to assist. The enemy of my enemy, kind of thing."

Ravi snorts, looking to Constance, a little surprised and alarmed that instead of outright refusing, she looks like she's giving the suggestion careful consideration.

"Have ye nothing more? Where to find him, mayhaps?"

"Look, I just learned this last minute that this demon prince is still alive and kicking, much less here in my neck of the woods. So no, I don't know where you can find him. But!" Calvin perks up, looking brightly from face to face. "It's helpful to know he's a prince, right? Lots of literature written about them. I don't specialize in that stuff myself, but it's out there."

"One research binge coming up," Nate says before Harry can even give him a significant glance.

"Of course," the broker continues, "word is that the Chosen One can kill anything. Even a demon prince."

Harry just gives Calvin a polite smile. She's got a hell of a poker face.

"If you do find anything," Calvin says, "and you need to get your hands on something not easily procured, I'm your guy. Not just info, I can get you all *kinds* of things; I've got the magic touch." He snaps his fingers, then pauses for a beat. Everyone stares in bemusement. Frowning, he looks down at his bare fingers. "Shucks, I forgot. That was supposed to make sparkles. Well, if that's all…"

"Not quite, Cal. One more thing." Harry motions Constance aside and nods to Ravi.

Ravi takes a deep breath. "Know anything about chronomages?"

Calvin slumps, crestfallen. "Brother, I could way easier get you a unicorn. Do you want a unicorn? They're annoying assholes, but I can get you one."

"Chronomages."

The broker sighs. "They're rarer than seers. Rarer than telepaths, or somamancers, or almost any wild magic talent out there. The available information is sketchy *at best*. Legends say there can only be one chronomancer on earth at a time, and they can only go so far back and forth in the timeline or else they bump into each other and unmake reality. Either that, or lots of them *do* get born, but they don't survive their powers developing. They pop themselves into a wall that didn't used to be there in the past, or whatever."

Interesting, but not particularly useful. "Any info about specific ones?"

Calvin rocks his hand from side to side. "Well, there used to be rumors. Old rumors."

"How old?"

"Roaring twenties, I'd say. Rumor had it there was this one guy who employed a chronomancer. He was some kind of big-shot crime boss in Paris. Not mafia or anything. Unaffiliated. They used to say if you crossed him, you'd be erased from existence." Calvin twiddles his fingers, adopting a spooky tone.

"Sounds like a bogeyman story," Nate says.

"Yeah, well, that's pretty much all there is about chronomages. The rumors could be true, but who knows for sure. Not me, man, and I know as much as anyone. Well…" The broker stops, screwing up his face in thought.

"What?" Ravi takes a step forward, unable to check his impatience.

"There's this one lady who claims she worked for that bogeyman guy. She's living in New York these days. I'll get you her address. Maybe she'll help you." He rifles through a thin drawer for some paper and starts scribbling.

Ravi gives the broker a narrow look. "Off the top of your head, you just happen to remember the address of some little old lady in at least her nineties?"

"Firstly, I remember everything, friend." Calvin taps his temple. "Steel trap. Secondly, she's not a little old lady. She's a vamp." He finishes writing with a flourish and hands the paper to Ravi. The address is in Manhattan, which makes things easy. There's a Trust branch in

Manhattan, and Ravi has been there before. "That's all I got. Y'all are tough customers, and I mean that literally. Busting up all my expensive golems and asking for two impossible things."

"At least we pay well, right, Cal?" Harry tips a handful of loose diamonds onto the desk.

His eyes go as wide as saucers.

Constance sets the broker's rings one by one along the far edge of the desk. "Almost all of these appear to be harmless enough. Mostly for defense and spectacle, though this one is a nasty bit of work." She holds up an understated ring of simple titanium. "A black bit of magic to permanently erase memories, I'd wager." She spins the ring in two opposite directions along some hidden seam. "Hark, it can be set for different durations. That's quite clever."

Calvin gestures at Ravi and whines, "Ah, c'mon, this guy's walking around with a *sniper rifle*. I can't have one little non-lethal offense spell in case of emergencies?"

"Get a nice, clean, evocation enchantment instead," Constance suggests, again wearing her usual chipper demeanor. "Fair enough to shoot lightning or some such in self-defense. This can sunder memories. Mind control magics are a perversion of free will. Most unsavory."

Ravi glares sidelong at the broker. "Hmm. Maybe we should take him in after all."

Calvin laughs brashly. *"Take me in*? What are you, the magic polic—" His humor drains away, along with all the blood in his face. "Oh fuck. You're Trust." He glances past Ravi to Harry. "So that old nugget of wisdom is true, huh? The Trust and the Chosen One, a package deal kind of thing?"

"Discretion, Cal," Harry reminds him with a wink.

"Do I *look* suicidal? I'm a helping helper, me. Plus, hey, fistful of diamonds. Consider my lips sealed." Calvin gazes yearningly at his rings but doesn't make a move toward them. "Any chance you need a CI? That a thing you Trusties do, work with us seedy underbelly types on the down-low? I'm way more useful out here than in your wizard prison, or whatever you have for people like me."

Harry quirks a brow at Ravi. He sighs, swallowing a grumble. "We can talk."

Chapter Two

A BULGING ACCORDION folder under his arm, Ravi lopes toward the front entrance of Constance's magic shop. Before he reaches the door, it swings open with a pleasant chiming of bells, and out barrels a girl with her hair up in twin afro puffs, dragging her parents behind her.

"It's Ravi!" she squeals and skips up to him, then stops and blushes straight up to her hair roots.

Twelve is a weird age. "Hey, Lucy." He smiles. Ravi shares a friendly nod with Fiona and Ethan, Lucy's parents. "How was the lesson today?"

"I learned how to make Griswold blue! And I gave him cool ears."

"And what else, Lucinda?" her father reminds her wearily. Having a kid who can rearrange bodies must be a harrowing ordeal for a parent, especially if that kid is approaching her teen years all too soon.

"I learned about personal responsibility," Lucy says as if by rote, rolling her eyes.

"That's good," Ravi says. "Very important."

Lucy frowns a little. "It is?"

"Of course."

"Oh," Lucy says thoughtfully.

Fiona clucks her tongue. "Typical. Won't hear a word of it from us, but anything *you* or *Dr. Corbin* say…"

Ethan leans toward Ravi with a stage whisper, "She's hitting her boy-crazy phase."

"*Dad,*" Lucy hisses, appalled. Despite her mortification, Lucy leans into her parents' hands as they rest on her shoulders, softening the tease, the gesture easy and automatic. The casual intimacy of a real family.

Just witnessing it makes Ravi feel like an intruder, an unwelcome guest. He looks away, feigning sudden interest in the folder he's carrying. "Good to see you three. I need to get this to Constance."

Ethan nods courteously. "Good to see you too. How have you been? Had some late nights?" A polite way of saying that Ravi looks like shit. The dark smudges under his eyes won't go away. If he could just get some sleep; he can't even remember the last time he got more than a couple of consecutive hours.

"I'm fine," he says.

Fiona checks her phone. "We've got to run too. If you see Harry, tell her to call! We're overdue for a brunch."

"Will do."

They say their goodbyes and Ravi watches after them for a few minutes, scanning the street for hidden threats or ambushes before heading into the store.

Griswold jumps out stiff-legged from behind the counter. "Aha, 'tis thee, witch-hunter! A fine day to thee." Constance spares a glance up from a massive book. She tosses him a quick wave and a smile before sinking back into her reading, transcribing notes and making small sketches in her grimoire.

"Hey, Griz." The cat isn't blue, so Lucy must have turned him back, but he does now sport long tufted ears, like a little lynx. "Nice ears."

"*Quite* fine, are they not?" Griswold struts a bit, then sits atop a table to lick his paw. Ravi keeps a polite distance, so he won't be set off sneezing and joins Constance at the counter.

"I don't have any matches," he tells her with slight smile.

She snorts, then pulls her nose out of the thick tome and rubs vigorously at her eyes. "Alas, thou couldst have alit a bonfire under mine canions to improve mine addlepation." She makes a face and shuts the book in a swirl of dust, her diction catching up on a few centuries worth of grammar. "Some of these demon accounts are most tedious, to my eyes. I thought I might make some headway after young Lucy's somamancy lesson, but in truth, I welcome the interruption. Need you anything?"

"Actually, I've brought something for you." Ravi slaps the folder down in front of her.

Constance opens it. "What is all this?"

"Everything The Trust has on demon princes. Cross-referenced with any mention of the name Hartnell, or the Heart's Last Knell. Sorry, there isn't more."

Constance's face brightens with delight. "Your aunt has been agreeable, then!"

"I wouldn't go that far," Ravi mutters. "I'm not going to get real access to intel at least until the…until the engagement is official." He clears his throat, fixing his attention on the plethora of mushrooms growing in bell jars on the back wall. One of them looks new, glowing faintly green.

Constance nods, attention divided as she skims through a few reports. "This is enormously helpful, Ravi. Between this and what Nathan will be able to dredge from folklore, that flensing cur shan't evade us for long." She sets the folder aside. "Tea?"

He checks his watch, but he's got nothing pressing the rest of the day aside from hitting the boxing gym much later. "Coffee?"

She wrinkles her nose a little, leading him away from the counter. Griswold jumps up to a nearby shelf and helpfully bats the store's sign to Closed. "I have chicory. 'Tis much the same."

"Sacrilege."

A peal of merry laughter. "I only jest. Harry has left a French press and fresh grounds." One of the back rooms has been set up as some kind of mix of classroom and fortune teller's tent. Constance pulls aside a star-strewn tapestry, revealing a small kitchenette. She sets the water to boil. "Just coffee? I have some lovely herbs that may ease thy spirit."

Ravi arches a brow. "By herbs, do you mean drugs?"

She clicks her tongue. "I mean *medicine*, whatever it is named in this bizarre age."

He can't blame her for trying. She's a healer by nature, with a different view on mind-altering substances. "Just the coffee, thanks."

"So," she says once they are seated at the table, drinks in hand. The steam from her tea smells like mushrooms roasting on a campfire. "I have told Robert Hernandez to remove himself from service. Now that we know my nemesis is no mere lesser demon, it is no longer safe for him to stalk the demon's steps."

"Yeah, I was going to ask. He checked in last week. Mentioned the trail had run cold." They'd had a brief meet-up wherein Robert had mostly regaled Ravi with his more amusing stories on the Boston police force in the '70s and '80s. Every time Robert asked about Ravi, he'd successfully managed to divert the conversation away from himself.

"Aye." Constance sips her pungent tea. "It might behoove us to contact James. We know he resides in the future, but not when or where. I had thought to maybe carve a huge granite edifice? That should last a fair while, yes?"

"You want to, what? Etch a note into a mountain that says *call me*?"

She makes a face. "Well, do you have any better ideas? How *does* one reliably contact a..." She minces warily through her question, as if she half-expects Ravi to fall apart at the mere mention of time travel. "—a time traveler?"

He shrugs with a barren little smile. "No idea. I'm just grateful no time travelers have tried to contact *me*. Thanks again for that threshold spell."

After the eternally long, immeasurably bad day a month ago in August, Constance had magically shored up defenses on everyone's place of residence. Now no one can find them without an express invitation. The downside was everyone had to get a PO Box for all their mail and deliveries, but hey, no Jehovah's Witnesses either.

"Ravi. You *are* well, are you not?"

"I'm fine."

Her fingertips ring against the ceramic mug. "It is all right to not be fine."

Ravi can feel annoyance creasing his forehead as he takes a drink of his coffee, welcoming the jolt of caffeine. "Are *you* fine?"

Constance meets his gaze and says plainly, "I am awash with remorse that I have unleashed a powerful evil into this world. Had not acted as I had, Hartnell would have long since been defeated by a more skilled hunter than I and sent back to Hell. This day and age would be safe from him, and those he has slain would still be alive." She picks up her mug and blows across it. "But alas, I cannot undo it. All I can do is move forward."

"We're going to find him, Constance. We're going to get him."

Constance smiles warmly and pats Ravi's hand. "Well said. Thou'rt stalwart."

In token protest, he shakes his head, dropping his gaze to a deck of cards on the table. Idly he picks it up and flips over the first couple of cards. "Is this tarot?"

"'Tis! There was no such thing in my time, but customers have been offering to pay me for readings, so I have learned. Like any other method of divination, it is mostly psychology and the subconscious working in tandem through the means of archetypal representations." When he glances up at her, she scrunches her nose into a cute grin. "I mean, oh la, good sir! I am but a simple peasant girl, thine world is strange and confusing to mine primitive eyes, and so on and such forth."

A laugh startles out of Ravi like a bird from the brush. "Right." He drains his coffee, debating whether another cup would even help his exhaustion. "I know you've got a lot on your plate, but I managed to get one more thing from my aunt I was hoping you could help with." He passes her a folded sheet of paper from his jacket pocket. "This is a list of all the magical artifacts that Cayenne stole from a Trust family. When you have time, could you look it over?"

Just saying their name brings a stab of guilt and remorse, and beneath, an undercurrent of longing that carries with it even more guilt. But knowing what powerful enchantments Cayenne has access to will be a big help. No reason to have an info broker in their pocket if the man can't alert them if certain artifacts pass through the black market. Maybe it'll provide a lead, a hint at where Cayenne will first strike.

Constance hesitates before looking it over. "These items were obtained from practitioners? Taken from witches and so forth?"

"Confiscated from warlocks. Not all of them, but many. Some are from various monsters or demon cults, but most are family heirlooms, I believe." The Bhagavatis can't trace their lineage back quite as far as the Abhiramnews, but they're still one of the oldest of the Trust families, joined well before the consortium had been formed with the Europeans. They've had a lot of time to accrue items of power.

Constance worries her lip. "Your Trust," she begins, tentative at first, then growing in surety. "Thou art very nearly an Inquisition, Ravi."

"We are not—" He swallows his automatic reaction to consider things from her perspective. "I…can see how it *looks* similar "

In the past month Ravi has had this problem often. The team can see he's passionate about the future of The Trust, but no matter how he tries to explain, no one can see what he sees. He can tell they're all wary and distrustful, and it troubles him. The Trust has gotten tarnished over time, but Ravi can fix it. He can shape the existing structure back into what it should be the way a blacksmith forges a blade.

"Constance, I'm not blind to its flaws and its faults. But I can also see what it could be, and I…I can *almost* see the path to get there…" He sighs in frustration. Words aren't his strong suit.

She traces a finger through a few errant drops of tea on the table. "The Trust has long taken down witches and such, yes, as well as monsters? Humans with magical abilities?"

He tries not to think of Cayenne. "You mean warlocks. Constance, *we've* taken down humans who misuse magic. The team, I mean. That guy with the dollhouse, shrinking people. And the woman who killed people with all those crystal bug assassins."

"Indeed! An important task. Shaws have often done such."

"You said as much back at the…last month. My aunt said Shaws used to hunt other magic users?"

"Many of us were mages ourselves, which is why it was of paramount importance that we keep our eyes on others. On ourselves, even." She smiles, a dangerous edge to it. Cut-throat. "Oh, we Shaws hath slain many a monster, but the line between man and monster does get fuzzy betimes, especially among those that practice the Art. Often my family would gather at our Moots to discuss if a fellow practitioner had grown sufficiently cackling to count as a demon. A monster, I should say; taxonomy is important, as our good professor would say."

She's been working very hard on her modern speech,

but Ravi wonders if she's using some Old English word he's unfamiliar with. "Cackling?"

Abruptly Constance wrings her hands together and demonstrates an evil cackle like a storybook witch. Ravi jumps a little at the sudden sound.

"Aye, cackling. Gone too far down the path of wickedness. An ever-present danger, for often those of us who crave knowledge find it impossible to know when to stop." She looks away, a shadow falling over her face. "It was far, far better for the task to fall to us, their fellow mages, than to call the attention of the Church, or superstitious townsfolk, or…"

"Witch-hunters," Ravi finishes, softly.

"Yes," Constance says. Then she sighs, tipping her head to one side. "You yourself kept my young pupil Lucy from The Trust's clutches when her powers were discovered."

"It's not *clutches*; she was just too young. I've…got a thing about kids being trained up too young. The Trust wanted to keep her safe, to keep others safe *from* her until she can be guided to—"

"Was that also what they intended with your former paramour? To keep them safe?"

Ravi goes completely still.

He is not an angry person by nature. Fierce, maybe. Protective, certainly. He enjoys the thrill of battle, the successful execution of his hard-won skills, helping people. Rarely is it accompanied by anything like anger.

But here in this little room smelling of sage and old books, he curls his hands tight enough around the edge of the table to make his fingernails go pale. He has to draw a deep, slow breath to cool the white-hot torch of his *rage*.

Don't be a child, his aunt had told him when he grilled her about it after the airport, refusing to dignify his accusations, *do you imagine that we are above using any means to keep the world safe?*

Cayenne could have been lying about their abduction. The torture. Just one more lie to spice up the banquet of falsehoods they kept serving Ravi. But they knew too much for him to discount it entirely, their vengeful fury too genuine.

If it was true, had his mother known? Was this the legacy she had always intended to leave him?

Padme wants to know who sent the urumi to Harry's door, who's meddling with The Trust and their family's legacy, with his birthright, wants to know why Ravi isn't itching to find the enemies lurking in the shadows.

He's more concerned with why The Trust has those enemies in the first place. If they deserve them.

Ravi has always been a light sleeper, but now he jolts awake every night, heart pounding and fists white-knuckled.

With a shaky sigh, Ravi rakes a hand through his hair. Graciously, Constance gives him a moment to collect himself, her attention on her cup of tea.

"If you can change any of that, then I wish you well of it, of course." She picks up the conversation easily, as if Ravi hadn't just had a small breakdown across from her. "I shall assist if I can. I think you shall be a valiant nephew, and a courageous defender of my niece."

His ears grow hot. "I, uh. Thanks."

"Do you want me to read your cards, nephew-to-be?" Constance playfully waggles her eyebrows and takes the cards from Ravi. He hadn't noticed he'd been absently shuffling them.

"I thought you said they were just psychology."

Constance's fingers flutter in a stage magician's flourish. "Lackaday, sirrah, you do not believe in such things, with all the magic you've seen in your life? What about astrology and chakras and such things my customers are always asking about?"

"Hey, my people *invented* chakras. And we've got our own horoscopes, thank you very much, astrology is kind of a big deal over there. But no on both counts. That stuff is…not for me." Lots of magic is real, Ravi knows from very personal experience. Vampires, lycanthropy, fairies, time travel, energetic fields, portals to other dimensions; sure. But the concept that some star billions of miles away means you get born with a certain personality? He's got to draw the line somewhere.

Sure, he'll *read* the horoscopes every morning, but that's just tradition.

"Indulge me, Ravi," Constance wheedles, setting the deck in front of her.

He tips his head back to demonstrate a beleaguered sigh. After a moment he gestures for her to go ahead.

Constance grins in delight and shuffles the cards. "Do not look so dour! This shall be most amusing. I have devised mine own method of spreading the cards, so it should not take over-long."

"Good." He settles into the chair, arms crossed over his chest.

Constance draws herself up, taps ink-stained fingers on the deck. "This first card is you." She flips it and lays it between them, the illustration facing Ravi. A golden painted sun shining its rays down to a flowery meadow. "The Sun."

Ravi shoots Constance a suspicious look. "That's me, huh."

She shrugs one shoulder. "So sayeth the cards. Two more cards to better hone the central one…" Another pair of cards go on either side of the Sun card. "Here we have the Hermit and the Page of Pentacles. You, my good fellow, radiate courage over the many evils of the world, and though thy body is young, thy mind is older. Thou often draw away from the world and enclose thyself in solitude."

Ravi frowns in mild irritation. "This is just what *you* think of me, Constance."

"It is certainly my interpretation of what the cards are said to mean, but I am not inventing anything." Her palm goes up in an eloquent gesture. "'Tis the nature of tarot to be vague enough to resonate with anyone."

Ravi looks at the Sun card again. Coincidence, after all, and not the result of Constance figuring out how to run a search engine or a translation app.

"Next, we have thy opposition. Thy struggle." Constance drops her voice low and sepulchral with a teasing smile. She flips a card, and her smile drops. "Oh."

Ravi eyes the card. The Moon.

"I...I swear thee I did not rig this," Constance assures him, grimacing. "By my troth. Perhaps this was a foolish idea."

"Well, now I'm curious. What's a Moon mean?"

She gnaws her lip a moment and sighs. "One who changes their face and walks in deception."

Ravi looks away, heart missing a step.

She flips two more cards and mutters to herself, "So

many major arcana." One fingernail taps the edge of a new card. "The Tower. And here, The Devil." She frowns at that one. "All three together would indicate that you are caught in an impossible illusion, trapped there and held hostage. The Tower means destruction wrought by an unwillingness to change, by the clinging of old ideas and falsehoods." Constance swipes her tongue over her lips. "Those are…bad cards."

He huffs a dry laugh. "I gathered."

"The next set represents thy strength." A bit hesitantly, Constance lays down the next three cards. "Ah! Good news at last. The Lovers." She laces her fingers under her chin, batting her lashes. "A fulfilling romance is in the cards for you."

Ravi rolls his eyes, relaxing a little at the change of mood. "Now there's some classic fortune-telling. Will I meet a dark and handsome stranger?"

"Ravi, you *are* a dark and handsome stranger. Here, the other two are the Ace of Cups and the Page of Wands. Thou must face thy fears to dispel them, and in doing so you will meet one whose passion is equal to thee and know an over-flowing abundance of love in your future." She simpers, saccharine sweet.

Ravi rolls his eyes. He's learned from his mistakes. He's not going to rush blindly toward the first person who's nice to him again, not going to hand a stranger his heart on a silver platter just because they say they want him. It's far safer to return to his old habits. Keeping to himself. Keeping his guard up. "Okay, is that it?"

"Patience, my fellow, one more set. This one represents thy road, the way forward. One extra card for this batch."

Ravi inspects the last four cards. Some crowns, some swords, a set of scales, and a man hanging upside down from a tree. Despite his vulnerable position, the man's face is drawn with an air of serenity.

"More major arcana. Thou hast an unusual overabundance of those. Justice flanked by the King of Wands and the Knight of Swords. The Hanged Man is your final card. Most interesting." Constance steeples her fingers and considers the cards for a long moment. "Wrongs have been committed against you, and against that which you call yours. You must beware of covert forces, and prepare to meet with your enemies, to make sacrifices. However, your cause is noble, and to succeed you must transform the fight into one of compassion instead of violence."

"Well, that's unfortunate. Violence is the only thing I'm good at," he half-jokes.

"Stuff and nonsense," Constance replies, her diction slipping back into her more archaic cadence, always harder for Ravi to follow. "Thou bearest a strategic mind and a kind heart under yon warrior's armor. 'Tis how I knowest thou will make the right decisions dealing with that red-capped skamelar."

Ravi looks away, arms tight over his chest. "Apart from trying to get something useful from that vampire in New York, I'm not sure there's anything I *can* do. So far, you're the only one who's figured out how to suspend a chrono-mancer's ability, possibly ever. We…we don't even know if Cayenne has *already* changed things, and we're all just stuck in that new timeline completely unaware."

Yet another popular nightmare for his seldom-slum-bering mind to dredge up; he'll awaken unsure if any of his memories are real, whether anyone he knows still exists or are only echoes.

"Hmm, mayhaps, although that seems beyond even their prodigious abilities. My wonder is what thou shall choose to do when they do show their many-masked face again." Her earnest hazel eyes meet his, her hands propped underneath her chin.

Everything she's said, how she interpreted his cards… Ravi looks away, skin prickling. "You think…you think I should forgive them."

"Piffle," Constance snorts contemptuously. "Forgive-ness is such a modern concept. 'Tis merely a ploy thought up by the powerful to keep the abused from seeking their rightful vengeance. Nay, *I* think ye should demand Cayenne's fealty."

Surprised, Ravi barks out a laugh. "Fealty?"

"Aye. They have wronged you most egregiously and done great dishonor. 'Twere it I, I would bind the chronomage to my service." She gives his arm a little pat, then gathers up the cards into a neat stack.

"I can't…I can't bind anyone, Constance."

Constance hesitates, looking at the Devil card, then makes a sour face. "Thou may be right. Mayhaps thou can find a better path?" She inspects the Hanged Man closely, then shrugs.

"What are you saying? What should I do?"

"God's blood, man, I cannot tell you that! Nobody can. Only thou mayest decide. None are going to give ye orders for this."

Ravi bites his lip. "Yeah." He rubs the back of his neck and stands up. "Thanks, Constance."

She waves away his thanks. "Soon we shall be as good as blood, whence thou marry Harry. Go ye well, Ravi. Mine gramercies unto thee for—yes, *sorry*, got a smidgen 'ye olde,' as Harry would say. Thank you for the files." She grants a little smile he half-heartedly returns as he buttons up his suit jacket.

"If you figure out what those artifacts can do, let me

know."

"Get some sleep!" she calls after him. He rolls his eyes, and the soft tinkle of bells follows him out of the door.

Chapter Three

NATE HEFTS THE reusable shopping bag higher up over his shoulder as he knocks on the door, deciding to spice it up with a little extra flourish, a quick playful rap. Why not.

The peephole darkens. Nate grins and waves. The door cracks open just enough for Ravi to peek out.

"Nate," he says, his rough timbre carrying a note of surprise.

"Secret Agent Man." Nate taps a greeting to his temple. "Busy? I brought stuff."

"Stuff?" Ravi opens the door, and his arm relaxes from its obscured position behind his back, revealing his gun. As much as Nate dislikes the things, he can't fault Ravi for being paranoid. He brushes past Ravi as he enters the apartment and kicks off his shoes.

"Yeah, *stuff*. I come bearing gifts."

Ravi's place is open plan, the entryway leading into a spacious but barren kitchen and extending into the living room. All the furniture is either jet black or stark white, with chrome fixtures and minimalist accents. It looks like a very expensive hotel suite; neat, bland, and unlived-in. The only personal touches are the gaming consoles by the TV, a glimpse of what must be a small household altar by the bedroom, and a potted cactus in the middle of the kitchen island.

Actually, it's three cacti now, Nate notes with interest, setting the bag down next to them. He turns around and leans back against the counter to give Ravi a business-like once-over from head to toe. "Well, you still look like death warmed over."

Sliding his gun back into its hidey-hole under the counter, Ravi tosses Nate an unimpressed look. "Oh, do I? Sorry, what's the normal amount of time to deal with this kind of bullshit? I could use your normal person perspective."

Nate grins, not taking offense in the least. Better this snippy, catty Ravi than the closed-off, mopey version he'd been right after the airport. A circumspect glance over at the barren spot on the far wall shows that the fucking Seychelles poster is still taken down, thank God. Nate wonders what Ravi has done with it. He doesn't seem the type to do the old burn-barrel thing after a bad breakup. "Bad" doesn't do it justice; breakups don't get much worse than what Cayenne did to Ravi.

"Studies show that the average amount of time to get over a breakup is three months and eleven days."

Ravi tilts his head, and as he does hair slides from its usually perfect swept-back placement and falls over his warm brown eyes. Today he's casually dressed, at least for him, just dark trousers and a barebones white button-up with the sleeves pushed up. No blazer, no tie, no cufflinks. Somehow, he still manages to make it look like haute couture. Nate, in his jeans and long-sleeved Henley, feels woefully underdressed.

"You're making that up," Ravi accuses.

"I'm really not. They do studies for everything. We academics gotta do something to justify all that grant money," Nate jokes.

Ravi scrubs a hand over his close-shorn beard, glancing curiously at the bag on the counter. "You want a drink?"

"Sure."

Ravi gets them both a beer, which Nate knows Ravi doesn't prefer. Looks like Harry's brand, that weird buckwheat stuff. Fortunately, the futuristic bar stools at the kitchen island are more comfortable than they look.

"So how are things going with Harry's new training regimen? Val's been laser-focused on it, I've hardly seen her all month." Not that she's particularly social anyway, but ever since Harry's weird new gig has been revealed, she's been even more reserved than usual, and rarely willing to leave Harry's side.

Ravi settles into a stool around the corner, at a pretty good angle to avoid eye contact. Nate doubts it's coincidence. "It's going," Ravi says, taking a small sip from the bottle.

"Yeah? The two of you having superpowered training montages?"

Ravi laughs. *Success.* It's a small thing, barely a laugh at all, but Nate will take anything he can get.

"Let's just say it's a good thing the urumi can't ever hurt the Chosen who wields it."

"Pretty smart design feature." Ravi's always been aloof. Hard to read. Like there's a wall running right down the middle of him, cordoning the really interesting parts of himself behind it. "My favorite thing about the urumi is how it kills stuff permanently dead. No monsters coming back from the grave to star in the sequel."

Ravi smiles in his lopsided way, and Nate has to mentally repeat the usual refrain; *don't flirt, don't flirt.* It's a constant battle of sheer will to hold back. Now, knowing Ravi's preferences, it's even harder for Nate than it always had been. Sure, the guy's got the kind of looks that make people accidentally walk into lampposts, but even worse, he makes it too easy, always setting Nate up for the most perfect lines. Once, Ravi mentioned getting beauty sleep and it took every ounce of Nate's self-control to not reply, *You've gotten plenty*, and that's just one example of hundreds.

"One of the few things in this world able to thwart necromancy," Ravi says with a tip of his beer bottle. And wow, that's unsettling information Nate is definitely going to want to research further on his own.

"I see my cactus buddy has sprouted a couple of friends." Nate gestures toward the trio of plants in the middle of the island.

Ravi's frosty smile thaws a little. "Yeah…the first one looked lonely."

"Well, thank you for making sure Mr. Cactus has some company."

"*Mr. Cactus*? That's the best you could come up with?"

"Why, what did you name the other two?"

The tips of Ravi's ears darken a shade or two, so Nate knows he's on the right track. "What makes you think I named them?"

Nate sets his chin in his hand and waits.

Ravi sighs. "All right, Rikkitikki and Tavi."

Nate bursts into a loud guffaw. "You did *not!*"

"Look," Ravi protests, hands up. "Despite my mixed feelings on Kipling, Harry called me Rikkitikki-Ravi when we first met and… It's my favorite story of his. So, yeah."

"Huh," Nate muses. "It's a good one. Brave mongoose protects defenseless family from evil cobras. Suits you down to the ground, my guy."

Ravi looks away. "You got a favorite myth, professor?" It's plainly an attempt to shift the subject away from himself, but Nate can't fault him for that.

"I specialize in European and North American folklore, but picking just one favorite of the bunch? I don't know. I guess it depends on the day." Unsurprisingly, Nate's usual favorites revolve around his heritage, a mongrel amalgam of Irish, Scandinavian, French-Canadian, and Sioux. Though he's barely got enough Native heritage to qualify him for a partial scholarship.

Ravi picks at the edges of the label of his beer bottle. Nate watches out of the corner of his eye. Impossible not to notice that Ravi gets fidgety when he's stressed, always wanting to move. Nate wishes he could help, do something to lighten his burdens. He wants badly to be Ravi's friend. In the field, when their lives are on the line, being around

Ravi always makes Nate feel safe. He wishes like hell he could return the favor.

"What about you, got a fave?"

Ravi glances up. "A favorite myth?"

"Yeah, I'd love to hear it."

"Hmm." Ravi's brow furrows. He taps his thumbs on his mostly full beer bottle. "Yeah, I guess I do." He tilts his head back, and the light spilling through the window catches him for a second. Christ, he's unfairly handsome: in the sun his skin is flawless bronze, hair lustrous black. The kind of bone structure people would kill for. The fact that he doesn't have a string of suitors is boggling. They ought to be lining up.

Nate himself is an attractive guy, but an affable, approachable sort of good-looking. Tall, blond, blue-eyed, works out, easy grin. The kind of guy you could get a drink with. Ravi, however, always looks like he just stepped out of a golden palanquin or something, like you'd be thrown in an oubliette for touching the hem of his garment.

Nate is aware that his opinion might be slightly overzealous and not accurately reflect reality.

"Okay, so long ago," Ravi begins, his voice taking on a rhythmic cadence Nate's never heard him use before, like he's reciting from memory. "There were a thousand serpents, all brothers, who spread fear and mayhem across the land. One of these snakes was named Sheshnaag.

"Sheshnaag grew weary of this life and disgusted with the actions of his brothers. He wanted to be better than he was. He climbed all the way to the top of the Himalayas, where he lived a peaceful life focusing on his spiritual growth. When the gods saw this, they were so impressed with Sheshnaag, a serpent who could change his nature, that they offered him a boon. Anything he wanted.

"Sheshnaag told them that he desired only to serve. So now Sheshnaag the serpent holds up the whole world in his coils, keeping it safe." Ravi takes a swig of his beer and makes a slight face. "Anyway. Better story than Atlas, right? That guy was always trying to find some sucker to take the burden from him. Sheshnaag volunteered. I've always liked that part."

"It's a theme with you, huh."

"What is?"

"Service. Personal sacrifice." Nate smiles, then points at Ravi's beer bottle. "Don't feel like you gotta drink that for my sake, man."

Ravi's ears darken again. "That's not... It's just a good myth." He keeps the beer.

"It is a good one," Nate agrees, not wanting to make Ravi uncomfortable by pressing the issue. "All right, present time." He stands up and pulls over the fabric bag.

Carefully, he extracts another potted cactus, this one a colorful succulent, and holds it up like Rafiki displaying Simba to all of Africa. "Another one you can add to your growing family here."

Ravi stands and takes the succulent with a small, genuine smile. "This is…really nice." He sets it next to the rest, carefully placing it so it'll catch an equal amount of sunlight. "Thanks, Nate."

"Sure thing, man." He's got a couple of inches of height on Ravi, but the way the guy carries himself, all lupine grace, sometimes Nate forgets that until they're standing a few feet away from each other.

"This one have a name too?" Ravi asks, tucking his hands underneath his arms. "*Mrs*. Cactus?"

Nate clicks his tongue in mock disappointment. "So heteronormative, man. No, this one is Spike," he says, plucking a name at random.

Ravi's eyes crease slightly at the edges, his crooked smile evening out. Another success. *Don't flirt.*

"Second and final present!" Careful to keep it flat, Nate pulls a pizza box out from the bag, its savory fragrance traveling with it. "Lunchtime pizza. This new place Downtown is no joke."

"Oh, ah." Ravi shifts his feet, scratching his cheek. "No, thanks."

"It's gluten-free," Nate says, sliding the box over to Ravi.

Ravi goes very still, his fingers twitching once on the countertop. Slowly, he turns his head and regards Nate with a narrow look that for the life of him, he can't parse. "I've never mentioned that to the team."

Confused, Nate cocks his head. "Mentioned what, the gluten thing?"

"Yes." Jaw tightening, Ravi draws himself up a little taller. "How do you know this about me?" It's a demand, with steel behind each quietly spoken word. Nate realizes with a start what that guarded expression is. Suspicion.

Sometimes he really, really hates that French asshole.

"Ravi," he says gently. "I like people. I pay attention. I have a doctorate in observing people, that's the basis of all anthropology. Aside from a few sips of beer, I've never seen you touch anything with wheat. Not even when Harry brings those incredible pastries to a meeting." He opens the lid and inches it forward. "No beef either. This one's veggie."

Ravi's shoulders fall just a fraction, and Nate feels a sympathetic pang at the exhaustion on his features.

"I... Yeah. Thanks." He snatches a couple of paper towels with a sigh and hands one to Nate. "Sorry, I..." Ravi shakes his head, looking disgusted with himself.

"Hey, don't worry about it." Nate waves his hand, smiling. "I know the whole team's coffee orders by heart too." He's the normal guy of the team. Gotta make himself useful somehow, beyond distracting monsters with his hockey stick and the occasional research binge.

Ravi gets himself a slice and heads back to the barstool. "Creepy," he finally says with the ghost of a joking smile.

"That's me," Nate laughs, making a face he's pretty sure reads more as goofy than anything else.

Ravi takes a few bites and looks faintly impressed. "This is pretty good."

"Not even a little cardboard-y," Nate agrees. "So, you observe the beef thing, but aren't vegetarian, right?"

Ravi shrugs one shoulder. "Not strictly vegetarian, no. Beef's more a cultural prohibition than religious. Depends on where you're from, your social class. Abhiramnews have lived all over India, so we're kind of a melting pot of traditions. Besides, cows are too cute to eat."

Don't flirt. Do. Not. Flirt.

Ravi's mouth acquires an ironic twist. "My family doesn't exactly follow social norms, in case you haven't been able to tell."

Yeah, Nate's been able to piece that together. Even putting aside their centrality in what seems to be, in all frankness, an apocalypse-themed death cult, Ravi's family has serious money. Anthropologically speaking, the super-rich act like a country unto themselves, no matter their place of origin. When you have unlimited funds and your own fleet of jets, things like borders and nationhood and cultural traditions cease to matter so much.

"And we've had close ties with Europeans for…well, a really long time."

With a cluck of his tongue, Nate shakes his head. "The scourge of colonialism, huh."

Ravi huffs a laugh. "It's where the power was. We went into the treaties with open eyes. Gave up some autonomy, but there were advantages too. Before, we were sort of no-madic, roaming around to whatever princely state would afford us the best opportunity to… Well. Run a monster-hunting cabal with as little interference as possible." He munches a few more bites. "Crazy how much beef they sneak into everything here. Once I ordered a Mediterranean salad and it had steak strips on it."

"It's the land of the cowboy, can't really blame 'em." Nate takes a hearty bite of the pizza. He'd love some pep-peroni himself, but this isn't too bad. He could give up glu-ten if he had to. "What's Sheshnaag mean?" he asks, unable to bite back his natural inclination to know every detail about a story. "*Naag* is snake, right? Like nagas and stuff?"

The look Ravi gives him is a little impressed, and Nate

resists the urge to preen. Ravi seems multilingual, and all Nate knows is English and a handful of Quebec French phrases from his mom's side. But he likes words and linguistics, enjoys finding the similarities and connections between different groups of people. Figuring out a new word's meaning just from its roots is always enormously satisfying for him.

"Yeah, naag is snake, but reptiles carry a lot of symbolism. *Shesh* can mean 'that which remains,' so Sheshnaag translates to 'that which will remain at the end of all things.'"

"Whoa. Badass."

Ravi smiles, finishing up his slice of pizza. Nate pushes the box toward him, pleased when he takes another slice.

"Is Ravi short for anything?" Nate munches on his crust, head propped on his fist.

"No, just Ravi."

"Hm. Does it mean anything, or does it just sound cool?"

This time Ravi smiles widely enough that it flashes white teeth. Nate's a little short of breath at the rare sight. "'Sounds cool,'" Ravi repeats, amused. "It means something. Doesn't Nathaniel?"

Nate suppresses a shiver at the sound of his name in that voice. "You first."

Ravi devours his second slice quickly, wipes his fingers clean, and takes another swallow of beer. "It means 'sun.' Not 'son' like a male child, but 'sun' like, you know, the big hot thing."

Don't flirt, don't flirt, Jesus Christ, he makes it too easy.

"Fitting," he says before he can think better of it. He means it; Ravi's like sunshine hidden behind a bank of clouds. "Nathaniel is a run-of-the-mill biblical name that goes back a-ways. Means something like, God has Given. Or close enough. I'm not religious, even though I hang around a real-life angel and an avatar of a goddess."

"Yeah, I get the impression from Val that there's an interdepartmental kind of deal with the whole…upstairs situation." Ravi motions vaguely upwards in a universal gesture for heavenly bodies.

"Boy, am I glad I went into the anthropology field and not into theology. This whole business would be giving me quite the existential crisis."

"I can imagine. Hindus probably have an easier time with the concept than monotheists do." Ravi suppresses a yawn with his hand.

Nate watches him carefully. "Be honest with me. How are you?"

Ravi shoots him a sidelong look. "You know the only one who doesn't constantly ask me that is Val? She doesn't do small talk. I really like that about her." He sweeps his hand back over his hair with a weary sigh. "I kinda wish society agreed with her sentiment. Niceties are hard. They do this thing here where they say, 'How are you?' but they don't really mean it. You're just supposed to say, 'I'm fine,' and then move on with your day."

Nate smirks. "So how are you?"

"I'm fine," Ravi deadpans.

Nate laughs, broad and wide, and Ravi smiles. "Hey," he says after a second's pause. "I should apologize."

"For what?"

"For snapping at you when you came in. I really *do* appreciate a normal perspective." He contemplates his hands for a moment before setting them flat on the counter. "This may come as a surprise to you, but I don't know anything about normal. Normal lives, normal childhoods, normal… Normal relationships. I'm figuring it out as I go."

There's a sudden pang deep in Nate's solar plexus. "Well, if it makes you feel any better, even so-called normal people don't always get that figured out either. Or have normal childhoods, for that matter."

"I guess so. Did you?"

"Yup, pretty normal."

"I'd…like to hear about it." He seems genuinely interested.

Touched, Nate looks away, scratching at his stubble. "Sure, man, but my life isn't interesting."

The little sound from Ravi's throat is split between disbelief and scoff. "Sure it is. Regale me with your exotic tales of normalcy."

What can a nerdy professor who only discovered the true nature of the supernatural a couple of years ago possibly have of interest to tell a badass secret agent? Nate busies himself closing the pizza box to stall for time. "What sort of exotic tales are you expecting?"

"I don't know. Suburban stuff. Riding bikes all over town with your little sisters, or something."

Now it's Nate's turn to look at Ravi with sharp surprise.

"I pay attention too," Ravi says, leaning in as if imparting some great secret, voice lowered.

Don't. Flirt. "I don't doubt it. Thought maybe there were some top-secret Trust dossiers on me or something."

"Oh, there are," Ravi says, and Nate can't tell if he's joking or not. "But really, I want to know. Did you…I don't know. Beg your parents for a dog, and they said, 'Only if you promise to take care of it'? Did you go on family road trips? Summer camp?" As he goes on, Ravi seems to warm to the subject. "Running after ice cream trucks. Baseball games. School dances. That kind of stuff."

Nate chuckles because that's easier than thinking about

the kind of childhood Ravi must have had to romanticize those things. There's a couple of faint old scars on Ravi's forearms that Nate would wager aren't his only ones. "Wow, is all your knowledge of Americana from movies and Norman Rockwell paintings?"

Ravi ducks his head with a chagrined smile. "Admittedly, some. I'd been to the States several times before I was stationed here. But always for work or Trust functions. Things like formal occasions at the Eaton Estate. Or special training at the Manhattan branch."

"Ooh, special training!" Nate doesn't bother disguising his interest. Not everyone gets to be friends with monster-slaying James Bond. "What did they teach you in Manhattan? Martial arts? Sharpshooting?"

Ravi's wall creeps up higher, his tone all business. "No, that was… Among other things, Manhattan focuses on non-combat skills necessary for the job."

"Like what?"

Ravi exhales sharply. "Enhanced interrogation resistance."

"*Jesus*," Nate says before he can muster up the appropriate amount of cultural relativism. He knows Ravi was as good as raised in a warrior culture, but sometimes it's alarming how casually he refers to it. What "normal" looks like for him.

"See, this is why I'd rather hear about you getting a dog," Ravi says coolly.

"Fair enough, okay!" Nate manages a laugh, which seems to put Ravi more at ease, the set of his shoulders loosening. "We did have dogs. All mutts and rescues. This one we had when I was thirteen, Leto? Sweetest dog in the world. Raised to be a hunting dog, but she was gun-shy and couldn't be trained out of it. My dad bought her from one of his hunting buddies, and she lived in the lap of luxury the rest of her days, getting doted on by me and four girls."

Ravi smiles in that way he does without actually smiling, only his eyes alight. "I'll bet."

"My parents do hunt; it's a lot easier feeding a family of seven with a freezer full of venison. Bow and arrow only. Taught all us kids. So, Leto still got to catch ducks and live her best life."

Ravi's paying attention more closely than Nate's students do at his lectures. Having all that keen focus on him is kind of intense.

"Why don't you use a bow in the field?"

"Because I don't own one? Because the last time I held a bow I was nineteen, and I missed half the shots I took? Because shooting a ravaging chupacabra is a lot harder than sitting safely up in a deer blind?"

"Okay, okay," Ravi allows, finally finishing his beer.

He's stopped peeling at the label to listen to Nate's story, which he'll take as a minor win. "Was that your first brush with the supernatural? Chupacabras?"

"Nope, fortunately." He's only seen pictures, but those things are *gross*. Animals shouldn't be so drippy.

"So how did you first get mixed up in all this, then?" Ravi leans on his elbow and rotates his wrist, his casual gesture somehow encompassing the totality of all weirdness in the world. He must have picked that up from Harry.

A hot flush begins to creep up the back of Nate's neck, and he coughs into his fist. "Oh. Thought you wanted to hear about the normal stuff."

"Sorry, yeah." Ravi shakes his head ruefully. "Can't seem to turn it off."

"No reason you have to, my guy. Dealing with the supernatural is an important part of your life. Makes sense it's where your head's at." His phone buzzes in his front pocket and he fishes it out just long enough to see a text from Harry before shoving it back into his jeans. "Maybe we should save that story for another time," he suggests, and he means it. He's willing to tell Ravi anything he wants to hear, even the sketchy stuff. "That's Harry, we've got a…a thing." A "thing." Brilliantly deflected.

Fortunately, Ravi isn't the type to pry and merely nods. "Sure. Thanks again for the 'stuff.'" He makes little air quotes with his fingers as he gets up to escort Nate to the door, a charming gentlemanly gesture.

"That's what I'm here for! Making sure everyone eats and has an oxygen-rich living space." He points a couple of fingers toward the little family of cacti before pulling on his shoes. "Spike was watered yesterday, you're good for a long while." The fabric bag gets folded and tucked into a neat square under his arm, and he pats his pockets to check for keys.

"Look, Nate…" Ravi pauses by the door, rubbing the back of his neck. "I'm not going to get in the way of Harry's…*anything*. If we do get…" *Married*, he doesn't say, but Nate hears it regardless. Clearing his throat, Ravi looks at Nate with another one of those small, low-banked smiles, no less devastating for its size. "So, I'm not going to stop you if you want to keep barking up her tree."

Another laugh is surprised out of Nate, and he automatically sets his hand on Ravi's forearm. "That idiom's about the *wrong* tree, so are you saying there are better trees I should bark up, sunshine?"

Ah fuck, that's definitely flirting. Nate quickly withdraws, turning the touch into a companionable clap on the back. "See you on the jet! Maybe we can find a decent pizza place that does a cauliflower crust for you in the Big Apple. Pretty sure a New Yorker would rather die than serve that, but who knows."

One of Ravi's thick black brows is hiked higher than the other, but to Nate's relief he just nods agreeably. The last thing Nate wants is to make him uncomfortable. He's been through enough lately.

"See you, Nate."

Nate taps his forehead in salute and heads out before he can find out if both feet fit into his mouth.

Chapter Four

NATE FINDS HARRY waiting on the roof of her apartment. He clambers up the fire escape and plops down next to her on the empty lawn chair.

"Another vision, huh?"

"Yyyyyup." Harry leans so far back in her chair she's nearly a straight line, head back, legs outstretched. Her sunglasses are so overlarge they cover half her face.

"How long we got?"

"No clue. That's the thing about divinely gifted prophetic dreams, they're still dreams. Light on specificity."

"Hey, I'll take any warning we can get."

"Yeah," Harry agrees with feeling, sitting up. "What's

up, Doc?"

He shakes his head, smiling. "Just balancing a whole mess of papers I gotta grade along with trawling every available legend on earth for information on demon princes. Different cultures have different names for them, so it's been a lot of cross-referencing and intuitive leaps, to be honest." He gives her the same searching once-over he did Ravi. "How's Chosen stuff?" The unpleasant rush of dying-Chosen memories had thankfully only lasted a few days. Harry was kind of a wreck during that, but she's both tough and adaptable.

"Oh, you know," she singsongs, "Val's been kicking my ass up and down the gym every day. My skin is maybe bulletproof, not that I am itching to test that, but my muscles are still plenty sore."

"Ooh, are you getting all buff? C'mon, flex for me."

Harry slips a hand in her pocket, extracts a quarter, and whips it at Nate. It hits him solidly behind the ear.

"Ow, fuck," he laughs. Harry is a ton of fun to flirt with; sometimes she plays along, and sometimes she flings things at him. It keeps him on his toes. He knows she doesn't take him seriously and isn't interested, which is the only reason he keeps the pretense going. Flirting with Harry is nice and harmless.

"I suppose you still haven't told Val about, ah, this?"

Nate indicates the empty rooftop with a sweep of his hand.

"*Hell* no. It'll just be hammer time for sure. I don't want to have to explain to my landlord why there's a big red smear all over the roof." Harry takes off her sunglasses to rub her eyes before putting them back on. "I appreciate you tag-teaming on this with me. The first time was…really, really fucking annoying on my own."

Nate leans over to clasp her arm. "Hey. Harry. You and me, we're the normal ones. Whatever magical destiny bullshit you've gotten roped into, that's still true. You need anything, I got you."

Harry throws another quarter at him.

"Jesus, what was that one for? I was being sincere," he grouses, rubbing his neck.

"Oh, I know," she says, sinking so far in her chair that her arms dangle off the edges. "That was a thank-you quarter."

It's then Cayenne appears, blinking owlishly as if they had just stepped out of darkness onto the sunlit roof.

Harry and Nate share a glance, then push to their feet.

Cayenne rolls their eyes and arranges themself with hips canted, elbow cupped in the palm of their hand. They're dressed in some kind of flashy designer suit with slim suspenders, the jacket tossed over their shoulder like they just popped off a fashion runway. The careless pose doesn't quite detract from how red-rimmed their green eyes are.

"Ah, and here we are once again, *mes amis*. I knew you lived somewhere in this building, dear Harry."

"Pretty funny watching you going up and down the fire escape trying to find which apartment is mine." Harry raises her arms above her head in a casual stretch.

Cayenne's smile is a blade's edge. "It's a cute spell your good witch Glinda devised, I must admit." They look away over the edge of the roof for a moment, gnawing on their lip, and turn back. "I just want to talk to him."

"You can fuck right off," Nate says with a ready shrug. He crosses his arms over his chest, making sure he's not in Harry's way if she needs to draw the urumi.

"Hm. So, like everyone else in his life, Harry, you're going to make decisions for him too?" They're ignoring Nate altogether, which suits him just fine. If he never had to see Cayenne again, it would be too soon.

Harry hums a low note, rocking back and forth on her heels. "How about we just fast-forward to the end of this conversation, Pep. We're not telling you shit, and we're not passing on any messages. Go away."

"At least..." They swallow, throat bobbing, and their voice goes plaintive. "At least tell me if he's okay."

Nate couldn't hold back the explosive words if he tried.

"*Is he okay?* Are you fucking serious?"

Harry sets her palm to Nate's chest, just a brief touch, but he subsides, unable to even look at Cayenne lest he throw a punch at their manufactured face and probably get himself erased from time.

She maintains her perfect, implacable calm. "We're not telling you shit. Go away."

They affect a charming lilt, running a hand through copper-red hair. "Really, darlings, there is no need for all this aggressive *posturing*. If you are truly his friends, you'll agree with me that The Trust has brought him nothing but pain. You should be *helping* me dismantle it, not stopping me at every turn."

A weird way to refer to a little rooftop chat, but whatever. "He doesn't want it dismantled. He didn't ask you to do that. Let him fix it the way he wants to."

"I'm trying to *free* him," they snarl, sudden and feral. Talk about aggressive posturing.

"He can do that on his own," Nate says, voice rising. "He's already doing great."

Cayenne sneers. "Yes, about to be trapped in a sham marriage."

"Hey," Harry says mildly. "I'm a delight, I'll have you know."

"You must have *some* idea what they've done to

him—"

"What *they've* done to him? *You've* done worse."

Cayenne spins toward Nate, eyes narrowed in real threat. "You don't know what the *fuck* you're talking about—"

"I've got an inkling. What I *do* know, 'Cayenne' or whatever your real name is, is that you altered time itself so you could get your hooks into someone you *knew* had been starved of any real affection for his whole life, knowing the whole time that you were responsible for ruining his life and killing his family. Then you *lied* to him so you could *sleep* with him." Nate straightens up to his full height, nearly six foot three in running shoes, shoulders square and broad. "You knew how to get him to say yes to anything you wanted. How many times did you rewind time because you couldn't take no for an answer? There aren't *words* for the kind of abuser you are."

Cayenne stands bristling and fuming, one hand slowly curling and uncurling, over and over.

"Ugh," Harry groans. "Grrr, testosterone, yeah. Listen." She runs an idle finger along the zipper of her jacket as if dislodging a piece of lint. "How many times have we had this conversation today, Cayenne? This exact one?"

Cayenne turns their glare on her, eyes widening a hair.

"Uh-huh. That's what I thought. And how many times

have we given you what you want?" Cayenne opens their mouth but before they can answer, Harry continues, "Well, *gosh*, wouldn't you know it, we're still here doing this bullshit for the god-knows-how-many-teenth time, so it must not have happened in any of those versions. Right?"

Nate takes a couple of deep breaths, trying to count to ten while Harry speaks. The highest he makes it to is seven before he loses count and has to start over.

"I'll save you the effort, Red; *it ain't gonna happen*. You can Groundhog Day this convo as many times as you like. It doesn't matter. We're not. Telling you. Shit." She ticks off each word on her fingers.

"So *protective* of you, o Chosen One," Cayenne says sweetly. "Such a shame you couldn't protect your mother when it counted."

"*Esti d'épais à marde*," Nate growls, the Québécois his mom taught him rusty but serviceable enough for profanity. "You stole some dossiers and you think you know us."

"Don't come at me with that *garbage* French, you moosefucker. And I think I *do* know something about you, Professor." Cayenne's hands fist briefly before they spread their arms wide, all derision and scorn. "I opened his doors, and you want to waltz right in and get comfy."

Nate spares Harry an incredulous look, mouthing, *his doors?* She makes a grossed-out face back. What an analogy,

Jesus. "Fuck right off. You're insane."

"And *you're* some boring nobody from nowhere, with a degree in fairy tales. Harry, you're aware you can easily replace this one with a Google search and a cardboard cut-out, *oui?*"

Nate has *two* doctorates in fairy tales, thank you very much. "Why are you still here? If Ravi wanted to talk to you, he wouldn't have destroyed his phones."

Cayenne looks up at him through their lashes, almost sweetly. "You know, Professor, for someone who's supposedly *so* intelligent, you don't seem to understand how foolish it is to stand between a chronomage and what is theirs."

Nate shakes his head with disgust. "You are *deeply* fucked up. You can't own people. He isn't yours."

"Oh, I *see*. You want him to be *yours*," they hiss, their tattooed hand twitching. It might glow faintly for a split second, but Nate can't be sure.

Harry lifts her brows. "Cayenne, if you make one move against any member of my team, I will find a way to end you." Every word is spoken as a solemn vow.

Cayenne's fury dissolves into a careless grin, their stance shifting to a harmless, amiable slouch. They flap a hand dismissively at Nate; how kind of them to decide not to toss him back into the Stone Age. "I just want to talk to Ravi. Tell me how I can reach him, and I'll go."

"You can't. You're broken up. Take the hint. Move on."

Cayenne's lip twitches down. Then they break into a sharp, flinty smile, dipping into a mocking bow. "I'll take that under advisement, *ma chérie* Angharad. And whatever means you have been employing to stop my plans, I'd *greatly* appreciate if you stop. Before I have to enhance my methods."

Harry crosses her arms. "Yeah, well, plenty more where that came from, Red."

Cayenne's smile drops completely as they glare daggers at Nate. They put a hand to their tattoo and disappear.

They've barely been gone a full second when Harry turns to Nate and says, "I have no fucking clue what they're talking about. I haven't been doing shit."

"Huh." Nate grapples for a sense of calm. Having a mystery helps, keeps his busy mind occupied on a problem to be solved instead of lingering over Cayenne's accusations. "So, someone else is moving against them? Stopping whatever their plans are? Fuck, I'd like to send whoever it is a fruit basket." He scrubs a hand over his face. "All in all, that could have gone worse."

"Maybe it did. Maybe they dropped us off the roof a couple of times just for funsies, and then undid it."

"Yikes, Harry."

She shrugs. "If you can control time, death's not

permanent unless you want it to be. Other people's death, at least."

Not for the first time, Nate is grateful there can only be one chronomancer at a time, assuming the black-market broker's information was correct. One is too many.

Harry sighs, plopping back down on the lawn chair. "This is the right thing to do? Running interference?"

"Well." Nate joins her, stretching out his legs. "Think of it like this. Say Cayenne was *your* manipulative, narcissistic, time-traveling ex. Would you like to deal with that yourself, or have a buddy tell them to back the fuck off for you?"

She sighs again, nodding. "Yeah." She looks over at Nate, pushing her sunglasses up into her hair, her weariness shifting into slight amusement.

"What?"

"You didn't deny it. That you like him."

Nate scoffs. "What? You like him too. He's very likable."

"Sure, I like him, I'm going to marry him."

"Ooh, is that official, then? Sending out invitations yet?"

"Don't change the subject, Doc." Harry glances at her nails, kindly giving Nate a chance to school his expression without her incisive scrutiny. "He didn't used to be likable.

When we first met, he came off like an arrogant prick."

Nate looks away, out over the treetops and scattered buildings. "You remember my first little foray into the field with you guys? That job up north with the cursed necklace. When he got in a snowball fight with those kids." After he'd consulted on the kappa case, Harry had invited Nate to ride along on a mission, to see how he'd mesh with the team, and if he could hold his own with something a little meatier than a stack of folklore translations.

She looks puzzled for a few seconds, but then her forehead smooths. "Oh yeah, I sorta remember that. Before we found the right graveyard. Fun times."

"I remember it," Nate says quietly. "Made an impression. This tough guy in a suit that costs more than my car gets thwapped upside the head by some strange kid's snowball, and he just smirks and throws a couple back."

Harry looks at him.

Awkwardly ruffling a hand through his hair, Nate sighs. "Yeah, okay, I don't deny it. But it's fine, I'm a grown boy. I can deal with a crush without making it weird for the heartbroken, grieving guy."

"He might be on the rebound," Harry snarks. "Maybe you should swoop in and offer some of your patented casual comforts. 'Relieve some stress,' I remember you saying."

"You've never taken me up on that offer, by the way."

"Aw, is yer widdle heart broken?"

"Shattered," he laughs.

Harry leans forward, elbows resting on her knees. "So, is that your thing? Going after the emotionally unavailable?"

Wincing, Nate lays a hand over his heart. "Ow, good aim, Harry. No need to get ugly."

"Uh-huh," she says knowingly.

She's not *wrong*, is the thing. It's a smart play to keep his dalliances light, to keep anyone from getting close enough to hurt. One heartbreak was enough for Nate, and he's enjoyed the casual blend of sex and friendship he's cultivated with interesting people ever since. Now he's got a code; never hook up with anyone he'd have a hard time letting go of. Definitely a good idea to keep things nice and friendly with Ravi.

"So, we're going to New York to talk to a vampire?" Nate attempts to change the subject.

Harry lets him because she is, in fact, a delight. "Yeah. Ravi's chartering us a jet."

"Ooh-la-la. Gonna be marrying into money, McAllister."

"Hey, I'm not marrying into nothin' until I see that ring." She wiggles her bare fingers.

Nate's smile softens into concern. "You really don't

mind?"

"Mind what?"

"You know."

Harry's chuckle is very cute, though she'd likely lob another coin at him for mentioning it. "Bless your heart. Do I mind being a beard for a millionaire monster-hunter who's pledged his undying service to me as essentially his liege lord? Gosh, Nate, what *hardship*!"

"Yeah, but…what if. You know." He shifts uncomfortably in his chair. "What if you meet someone? What if you fall in love?"

Harry's mouth drops open. "Oh my *god*, Nate. You play the slutty professor pretty well, but you're a closet romantic." She sets her hands on either side of her face in a sweet simper. "What if I fall in *looooove*," she drawls, looking tickled by the very concept.

"Hey, I'm not a closet anything. My parents have matching 'I love my bi son' T-shirts with rainbow bison on them, it's great." He crosses his arms over his chest. "And you're avoiding the question."

"Okay," she says sarcastically, as if she's willing to play the idea out solely for Nate's benefit. "If I meet a guy I like, then I'll see him. I know *you're* familiar with the concept of an open marriage, Doc. Or a, wait— What did they used to call them? Right, a lavender marriage. What's the confusion? Ravi's obviously free to bang any dude he wants once he's over his tragic first love."

"Sure, but what if the guy you're seeing— Hold up, *first love*?" He can't have heard that right.

Harry stares at him, at the way he's sat bolt upright in his lawn chair. "That wasn't painfully obvious?"

Nate's mind whirs for a few seconds. "Not to me." He drags a palm over his face. "Huh. That does paint a clearer picture." A way, way worse picture. Shades of worse than just some crazy ex; a fucked-up, time-twisted-up-in-knots, mom-killing whirlwind romance was one thing, but add first love to that? Fucking hell. And Nate had told Ravi he looked like death warmed over.

Nate sucks his lips between his teeth. "Damn, I think I've been a bit of an asshole."

"Join the club." Harry sighs. "Look, Nate." Harry sits up, taking out her disguised urumi, a silvery coin with a scalloped edge. She contemplates it for a second before sliding it back in her pocket. "We've got a lot going on these days. We're working on finding Constance's big-shot demon and finally killing it. We're trying to help Ravi uncover and dismantle the unsavory elements in his ancient, filthy-rich MI6 Illuminati with virtually zero info to go on. Still coming up dry for whoever sent the noodle sword my way, and now we're trying to figure out how to keep the chronothot from fucking up all our lives if and whenever they feel like it. Plus, if an apocalypse crops up, guess who's on deck to stop that?" She jerks both thumbs back at herself. "What I'm saying is: life's short and have fun, but be careful." She leans over and punches him on the shoulder. "Don't go getting that delicate himbo heart of yours all tangled up in an impossible situation."

"There's nothing to be careful of. It doesn't seem like Ravi's had many friends in his life, and I want to be one. I'm not going to complicate that."

Harry regards him for a while through her oversized shades. "You're a good egg, Doc."

He widens his eyes in mock fear. "You're going to replace me with Google, aren't you?"

This time he's ready and ducks the quarter with a laugh.

Chapter Five

A HAND SLIDES over Ravi's ribs and comes to rest over his heart, the touch rousing him from slumber. He murmurs in encouragement, clasping the smaller hand within his own, pressing back into the hot body behind him.

"Are you awake, my sweet?" A thumb sweeps across his nipple, kisses pepper the back of his neck.

"Mm." Feeling warm and wanted, Ravi smiles. "No, I'm sleeping."

A soft chuckle presses to his ear. "Is that so?" Sharp teeth latch on to his earlobe. Ravi gasps, goosebumps spreading over his skin. "Maybe I can be a good dream." Snaking a hand down, Cayenne maps the topography of

Ravi's chest, tracing over his abs lower and lower until their hand wraps around his half-hard cock.

A low, wanton growl in Ravi's ear kicks his arousal into high gear. "What do you want?" he asks, breath coming fast, thrusting lazily into their touch. "I'll give you anything."

"I'll take it all," they chuckle, rolling Ravi onto his back and slithering on top of him. They slide down easily onto his aching cock, so easily, already ready for him. As ever, they feel so good Ravi is sure he's going to come apart at the seams, unraveled and tattered.

Something about thresholds niggles at the back of his mind. He wonders aloud, "How…how did you get in here?" All the while he sets his thumbs into the slope of Cayenne's hip bones and guides them as they rock, his thighs already trembling with eagerness. Mouth watering, he watches as a bead of moisture wells up at the tip of their cock and spills over to pool on Ravi's stomach. His admiring gaze travels up to their gem-cut eyes, rimmed in gold and shadowed with dark grays and purples, storm colors.

Cayenne moans instead of answering, driving their silk-smooth heat down around him, faster, harder. They use him for their own pleasure, and *fuck* if that isn't exactly what Ravi needs, shivering and swearing under his breath. He rolls his head back into the pillow, letting Cayenne take what they want from him.

"You're perfect like this, *mon coeur*." Cayenne grins and braces themself up on his chest, and that's when he notices their hands are dripping red to the elbows with blood.

He jerks awake, hand flying on autopilot for the gun on his nightstand. Ravi barely gets a hand around the grip before realizing it was another dream. The worst kind, the kind that leaves him hard and hating himself, as shattered as those clay golems.

Ravi sets the Glock back down and sits on the edge of the bed, dragging in ragged breaths, scrambling for his well-worn techniques to regain control of himself. He sinks his head into his hands, scraping his nails over his scalp. Faint light pours in through the window, pale and gray. Not even dawn.

"Fuck," he hisses, pressing the heel of his hand to the base of his insistent cock. A cold shower won't help, he knows that from experience. He's desperately tired, desperately turned on, and desperate to not come while thinking about his mother's murderer.

So, he gets up and starts his morning routine. Push-ups followed by sit-ups, getting his blood flowing somewhere useful. The flight is in a handful of hours and Ravi could use a lot more sleep, but when he looks at the tangled sheets, something like dread creeps in his gut.

Instead, he runs through his routine once more for good measure, adding in more reps and pushing himself harder, and pulls on some clothes to take a run. Exercise and coffee don't replace real rest, but they'll have to do.

*

"ANY LAST-MINUTE tips on dealing with vampires, Doc?" Harry asks as they round the second-to-last flight of stairs. The vamp lives in a well-heeled brownstone in a fashionable part of town, recently updated but still keeping most of its original charms intact. Maybe a historical site, Ravi has no idea.

"Beheading," Val intones.

"Or direct sunlight," adds Constance.

"Stake through the heart's a classic," Ravi mutters, bringing up the rear.

Nate turns and looks at the rest of the team, appalled. "I was going to say, 'mind your manners.' Jesus Christ, you guys." He shakes his head. "According to my buddy, Genevieve is like him; a human-friendly vamp. Cuddly. Gets consent for a little hemoglobin, all cool."

Ravi snorts. "There's no such thing as a human-friendly vamp. Some have just figured out a more survivable hunting strategy."

"Oof. Then you really don't want to hear that story

about how I discovered the supernatural, my guy."

"Ravi is wise to be wary," Constance agrees grimly. "These demon-blooded beasts play nice as long as it is convenient to do so. Once they get hungry enough, the veneer drops and the monster is revealed."

"I disagree," Val says, shrugging as everyone regards her with shock. "Occasionally the rare vampire has overcome their natural bloodlust and been of benefit to humanity. Not often, but it is not unknown."

Ravi grimaces, grudgingly recalling a few family history lessons that have suggested as much.

"*Thank* you, Val," Nate says. "Exactly. So, Harry and I pull the old tried-and-true charm offensive, and you three are here to be a subtle, muscley hint that we're not for snacking on."

"Offer diplomacy with one hand and wield a sword in the other." Val nods in approval. "I shall not move against this Genevieve unless her actions demand it."

At her familiar words Ravi looks away, adjusting the set of his cuffs. He opted for something nondescript today, a simple slim-cut charcoal suit with a dark shirt. Naturally, he still has his 9mm and both brass knuckles hidden in his shoulder holsters. The thin flask of holy water in his jacket pocket is just extra insurance, in case this vampire turns out to be less cuddly than promised.

Constance moves her hand in some kind of archaic flourish. "We shall be quiet as little church mice, my fellow, fret ye not."

"Maybe best to rein in the 'ye olde' speech, Constance," Harry reminds her as they approach the vampire's door.

Constance murmurs to Ravi, lengthening her vowels in an exaggerated North American accent, "Well, gosh, pals, how is this? Better?" It's a truly terrible impersonation, and Ravi coughs to cover a laugh.

Harry raps on the door. A petite pixie of a woman with short auburn hair opens it, giving them all an interested once-over. "I don't remember ordering out," she says silkily. To Ravi's eye, she appears unarmed and untrained for martial combat, her frame soft and willowy; but the way her eyes move gives her away. Pure predator.

Harry gives her a winning grin. "We're not delivery, Ms. Zabek."

The vampire lays a hand alongside her face, tapping her foot. "You are those visitors Miles told me to expect. He said it was very important."

"Yes, ma'am," Nate says earnestly. "Miles is a friend of mine. We have a few questions we were hoping you could help us with."

"Miles and I go back several decades, but he did not mention there would be so many of you." She purses her lips together in disapproval, eyes catching on Val's intimidating frame.

"We're not looking to cause trouble, Ms. Zabek," Harry assures her. "We've come a long way to get your expertise on a historical matter."

"Flattery," the vampire murmurs, looking even chillier. She narrows her gray eyes for a moment, then sighs. "I owe Miles a favor. You may come in." She abandons the door altogether, disappearing into her apartment.

Harry and Nate look at each other. "The old charm offensive," Harry mutters sardonically, waving everyone in. Before she can enter, Ravi stops her with a hand to her shoulder, then slinks through the door before she can protest. If Harry thinks he's going to let the Chosen enter a vampire's lair without him checking it out first, she's got another think coming.

Ravi quickly scans for hidden inhabitants, checking behind the door, the corners, noting all possible points of entry. The vampire has her back to them on the far side of the room, occupied with her bar cart. He turns back to the group with a brief nod.

Harry gives him a half-lidded look. "Is this going to be a regular thing?"

He shrugs and takes position by the wall as the group files in, standing ready for anything.

"You have a lovely home, Ms. Zabek," Nate says. It's not an empty compliment; the apartment is beautiful, high ceilinged and well-lit despite having no windows, and tastefully furnished with decor and artwork ranging from multiple eras.

The vampire turns back to the team, holding a violet cocktail in a martini glass in her small hand. She keeps a couch between herself and them, Ravi notes. He divides his attention between her and the rest of the room, alert for any hidden persons or evidence of spellwork, eyes constantly roving.

"Why don't you just tell me why you are all here?"

"Of course," Harry says, glancing at all the available seating they haven't been invited to sit on, and clears her throat. "We're looking for information about someone you used to work with."

"I used to work with a lot of people. An industrious vampire has to make a living." She sips at her cocktail, tone icy.

Ravi's eyes catch on an unframed painting on the wall, and he steps in to inspect it.

"Ms. Zabek," Harry continues in her most charming tone. "Did you used to work for a man in 1920s Paris?"

"That was a long time ago. I'm sure I can't remember."

Harry drops some of her sweetness. "Pretty sure I'd

remember if one of my coworkers was someone who could alter time."

Keeping a careful ear on the conversation, Ravi leans close to the painting, brow furrowed.

The vampire laughs, a throaty sound that belies her small frame. "Alter time? You're talking about a chrono-mancer? Ridiculous. They're practically a myth."

"This is important, Ms. Za—"

Ravi interrupts. "Is this a Tamara de Lempicka?"

The room goes silent. Ravi doesn't turn around. It's an original. He can see the brushstrokes.

The vampire weaves her way through the team and joins Ravi with an appraising nod. "Good eye. Yes, it is."

Ravi shrugs off the praise. "Her work is distinctive." He angles his head to the side, taking in the bold colors, the sensuous lines. "I've never seen this one before."

"Nobody has," she says with clear pleasure. "She painted it for me." She turns back to the team, lips pursed, then motions Ravi to face her. Warily, he does. "Where are you all from?" she asks him with her steely predator's eyes.

"Atlanta."

"I've never been. What's it like?"

Ravi thinks for a moment before tidily summing up all the operational knowledge he's gleaned from his years being stationed there. "The traffic sucks. Macaroni and cheese counts as a vegetable. If someone says, 'bless your heart,' it's an insult."

She laughs richly, hand aside her face. She curls her small cupid's bow of a mouth into a closed-lipped smile. "The little redhead always hated humidity. Complained about it constantly. Surprising they'd spend any time in Georgia at all."

Ravi doesn't react. Not even a twitch.

She smiles widely, her fangs peeking from behind her upper lip. "Your heartbeat is uncommonly calm, even when walking into a vampire's den. Except when I talk about *le petit renard*, and then it goes tripping in your chest. That's interesting, don't you think?"

Not waiting for a response, she pivots on her heel and seats herself in a green wingback armchair. She gestures magnanimously to the velvet sofas. "Come sit, all of you. I will talk to you."

Exchanging glances, everyone makes themselves comfortable. Harry sits next to Ravi and whispers, "Those art history lessons finally came in handy, huh?"

He shrugs, a little embarrassed. When he was younger, as long as he ran his laps and hit his targets, no one really cared what electives he took.

Harry turns to the vampire and says, "We appreciate it, Ms. Zabek."

"You may call me Genevieve." She smiles with closed lips again, fangs hidden away. "An old woman like me does enjoy the occasional trip down memory lane."

Harry offers brief introductions, giving first names only, then asks again about Genevieve's old boss.

"He went by Marquette. You have to understand, after the war, Paris was…" Genevieve goes misty, eyes fixed in a faraway time. "It was the center of the world. Where all the great minds met. Of course, there was money to be made there, or fame to be won, and the most beautiful of people to be seduced. Whatever type you fancied." She contemplates her drink for a moment before taking a sip. "Marquette wasn't interested in any of that. He was only interested in power. He himself had a unique talent; he could create doors out of nothing."

Constance gasps, sitting forward. "A Keeper of the Ways!"

Genevieve gives her a perplexed blink. "An odd turn of phrase. Thyramancer, he used to call himself. I've never heard of one before or since."

"Anyone else heard of this?" Harry asks, looking at each of them in turn. Ravi shakes his head. Even Nate and Val are clueless. Only Constance nods, adding, "A gate wizard. An uncommonly rare talent, though not unheard of. Perhaps there used to be more of them in my day. They possess the magical talent to open doors anywhere they can visualize, even places they have not been before."

"Yes," Genevieve says with a hint of nostalgia. "We could go anywhere we pleased, and often did. Marquette had quite a stable of us; little pets of various dangerous talents he would use to take care of his enemies. The man collected both enemies and pets the way another man might collect stamps." She sets her drink on the glass table beside her. "I was just a young leech, newly made. Eager to taste the world. I did a lot of things I am not proud of, but nothing I did compared to what Marquette had his little fox do."

Ravi can *feel* the way the rest of the team carefully avoid looking at him. He hates being the center of attention, and keeps his impassive expression tightly controlled.

Genevieve curls her feet up under her, rests her chin on her fist. "They showed up one day fresh off a boat, no name given, speaking the most deplorable dialect of colony French, and dressed in clothes that were fashionable over fifty years ago. I'm not sure how Marquette found them, or how they found Marquette, but when le petit renard joined up with all of us seasoned supernatural thieves and killers, we suddenly had a lot more time to ourselves. That kid put us out of the job." She shakes her head, smiling faintly. "I took up a few hobbies, I had so much free time. Met many artists at Montparnasse, became a muse for a while." She goes distant again, gazing away into her paintings.

"The chronomage, Genevieve," Harry gently prods.

Genevieve turns back and shrugs. "Turns out there are very few problems that can't be solved by being able to go anywhere and anywhen you like. The two of them were the perfect duo. Not just a knife in the dark, but an invisible knife; and then it turns out the knife that made the cut was never there at all." The vampire turns up her palms, fingers whisking over each other as if she had been holding something made of sand that had blown away.

"Any information you have about them could be useful. Anything else you can tell us?"

Genevieve considers this, a thumb to her cupid mouth. "The little fox was fun, can't argue with that. A firebrand in the sheets, as I recall." Ravi's heart skips. She glances at him knowingly but continues without pause. "They were young, but had figured themself out fairly early, it seemed to me. Had a few forays forward into time that gave them a unique perspective on many things. The *Années Folles* were the perfect setting for such a thing, awash in free-thinkers and iconoclasts, people who turned their nose up at conventional thinking." Genevieve pauses, then asks, "What are you intending to do with this information, I wonder?" Her eyes slide over to Ravi.

Harry has dropped her overly polite approach, her

usual brash demeanor edging closer to the surface. "Well, here's the thing; we won't know until we have the info. We're not looking to hunt or capture them or anything like that. Honestly, Genevieve, we're trying to stay off their radar and keep them from messing with us."

Genevieve's thin brows rise. "Interesting. Would you agree with that?" She looks to Ravi.

He grunts. "Pretty much. Why? Are you going to warn them we were here asking questions?"

Her slim shoulders rise in a shrug. "I have no loyalty to the little fox, as they have none to me. They were dismissive of the idea of family, which some of us at the time believed we were. Even in our tribe of misfits, they always stood apart. I got the impression that they never truly believed any of us were *real.* Not real people, as such, and not just because some of us weren't human. Fun to play with, maybe, but they bored easily of that once they had gotten what they wanted. They were impulsive, a poor strategist, but that hardly mattered with all of time at their disposal and with Marquette pulling their strings. Marquette was the only one they had any real respect for. Marquette, however…" She shakes her head.

"Greed isn't satisfied even with the whole world set at its feet. Marquette was only interested in power, and another word for power is *control.* We were favored pets, to be sure, living in clover. But all of us were under Marquette's thumb in one way or another. He had me kept under the leash with blood, others by debts or blackmail or addiction; whatever it took to keep us loyal. Le petit renard was his favorite by far, but Marquette just couldn't help himself, and had to exert his grip over them too." She makes a fist in demonstration.

There's a pause in which no one else seems willing to ask, so Ravi does. "What happened to Marquette?"

She picks her drink back up and sips. "There was a shop Marquette liked to make deals out of. Every year for ten years on the very same day, they would find one piece of him displayed in the shop window, fresh as the day he died."

"Jesus." Nate recoils.

"As I said, it was a long time ago. After Marquette was gone, we pets scattered to the winds, and I think at last count very few of us still live. I had no idea the little fox was among that number until now. I haven't seen them since, oh, 1926, I'd say." Genevieve finishes the last of her drink and motions it toward the team. "Can I make anyone an Aviation?"

Is this it? A little backstory that merely colors in what he already knew? Ravi crosses his arms over his chest, tamping down a flash of irritation. "None of this is helpful."

Genevieve cocks her head. "What information were you hoping I'd have?"

"*Something*," he growls, fighting a sudden wave of exhaustion. "How to anticipate what they'll do. How to stop them from doing it. Weaknesses we can reliably use. How to…how to lock them out of a timeline, or keep them from using their ability on you, or…"

"You want to know how to control the uncontrollable," Genevieve says. "You want to know how to rein in a storm."

Despite himself, Ravi startles and stares at her.

"You cannot," she continues softly, and if she wasn't a vampire, he would have sworn it was with kindness. "All you can do is try to stay dry." She rises to her feet. "I really don't know anything more. I wouldn't have the first idea how to contact them even if I wanted to, and if there is anyone alive who might know more than I, I don't know of them. A time traveler can be a ghost in the world if they wish to be."

"Ghosts are easier," Constance mutters, standing with the rest of the group. "A little salt, a little silver…"

"Give my regards to Miles," she remarks to Nate, then favors the rest of them with a small smile. "If you do make any attempts on the little fox, do be cautious. Marquette learned the hard way that if you ill-treat your pets, they will learn to bite." She flashes her fangs.

Bites, Ravi thinks.

"Thank you for talking to us, Genevieve." Ravi is dimly aware of Harry speaking. "Sorry to have made you nervous when we arrived."

"You are forgiven. There was recently a mass die-off of vampires. It pays to be cautious."

Nate sounds sympathetic. "Yeah, we, uh, heard about that. Did you lose anyone?"

Genevieve hums a note, a musical negative. "The fewer of my kind out there leaving corpses, the less suspicions get cast on me. As your sharp-eyed, well-dressed friend might be able to tell you, I enjoy immortality for its access to the finer things in life, not to glut myself on bodily fluids any more than I have to." She waves a hand at her decorated walls like a proud gallery curator.

Bites. Fuck, he's been an idiot.

Val stands fully head and shoulders above the vampire. "Impressive that the loss of your soul has not defined your actions, Genevieve Zabek."

"…Thank you?"

A round of farewells that Ravi barely hears, as the team leaves the apartment and starts heading down the stairs.

"Well," Nate says brightly. "She was nice. I liked her."

Ravi remembers that night on the dock, night-black waves lapping at the wooden posts, the smell of saltwater.

The inky needle-strewn mouth of the nix, the way Cayenne had swayed and clung to him, terrified and trapped with the venom in their system.

Of course. Get nix venom from Guinto. The black marketeer said he could get anything. Enough venom for tranq darts. Maybe The Trust can synthesize it. That, along with Constance's spell and—

The second realization comes on the heels of the first so suddenly Ravi's head spins, as dizzy as if he had been drugged himself.

"Fuck," he says thickly, leaning his full weight against the railing.

Dimly he feels Nate's hand on his shoulder as the rest of the team circles around him.

Harry slides into his field of vision, bending down to meet his eyes. "Hey, Rav, hey. You okay?"

"It's me," he says hollowly. "I've done this."

"What do you mean?"

He puts his hands over his face, trying to remember how to breathe.

"Ravi," Val says, "are you unwell? Do you wish me to teleport you back home?"

He lets his hands fall. "It's my fucking fault." He drops to his haunches, sitting in the middle of the stairs of some anonymous brownstone in the heart of New York. "I'm responsible."

Harry sits next to him, her hands reaching for his before pulling back in uncertainty. "What is?"

He looks her in the eye. "I know how to get them. I know how to fight Cayenne."

"That's…good? That's great, right?"

He laughs. "No." It's an absurd joke. A snake eating its own tail and choking on it. He laughs again, while everyone exchanges concerned glances and arranges themselves on the stairs around him.

"Let us in on the jest, mine fellow," Constance says while pulling a metal thermos from her satchel. Steam billows up when she unscrews the top.

"I've been thinking it over. How The Trust even got their hands on Cayenne in the first place. How…how the whole inciting incident got started, in our future."

Constance presses a warm cup into his hands. He sniffs it.

"It is merely tea."

"I don't like—"

"*Drink the tea, witch-hunter.*"

After a pause, he takes a sip. "It's not as simple as they lure Cayenne onto a fast jet. That's not sustainable. Not long-term."

"Okay?" Nate leans back against the stairwell wall with

his feet on different steps. "That makes sense. What else would they need?"

Ravi looks into the mug of tea as if directing his words into the cloud of steam. "They would need to drug Cayenne to have any success at keeping them in one time without shifting away or rewinding their consciousness." He takes another sip, not tasting anything beyond hot leaf-flavored water. "I know what drug would be effective, and I know how to get it."

Harry's eyes widen. "Oh, balls," she whispers. Harry is an excellent detective; she gets it already.

"I didn't get rid of that poster. There's…there's DNA on it. It's in a safety deposit box along with a memory card that has the only known picture of them on it. It's recent, but there are enough similarities to their past self that…" Ravi swallows, focusing on the bitter tang of the tea, the warmth of the cup on his palms. "I kept them. Just in case," he rasps through a clinging net of guilt. The present they sent him, purple kiss on the corner, a reminder of how freedom felt. The selfie they sent, a gesture of unconditional trust. And here Ravi is, ready to make them into weapons.

A thug in a suit. A loyal little agent.

Tentatively, Nate gives Ravi a smile. "That's smart, man. Nothing wrong with being prepared. You're a secret agent, you gotta think about that kind of stuff."

Ravi takes a slow, centering breath. "They'd also need some kind of magic that could control them even while undrugged. Some kind of 'off' switch." He gestures a hand toward Constance. "Like the version of Constance's spell that I was going to ask her to refine into something more reliable, after we've dealt with her demon."

Sheepishly, Constance raises her hand. "I have already been working on that in my spare time, in truth."

"*Don't*," Ravi says harshly. "These are all… These are the fucking puzzle pieces, and I now know how they fit together. It doesn't matter that it's not going to be me in the future who uses it on Cayenne, or even me who orders it." And it won't be, there's not even a slight wavering in his iron certainty on that. "*I'm* the one who puts it all together, who figures out the formula to catch and control a chronomage. Sometime in the future, someone uses it on Cayenne. Someone captures them, tortures them, and radicalizes them. And that creates this whole fucking situation."

A snake eating its tail, an ouroboros in which Ravi is both perpetrator and victim.

Harry says, "You think maybe someone in an opposing faction? Or your aunt?"

Ravi shrugs. He is so fucking tired. "Who can say?"

Nate whistles low. "Wow, okay, so this is some serious cyclical Greek tragedy shit, my guy. But…hold up. I'm following, but…how do time paradoxes work? I'm thinking about Marty McFly vanishing from that photo. Doesn't just knowing this change the future?"

Ravi shakes his head. "I only have…hints and clues to go on. But I think…time doesn't get rewritten as we experience it. If I can change things, then we'd have to wait until that moment in time does or does not occur, in order for the changes to take hold."

"Shoulda taken Genevieve up on that Aviation," Harry says wistfully. "This is not a concept to be handled by sobriety." She rubs the bridge of her nose. "What do you want to do, dude? None of this changes our present reality, that Cayenne is a very real threat to us, to your organization."

Ravi hands the empty cup back to Constance. *All you can do is try to stay dry*. "We do nothing."

Val glowers. "We do nothing?"

"It's the only thing we *can* do," Ravi grits out, gripping his hair with both hands. "I destroy the evidence I already have. Constance scraps the spell. And I take the secret of the drug to my grave. That's the only way we can break the cycle, change the future. The past. *Fuck*, you know what I mean."

"So, whatever Cayenne is planning, we just let them do it? You want to do *nothing*?"

"Yes, I love being useless," Ravi scoffs, borrowing a cup

of Harry's sarcasm. "I don't *want* to do nothing." His hands flex on air. He wants to move, to take action. To not feel so fucking helpless.

"We may guard against the chronomancer's capture in the future while still opposing their machinations in the present," Val suggests. "We stand vigilant for any moves they make and foil them as we can. Should we see them, we seize opportunities as we may."

Harry and Nate exchange a swift, indecipherable look, but before Ravi can inquire, his phone buzzes.

The number on the caller ID is redacted. His aunt. He makes a sound that resembles a laugh the way an empty husk resembles the cicada left it stuck to the tree bark. He swipes into the call. "Ma'am."

"Ravi. You and the Chosen are still in New York, yes? There's a possible incident with the Manhattan branch. We are not sure what's going on, only that the new Branch Director is missing and the hub has gone dark. We can't get in touch. Are you nearby?"

"Ten minutes out," he answers, squaring his shoulders, head clearing. When Ravi stands, the rest follow his lead. "We're on it. I'll keep you posted."

Padme takes the briefest of pauses before saying briskly, "Good luck, agent." One eyebrow jumps up Ravi's forehead; it's practically an outright declaration of fondness. She hangs up.

Smoothing the lines of his suit, Ravi says, "The Manhattan branch has gone offline."

"Speak of the devil," Harry drawls, arms crossed. "Let me guess, they're making a move on the New York family?"

"There is no New York family. Manhattan is an intel hub. And yeah. Seems likely."

"An intel hub? Even worse."

"Considerably," Ravi sighs, drawing his gun to run through a quick magazine check. "But at least it's something we *can* do. Damage control."

Chapter Six

THE LOBBY LOOKS like any other nondescript hub of sky-scraper offices. No logos or branding, which is standard. No people either, which isn't. Lobby completely empty, emergency lights flashing. Eerily still and quiet.

"Nobody home," Ravi says grimly, slipping his access card back into his pocket. "Not great."

"How *incredibly* lucky that we just happened to be in the city while this is happening, isn't it?" Harry's words are so full of irony they're rusting at the edges. She hops over the security desk and parks herself at the computer.

"I hath ceased to believe in such things as coincidence," Constance sighs, rummaging through her bag for magical supplies.

"So, trap?" Nate asks conversationally, rolling up his shirt sleeves to the elbows.

Val takes off her sunglasses, her eyes burning white fire. "I have received no worthwhile information from my superiors in some while. All this twisting of time has left even the celestial plane in uncertainty." Her meter-long maul appears in her hand, and she rests it on her shoulder while clapping a hand to Nate's back, sending the professor staggering forward. "Trap or no, I am confident we shall prevail."

"Atta girl, Val," Harry absently mutters, clicking through menus. "An evacuation notice was sent out to all staff twenty-five minutes ago. Then shortly after, the building's alarms were pulled. But I'm not seeing any useful details. Everything here is very vague."

Ravi stretches over the desk, reaches under the counter, and keys the secret button. The nearest elevator dings and the doors slide open. "What are we, amateurs? Critical information isn't available in the lobby. This way." He draws his gun and clears the elevator first, even checking the maintenance hatch. "All good," he says, holding the gun low at his side and stepping aside for the rest to file in.

"Aren't you supposed to take the stairs in an emergency?"

"Stairs don't lead up to the working floors," Ravi explains, "just the dummy offices. The real offices can only be reached by reinforced elevators or helicopter access." He punches in a series of numbers using the call buttons. A panel pops open and he swipes his access card.

"*Cool*. Please tell me it takes a handprint, or a retinal scan or something," Nate says, eyes round and impressed.

Ravi smirks. "You watch too many movies, Doc."

The doors shut and they begin rising. In the moment of silence, Harry clears her throat and bumps her shoulder to Ravi's. "You good?"

"Yup," he replies, feeling almost cheerful. It's a pleasure to have something to do, something he's good at.

"You've been to this branch before?"

"Yeah, a couple of times. Been a few years though." More than a few. Since before Tanvi and Nirav died.

Nate turns to him with a look of concern. "Are you okay being back here?"

He doesn't hide his confusion. "Yeah?"

A peculiar mix of wryness and disquiet crosses Nate's features. "Right, right. Why wouldn't you be."

Harry watches the slow crawl of numbers on the digital display as the floors rise. Her tone shifts a little, into the capable cadence Ravi secretly thinks of as Leader Voice. "What do we need to know?"

Delivering a brief is comfortingly familiar. Ravi stands a little straighter. "Manhattan branch is the main North American hub for intelligence agents and network specialists. Mostly comprised of intel agents with occasional field agent coverage. Except for select Directors, these people don't know anything about the Chosen, Harry. Only the old families know much about that part of The Trust. These are career agents and contractors. They're not going to take orders from you."

"Fine by me, I'm not big on giving orders to strangers anyway. We run into Trusties, you take point."

"Understood. Chances are low that we'll run into an agent I've worked with before, but that shouldn't be a problem. There's inter-branch cooperation all the time during emergencies." While he speaks, he holsters his gun long enough to slip on both knuckledusters, specially shaped to accommodate a pistol grip. *No such thing as overprepared*, one of his combat tutors liked to say.

Harry zips her leather jacket up to her chin. "All right. I want Val and Ravi sweeping first, Constance and Nate in the middle, and I'll take caboose." The urumi unfurls from its disguised form in Harry's hand as the elevator comes to a halt, ribbons of steel blades ringing. "We have no idea what's going on here, so let's be ready for anything."

The elevator dings. The doors slide open. A twisted,

hulking quadruped whips around to face them, snarling through rows upon rows of jagged teeth.

Val strides one step forward and backswings her maul into its chest, the force propelling it clean into the wall where it makes a significant dent in the plaster. The creature shakes his head, making a terrible gibbering sound as it struggles to its clawed feet. Stepping in, Ravi puts three bullets into its head before it can stand. He swiftly checks the hallway for more movement.

"Clear," he tosses over his shoulder.

"Jesus *fuck*," Nate mutters beside a wide-eyed Constance.

"Aye, I admit I wasn't *quite* ready for anything, my niece."

"No shit." Harry's fingers are white on the urumi's handle.

Gun at the ready, Ravi moves to study the body. The creature looks like some unholy mating of a mastiff and a snake but covered with two lines of multiple eyes that trail from snout to ears. Each eye has an unsettling triplicate of pupils. Its surface doesn't look like anything Ravi's ever seen before; not covered in fur or scales or skin, but an oil-sheened film that reflects the light oddly. After a few seconds, the body begins to froth and dissolve, leaving a smoky, stinking burn in the tiles.

"Well, that's pretty fucking gross." Nate sidles alongside him to also inspect the corpse, their shoulders brushing. "I've never heard of anything matching this description. Very cool. Know what it is?"

"Unknown," Val declares. "A being not of this world. We should assume there are more of them."

"Percussive force kills it," Ravi says with a shrug. As far as he's concerned, that's all the information currently required.

Nate doesn't respond, staring at the stain on the floor while he nibbles at his lower lip, brows drawn low. Ravi bumps his shoulder in a steadying nudge, and Nate's nervousness dissolves into a grateful smile.

"Indeed." Valiance hefts her maul, looking downright jaunty to have something tangible to smite. "Where do we go?"

Ravi cautiously pokes his head around the corner, hand-signaling the group to move forward. No bodies or blood. Maybe the evacuation was complete before things went to shit. A surprising turn of good luck. "Through this room. The most secure area nearby will be the server room. Anyone under attack here would have fallen back to that location."

"Then that's where we're going." Harry edges her boots carefully around the acid-etched part of the floor.

"We're a little light on firepower."

"Oh, I'm fine," Constance says, stuffing a few bundles of herbs into her pockets for easy reach.

Nate raises his hand like a kid in class. "I'm not fine. We were just gonna have a friendly chat with a vampire today, I left my stuff back on the plane." Without hesitation Ravi flips his gun upside down and offers it to Nate, who grimaces and shakes his head. "No way, man. You've taken me to the range enough times to know I'm next to useless with those."

"You have to have *something*, Doc. I can make do with these," Ravi insists, displaying one be-knuckled fist.

"I can teleport," Val mentions.

Harry smacks her forehead. "Fuck me, all this time doing this crazy shit and I still forget you can just *bamf* anywhere you've visited before. Val, can you be a lamb and grab our stuff?"

Without a word Val disappears. She pops back into the hallway with an oversized weapons bag hefted easily in one hand. Harry unzips the bag and hands out Nate's hockey stick, then affixes her gun onto her hip with a sigh of relief. She tucks a few more clips into her pockets and throws a couple to Ravi. "That's better. Heads on swivels, folks."

Ravi and Val lead the way in a quiet, cautious advance through the building. Aside from hastily moved ergonomic chairs and scattered papers on the floor, nothing appears amiss. Computer screens still on and glowing, a few lunches left half-eaten. No sign of movement anywhere.

"Nice offices," Harry mutters. "Intel must be cushy work." Ravi suppresses a smirk. Harry unknowingly hit upon the main point of contention between field and intel agents.

The door to the server room resembles a bank vault. After Ravi swipes his card, keys in the code, and lets the reader take a thumbprint scan, the door buzzes, a series of internal bolts noisily unlocking.

He carefully leans around the open frame. "Anyone alive in there?"

A few tense seconds pass before a reedy tenor calls, "You field?"

"Yeah. Intel?"

"Yeah." The sound of scrabbling feet. "Come on in, but weapons up. It's been a weird day."

"Looks like," Ravi says, holding his gun low. He gives the team a nod, and Harry's urumi snakes up into its disguise. Nate lowers his stick, Val puts on her sunglasses and holds her maul down at her hip, which is the most disarmed she's likely to get. Constance trots along behind, looking as deceptively harmless as she ever does. "We're coming in."

Ravi enters first, scanning the room as the others pile in

behind him. Behind the glass partition, banks of servers hum away while the front area looks like a hurricane's been through it. A face peers out from behind an overturned desk, the muzzle of a shotgun beside it. Lowering his Glock, making it clear he's no threat, Ravi approaches with one hand raised.

"Agent Abhiramnew from Atlanta branch. This is my team. Freelancers. We were in the neighborhood and got a call that you went dark."

A lanky intel agent with square glasses and a hi-top fade stands up, wearing business casual attire that's torn in several places. "Agent Williams. Thank God, yeah, there's been a brea—" Williams loosens his grip on his shotgun, and he blinks a few times. "Wait, *Ravi* Abhiramnew?"

Ravi frowns. "Yeah. Have we worked together? Sorry, I don't remember you."

Williams's laugh is just shy of hysterical. "Have we worked together! No, we have not." He shakes his head. "Sorry, I'm just really glad someone's shown up. I've been holding position by myself for the last half-hour." The agent straightens up as if his morale has been boosted considerably.

Odd. There's no reason for another agent, even an intelligence agent, to know the first thing about the old family names, even the Abhiramnews. And even if they did, recognizing Ravi's name specifically? It's strange, but ultimately not important, so he shoves it aside. "What's the situation?"

"Right. A bit ago a mysterious branch-wide evacuation was called, warning us about an incoming dimensional breach. Somehow a rift was opened inside the premises. The communication network went down, like a damned EMP or something. Then those snake-dog things started pouring through, attacking anything they saw. Did you spot any on the way in?"

"Just one. It's dead."

"There's a *lot* more," Williams states grimly. "Most people got out, as far as I know, trying to alert other branches. There's still a strike team in the facility, working on extraction of…a high-priority asset. I think the bulk of the horde has them pinned down."

"Why didn't you evacuate too?"

"I, uh. I'm mainly IT. I…get a lot done when everyone's away from their desk, not messing up their computer. I didn't realize the evac was legit until those things started running through."

Nate chuckles. "Some office drama is universal."

"What about the Branch Director?" Ravi asks. "We were told he's missing."

Williams shrugs. "Yes, kind of. But he does that. He's

sort of infamous for it."

"I haven't heard about him."

"Javier Mason? He was promoted to the position a couple of months ago."

"Oh," Ravi says with surprise, "I *have* heard of him." Mason was something of a Trust legend. Five years ago, he was presumed KIA in Anchorage for several months until he showed up wearing a yeti skin for warmth. Ravi has always wanted to meet him. "Mason's out of house?"

"Yeah, he goes on walkabouts sometimes to investigate stuff on his own. He says it keeps him sharp. He left yesterday. Bali, I think?"

"It wasn't him who sent out the evac order?"

"No. I took a look at the message, and all the metadata had been scrubbed. I didn't have time to dig deeper, but whoever sent it saved a lot of lives."

A mystery for later. "The strike team on site. What kind of asset are they securing?" Williams gives the rest of the team a wary look. "You can speak freely, Agent."

Williams stands up a little straighter, almost at attention. "We have a seer visiting, sir."

Ravi sucks in a breath. If this attack was of Cayenne's design, which Ravi still holds out thin hope it wasn't, then they're making a hit on a Trust seer, one of the most valuable resources The Trust possesses. Smart play. Even though time travel played havoc with clairvoyance, the seer must pose a significant enough threat to warrant taking out.

If it is Cayenne. There's still a chance it's not.

"I'm not a sir, Williams. Just an agent."

"Yes, s—uh, right."

This random agent's high regard for him is *weird.* Another mystery for later. "Relevant details?"

Williams nods sharply and trades his shotgun for a laptop, bringing up a map. "An unknown incident caused a rift to the Outside to open in the middle of the armory. That's the epicenter. Seconds later, the feeds shut down along with comms. I haven't been able to get them back online."

"Fuck," Ravi mutters. The armory is the worst possible place the branch could be breached. It was extremely good fortune that the evac order came when it did, or there would have been a lot of agents unable to arm themselves against the attack.

Constance steps forward, her eyes wide. "The Outside?" She shoots a meaningful look at Ravi, jerking her head aside.

Harry catches this and turns to Williams with a reassuring smile. "We're on it! We're gonna need some floor plans." She takes the agent aside to look over his laptop while the rest of the group forms a loose huddle around Constance.

"Ravi," she says urgently, "I have not yet finished looking into your list of stolen arcane artifacts, but this occurrence was most assuredly caused by one of them."

"One of the Bhagavati's lost items? You're sure?"

"Aye, an obsidian mirror that opens a rift to the Outside. Called the Darkling Eye."

So much for Cayenne not being responsible. Ravi swallows bile.

Nate hikes up his hockey stick over both broad shoulders. "What's the Outside? Another word for the Faerie Realm or something?"

Constance shakes her head, braids spilling over her shoulders. "Nay, 'tis the space *between* realms. A dark place of madness and eldritch beings who seek to enslave lifeforms on the material planes."

"Ah. Lovecraftian horrors. Got it."

Ravi snorts. "Basically, yeah."

Nate flashes a buoyant smile. "That's easy, then. Nobody read any old books, and if you see any fog or mist, don't walk into it."

Harry comes back while tapping at her phone, no doubt syncing up with Agent Williams's information. She checks her gun again. "Nothing about avoiding tentacles, Doc?"

"Hey, I don't kink shame."

From a respectful distance away, Williams hefts his shotgun and pipes up, "I'll keep this area secure. A defensible position in case you need to fall back."

"Okay." Ravi nods. "Good thinking." Agent Williams looks inordinately pleased, narrow chest swelling.

Constance ties her skirts into a pair of knots over each knee, freeing up her formidable boots. "Likely these hounds are merely vanguards. We need destroy the mirror before anything larger comes through."

Ravi takes a long breath and adjusts the fit of his knuckledusters against his palms. "Okay. Shut the rift, find the strike team, save the seer. Those are our objectives."

"Unlikely that our adversary is still here after setting their trap, but we should still remain vigilant," Val says. Ravi hopes fervently that she's right, that Cayenne *isn't* still here. He can plan for or adapt to any battlefield situation, but when he grasps for what he'd do if he saw Cayenne, he just…blanks. Like a map with a hole cut in it.

"Vigilance, yeah. Always, big gal," Harry mutters. She checks her gun a third time. Ravi inspects her a little more closely. The whites of her eyes are wider than normal, her skin pale as wheat.

"Hey," he says, gently. "Harry."

She looks up with false brightness. "Mm-hmm?"

"We're going to be fine."

"Oh, yeah, for sure," she says with a careless wave. "Just kinda seems like the sort of apocalyptic event that Chosen Ones tend to get chewed up by, y'know?"

This is several orders of magnitude worse than the few small skirmishes Harry's had since getting her newfound abilities, and though she's been training hard the entire month with both Val and with Ravi, her introduction to what it meant to be Chosen was a front row seat to the memories of countless deaths.

Ravi wishes fiercely he could take that burden from her; not the urumi, that wasn't his place. But if he could take the fear from her, he would.

So, he gives it a try.

"This?" he scoffs. "This isn't an apocalypse, Harry." He grins and cocks his gun for theatrical effect. "This is a Tuesday."

*

"YOU KNOW WHAT I wish we had? Flamethrowers." Harry drags back on the urumi, its whiplike blades scissoring deep into a hound's hamstrings. It howls furiously, struggling until Nate staves in its skull with his hockey stick. The professor's eyes are a little wild, but he's handling himself well.

While the others take care of the straggler, Ravi and Val

continue covering the hallway. A thick mass of hounds waits for them. Hundreds of eyes reflect the fluorescent light in unearthly green flashes. The beasts writhe around each other in a confusing knot, making it impossible to pick out just one. An oil-sheened ocean of menace waits to crest over them. The chorus they make, a terrible gibbering, chattering whine, sets Ravi's teeth on edge. Enough time spent listening to that might drive a person mad.

"There would have been some flamethrowers in the armory," he says wistfully. "And grenades." Now it's all likely floating away in the hollow space between worlds.

"Throwing flame is no problem, mine companions." Constance dips her hands in her pockets, then draws her fingertips across each opposite palm, smearing gritty ash over them. "Plan, mine niece?" Two small sparks ignite in her palms, illuminating her strangely, gilding her hair as it slips out of its plaits.

Double-wielding gun and urumi, Harry asks, "Rav, how much further?"

"Down that way past the foyer, and then two more rooms to the armory." Which is now a gaping hole into the Outside, spilling out more monsters the longer they linger.

"Okay," Harry says. "There's a lot of these things, and we can't let them surround us or separate us. We stay close to the wall. Constance, clear a path. Nate, you cover her.

Val, guard right flank, I'll take left. Ravi, can you keep them back with some suppressing fire?"

"I'll keep them off you. Though headshots would be more effective than suppression." He slides in a new magazine. If he had an automatic weapon and unlimited ammo, that would be another story, but with a 9mm, he's got to choose each shot carefully.

"I mean, if you can get some, sure, take 'em."

He attempts to keep a wolfish smile off his face. "Can do."

"You're enjoying yourself way too much, my guy," Nate remarks, though he's smiling himself.

"Let's move," Harry says.

Her tactics are sound; the cumulative wisdom of the Chosen weapon added to Harry's natural affinity for leadership make a powerful combination. Constance keeps a steady sweep of flame aimed ahead of them as they hug the wall, occasionally catching a hound aflame and sending it panicking into the mass of its pack, causing further damage. And as much shit as Ravi gives him for stubbornly fighting with only a wooden hockey stick, Nate is impressively accomplished with it. The professor aims for the eyes of any creature that gets close enough, blinding it for Val to bring down her mighty war-hammer onto it. Hound after hound gets smashed into frothing ichor. Exultant, eyes aflame, Val roars battle cries with every pummel of her maul. Ravi's never seen her smile so much. No doubt, like him, she's pleased to finally have a problem she is suited to solving: a hammer among nails. Emotional tumult and intrigue aren't her forte.

Harry's attacks are neat and quick, constantly aware of their placement and gauging distance. Economical movements of both sword and gun work in tandem to hobble hounds that stray too close.

Another hound separates from the main knot and tenses for a leap at her. Ravi's shot catches it square in its centermost eye. It topples, body disappearing under the mass of creatures that undulate around them as they keep moving.

"Dude," Harry laughs back at Ravi. "You weren't kidding about headshots."

One monster bounds up to him from their flank, shark-like rows of teeth gnashing too close to shoot. He takes a swing with a left hook. The metal does no special damage—his "brass" knuckles are iron for fae and silver for undead—but the weight of them added to his well-placed punch sure has the intended effect. Bones and cartilage crunch as the beast falls short, catching his forearm with a shallow rake of claws. Ravi ignores the scratches to skip back and put a bullet in its head, keeping his attention on the ever-changing battlefield.

"A great shame my noble familiar Griswold is not here," Constance calls back, furling a fresh gout of flame to clear the way, beasts cringing away from the heat. "He has been complaining about getting fat and complacent without battles to keep him sharp."

"I share your cat's sentiment," Val declares, stepping out between two straggling hounds. She kicks one in the face, while her hammer swing collapses the ribs of the other. The kicked hound bites her savagely on the calf before Ravi and Harry fell the creature with a flurry of bullets.

"Stay in formation, Val!" Harry darts forward, covering Val's side as the angel rejoins the main group.

Constance staggers a little. Nate is quick to shore her up, bracing himself against her back. "You okay?" He thwacks an approaching monster square in the mouth, then sweeps its legs out from under it.

Her voice sounds faint. "'Tis a great deal of magic to channel without surcease. I am well enough." The hounds' terrible chittering joins into one menacing yowl, like they've scented weakness.

"We have to pick up the pace," Ravi shouts, shooting the creature Nate had dropped before it gets back up. The sound of the shot gets swallowed up by the cacophony, like a thousand hyenas screaming.

Harry uses her forearm to swipe a spatter of oily ichor from her cheek. "Fuck, that noise is giving me a headache. Just a little more to go before we get there, guys. Once the mirror is in view, you can teleport over and smash it, right, Val?"

Val winds up a hit and slams a hound back into the pack. Bones crunch. "Yes."

"Will that do the trick, Constance, or is there an incantation or something?" Harry slices a hound clean in half with the urumi. A second one slinks ahead, but Ravi's shot takes it right at the base of the skull. The team steps over their bubbling, dissolving bodies.

The line of fire gutters for a heart-stopping second before Constance leans into it with determination, bracing her boots wide. "*God's wounds*, how should I know? This is all new to me."

"My hammer will suffice," Val asserts. She spins her hammer fast enough for it to hum in the air before crushing another beast into paste. The mass of snarling hounds closes in tighter, crowding the team against the wall. One snaps at Ravi's leg, and he kicks it away with a sharp curse.

Distance is gained with agonizing slowness, step by step. Sweat beads on Constance's brow, fire pouring from her hands. At last, they round the final corner. A long tear of blackness ripples in midair like a torn sail, the area around it a twisted mess of concrete and rebar. The sheer force of it opening must have ripped the armory apart, and the very walls from their moorings. The only thing untouched is a round, impossibly black circle of glass flat underneath the portal. As they watch, another slavering hound wriggles through the rift, unsettlingly reminiscent of a thing being given birth. Rows of triple-pupiled eyes blink independently, claws clicking one by one on the concrete as the hound sets foot into their reality. The creature fixes every one of its many eyes on the group, then starts running toward them, ichor dripping from its jaws.

The arc of shielding fire flickers and dies. Constance looks at her palms with alarm.

Ravi drops to one knee and sights down the barrel. He pops off two rounds, and the beast's head jerks back once; twice, and its legs crumple underneath it. The hound slides lifelessly the rest of the way to Constance's boots, already sizzling into acid.

Harry spins around to cover their rear. "Val! You're up!"

Ivory wings fan out with a loud snap as Valiance teleports next to the rift. She grimaces, as if the air itself hurt. Bracing herself with wings spread wide, she slams the head of her maul down on the obsidian mirror.

There's a reason why Val is the team's tank; so far, they

haven't run into anything that can withstand a direct hit from her celestial weapon, and the Darkling Eye is no exception. Glass shatters, the rift twisting and twitching as it sucks in a massive draft of air. Val gets dragged across the floor toward it before she slams her maul into the concrete, wedging herself firmly in place.

Everyone's hair swirls wildly in the sudden wind, then just as abruptly as it started, it stops. The rift winks closed like a weary sideways eye, and the air itself loses a slimy, oppressive quality Ravi hadn't even consciously aware was there. The destroyed section of building looks a lot bigger without a massive hole in the middle of it.

With ear-splitting howls, the hounds disband and scatter, no longer twining together in their protective pack formation. Shoulder to shoulder, Ravi and Harry together pick off as many as they can before the rest retreat deeper into the facility.

A long moment to catch their breath. Val kicks at the shards of obsidian. Constance slides down a wall and sits with her legs splayed, rubbing at her ashen hands. Nate joins her, talking softly. She nods and pats his hand.

Harry leans into Ravi for a second. "Objective one complete."

Switching out his clip, he returns her grin with a crooked one of his own, adrenaline high. "And look at that.

Still alive."

She gives a comical roll of her eyes. "Well, now you've jinxed me. Nice job, dude." She nods her chin over at the rest of the team in silent suggestion to join them as she trades her gun for her phone. "I'll keep watch and check in with Williams. Find out where the strike team is. We could use a hand mopping up whatever hound-things are left."

Ravi leaves her to it. He holsters his gun and crouches down next to Nate. "Nice work, Constance."

She smiles with a little scrunch of her nose, wiping ash from her hands. "Fair shooting, as well. Mine thanks."

"None necessary." He looks them both over. "Any injuries?"

Constance shakes her head, and Nate says, "I'm good, but it looks like you took a hit."

"Hm?"

Without another word, Nate takes Ravi's arm, shoving up his tattered sleeve. Ravi blinks. "Got something for this, Constance?" She leans over to look at the sluggishly bleeding claw marks. She purses her lips and digs through her bag.

"It can wait," Ravi insists. "Val took a bite."

"And I shall require healing for it, as well." Val sets herself down beside Ravi, stretching out her injured leg. The wound appears to be sizzling, though she pays it little mind.

"We both need to stay in top form to be most effective on the field."

Grudgingly, Ravi drops into a cross-legged seat. Constance gets to work patching Val's bite while Nate still holds onto Ravi's wrist, his fingers warm and gentle.

"Hey," he says seriously. "Tell me the truth, Ravi."

Ravi lifts an eyebrow.

"Last time you invited me to the range, to teach me to shoot."

"Yeah?"

"Did you miss those shots on purpose, to make me feel better?" Clear blue eyes twinkle as Nate's serious expression breaks at the edges, a smile creeping through.

Ravi looks away, ears growing hot. "I, uh. I didn't want to demoralize you."

"*Demoralize* me, geez, man. You're not my commanding officer."

"Okay," Ravi admits, turning back to meet Nate's gaze. "I didn't want you to think I brought you there just to show off."

Nate's grin is wide and admiring. "I think you're entitled to show off a *little*, Annie Oakley."

Ravi snorts and looks away again, warmth creeping across the nape of his neck.

Constance takes Ravi's arm, pulling him into an

awkward lean as she cleans and dresses his wound. He murmurs his thanks and pushes himself to his feet.

Harry steps over, putting away her phone. "Williams says the strike team is pinned down over by the archives, with the seer safe for now." She bends and helps Constance to her feet. "You good, hot stuff?"

"Indeed, I just needed to catch mine breath. Channeling the same spell for so long is akin to straining a muscle."

Val tests her leg before she extends a hand and pulls Nate upright. "That was a very refreshing battle. Let us seek out another."

*

ASIDE FROM HOCKEY (and a few abysmal seasons of standing in the left outfield of his Little League, catching more Zs than fly balls) Nate hadn't been a particularly sporty kid. He had been an extroverted Honors Roll vale-dictorian with AP courses in everything except math and physics. It wasn't until grad school, after his big breakup, that Nate hit the gym and discovered he was secretly kind of a jock under the nerdy leanings.

He's never been more grateful for that discovery than he is now, bashing in an eldritch abomination's head as it tries to latch onto his face. Its chattering screech cuts off as it falls dead at his feet, flesh bubbling into foul ichor. The things have a strange chemical stink, inorganic, like ozone. Nate wishes their bodies wouldn't dissolve *quite* so fast; he'd love to catalog a few pictures for later research.

The hallway roils thick with snarling hounds, slamming and clawing at the far double doors in repeated attempts to break into the room. They've got the strike team well pinned down inside, with only about a jillion otherworldly monsters in the way. No problem. Nate's heart feels like it's dancing a rumba.

The team is holding the advantage so far, Harry having led them in wedge formation right in the thick of things. Constance switches to casting hedge-witchery spells, growing tangles of vines up through the floor that wrap around the beasts, keeping them frustrated and corralled. Easy to pick off. Nate resolves to bake Constance a dozen chocolate cupcakes after they get back home. Two dozen.

Gun hand propped on his bandaged wrist, Ravi rocks off another series of swift shots, serenely lining up each one to find purchase through a different monster's eye. The team has never encountered a horde like this before, or at least not since Nate joined up. Seeing Ravi get a few perfect shots on a single foe is one thing, but this is a whole other ballpark. His distaste for firearms notwithstanding, Nate's always had a thing for competence, and Ravi is a dead shot. Good aim is a big deal in most South Asian folklore, nearly synonymous with virtue. Seems about right.

Val teleports around the hallway in flicker-swift dashes, taking out hounds while Constance's vines snag them in place. She appears, strikes, then disappears before any snapping fangs can catch her. That much teleportation will wear her out in pretty short order, so they can't drag this out too long.

With a clear path to the doors, Harry takes out a trio of hounds with a complicated sweep of the noodle sword. Nate almost laughs at how surprised she looks with her own success.

Harry knocks on the door with a shave-and-a-haircut rap. "Hey in there, fellow humans to the rescue! Well, human-ish."

"Thank *fuck*," comes a muffled Brooklyn-accented female voice. "We've got the way barricaded. Hold out a minute while we clear it."

"Easy-peasy," Harry says sarcastically, taking out a hound with a noodle sword/gun combo. As Nate watches, another creature tears free of its ensnaring vine while Harry is distracted and takes a running leap at her, rows of teeth glinting in its oil-slick mouth.

Before the thought even registers, Nate intercepts, blocking with his hockey stick with the intent of checking the thing into the door. It's far too heavy, and Nate slips on an oily film left by the melting bodies. Next thing he knows he's flat on his back, bracing the stick against the monster's slavering jaws. His heart thuds a wild tattoo in his ears, vision tunneling down, but he keeps his arms locked and attempts to kick up into this thing's gut. Spittle flies from its mouth, and every droplet that lands on Nate's face burns with pinpricks of fire. His arms strain as the creature bears down on him, seeking his throat.

A silver flash slams into the back of the hound's skull. It gives a pained whine and falls off him. Nate scrambles to his feet. He's always happy to see Ravi, but this is something else. Ravi grabs the creature's jaw in one hand, and the other digs into the loose skin at the scruff of the neck. He twists up sharply. There's a muffled crack, and the beast goes limp, spine broken. Ravi drops the beast as it falls, avoiding the corrosive effluvia, and draws his gun again. He glowers through lowered brows like a panther, all deadly grace.

"You've got to stop charging in like that, Doc."

Breathing fast, knuckles bloodless white on his chewed hockey stick, Nate can only shrug as he wipes his face with his shirt, adrenaline making him a little shaky. He's saved from thinking up a response by the doors finally cracking open. Attired in classic Men in Black suits, two agents flank the narrow opening, pistols ready. They wave the team inside as they lay down covering fire and bar the doors behind them.

The strike team is split into two groups, one covering the door, and a secondary smaller group back in the farthest part of the office, where filing cabinets and desks have been piled up in a defensible position. It's a fancy office, bigger than it needs to be, in Nate's opinion, with a bank of windows looking out over the Manhattan skyline.

Harry shoots Ravi a look, and with a barely perceptible nod, he steps forward, gun down at his side. "Casualties?" he briskly asks, taking lead. The doors behind them rattle, hounds renewing their attack. Nate jumps a little, but Val puts her back to the door. Even without her wings, she looks as if she could stand firm there for eternity.

A woman steps forward. "A couple of us sustained minor injuries, but nothing serious. You from this branch?" She's cute, a black-haired Latina in a pantsuit with an air of command to her.

"Atlanta," Ravi replies. "You're not local?"

"Nah." She jerks her head back to the far side of the office where the rest of the team are still in cover. "We're an escort unit for the seer. We've been expecting a rescue, actually. Glad that prediction was for real. Not sure how much longer the doors would have held out." She extends her hand. "Agent Rojas. Team lead."

"Agent Abhiramnew." Ravi shakes her hand. "Liaison for this freelancer team. The portal has been destroyed, so when you're ready we can run a clean-up on remaining hostiles."

She breathes a sigh of relief. "Great news. We've been saving ammo since the armory was—hold up. Abhiramnew?" She sizes Ravi up head to toe, then grins. "Callum's gonna lose his *shit*." Rojas calls to the group in the back. "Hey, youngblood, move up. We're clear for now."

Nate watches Ravi's face screw up in confusion. Seems like he'd been equally surprised to be recognized back with that Williams guy. "I thought you said no one was going to know who you are?"

Ravi levels a blank, puzzled look at Nate and shrugs.

From behind cover, a couple of new agents pop up, as well as a very distinctive individual, androgynous and elegant in a slim white suit, platinum hair sheeting to the waist. Nate can only assume this is the seer, who looks like they saw the Lord of the Rings movies and leaned *hard* into the elf aesthetic. Nate's a little surprised they don't have pointy ears.

One of the agents from the back can't be older than twenty, and when he spots the team he stops in his tracks, mouth hanging open. "Bloody hell," he exclaims in a plummy, aristocratic accent.

Both of Ravi's brows arch high. "Callum Harbridge?"

Constance keeps behind Nate, obscuring herself from the Trust agents. Can't blame her. Though she seems to trust Ravi now, no doubt she's still wary of these new "witch-hunters." He tries to oblige her, keeping her blocked from view as much as possible behind the shield of his body. "Harbridge," she murmurs for his ears only. "They were on that plane, were they not?"

Nate nods. Last month they managed to keep Cayenne from killing two planes full of people, including one with the entire Harbridge family on board. According to Ravi, they're some big Trust deal in England. Nate's not sure of the details.

This Harbridge kid is younger than most of Nate's students, this little James Bond Junior. Actually, he looks like… Nate suppresses a smile, glancing at Harry to see if she picked up on it too, and judging by her amused snort, she definitely does.

"Sir! Er, Agent Abhiramnew, rather," the kid says, eyes wide. His hair is swept back and shaved down at the sides. An unsuccessful attempt has been made at a close-trimmed beard. He's wearing the same black attire as the rest of the agents in his unit, but he's added to his ensemble a set of flashy cufflinks, a fashionable pocket square, and a thin tie that he hastily adjusts.

Looks like Ravi has a little admirer. *Adorable.* Nate has to bite down on a smile.

"Well, I see you two are acquainted," Rojas says, directing her team into position by the door. "Your team cleared a way in, it's only fair that my team starts clearing out. Harbridge, stay with the Atlanta crew and keep watch over the seer."

"Yes, ma'am."

Val hefts her maul and leaves the door to the strike team, looking a bit regretful to be walking away from the battle as she rejoins the team. Rojas and the rest of her agents head toward the double doors, and soon the office rings with the sounds of gunfire and chattering howls as they start thinning out the monsters through a gap in the door. It's loud as hell, but Ravi ignores the racket completely, tucking both his gun and those flashy brass knuckles under his jacket. Nate relaxes a little; if Ravi thinks they're okay, they likely are.

"I didn't know you had graduated to fieldwork, Harbridge." Ravi gives the Harbridge kid a swift, firm handshake. The kid's chest puffs up a few inches.

"I was cleared two months ago, in fact."

Ravi raises a single brow. "And already on protective detail?" He dips his chin toward the seer, a respectful gesture, and the seer grants a lofty nod back.

"Er, well." Harbridge coughs delicately into his fist. "My family insisted." Nate thinks he can read disapproval in the set of Ravi's mouth, but he's unsure if it's the nepotism or Callum's inexperience that Ravi takes issue with. The kid's eyes widen. "My family! Where are my manners, do forgive me. I am glad to have this chance to thank you. All of you," he adds, sweeping his gaze over the entire team. "We were told we narrowly avoided a nasty fate thanks to your intervention."

Pretty Machiavellian move on Padme's part, to inform a valuable family they owe their lives to Harry's team for an incident that technically never occurred. Get them indebted. Seems like Padme's style.

"A confusing day," the seer speaks up. Nate's no expert, but the accent sounds kind of Björk-ish. Maybe Icelandic.

Harbridge goes red and sweeps his hand. "My manners again, apologies. This is Ikshana. Ikshana, this is—"

"I know who they are." The seer immediately offers a hand to Harry. "It is a unique pleasure."

After a swift glance to Ravi, Harry accepts the handshake. "Hi there, nice to meet you, Ikshana. I'm Harry, I go by she/her, you got some pronouns you prefer?"

Ikshana's ageless smile widens. "They/them will suffice, thank you for asking. You, Miss McAllister, came as quite a surprise."

Callum smacks his forehead. Nate's pretty sure the right word here is "gobsmacked." "Bloody hell, you're the Chosen." Hastily, he puts his hands together in a recognizable *namaste* bow.

Harry winces. "You really don't have to do that."

"Er. Quite right. As you wish, ma'am."

Ikshana continues with eerie calm, "Quite an irritating time we've had, we seers. Things have been uncommonly difficult to predict with any certainty." Their pale gaze sweeps over each of the team in turn, from Val to Constance to Nate, but when it lands on Ravi it sticks there. "I've seen you. Long ago."

Ravi's throat bobs very slightly.

Ikshana raises both palms up, as if in supplication. "I sincerely apologize for the mistake. I was very sure. We all were."

The corner of Ravi's mouth pulls suddenly as if caught by a fishhook, then he composes it back into stillness. "Not your fault," he says harshly.

Ikshana squints. "You wear time very oddly." They lean in, peering at Ravi as if inspecting him for imperfections. "Folded on itself. Or perhaps like those Russian toys, the smaller ones fitting inside the larger. I have not seen the like before."

Ravi steps back, his ears darkening, and Nate has to look aside before his face gives him away. He's got a pretty good imagination, and he can think of a couple of time travel scenarios that would get those results. He's not jealous. He's glad Ravi had a fun time with all that time wizard sex magic, he truly is. Too bad time couldn't be rewound just to take away all the horrific abusive shit and leave the fun stuff behind.

Ravi rescued Nate; maybe he can return the favor. He reels the seer into a hearty handshake, pulling their attention off Ravi. "Hey there! Doctor Nathan Corbin, nice to meet you. So, you're a seer, that is incredibly cool! There are many fascinating tales about seers. I have so many questions!" A diversion, sure, but also the enthusiastic truth.

"You have a vital part to play, Dr. Corbin," the seer tells him, and whoa, Nate's seen eyes this pale blue before, but Ikshana's are especially piercing. It's like they can see all the way beneath his skin down to his spine. "Each one of you do. Threads of a tapestry."

Over Ikshana's head, Ravi gives Nate a tiny lopsided grin and a very slight roll of his eyes as if to convey: *Seers, man.*

Nate swallows a laugh.

Val moves out from her vigil at Harry's shoulder and approaches Callum. The kid has to lean his head back to stare up at her, face agog. She bends down and looks him over like a general inspecting a new recruit. "Your ancestor was Chosen."

Callum blinks. He might be trying to imitate Ravi, but the kid is nowhere close to achieving his cool, collected demeanor. "Er, that's right. William Harbridge. Not directly, of course, he married into the Abhiramnews. He was my great-great uncle. Chosen at the start of the first World War." He lifts his chin, obviously proud. Then he darts a glance to Ravi. "And, er, he was Agent Abhiramnew's great-great grandfather, of course."

These bluebloods and their obsession with lineage and bloodline. Nate gets it professionally; history is full of that kind of thing. But personally? He's way too working-class for that "legacy is everything" crap. The fact that this whole monolithic organization seems built on an archaic idea of the worthiness of birth over earned merit is unsettling enough, but after seeing the size and scope of this facility, the resources at their disposal... How often do the rich and powerful claim they are devoted to the greater good and actually follow through on that? Yeah, Nate doesn't believe in The Trust. He doesn't buy what they claim about themselves.

But he does believe in Ravi.

Val, having satisfied whatever curiosity motivated her

in the first place, returns to Harry's shoulder. Harry is wearing her detective face. No doubt later she's going to grill the angel on what *that* was about.

Harry turns to the seer. "If you have any useful info for us, Ikshana, I gotta say I'd be pretty thrilled to hear it."

The face Ikshana makes is almost a pout, a very normal human expression, the first Nate has seen beyond an enigmatic smile or a mysterious arch of their brow. "Would that I could. The way these past months have gone, you may be better off with a Magic 8 Ball than with a seer. Short-term divinations might still be somewhat effective, albeit limited in scope. But for us seers it's been nothing but migraines and conflicting visions."

Ravi and Harry exchange a quick look that Nate can't parse, a flash of silent communication. "I'm sorry to hear that," Ravi says, pulling a pen and a small notebook from his jacket pocket. He scribbles something on a page and hands it to Ikshana.

"What is this?"

Ravi closes the notebook with a snap. "That's the Chosen's cell number. A direct line."

Callum Harbridge's jaw drops for a moment before he gathers himself, clasping his hands behind his back and looking straight ahead with the air of somebody worried they'll get into trouble for witnessing something they're not supposed to.

"Hm. There are proper channels for these things," Ikshana says mildly.

Harry grins, all easy charm and engaging charisma. "Oh, for sure, proper channels. But, ugh, bureaucracy, right?" She leans her elbow casually against Val. "All that waiting, the red tape, you know how it is. You and your seer buddies need *anything*, you can just let me know, and me and my team will be right at your side ASAP, no problem."

Ikshana gives her a long look before inclining their head, a faint smile tracing their pale features. "A generous offer. Thank you, Chosen."

"Just Harry is fine."

There's an especially long moment in between gun-shots before Nate realizes the firing has ceased altogether. Rojas calls back, "Hall's clear," before trotting up to the group, oily ichor splashed on her hands and face. "I'm going to leave Harbridge and one other back here with Seer Ikshana. Abhiramnew, your team all-in on the facility sweep with mine, or do you want to leave anyone back?" Her eyes flicker to Constance, who is dressed in skirts and has no obvious weapon, still trying to shy away from all the agents' sightlines.

"Yeah, we're all-in."

"Great," says Rojas, sliding in a new magazine. "The

more the merrier. And a chance to work alongside you is gonna have all my guys strutting around for a while. Probably won't have to pay for their own drinks for months after word gets around."

"That's it," Ravi says, voice going stony, his brows drawn forbiddingly close. "How does everyone here know me? Harbridge, sure, we've met. But I haven't been to this branch since I was sixteen—"

Remembering what "special training" at this branch involved, Nate has to take a moment, swallowing hard against a rise of nausea, before he can pay attention again.

"—you wouldn't mind enlightening me?" Ravi crosses his arms over his chest.

Rojas grins, as if he just told a hilarious joke. "Yeah, how's everyone know about the highest record-holding agent in any department."

Clearly just to fuck with him, Harry slaps Ravi on the shoulder with an overly cheerful noise of approval.

Ravi stares blankly at Rojas. "I don't… What records?"

Rojas shakes her head incredulously. "Are you serious? Jesus, Mary, and Joseph. What kind of bubble do they keep you Atlanta guys in? Don't any of you gossip?"

Nate can't suppress a laugh. "Secret agents gossip, huh?"

"*People* gossip." Rojas shrugs. "We're careful about

stuff that matters, but this is just for some friendly, inter-branch competition. You know how it is. You make bets with your teammates, you keep in touch after you transfer, you make intel buddies, you go to office parties."

One glance at Ravi tells Nate that he does not, in fact, "know how it is."

"Intel keeps a spreadsheet of everyone's kills, assists, captures, retrievals, and rankings in all the refresher courses. Guess who's top fuckin' dog? Mr. Big Deal right here." Rojas tosses a wink at Ravi, and if the wink had been a physical thing he would have fumbled and dropped it.

"Uh. That can't…"

Rojas slams her shoulder into Callum's, rocking him off balance. "Besides, the kid here talks about you constantly. Full-on hero worship, it's embarrassing."

Harbridge goes as red as a beet and starts stammering.

Clearing his throat, Ravi turns to Rojas, adjusting his cuffs with two quick flicks of his wrists. "We should clear the building."

"Modest too," Rojas mock-whispers to Harry, giving her a just-between-us-gals smirk that Nate knows well from growing up with four sisters. Ravi looks like he might shoot a big hole in the floor to jump into, so Nate takes pity on him, kicking the hockey stick with his heel to send it up onto his shoulders.

"So, how do you wanna do this? Top floor down? Bottom floor up? A…pincer strategy?" Now Nate is just throwing out stuff he's seen in movies, but the grateful look Ravi gives him makes it worth it.

Rojas immediately gets serious. "We head down, you head up?"

"Sounds good," Ravi says with a brisk nod. He gives another to Ikshana, turning it into something a bit deeper and more respectful, almost a bow.

Ikshana returns it, then smiles enigmatically. "I foresee we shall meet again."

*

BY THE TIME the branch is cleared, it's just gone morning, and the team crashes at a Trust-provided hotel. A really nice hotel, probably the nicest one Nate's ever stayed at. Agent Williams sent them each an Edible Arrangement, though Val gave hers to a delighted Constance. She still hoards fresh fruit like she's trying to stave off rickets. You can take the girl out of the Dark Ages, but maybe you can't take the Dark Ages out of the girl.

Nate munches on a strawberry while jotting notes on the day's events in his Moleskine. Updating chronomage lore, starting a new page on Marquette's hitherto unknown brand of wild magic, scribbling observations on every detail he's gleaned of the Outside. It's been an educational day.

Perhaps the most educational bit had been finding that all the Trust agents he'd met were actually good people. He'd learned a lot in a few short chats. Rojas had been a paramedic until she saw enough weird shit to get her on The Trust's radar. Likewise, another of the MIB-looking agents had left an impressive career at the FBI to "fight the good fight," as he put it, after a monster killed his partner. Ikshana was a certified weirdo—but Nate *likes* weirdos, some of his best friends are supremely weird—who gave off solidly positive vibes and spoke often of helping others. Even rich-kid Callum Harbridge, the little James Bond Junior Ravi-wannabe, had seemed like a good guy. Nate knows how to read people, and nobody he's met appeared capable of the kind of thing Cayenne had accused Padme of. They just seemed like…people.

Maybe he's starting to get it, what Ravi sees in preserving the institution. It was easier to think it was some irredeemably evil secret society before Nate met the folks who make it up. As with all societies, ancient and modern alike, things were more complicated once you looked under the surface.

On the jet back to Georgia, Harry pours herself a tumbler of whisky, clears her throat, and asks out loud, "So how'd that obsidian mirror get there? I'd love to hear theories."

Ravi looks out at the tops of clouds. He's been quiet all morning, more withdrawn than usual, which is saying something. But clearly, he's been mulling over this question too, because he answers right away. "Cayenne could have stood exactly where the armory stands now and just jumped in and out from years in the past. Or future."

"Yeah, but how did they know the exact location?"

Ravi frowns, finally turning away from the window to face the rest of the team. "They could have…found blueprints. Or gotten to the builders."

"There could be a simpler solution," Nate suggests. "Paying an unsuspecting intern a thousand bucks to put the mirror there is way easier than tracking down super-secret blueprints."

Nate can hear the slight scrape of Ravi's calloused hand running over his beard. "We don't have interns, but point taken, Doc."

Constance sighs. "To be frank, my fellows, there are a plethora of ways a chronomage may accomplish near anything they wish. We are extraordinarily fortunate that we have managed to avert their plans without them merely trying again until they succeed."

"An unsettling thought," Val opines.

Harry rubs the bridge of her nose. "But a fair one. Well,

crisis averted, great job everyone. Have yourself a cocktail, you've earned it." She stands up and heads to the entryway, into the more lounge-like section of the jet. As she passes Nate, she surreptitiously kicks his ankle with her boot.

"Ow, fuck," he silently mouths, rubbing his ankle before getting up and following her.

When it's just the two of them, Harry crosses her arms with a wry smile. "So that actually went shockingly well for us."

"I noticed. Pretty much saved the life of someone with one of the rarest and most powerful magical talents on the planet. Saved a whole branch full of useful intel agents, *and* we learned that Ravi's name is well respected by the boots-on-the-ground level of The Trust."

"Now, theoretically, Professor. If someone was trying to thwart the Pepper's plans and give us a leg-up, do you think it might have looked *just* like that?"

"You know what, Detective Chosen PI? I think I do."

"Let's just hope whoever it is keeps it up." Harry takes a practiced swallow of whisky. "I'm gonna have a chat with Val. She's been more talkative with me lately, but that's a…process."

"I'll bet," Nate chuckles. "I don't know how many times I've begged her to let me interview her."

"Good job in the fight, by the way. You know you

didn't need to run interference for me, Doc. I'm invulnerable, remember?" She makes a face as if the words taste as ridiculous as they sound.

Sheepishly, Nate says, "Yeah, in the moment I kind of forgot."

Harry gives him a rare, real smile. "It's appreciated, nevertheless. I know we haven't had anything go down quite like that before. You did all right. Nice stick control." And Nate knows she's talking about his hockey stick, but it would take a stronger man than him to resist a set-up like that.

"Harry, you just used the words 'go down' before complimenting my stick, whatever is a gentleman supposed to think?"

Her eyes narrow dangerously. "I'm going to take your books out of alphabetical order, or whatever nerd shit is going to drive you crazy, you total dweeb."

"Throwing insults now? Guess you're out of quarters, huh?"

Nate has to run out of her reach back into the main cabin, chortling and smoothing his hair. Who tries to noogie a grown man? Honestly.

He plops down in the cushy chair next to Ravi. "Am I allowed to look upon thy face, Your Highness?"

Not dignifying him with a verbal response, Ravi rolls

his eyes with a scornful snort.

"You really didn't know any of that, man? All that Trust gossip missed you?"

"I never…made close ties with other agents," Ravi admits, pushing a loose lock of dark hair up off his forehead. "I stayed a few steps removed from almost everyone, even when I had been assigned to a team." He taps his fingers restlessly on the armrest. "I just don't understand…Why didn't anyone tell me? My aunt never mentioned…"

"That you're the best agent in the entire Trust?"

Ravi flushes dark all the way to his high cheekbones. "I thought… It always seemed like—" His lips press into a thin line.

"Like what?"

"Like I've come up short."

Nate brushes the back of Ravi's hand. "Confident people are harder to control."

Head jerking back, Ravi levels his sniper's focus on Nate. "That's true," he says, a thoughtful furrow between his eyes. "Raise up a kid to think he's important, supposed to be somebody, and you might end up with a real arrogant asshole on your hands."

"Oh, absolutely," Nate teases. "Better to give him the Cinderella treatment until he reaches majority."

Ravi's sharp exhale is almost a laugh. "I didn't say that.

Can't there be a happy medium?"

"If there is, you can find it, my guy. That goes for the whole shebang. You have a vision of how The Trust should be run. You're going to do great," he says with a squeeze to Ravi's forearm above the healing claw marks. "If I can help in my nerdy little way, lemme know."

Sometimes it's hard to meet the intensity in Ravi's eyes, the endless topaz depths of them. Feels like burning his tongue on hot coffee. But it's really good coffee, the kind you want to keep drinking anyway.

"You really think that?"

Nate crosses one leg over the other, ankle dangling over his knee. "Sure, I do. In my professional opinion, you don't have to destroy something to fix it. It's harder, *way* harder, going step by step. Figuring out what works, what doesn't. Like writing a dissertation. It *feels* easier to rip the whole thing apart and start over, but it never works out that way. You gotta have an outline. No revolution in history has succeeded building something from nothing; without a working infrastructure, the new system fails."

Ravi bites his lip, running a hand over his beard. The rasp of it makes Nate wonder how it would feel against his tongue, and he wrenches his wandering focus back to the present. "I feel like…" Ravi sighs, head dropping low. He looks exhausted. Nate wants nothing more than to bundle him up in a blanket and turn down the lights. "I feel like any progress I *might* make is just going to be undone. Like it's all going to be torn down, no matter what I do."

"Maybe so. But I don't think that'll stop you for long, sunshine."

Ravi glances away sharply, his Adam's apple bobbing. A long moment passes before he says, low and rough, "Thanks."

Worried he might have stepped on a sore spot, Nate attempts to lighten the mood. "You know," he says with a lascivious wiggle of his brows, "I think Rojas was flirting with you."

Ravi snorts. "You think? Seemed like she was making fun of me."

Nate squints in pretend speculation. "Hmm, yeah, pretty sure that's Brooklyn flirting."

"So, what's Canadian flirting?" The sideways glance Ravi slides over is worse than grabbing the end of an electric wire, Nate suddenly shocked and buzzing all over. *Don't do it, Nate, don't flirt, don't you fucking flirt.*

"Been a couple decades since I counted as one, but everyone knows we ride over to our intended on our favorite moose and pledge our troth with the finest poutine."

With a bark of laughter, Ravi fully turns to face Nate. "The gravy fries thing?"

Nate gasps theatrically. "*The gravy fries thing*, Jesus, man. That's it, we're diverting this jet to Toronto for the sole purpose of getting you real poutine. There are places that do a flourless chicken gravy, you should be fine. See, the important thing is to get the cheese curds fresh, so they're still nice and squeaky."

Ravi's mouth twists in a unique blend of horror and intrigue. "That sounds disgusting."

"Oh, ye of little faith. You know what," he decides, tapping a hand to Ravi's knee, "we don't have to take that detour. I'll just make you some. You're gonna be very surprised."

"If it's at all edible, I will be."

"That's either a slam on my cooking skills or on my birthplace's most favored dish. Either way, you trying to pick a fight, Abhiramnew?" Nate squares up, adopting a glare.

Ravi laughs again—*success*—holding up his hands. "I take it back. I don't want to meet the business end of that hockey stick."

"Speaking of, I didn't thank you yet for saving my life back there." Nate scratches at the nape of his neck, a little embarrassed. "I slipped on some monster goo."

"Oh, that's... No need."

This time it's Nate's turn to snort. "Yeah, all in a day's

work, right? Just punched an eldritch horror in the face and then broke its neck with your bare hands. *Yawn.*"

Ravi stares at Nate for a long stretch, long enough that Nate wonders if he said something wrong. "You put yourself in harm's way to protect Harry. Least I could do was make sure you were safe too."

"Teamwork makes the dream work," Nate says easily, pushing himself to his feet. "Well, we got about forty-five minutes before we land. If you want to take a quick nap, I'll get out of your hair."

"I'm fine." The words seem automatic, like Ravi has been programmed with self-effacing software.

Nate tuts. "You didn't even let me ask the great North American question first, man. Bad form."

Ravi's teeth flash in a lightning-quick snapshot of a smile, blink-and-you'll-miss-it. "Sorry. Go ahead."

"Thank you. Ahem." He leans his elbow on the back of his chair in an overly casual manner. "So, how are you?"

Ravi smiles, eyes creasing at the corners, and Nate wonders if he's ever going to see anyone more attractive in his entire life.

"I'm fine," Ravi says, and for the first time, Nate is almost convinced it's true.

Chapter Seven

USUALLY, RAVI ONLY takes runs in the morning, but even after his bi-monthly bouts at the fencing club, he's still left with a tangled knot of restlessness and exhaustion lodged under his skin. Every night since Manhattan, his dreams have only gotten worse. His sleeping mind kept imagining how much worse things could have gone there, maybe *had* gone in another timeline, maybe would *still* go if Cayenne decided to turn back time and undo everything. And then inevitably his dreams shift, warping into memories of want denied and desires fulfilled, a hot tongue running over his collarbone and elegant hands pushing apart his thighs.

So here he is, running a few more high intensity

intervals in the early October evening, at the park nearest his apartment, trying to overwork both his body and brain and tire himself out enough to sleep.

It's nearly sundown by the time he walks back to cool down, using the long sleeve of his compression shirt to wipe his brow, legs pleasantly twitchy from exertion. The route is quiet today, not as many fellow joggers as usual, and only a few spandexed bicyclists. Ravi slows down to admire a new graffitied mural that wraps around the side of a closed coffee shop and into the narrow alley lane. Atlanta has a vibrant street art scene, and a few local artists use this block as their regular canvas. Ravi's annoyed to see that someone has tagged over part of the mural, obscuring the design with jagged, hastily done lettering. Then he freezes in his tracks, heartbeat running wild and unchecked.

Your Monsoon has been spray painted on the corner of the coffee shop in bright purple letters half his height over the existing graffiti.

Ravi's eyes dart, checking his six. After a few minutes of no movement but the usual passage of cars and the occasional unconcerned pedestrian, he sidesteps toward the alley, his pulse galloping. He peers around the corner, ducks back, peeks a second time. No movement. There is an odd faint light a few dozen yards down the brick-lined alley.

On the opposite corner, next to *Monsoon*, a simple

arrow points further into the alley.

Ravi follows the arrow.

The thought occurs to call one of his teammates to back him up; he doesn't. A second thought insists he should arm himself first before going in; he doesn't. The third thought yells, *what the fuck are you doing, this is a trap, this is bait, be smart for once in your fucking life, keep your shit on lockdown, kid.*

He ignores it.

The source of the odd light is from a lit candle in a hurricane glass set at the edge of a small chalk circle. Pocket watches have been placed along the chalk. On the wall above the circle, a scrawl of violet paint reads: *Please? I'll be good.*

Ravi isn't sure how long he stands there, frozen in indecision. Maybe minutes, maybe hours.

He steps in.

After blinking back the nausea, Ravi spins around in a tight, guarded stance. He's alone in a small living room, the furniture modular and suited for compact spaces, more European in design than he's used to seeing in Atlanta. In place of the alley, a full window faces out onto the street. It's still evening, and Ravi can see over the nearby rooftops that the skyline has been redrawn with new shapes, more crowded with unfamiliar buildings. More lights, more ads, the quick dart of flying drones.

He's in the future.

A gasp jolts him out of his wonderment, the sound of indrawn breath achingly familiar. Cayenne dashes into the room, hastily raking their hair into place. As soon as they see Ravi they skid to a halt, green eyes round and wild. They exhale shakily, taking an abortive half-step toward him.

"Ravi," they say, shading his name with a million unsaid meanings.

He didn't expect to feel like this. Like no time had passed since that night on Harry's roof.

"Cayenne." He swipes his tongue over dry lips. "What do you want?"

They try on a hesitant, uneven smile, the shape not quite fitting on their face. "*You* visited *me*, sweetheart. I should be asking what *you* want."

That's what got Ravi in trouble in the first place, thinking that what he wants matters. He keeps his face impassive, arms crossing over his chest. "I want to know why I'm here."

"My little circle was only an invitation, *mon chéri*. You'd know better than I why you accepted. I suppose…curiosity?" They sidle a little closer, smile fitting better now, more genuine. "You know what they say about *le pauvre petit chat*."

"But satisfaction brought it back."

"*Quoi?*"

"Curiosity killed the cat, but satisfaction brought it back. Everyone forgets that part of the idiom."

"I suppose it holds true enough if you have nine lives. Most of us only get the one, *oui?*" Their smile fades, and the naked, open sorrow on their face hits Ravi like a sudden slap. "Ravi...I am so, *so* sorry."

He shakes his head, breath coming harsh and fast. "I don't want to hear it."

"But I..." They run a hand over their face, looking as tired as Ravi feels. "Guilt. Regret. Remorse. How does anyone live with those terrible things inside of them?" They press their hands over their chest, then pull them back as if expecting their palms to be filled with blood. They look lost, vulnerable.

Ravi looks away and swallows hard. "You once told me it's surprising what you can live with." More meaningful now, knowing Cayenne used to be a hired killer for a syndicate of supernatural criminals.

"No doubt this will shock you, but past-me is an *idiot.*" With a self-deprecating laugh they run a hand through their hair, rumpling it into a fetching mop. "This is true no matter if we're talking about me ten years ago or me ten minutes ago."

They smile, open and yearning and sincere, and it's bait, Ravi *knows* it's bait, but the knowledge doesn't help. He aches to return the smile, to set a hand to their cheek. To let his hands relearn the curve of their spine, trace the folds of their ear with his lips, to feel their skin flushed and wanting against him…

"Why are we here?"

"I…I just wanted to know that you are okay, *mon amour*." Cayenne wraps their arms around themself, a half-done embrace, looking up with beseeching eyes. "I needed to see you."

Ravi keeps his arms crossed over his chest, as if that could be any kind of shield against them. Usually, monsters have a weakness hunters can exploit to take them down: silver, or salt, or a particular type of magic, all kinds of things. For Ravi, everything about Cayenne is a weapon; their magic, their soft words, even the way they stand there separate and apart and alone, so easy to want to comfort—all his weaknesses honed into one beautiful strike.

He takes several steadying breaths. "The only reason I came is because I want you to stop. The things you've been doing, you've…you've been making my work harder." They almost collapsed an entire branch full of agents, and it's far easier to swallow his pride when others' lives are on the line, when more still may be endangered. *"Please,*

Cayenne."

Their head tips to the side in mild interest. "The things I've been doing? What things are those, *mon trésor?*"

He scoffs. "I'm not falling for that again." Back on Harry's rooftop, he'd caused Isabella Cattano's skiing accident by telling Cayenne about a personal grievance against her. They'd taken umbrage enough to exact revenge on his behalf. Ravi's fault. "I'm done giving you ammunition to use against me."

Cayenne groans loudly. "It's not against *you*, Ravi, I'd never hurt *you*. It's against those fucking monsters you work for. Why can't you *understand* this?"

"Because they're not monsters, Cayenne, they're *people*. And yes, people are—"

"Flawed, *oui*, and people make mistakes, but guided on the right path, etcetera, etcetera, I *know*, darling, but if you would just *listen*—"

Body outrunning his sense, Ravi snakes forward and grabs their wrist in his hand. They gasp and go still, looking up at him with mingled hope and wariness.

"You're rewinding this," Ravi hisses. Their impatience is a dead giveaway.

Dropping some of their wounded pose, Cayenne lifts their chin, pulse throbbing under his fingertips. "Let go of me."

"Not if you're going to keep doubling back." He feels ill, and not just from the jump forward in time. "You can't keep *doing this to me*," he says, voice breaking. "How many times have we had this talk?"

They jerk their wrist, though not hard enough to break his grip. With all their lethal capoeira moves, they easily could if they truly wanted to get loose, so this too is just another ploy. *Fuck*, he's so easy to manipulate. He wants to kick himself. "Just *stop*, Cayenne."

"You can't make me do anything, *ravageur*," Cayenne goads with a sneer. Their pulse has gone jackrabbit quick under his fingers, and they're breathing hard, eyes flashing like bright leaves in moonlight.

"Obviously," Ravi grits through his teeth. "If I could, I'd make you get out of my life."

Cayenne rears back as if he had struck them, blinking against tears. He feels like the lowest kind of worm. "You *are* my life, Ravi. Everything I do, I'm doing for *you*, my love." Arm going lax under his grip, they move close enough for their scent to fill his nostrils, that same warm, spicy cologne he's had dreams about hitting harder than Val's hammer. "If you'd just *trust* me, you'd be so much happier."

Ravi's throat dries out, and his own voice sounds as muted as if it's coming up from miles underground. "I *did* trust you. And even if I could forgive you for…" He can't bring himself to say it, can't even think the words, for a single heartbeat can't see anything but ashes floating on water. "But you *lied* to me. The *whole time*, you *knew*. You knew I'd find out, and you chose to—" He gasps for air. "I let…I let you see parts of myself that I've never shown anyone before. I *trusted* you."

"More the fool, you, my love. I told you not to, didn't I?"

"So, it's my fault? That I didn't listen?"

They bite down on their lip, looking up through lowered lashes. "I wish you'd just hit me, already."

Recoiling, Ravi stares in disbelief. "What?"

"You'll feel better," Cayenne remarks as lightly as if commenting on the weather. "I'll feel better too, I must admit, sweetheart. A little well-deserved punishment, no?" They wink, leaning in close enough that he can feel the heat of their body, hear the slide of tongue over lips. "I want you to, darling. Can you be a good boy and do that for me?" The low, sultry croon hits him hard below the belt.

Shocked and stung, Ravi drops their arm and steps away. "You…you can't talk to me like that anymore." He drags the back of his hand across his mouth, shaking. "I don't want to hit you. You…still think I'm just some thug in a suit? You know me, know how I was raised, and you think

I'd want…"

Cayenne closes the distance until they are inches away. Their tattooed hand on his chest, slender fingers set right over the claw-shaped scars hidden under his shirt. Their eyes bore into him, deep, searching, sincere.

"I do know you, Ravi. I *know* you. I *see* you. And you know me, my love." They snatch up his hand and place it over their own heart. It thrums wildly under his clammy palm. "Nobody is ever going to know either of us the way we know each other, Ravi. Nobody can give you what I can. *Please*. Come back to me. I'll make it all up to you."

Ravi's arm is numb and won't respond as he tries to pull it back. His feet are locked in place, made of stone. "I shouldn't have come here."

In a slow glide, Cayenne runs both hands up Ravi's shoulders. It might as well be some kind of magic, the way the sensation saps away his strength. He's got nothing in him, can't move, can't push them away. He can barely breathe.

Cayenne licks their lips, their mouth red. "My beautiful boy. I can say I'm sorry a hundred times, but it won't ever change what I did. What if I tell you something else instead, hm? Say that a hundred times? I will, *mon cher*." They lace their fingers behind his neck, trapping him in place, and he shivers as their breath gusts hot across his throat. "I love you."

"Stop," he whispers, no louder than an autumn leaf skittering over the ground.

"I love you, Ravi."

"I don't want to hear it."

"Liar." Their smile is a slow curling thing of soft lips and sharp teeth, a hairsbreadth from his throat, close enough to bite, as the words spill across his jugular; "I love you; *je t'aime; ti amo; main tumse pyaar*—"

Ravi buries his fists in their hair and grinds their mouths together, more attack than kiss, a desperate bid to stop the unbearable tumble of endearments.

Cayenne gasps into Ravi's mouth, familiar and sweet, and he feels truly awake for the first time in weeks.

"*There* we go," they hiss against his tongue, triumphant. Their teeth are sharp on his lip, nipping wildly, breath hot and quick. They twine their hands up into his hair and cleave tight, lithe body fitting against him like the sea to the shoreline.

Fuck, but they feel good, overwhelmingly good, as if they were carved to fit against him. Ravi sinks, drowning, sucking on their tongue and grabbing fistfuls of their shirt. Cayenne surges forward, walking Ravi back until his shoulders hit the wall. They moan into him, holding his jaw open with tight, grasping fingers so they can devour him, swallowing his breath and leaving him lightheaded. They smile, rake their nails down his chest, and dive a brazen hand straight under the waistband of his joggers.

Later, he can at least take the barest solace that he does push them away. It's a close thing, but he manages it.

"*Fuck*," he growls, hands braced on their shoulders, trembling at the effort of keeping the distance. Grappling for words, for any scrap of his tattered willpower to cling to, he gasps, "Undo it."

Panting with want, Cayenne sways forward, stopped from resuming the kiss only by Ravi's firm grip. They roll their eyes. "Make up your mind! You don't want me to rewind, you *do* want me to rewind. You're *so* inconsistent, *mon trésor*." They touch the tip of their tongue to their lip and grin, face flushed lotus pink. "*You* kissed *me*."

"*Undo it*," he breathes, a note of desperation creeping in.

"No," they scoff.

Cayenne's shoulders are the only thing holding him up. Ravi bows his head, hair falling into his eyes as he drags in breath after breath. "Cayenne…"

Sagging a little, Cayenne sighs and sets a hand to their tattoo. It flashes and Ravi feels that familiar tug in his gut, head briefly set to spinning. They now stand apart, back to the positions they had been in a handful of minutes ago.

"There," Cayenne says with a pointed showman's flourish of their hand. "Did that help, my sweet? Did that undo what we have done?"

Ravi drags a trembling hand over his face. He can still feel their nails on his scalp, still taste them in his mouth. It's only a memory in his mind, but it feels as real as anything.

"No."

"No." A wolfish grin. "So, what harm if we do it again, hmm?" They move in.

Ravi steps back, hands going up. "No."

Reluctantly Cayenne pulls to a halt, crossing their arms with an annoyed pout, as if Ravi was acting very silly. "All right, all right. I can wait. Here." They fish out a red phone from their pocket and hold it out to him. "So, I don't have to draw chalk circles all over Atlanta every time we want to speak, *mon amour*."

"Stop calling me that," he hisses. Each endearment is another needle under his skin, his willpower already dangling by a thread. "I don't want to speak with you, I just want…" He's not sure how to end that. *I want you gone? I want you to help me fix The Trust? I want you to take us back to the way things used to be, to spin us all the way back to before I knew the truth?*

"Just…take the phone, Ravi."

"No."

The phone clatters to the floor. Cayenne yanks on their hair with both hands, sending it into a disordered mess. "*Arrgh,* you are so *frustrating*! I just want us to be *happy*, why is this..." They turn away from him, arms crossed, drumming their fingers against their elbows. When Cayenne turns back to him, their expression has gone flat and serious. "You may want to ask your little friends if they've been keeping any secrets from you, dearest."

"What are you talking about?"

Their shoulders rise in a graceful shrug. "I'm sure it's not for me to say." They take a small sidling step toward him, arching their head back, hair sliding into a fiery tangle, pale throat exposed. "Just stay the night, my sweet. Just one night. I know you want it too. I'm not going to beg. We can snatch away a few more hours of happiness together. No past, no future, just like it was back at the lake house. Like the kiss we just didn't have. One night, then I'll take us back to before, so it won't count. Hm?"

It's only due to the memory of those ashes that Ravi has the strength to say, "No."

"Okay, you called my bluff. I will absolutely beg; *please,* Ravi, let me make it up to you."

He stares at them, then barks a sharp, joyless laugh. "Make it up to me?"

Cayenne's shoulders drop, and it's like a mask has

fallen away. Harder at the edges, their words all sharp corners and angles, slanting him a bladed smile. "Do you think I had to do this?" They wave a hand behind him at the circle. "Set a snare and vainly hope you'd keep to your regular route for your little jogs, darling? Anything you've seen me do, anything I've *let* you see, you must realize I can do much, much worse. You can have Constance set any kind of magic spells to keep me from finding you all that you wish, *chéri*." With a placid smile, they say, "Fairly simple to remove her from the equation, one way or another."

Between one word and the next Ravi goes utterly still.

Instantly Cayenne holds up their hands with a disarming grin. "Ah, no, not a threat, *mon tigre*, whatever do you think of me? I am merely saying that I'm not doing my worst. I'm trying to be *better*. For you."

"This is you trying?" Ravi manages in a strangled voice, dragging in air.

Cayenne's face scrunches up in exaggerated disdain. "*Ugh*, I know, I'm not very good at it, am I?" Another small sideways step toward him. "If *you* helped me, I think I could be better. My north star, my guiding light." They break into an achingly handsome smile.

That's…more tempting than it has any right to be. Side by side, what they could accomplish? Being together—really together. Their combined strengths and abilities.

Was the inevitable price of love betrayal? How should Ravi know? He has no frame of reference to know what's normal. It's a common enough refrain in pop culture—that love hurts, love is pain, love is a battlefield, love is a knife in the back.

Fuck, he can still taste them on his tongue.

"I don't…" He swallows, teeth catching his lower lip. "You would listen to me?"

"You've *inspired* me, Ravi." Cayenne steps closer. "*Je suis ton monstre.*"

His gaze locks on theirs, his will wavering, steel melting into quicksilver.

And there on their face, the face he's come to know so well, is a tiny, nearly imperceptible shift. The tapered end of their eyebrow lifts just slightly in interest, marking a bullseye.

Ravi tips his head back and puts his hands over his face, heart sinking down to his feet. "I can't believe that I… *Fuck*, Cayenne, how many tries did it take to find that tactic?" He drops his hands, a bitter laugh on his lips. He should be furious, but instead he just feels exhausted. Wrung out and empty.

Cayenne tsks. "You're so difficult, *mon amour*." They pick up the dropped phone. "Look, Ravi, if you do want to get in touch, or if you're in trouble in *any* way, this will be under that little garden statue at the lake house."

He rallies, scraping together a bit of fire. "You might as well throw it in the fucking lake."

A fond smile. "So fierce, *mon tigre.* It's very attractive." Their eyes sweep over him, hungrily. "Don't try and claim you don't miss me. You've always been so honest with me." Cayenne drags their plush lower lip between their teeth, head at an inviting tilt. "Here's some honesty in kind: I miss you, Ravi, so much it's like I'm missing a piece of myself. I miss touching you. I miss the way you smell. I miss the *taste* of you, the way your body is always so—"

"*Stop,*" Ravi begs, stepping back. His shoulders bump into the wall behind him. Trapped. Cornered.

Cayenne's lips purse into a rueful bow. "I suppose I can't entice you into one little *tête-à-tête* for old time's sake, can I?" They don't reach for their tattoo, but their hand does twitch minutely, as if on instinct.

Swallowing dryly, Ravi shakes his head. "Can I entice you to help me fix The Trust instead of tearing it apart?"

They laugh, long and derisive. "Hmm, fuck me good enough, and I'll think about it." Their tongue flashes, pink and wet, over their lips. "Can't ask for fairer than that."

Ravi turns his face away, more disgusted with himself than Cayenne, at his body's reaction. "Then I guess we don't have anything else to talk about." He forces his feet to move, back to the chalk circle.

"Wait…Ravi, *wait*. Don't go, *s'il te plaît*, I'm sorry."

He whirls around. "You're free and clear, Cayenne. I didn't tell The Trust about you. You got away with it. So just *go*. Stay out of my business, out of my team, out of my life." Funny how the words taste like lies on his tongue, even though he's certain he means them.

"Why don't you go ask your little teammates if *they* are staying out of your business, pet?"

"I'm not your *pet*," Ravi chokes, and walks back out into the past.

Chapter Eight

HE KNOCKS TWICE, brisk and efficient, then waits, arms tight across his chest, barely restraining himself from tapping a foot.

The door opens on Nate's friendly face. "Hey! Knew it was you. You're the only one on my short list of magically allowed visitors who knocks like a robot." Nate is dressed like he's settled in for the night, in comfortable clothes and a pair of wire-rimmed glasses. He waves Ravi inside. "Val just knocks once, extremely hard. And that's after she teleports on the *inside* of the door. C'mon in."

Silently Ravi stalks in, barely slowing to toe off his running shoes. He's been to Nate's apartment once or twice, but never without the rest of the team. Cozily appointed, all soft furniture and plush rugs. Lots of family pictures and world art on the walls, artifact replicas displayed on the many bookshelves. Anywhere space exists for a bookshelf, one has been squeezed in and loaded full.

Brushing past Nate, Ravi goes over to a shelf and angles his head to read the spines. A mix of textbooks, field journals, fairy tales, and pulp paranormal fiction novels. His attention shifts to a framed picture propped up between *Bullfinch's Mythology* and a decorative canopic jar of Anubis. A younger, lankier Nate, hair shaggy, with his arm around a white girl about the same age. They're both grinning happily at the camera.

"So, can I get you anything? You want a drink? I think I only have beer. I can maybe make a gin and tonic? Eh, the tonic might be flat. I'm overdue for groceries. The beer's probably the better option, to be honest. You can do regular beer, right? I've seen you drink it. Well, sip it. There's, uh, water? I've got a Brita."

That's a whole lot of nervous babble. Ravi doesn't look around. "It's a mild intolerance, not an allergy. I can have a beer."

"You're sure? Great! Okay. I'll just go get that, then."

Other photographs line the shelves and walls, and Ravi moves slowly from one to the other. Nate with both arms slung over the shoulders of four young blonde women nearly identical except for age; Nate with a diploma and two middle-aged parents at his side beaming with pride; Nate at a bar with a cluster of friends all wearing rainbow themed attire; Nate and his college hockey team holding up a trophy; Nate brandishing a fish while he sits in a boat with that same auburn-haired woman from the first photo. She's leaning into him, holding a much larger fish. They both are a little older than they were in the first photo. They look happy.

"Here ya go." Nate comes back and hands Ravi a bottle with the top already popped off. Ravi takes a long swallow, eyes on the photo. Nate clears his throat. "You didn't jog here, did you? It's a little chilly by Georgia standards, even with long sleeves." After a pause, Nate asks more softly, "Are you okay? Did something happen?"

Ravi's throat immediately goes tight. "Who's this?" he asks in a sandpaper rasp, pointing his beer at the woman in the picture.

Nate lets him change the subject without protest. "That's Trish. We used to be engaged."

Ravi swings his head around, really looking at Nate for the first time since he arrived. Ravi's never seen Nate wear glasses before. They highlight the blue of his eyes and the angle of his jaw.

"This…was your fiancée?"

"Yup, high school sweethearts." Nate smiles. It's a little sad, but also a great deal fond. "Then we went to college, tried long distance, and it fell apart. Nobody's fault. It was a rough time, but we stayed friends. We check in every few months, catch up on news, see how our families are doing." He takes a drink of his beer. Ravi watches the bounce of his throat as he swallows. "After the breakup, I did what fifty percent of guys do when their hearts get broken."

"And what's that?"

"I hit the gym. It was either that or get a beer gut."

Unbelievably, Ravi laughs. It's a dry little thing, but it's there. He chokes on the end of it, chest rising and falling unevenly, and pours about half the beer down his throat in one long swallow.

"Ravi," Nate says softly, shifting toward him. "What happened?" He radiates concern, nothing devious behind it that Ravi can detect, but his judgement hasn't been so great lately.

"Is there anything you haven't told me?"

Nate's eyes flash wide for a split second, a pink flush creeping up his neck. "Like what?"

Ravi sets the beer bottle on the shelf with a precise *click*. "Cayenne said my friends are keeping secrets from me. Are you?"

Nate's arms drop to his side and he takes an instinctive, halted step toward Ravi. "Jesus Christ, you're saying they told you that *recently*? Are you *okay*? Did they —" Nate starts to run a hand over his face before it bumps into his glasses. Hastily, he takes them off, face going scarlet, and sets them on a shelf along with his beer. He inspects Ravi from head to toe the same way Constance does when checking for injuries after a battle. "What did they want?" he asks, though his lips screw up to one side, as if he already knows the answer before he finishes the question.

"Is it true?"

Nate sighs. "Yeah. It is."

It stings, but Ravi merely waits, taking a page from Robert Hernandez's book, creating an uncomfortable silence to be filled.

Jerking a thumb at the couch, Nate asks, "You wanna sit down for this?"

Ravi sits. Nate joins him, turning sideways to face Ravi head-on, and without hesitation says, "Harry and I have had run-ins with Cayenne over the last couple of weeks. They figured out Harry's apartment but not what floor, so every so often they'll pop in and look around for her."

"Why?"

"To get to you," Nate says earnestly. "Constance layered so many protection spells on your building that I think

Cayenne's hair will start on fire if they even *look* at it. Obviously they weren't going to get very far talking to Val, they hate even being close to Constance, and they don't like *me* much either; so that means it's been Harry."

"I meant, why didn't you tell me?" Ravi asks through a throat full of thorns.

"Because Cayenne is a manipulative, abusive prick and will say any bullshit they think will work to make you feel sorry for them." Nate's steady gaze does not waver. "Harry and I discussed it extensively. Neither of us were thrilled about keeping it from you, but we thought—I *still* think it's the right call." Nate doesn't often use his hands to gesture as he speaks, so instead his sincerity is written in the set of his eyes, the evenness of his voice. "Look, Ravi, I've been in a lot of relationships—let's just assume you made the appropriately catty joke here and move on—and I've been involved in a few nasty breakups. I'm really sorry Cayenne got to you. I wish there was a way we could have prevented it better. In a normal relationship, you can just block your ex on social media and throw out their hoodie and that's the end of it, but this fucking time travel bullshit makes things tough. Did they… I can tell you're not okay, so I'll stop asking. But did they—"

"We just talked," Ravi interrupts, back straight with both feet on the floor. A technical truth, chronologically speaking. "They just wanted to talk."

"Uh-huh." Nate slouches, running fingers through his short blond hair and making it stand on end. "Let me guess. They're feeling this new scary emotion called regret. And they're really sorry, and they want to make it up to you, right?"

Ravi doesn't say anything, forehead furrowing.

"Ah, geez, man, I'm sorry." Nate gives Ravi's knee a quick pat before drawing back. "That's classic manipulator stuff. And then telling you that your friends aren't really your friends on top of it, right? Trying to isolate you? Christ, that fucking asshole," he snaps swift and furious, as if the sentiment could no longer be contained.

Ravi runs back the evening in his head, this time a step removed, thinking tactically for once instead of like a brokenhearted idiot who hadn't had years of secret agent training. "They were..." He drags a hand over his mouth, thoughts clicking into place. One minute contrite, the next aggressive and goading, and the next tender and loving; even for Cayenne, it had left Ravi with emotional whiplash. "They were all over the place. Scattershot. No unifying... strategy, I guess you'd say."

"Trying everything to see what works, maybe?"

Head sinking into his hands, Ravi hisses, "*Shit*. Yeah." Marking hits and misses. Rewinding when they could, and tallying wins for next time when they couldn't. He *knew* they were playing him, but still let himself fall for it. *Fucking pathetic.*

Nate's arm twitches, like he's restraining himself from reaching out. "I get that you haven't had a lot of experience in this arena. So let me help, my guy."

Ravi pauses. He looks up. Every syllable, every tiny tell of his body language, is drawn into a challenge. "Yeah? You want to help me?"

He's noticed the way Nate looks at him. He's not blind.

Nate's easy smile dissolves any tension before it can even really build. "Course I do. Look, Ravi, I can't tell you what to do, but friend to friend? Do *not* take Cayenne back. This is seriously fucked-up behavior, even for a time assassin. This is textbook toxic manipulation to make you feel like they're the only person you can turn to, but that's not true. You have people. I'm aware this sounds like a terrible pun, but *chosen family* is a real thing. You have friends who care about you. You have us, have this team. We keep each other safe, patch each other up, teleport each other around, and get cacti to cheer each other up." He grins, flashing a little wink.

Twining his hands in his lap, Ravi swallows, chest tight. "It's... I've never been through anything like this. I don't know what..." He's lost and adrift without a map. He feels like he's about to come out of his skin. He wants to *do* something, needs to take action, needs to be useful. He digs the heels of his palms into his eyes.

"My guy, *nobody* has been through what you're going through, for real. Some of it, sure. Getting your heart stepped on is a nearly universal experience." Nate does touch him this time, a sympathetic hand on the shoulder. "But eventually you figure out that anyone who says love hurts isn't doing it right. I promise, Ravi, things will get better. You just gotta give yourself time. There's plenty of fish in the sea."

Shrugging out from under Nate's hand, Ravi pushes himself up to pace across the brightly patterned rug. "Plenty of fish?" A hollow, mirthless laugh. "Cayenne was the first person *in my life* who wanted to know me. Really *me*, not whatever they expected was already there. They *saw* me. That's the worst *fucking* thing, no one has ever, *ever*, seen me before. I know it was all lies, every second of it, but it was *real* too." The words burn their way out of his throat. He drags his hands over his face, willing himself to stop trembling. "I look at them now and I see a stranger. Did I ever really know them? Did I just see what I wanted to see? I feel *so fucking stupid*."

"Ravi. You're not. You're—"

Ravi spins on his heel. "You lead this charmed life,

you're a…a fucking dreamboat professor with a supportive family and an emotionally healthy relationship with his ex-fiancée. For you, the sea is nothing *but* fishes."

Nate stands up too, and his words ring out like a struck tuning fork.

"You've been taught to hide anything unique about yourself your entire life. You think you're worthless unless you're useful. You always feel like you're on the outside looking in. You're intelligent. You're loyal. You're funny, but don't think you're allowed to show it. You think of yourself as a shield and the whole world a battle you have to guard against. You're allergic to cats. You're into art. You're good with kids. You're kinder than you think you are. You're so much more than just a guy with good aim, Ravi." Nate spreads his hands wide, smiling softly. "See? Just because they were the first to see you doesn't mean nobody else ever will. Plenty of fish out there with vision as good as mine."

At his sides, Ravi's hands curl into fists, and he stalks toward Nate.

*

MAYBE HE'S PUSHED too far, Nate realizes. He doesn't believe for a second that Ravi would hurt him, but yell at him to mind his own fucking business? Probably.

Ravi stops less than a foot away. His chest is heaving, like he's sprinted miles. He glares up at Nate with clear challenge and demands, "Do you want me or not?"

That's not anywhere close to what Nate was expecting.

He's never seen Ravi in anything more casual than a bespoke collared shirt before. Showing up on Nate's doorstep, all windswept hair and broodiness, those long, lean lines of him outlined in a skintight athletic shirt, had come alarmingly close to some fantasies Nate's had. It caught him off-guard. And now this is… Well, it's unexpected, is what it is.

"Uh, that's…" It's the best he can manage.

Ravi licks his lips, and the pinkness of his tongue is all Nate can focus on, his brain short-circuiting. "Just tell me you want me, and you can have me."

And, whoa, zero to sixty in under a second, Nate is so turned on he's literally dizzy with it. "Wow, sunshine, that's a hell of an offer." He clears his throat. "Is that what *you* want?"

A wry huff. "I thought you had good vision, Doc."

"Pretty good hearing too. Sounds like you're only concerned with what *I* want."

Ravi bites down on his lip, and Nate's vision again tunnels down to his lush mouth, which isn't helpful in the least. "That's…easier," Ravi breathes, his octave dropping low.

"Say that you want me, and I'll do anything you like."

Every drop of blood rushes down from Nate's brain to his dick, and he sways a little from the force of his arousal. "Hell of an offer," he croaks.

Ravi's eyes darken, and he moves in with a silent step. He bumps into Nate's upraised hands. Fuck, it's hard to keep his palms flat on Ravi's chest, to not let them wander, explore all that toned, sleek, taut-muscled—*fuck.*

"Whoa, hey, Ravi. Wait."

A thin line appears between dark brows.

Nate hastily drops his hands, but Ravi's heat clings to his skin. "Is that what *you* want?"

A complex array of barely perceptible emotions chases across Ravi's features. "It's so *easy* for you," he says, with something like envy. "You get to say yes to things you want, and no to things you don't. You're safe no matter what. I want all kinds of things I can't have and have all kinds of things I don't."

Under his breastbone, Nate's heart gives a little tug. "You should get that too, Ravi. You get to say no. To have a choice. You deserve to feel safe."

As he looks away, Ravi's throat moves, breath visibly hitching. "I...don't think I remember what safe feels like," he finally says, like it's been pried out of him, so soft it's almost a whisper.

Nate wants to punch Cayenne in their perfect lying face. He wants to…

"Can I hug you? Would that be okay?"

Ravi shoots him a startled stare.

"I'm a huggy kind of guy," Nate explains. He was raised in a touchy-feely family; none of that typical Midwestern restraint for the Corbins. Nate's always been tactile with his friends, and Ravi looks like he could use it.

Ravi eyes him, wary, before nodding once.

Without hesitation Nate pulls him in, carefully angling his hips away but otherwise folding Ravi completely into an embrace, arms wrapping around the breadth of Ravi's shoulders, holding him close.

Bit by bit, Ravi sinks into it, his hands crawling up Nate's ribs until they rest tentatively at his mid-back. After a minute, his heartbeat steadies against Nate's chest.

"This is nice," Nate says. Just the smell of Ravi is enough to make him a little light-headed; masculine musk and a rich woody scent that Nate knows but can't place. It takes some extra effort to compartmentalize his longing into a neat little box, to keep this friendly embrace from turning into something else.

Fingers slowly wind into Nate's shirt until Ravi is clinging on. Face turned into Nate's collar, he makes a low sound in his throat that Nate interprets as agreement.

"You can stay, if you want." Nate gives Ravi's back a friendly little rub. "As long as you like. We can keep doing this. Just this." People need physical touch, and all too often, men don't get to have it without first paying the toll of sex. Nate's willing to bet Ravi's no stranger to that exchange.

"You…aren't interested." Ravi's shoulders slump, his voice regretful, lost. "I'm being an asshole. You and Harry —" He starts to pull away, but so slowly and reluctantly that Nate thinks it's probably okay to tighten his arms a little, encouraging Ravi to stay. Seems like that's the right call, because Ravi instantly subsides, his hands again tangling in Nate's T-shirt.

"Oh, no, no, Harry and I are just friends. You're not an asshole at all. And of course I'm interested." There's no point lying to the guy; he's already got Nate's number. The jig is up. "But I don't think you're in a good headspace right now."

Ravi's throat clicks as he swallows.

"Hey, it's okay, my guy. You wanna move back to the couch? We can get comfy and I can hold you for a bit. I'd like that. Does that sound good to you?"

Ravi drags in several shuddering breaths before he nods, face hidden against Nate's faded old college shirt. Patiently, Nate waits until he hears a small, gravelly, "Okay."

After a bit of maneuvering, Nate ends up on his back

with Ravi tucked beside him, head pillowed on Nate's chest. Nate drapes his arms over Ravi lightly, offering the comfort of his touch without blocking off a way to escape.

Ravi doesn't speak, doesn't look up. He just takes long measured breaths like he's counting them out, one by one. He's a warm and pleasant weight, far better than a blanket, and he relaxes even further as Nate strokes Ravi's hairline with his thumb.

He's a caretaker by nature. It's a rare thing for a tough, independent guy like Ravi to let himself be cared for. He wants Ravi to know that he can trust Nate. That he's safe with him.

So, Nate is *not* going to fuck this up. He's not going to complicate a friendship with sex just because it's offered while in a state of distress. If Ravi does ever decide he wants something more… Well, friendship is a pretty good foundation to build on.

*

RAVI JOLTS AWAKE, heart pounding, sweat cooling at his temples. It's dark, the shadows strange, and he jerks away from the unfamiliar bulk under him.

Nate shifts beneath him, murmuring "S'okay, s'okay," in a sleep-rough voice that rumbles up through his chest. A hand smooths over the disordered tumble of Ravi's hair, heedless of his clammy skin. Nate shushes softly, stroking Ravi's forehead like he's an oversized cat.

After a frozen moment, Ravi leans into the soothing touch, still shaky with nightmares. Strong arms tighten around him, squeezing protectively. Ravi slowly drops his head back to Nate's chest, pulse calming. He closes his eyes and listens to that steadfast heartbeat, the swell of it like an ocean buoying him up, the soft rise and fall of a tide lulling him back to sleep. Before he drops off, Nate must be conscious enough to mumble, "I've got you," and it's the last thing Ravi hears before he sinks into slumber.

He sleeps, deep and dreamless.

When he wakes again, it's morning. Judging by the light through the windows, it's maybe an hour later than Ravi usually sets his alarm. His top half sprawls across Nate's torso. At some point in the night, a thin blanket has been pulled off the back of the couch and thrown over them.

He'd shown up at Nate's door last night intending to provoke either a fight or a fuck. He hadn't expected he'd be waking up warm and well-rested after a night of what could only be defined as platonic cuddling.

Nate rouses after a small, sleepy grumble, lashes fluttering. "Sandalwood," he says with muzzy satisfaction.

"What?"

"I've been trying to place it." Nate sets his nose to

Ravi's temple and breathes in. Ravi shivers. "Mm. Is that a shampoo?" The touch is intimate but not seductive, not something Ravi has any experience with. Like waking up together is no big deal, not trying to turn it into anything more. Touch offered freely without ulterior intent.

"It's…it's hair oil." Ravi tries to match Nate's casual tone. "I'll bring you some," he offers, ready to jump on any opportunity to pay Nate back for this, for giving him…a *lot*, not the least of which is comfort, and the best night's sleep he's had in months.

"Aw, that's sweet, man." Nate smiles and stretches his arms over his head. "You want some eggs?"

"And you can cook too," Ravi murmurs, mostly to himself, the corner of his mouth curling up.

Nate rolls his eyes with a chuckle. "It's just eggs. I've only got regular toast. I'll get some non-glutenous stuff next time I hit the store. Then it can be eggs *and* toast, and you'll be rightly impressed by my superior culinary skills."

The implication being that Nate wants Ravi back here in his home. Wants to cook for him.

Ravi's pulse increases, not a sharp spike but a warm, steady build, and he turns his face to the side with a shy smile.

All the details he's been cataloguing in the back of his mind for the last several months march to the forefront; the professor is handsome enough that it's likely to get him in trouble with students if he's not extra careful; blue eyes and blond hair that are kept from reading as "boy next door" by the clever angle of his brows and the rakish shadow of stubble; a warm smile, an easy laugh, nice shoulders, narrow hips, long-fingered hands that would look very good on—

Nate's phone chimes from the coffee table. The text tone must be customized because Nate grunts, "Harry," and reaches for it.

Ravi pulls himself to the far end of the couch and fishes his own phone out of his joggers. There's a missed call—and the fact that he slept through his phone buzzing in his pocket is certainly unusual; Ravi's a light sleeper—and a text that reads, *Hey, gotta job! Can you get us a jet by 9?*

He doesn't have to check before he texts back, *Yes.* If the Chosen wants a jet, The Trust will get her a jet. *Where to?*

- Harry-

Indonesia. Val's gonna zap around and pick everyone up at 8:45. Supposed to be combat light, I've been assured.

He snorts and texts back an affirmative while attempting to finger comb his hair into place. "Combat light, she says."

Nate laughs and tosses his phone back on the table. "So

lemme guess, you're gonna roll up with a bandolier of grenades?"

"You'll thank me later."

"No doubt. You still want those eggs, or do you have stuff to take care of?"

"I do," Ravi says, the honest regret taking him by surprise. "But I appreciate the thought." He has to head home, shower, suit up, and make some calls before hitching a ride on the angel express.

"How about a ride home?" Nate sprawls against the plush armrest and covers a yawn with the back of his hand.

"No, I'm good. I'll enjoy the walk." It'll eat into his time, but he's feeling alert and full of energy for the first time in weeks. And if he sees any chalk circles, this time he's going to be smart and avoid them.

"At least let me make you some coffee for the road. I've got protein bars too."

"Yeah, that sounds great." Nate's almost to the kitchen by the time Ravi adds, "And…thanks, Nate."

Nate pauses in the doorframe to toss him a smile. "You're welcome, Secret Agent Man."

Soon, Nate hands Ravi a lidded paper cup and the protein bar, waving off more of Ravi's thanks. "Anytime, my guy." He gives Ravi's shoulder a squeeze and adopts a fanciful yuppie accent. "I'll see you on the jet, old boy."

"No, no, you need to look down your nose more, if you really want to pull off the filthy rich impression." He gives Nate a quick demonstration.

Nate laughs. It's a very nice laugh. "See? You're *funny*."

As Ravi walks down from the apartment and steps into a pleasantly mild Atlanta morning, he takes a sip of the coffee. Blonde roast, no cream or sugar, with a dash of cinnamon. Warmth suffuses through his chest and into his limbs, bolstering his steps.

Chapter Nine

"SO, IN MY vision," Harry explains, "which I guess are things I get now, I dreamed about a ruin in a jungle. Not like a hidden ruin; there were signs in English and tourists all over, people walking around with cameras. And then I saw a bunch of…horrifying shadows emerging from the ruin. I woke up, and guess who called me?"

Her relaxed tone doesn't lead Ravi to become too alarmed, but nevertheless he says, "You have no idea how much dread that question filled me with."

"Sorry, yeah. With our track record, right? Ikshana called." She gives Ravi finger-guns and smirks. "Direct line to the Chosen, nice play. They got a vision very similar to mine, said we should handle it directly, and gave an exact location. Weirdly, they said even though it's going to be a critically important problem for us to solve, it should be a low-key mish. Not that I don't agree that fortune favors the prepared," she adds, toeing the drag bag Ravi set by the door.

"Please don't kick that. These jets are expensive."

Nate laughs nervously. "You didn't *actually* bring grenades, did you?"

Ravi looks at him, expressionless. Then winks. Nate relaxes and turns away, smiling as a flush creeps up his neck.

"Anyway," Harry continues, eyes flicking back and forth between them. "This is good for us. The seer contacting us directly cuts out the middleman, and the Chosen's team gets a reputation for sweeping in and fixing problems before they're even reported to the top brass. This is advantageous because…" She looks at Ravi expectantly.

"Because Harry's position is extremely precarious right now." He leans back into his chair with his arms folded. "It's been nearly a decade since the last Chosen, and nobody has any idea how the urumi got to her. Rumors are flying. Some families suspect a trick or a trap, that somehow the Choosing has been falsified. The more evidence mounts that Harry truly is Durga's Chosen, the more good she does, the better off we'll be for the Gala next month."

Ravi would rather chew glass than attend yet another formal Trust event, but this one is going to be the most important one he's ever faced. The introduction of Harry McAllister as the new Chosen One to the Trust families. His aunt Padme's been busy setting it up for weeks.

"The more people convinced that her claim is legitimate, the more we'll have on our side." Of course, there's one surefire way to secure Harry's place—just seven little steps around a fire. But Ravi hasn't brought up the marriage talk just yet, and Harry hasn't pressed the issue either. They're not going to be able to dance around it much longer. By tradition, even their engagement alone will get them more access to intel and resources than they currently have.

"My *claim*," Harry mutters under her breath. Then she straightens, pulling her hair into a high bun. "Saving the Manhattan branch and then fixing today's mystery problem? Gonna make a strong impression. We should really write Ikshana a thank-you note."

"I quite liked that comely platinum beanpole," Constance says cheerfully. "Doth you know how long it has been since I've been tupped?"

"Tupped?" Ravi isn't familiar with the word, not even sure if it's English.

Nate coughs as if covering a laugh, going floridly red. "Tell you later. Constance, I can introduce you to some folks."

She looks dubious. "Are any of them guaranteed to not be demons in disguise?"

"I guess you could throw holy water at them before you take anyone home."

Constance brightens. "A fine idea."

"I bet there's people into that," Harry says, slouching down into her seat. "A little Exorcist roleplay."

Nate makes a face. "Gross, McAllister, have some class."

She flings a quarter at him.

"Where in Indonesia is the ruin, exactly?" Ravi asks, rolling up the sleeves of his lightweight linen suit, tucking his pant cuffs into waterproof combat boots, and making sure the ceramic knife hidden by his ankle is secure. His drag bag does in fact have a few explosives in it along with his rifle case, just in case 9mm and knuckle dusters aren't enough for whatever "combat light" scenario they're going to be walking into. Not for the first time, he envies the easy portability of Val's magic maul.

"Uhhh, Boro-something." Harry checks her phone. "Borobudur."

"Oh shit! That's the world's largest Buddhist temple," Nate exclaims. "I've always wanted to go, this is great! Y'know, assuming there's not some ravening beast we gotta take down there. If there is, we *cannot* damage the temple. It's a World Heritage Site."

"And a Trust network waystation." Everyone turns to look at Ravi except Val, who keeps gazing out the window over the white blanket of cloud tops. "They're scattered all over the globe," he explains. "Places where local contractors and volunteers gather information on the supernatural in the area, and where field agents can stop and resupply in case of emergency. Waystations were more vital hubs before satellites and cell phones, but they're all still in operation." He checks his handgun with quick, practiced motions. "I've never been to this one, but we'll find a contact who will know what's going on. They should be able to direct us."

"Okay, that actually sounds pretty cool," Harry says. "Is there a super-secret spy way to tell who the contact is?"

"Yup." Ravi smiles and leaves it at that.

She tilts her head to one side with a tiny smile of her own. "You're in a good mood today."

Ducking his chin, Ravi turns his attention back to his ammo clip.

Constance rubs her hands together. "I profess I am greatly looking forward to seeing this hallowed temple. All things in America be so new; it shall be a pleasant thing indeed to see some remnants of true history still around. Like myself."

"I could have teleported us there." Now it's Val's turn to get stared at.

Harry says, "You've been to Borobudur before? Which is a fun new tongue twister I've just invented and trademarked."

"I have existed for over a thousand years." Val doesn't turn, still gazing out at the clouds. "I have worn other human forms. I have been to many places in the world."

"Val," Nate pleads. "I know you don't like us to pry, but I need to ask again, for the sake of anthropology: please, please, *please* let me interview you."

Finally turning, Val regards Nate for a long moment. "I will consider it."

Nate's grin is radiant. It takes a second for Ravi to realize Harry is speaking.

"Well, we already got the jet, Val, but good to know. Don't suppose you've also been to Manhattan before we flew there?"

"I have."

Harry pinches the bridge of her nose. "Okay, well, in the future if you ever want to volunteer to take us via the Angel Express, you can offer. You're allowed to offer things. Or to ask for things." Ravi glances between Harry and Val. This has the weight of a long-continuing private conversation.

Val's only response is a slow nod as she turns back to the window, watching clouds swirl around silver wings.

*

BOROBUDUR IS THE largest tourist attraction in Java, and the temple is predictably awash with sightseers. All the easier for them to blend in with the crowd: a colorful sea of tourists, pilgrims, and students of various ethnicities and faiths. A few people pose in front of the carved andesite reliefs, mimicking Lord Buddha's descent from heaven, while others conduct themselves more respectfully.

"Look for a tiger," Ravi tells the team as they ascend the steep stairs onto the next terrace. Only Harry and Val are really paying attention to him, as Constance and Nate keep getting sidetracked with sightseeing. Nate's phone has got to be reaching its memory limit, with the number of pictures he's taking.

"Whoa, whoa, there are tigers here?"

"No, that's Sumatra, not Java. But I meant an image of one. There will be a carving or a painting, something like that. It'll mark our contact."

"The tiger's a Durga thing, right?" Harry fans herself with both hands; the temple stones absorb sunlight, and the lower levels are hot and sticky without the benefit of the breeze higher up.

Ravi gives her a reproachful frown. "Have you done *any* research into the goddess who has Chosen you to be her living avatar? At least look at a Wiki?"

Harry slings an arm over Ravi's shoulder as they weave around a group of wannabe influencers taking pictures of each other on the bell-like stupas despite ample DO NOT TOUCH signage. "Look, the fact I know even that much is pretty spectacular for an until-recently adamant atheist. Take what you can get."

Ravi sighs. "The tiger is Durga's *vahana*, her... The translation is vehicle, but that falls way short. He's Durga Devi's spirit animal, her connection to rightness of purpose, to her divinity. He's a symbol that she protects virtue and destroys evil."

Harry eyes Ravi with an odd sort of calculation. "Symbols are important." She taps her fingers a couple of times on his shoulder, as if in thought, before she points her chin toward an isolated stupa. "A tiger like that?"

Ravi follows her gaze. A bald man in saffron robes sits in prayer pose on a rolled-out tapestry, a stylized tiger depicted in the design. "Nicely spotted, detective."

The group gathers up, Constance grinning ear to ear and chatting merrily to an equally enthused Nate. His eyes are practically sparkling as he launches into an animated lecture about the temple's history. Ravi tears his attention back to the robed man.

He passes Val up his heavy sniper kit bag in unspoken request. She hikes the bag onto her shoulder without hesitation. Ravi approaches the monk, motioning the team to stay at his back. He kneels with a deferential nod. "I trust you know the way."

The monk raises his head. "Trust is answered in kind," he says in barely accented English. Tourists move around them, oblivious. "How do you stand?"

Ravi's hit with a little unexpected wave of nostalgia. He hasn't visited a waystation since he was in training. "Unflinching."

The monk regards him. "You must be related to the Field Director."

Ravi hides an exasperated sigh. "Oh?" A little odd that his aunt has visited before; waystations are for field agents.

"The cheekbones are distinctive. I am Suharto." Suharto bows slightly, hands together.

Ravi returns the gesture. "Ravi." The man isn't an agent but a volunteer; given names are appropriate. "My team. Freelancers." In other words, not regular agents who will know all the ropes.

"Ah, specialists. Most fortunate. Are you here to help?"

"Absolutely," Harry cuts in. "Help with what?"

"It will be easier if I showed you." The monk gets to his feet, dusting off his knees. "This way." He leads them up, almost to the topmost terrace, around a more secluded area of the temple complex. Ravi takes note of the way the man moves, of the lay of his robes. Likely unarmed but knows his way around a fight.

Nate sidles next to Ravi as they follow along. "That was *so cool*, dude. Real secret agent stuff. The crow flies at midnight," he whispers, eyes darting shiftily, then relaxes into a grin. "Also? Spy monks. Hell, yeah."

"You're easily impressed, Doc." Ravi has a hard time wrangling back a smile. "Let's see if you can keep that energy up through the security measures."

Nate's smile drops. "Security measures?"

"Nothing crazy," Ravi quickly reassures him, regretting making that golden smile disappear.

Suharto stops in front of a well-worn wall tucked away behind a large statue, takes a swift glance around for onlookers, and twists an innocuous brick. The wall swings inward to a stone staircase heading down.

It descends to a small entry room, built of rune-etched steel with a bulletproof glass partition, like most waystations. Safely ensconced behind it, a second monk is frantically flipping through the pages of a large book. This monk appears to be getting on in years, and blinks up owlishly through thick, round spectacles.

"Now *that's* quick." While Suharto sounds Javanese, this monk has a perfect Yorkshire accent. "I haven't even sent in the report yet! Are you here about the malfunction?"

"Malfunction?" Ravi asks. "In a waystation?" There should be field bunks, a stock of MREs, and a weapons cache for visiting agents. Aside from a secure uplink to The Trust's hubs, there shouldn't really be anything *to* malfunction here.

"Right," Suharto says firmly, "security first, questions later." He motions toward a narrow opening in the glass partition, and the older monk sets aside his book to open a small wooden trunk, intricately carved, its copper banding gone green with verdigris.

Ravi nods encouragingly back at his team and sticks his hand through the opening. The monk removes a bottle of clear liquid from the trunk and sets it aside. Then he draws out a series of long needles, some metal and some not, and lays them all out side by side.

"Uh." Harry and Nate echo each other in uncertainty, and Constance shrinks back into Val, who sets a supportive hand on the witch's shoulder.

"It's just to make sure we're human." Ravi looks to Val, with her dark glasses and statuesque frame. She has a mostly human body. "Should be fine," he says, and holds his hand outstretched, palm up and fingers relaxed.

With practiced efficiency, the monk pricks the meat of Ravi's fingertip with the first needle. "Silver," the monk explains as he continues piercing skin with the other needles, testing fingers at seemingly random. "Then iron, then this one is solid salt—sorry, that one's the worst—and this one gets a dip in holy water first. Good so far." He gives Ravi a grandfatherly smile as he twitches through the sting of the salt. "This one to pierce through illusions. Looks good! And this one to verify truth." The last needle is a sharp-honed wooden splinter. Instead of drawing it quickly back out, the monk leaves it in the meat of Ravi's fingertip as if it were for acupuncture.

"Your name?"

"Ravi Abhiramnew."

"Designation?"

"Field agent of The Trust."

"Are your intentions here to cause any ill will or harm?"

"No."

Usually, the truth compulsion ends there with those three questions. But the monks share a look, then the older one asks, "How is it you came to be here right when we discovered we had a serious potential disaster on our hands?"

"A Trust seer told us we should be here." The words

are drawn from Ravi like poison from a wound. He frowns down at the wooden needle on principle. He would have told the truth anyway, but it's an unsettling feeling, the compulsion extracting truth without the mind's volition.

Suharto makes a small exclamation of surprise. The older monk simply nods and says, "Well, I am not one to look a gift horse in the mouth. Time is a factor, so do you vouch for all your companions here today?"

"Yes. I trust them with my life," he says, and whether it's the needle or his own choice to say it, it hardly matters.

Constance clucks her tongue softly. "Bless," she says in a tone usually reserved for baby animals.

The monk removes the needle. He wipes a tiny dot of ointment over Ravi's pincushioned fingertips that tingles briefly, a familiar brush of healing magic Ravi knows well from Constance's ministrations.

"Appreciate it." The weathered monk waves away his thanks.

"This way," Suharto beckons, leading them back to a pair of elevators. Once they all pile in, he digs out a card from the saffron folds of his robes and pops open a panel at head height. "One moment, if you please." He leans in, placing his hand over a black screen while a tiny blue light flickers over his face.

"Oh my god, I *knew* it," Nate exclaims. "Retinal

scanner. So cool."

"This is higher security than we met at the other branch," Val says with clear approval, handing back Ravi's bag as the elevator starts to descend.

"This isn't a waystation, is it?" Ravi observes.

"Not just a waystation, no. We do have separate facilities for agents on errantry, but we are first and foremost a secure hazardous materials site."

"Hazardous materials?" Harry gives Ravi a warily inquiring look, but he can only shrug in response.

The elevator comes to a halt, and Suharto keys in a code before the doors slide open. A set of steel vault doors opens with a prolonged hiss, like an airlock, and they are met with a draft of cool, nearly refrigerated air. The space beyond is made up of rows upon rows upon rows of brightly lit glass cases, varying in size, like hundreds of museum displays crammed together in one place.

"Welcome to the Ossuary," Suharto says. "We keep the bones of monsters Trust agents dispatch in the field. As well as a few recovered remains of non-violent supernatural entities that are nevertheless quite dangerous if stumbled upon. Everything secured in this facility can't be destroyed by mortal means—some beings are too resilient, or regenerate if left unchecked."

Ah. This explains why Ravi's aunt has been here; it's a

vital resource of a kind Ravi had only ever speculated on the existence of before.

"Wait," Harry says. "Don't monsters melt when they die?"

"Beings from other realms do," Nate says, almost whispering, as if on hallowed ground. "They don't last long on this side of the Veil. But if Earth is their native soil…"

Constance stops in front of a case, mouth agape. "Are these *dragon teeth?*"

Suharto joins her. "Indeed, well spotted. I'll admit, that's one of my favorites in the collection. A small dragon was ravaging the coast of Liberia. It killed three agents before it was taken out."

"Dragons are real, check," Harry says, peering over Constance's shoulder.

"Aye. And the teeth of a dragon sown in fertile ground will grow a band of fully armed earthen warriors. Or so I've heard," Constance adds hastily.

Nate walks from case to case with a dazed expression. "This is…" He glides along as if in a dream. He's practically lit up from within, leaning in close to the glass and absently patting his shirt pocket, looking for glasses that aren't there.

"There's so many," Harry breathes, looking down the long labyrinthine halls. Ravi wonders if anything the twins killed is here. Or anything he killed.

Beckoning again, Suharto takes them to the furthest row. "The heart of our problem lies here. This whole wall is kept under special protection. You'll notice the protection glyphs?" Faint green markings cover the face of the glass, flickering unsteadily. The remains inside look unsettlingly human, each vacant skull in a grinning leer. Suharto taps the glass, his face deeply grooved with concern. "They're drawn in basilisk venom, and meant to be much brighter, keeping the bones in stasis. But something has disrupted them. We haven't had time to determine what, perhaps a dissolving compound, or a counter-spell... Honestly, we don't have time to investigate. By the rate of decay, the glyphs will be rendered inert in three days' time."

"What are these bones?" Nate asks. "They appear hominid."

"A breed of lesser demons. They regenerate completely if their remains aren't controlled."

Nate steps back, taking dozens and dozens of cases into his field of view. "Wow. That's...a lot of demons."

Harry sets her hands on her hips. "So, you just need to redraw the glyphs? Strengthen them back up?"

"That is the other problem," Suharto says grimly. "Our supply of the venom is gone."

Ravi frowns. "What happened to it?"

"We have no idea. We have a supply chain we can

requisition from, but there's very little chance they can get five gallons of basilisk venom to us in under three days. By then the glyphs will have degraded completely, and the demons will be able to reform themselves. Our only option is to call in as many field agents as possible in the narrow time frame, and set up a perimeter to take out as many demons as we—"

"Okay, wait, back up." Harry holds up her hands. "We'll just get you some more! Seems like that'll be way easier than cordoning off the whole temple. Logistical nightmare."

Suharto shakes his head. "Basilisk venom is a highly controlled substance. Dangerous and rare."

"Are we going to have to milk a basilisk?" Nate sounds equal parts excited and alarmed.

"Hey, what you do for fun is none of my business, Doc." She regards the cases thoughtfully. "Rav, think you can put in a call? To our buddy with all the rings?"

"Ah. Yeah." Ravi takes out his phone and asks the monk, "Do you get cell service down here?"

"Do we get..." Suharto blinks. "Actually, if you stand near that case over there, the thunderbird skull has been known to boost signals." The case in question is a freestanding floor-to-ceiling display of an enormous bird skull.

Nate practically vibrates with excitement. "A real

thunderbird?" He darts in for a look.

Dialing up Calvin Guinto, Ravi puts the call on speaker. The broker's voice comes through tinny and nervous. "Uh, hey. Hi. Hello. You, uh…you need something?"

"Basilisk venom," Ravi says by way of greeting. "Can you get it?"

"Basilisk…yeah, I can get my hands on some. How much you need?"

"At least five gallons."

"Okay, so, a lot. I'm pretty sure…yeah, still yes, I got you covered. It'll be pricey though."

"Money isn't a concern."

"My favorite words in the English language," the broker says fervently. "You called the right guy. I can get all of it by the end of the week."

"We need it today or tomorrow at the latest."

A long pause. "Y'all never want anything simple."

"Can you do it?"

A heavy sigh. "I'll need to call in some favors, but yes. If your teleporting Wonder Woman can lend a hand, it'll be even faster."

"I can," Val says. "The place where we met in battle will be an acceptable rendezvous."

Constance leans over the phone and shouts, "Hello, Calvin! This is Constance. I was the wolf. Do you remember?"

"Pretty sure he can hear you, Constance." Harry shares a disarming little "whaddya gonna do" shrug with Suharto, who appears both perplexed and mildly amused at the turn of events.

A nervous laugh. "Uh, I remember, yeah. Gang's all there. Cool, cool. I'll text as soon as I get the stuff. Meet me there with a big, repeat big, briefcase of money."

Ravi rolls his eyes. "Little clichéd."

"Well, you don't get into this line of work unless you enjoy a little theatricality, brother. Need anything else?"

"Not at the moment. Thanks."

"Thank *you*." Ravi hangs up.

Harry claps her hands together. "All settled, Suharto. By the way, I'm Harry McAllister." She extends a hand then immediately draws it back, apologetic. "Oh sorry, Buddhist, right? That's not a disguise, is it?"

"It certainly is not," Suharto says mildly. "I appreciate the gesture though, Miss McAllister. I prefer not to shake hands, and it is also not customary to thank others for their services. If I were to offer thanks for your generosity, that would imply that you have done it to receive something in return. Even if only my humble thanks. I would not disgrace you in such a manner." He grants a small but sincere smile.

"Read ya loud and clear." Harry grins back. "In that

case, you're not welcome."

"Another mission nearly in the bag." Tearing himself away from the skull, Nate throws the group a double thumbs-up. "We're crushing it."

Constance putters around from case to case, though she always seems to end up back at the dragon teeth. "I confess myself greatly curious, how old is this place? I am sure 'twas recently—what is the word? Ah, yes, *updated*—but how many centuries does this facility go back?"

"Oh," Suharto replies, "the Ossuary was only added to the waystation since Borobudur's restoration in the 1970s."

Harry turns to him in disbelief. "You're telling me *all* these monster bits are only from the *last forty years*?"

"Whoa," Nate says in a hushed voice, staring down the long aisles. "And just the ones they couldn't destroy."

Ravi doesn't get why they are so surprised. "The Trust deals with a lot of monsters."

"Well, yeah, but...huh." She blinks, looking around with renewed interest. "Val, wanna help me coordinate basilisk goo drop-off with our friend here?" Harry and Val step aside with Suharto, but not before Harry calls over her shoulder, "You don't have room for a bunch of tooth soldiers, Constance."

The witch wrinkles her nose and finally abandons the dragon teeth case to join Harry, a little sulkily.

Ravi stays back. He watches Nate inspect case after case, his nose nearly touching the glass. As Ravi approaches, Nate glances up with a blinding smile. "This is hands-down the coolest thing I've seen from The Trust to date, my guy. You must have had anthropologist input during the construction here. Climate controlled atmosphere, archival lighting. Everything is top notch."

"We spare no expense."

"No kidding." Nate takes Ravi's elbow and drags him a few cases back, to the huge raptor skull. That wickedly curved beak looks like it wouldn't have much trouble taking off a grown man's arm. "Smart to keep this secure. My research suggests the skulls of thunderbirds can electrocute people if touched."

"Yeah?" Ravi isn't looking at the skull. Nate's got that lit-up look again, eyes the clear blue of a mountain sky. It's chilly in the Ossuary, far too cool for Ravi's light linen suit, but the warmth of Nate's hand travels right through the fabric.

"Makes sense, if you know the myths. In the Sioux tradition they're called Wakinyan, powerful sky spirits that control storms. They're said to protect people from evil, but also can punish the same people for not paying the thunderbirds enough respect. They also— Sorry," he says sheepishly, rubbing the back of his neck. "Nerded out a little." He glances at Ravi sidelong, cheeks pink.

Something flutters in Ravi's belly. "I'll bring you back here later, if you want."

"Yeah?" Nate grins at him, a bright, golden thing, and Ravi forgets where they are for a moment. He quickly tears his gaze back to the thunderbird, a faint buzz running through him. Is the skull giving off electricity?

"Yeah. You can take pictures, notes, whatever you want."

After a slight pause, Nate's voice goes soft, almost layered. "I would really like that, Ravi."

"Hey fellas, you ready to rock and roll?" Harry sidles up between them, slinging her arms up as high as she can reach over their shoulders. "We might as well get to gettin'. Val can teleport to Cal from anywhere." She lowers her voice. "And I'm pretty sure Constance is close to figuring out how to bust into that dragon tooth case."

"Yeah, we're ready. Let's get topside before Ravi has to fight a vengeful monk."

Ravi snorts a laugh.

*

LATER, THE SUNSET meets the towering emerald palms of the surrounding forest, casting a warm glow over verdant hills as they all sit together on the steps outside

Borobudur. The nearby museum has closed, and they have the stairway to themselves, watching tourists pile into buses down below. The air grows heavy and still as the sun lowers, but no one makes the first move to leave.

"This is nice," Harry says with a note of surprise, clearly not just talking about the spectacular view.

"A fine thing," Val agrees, "to see such a vast number of vanquished evils kept safe and well-guarded by those pure of heart."

"Yeah," Harry says thoughtfully. "It is."

"It's mostly like this." Ravi punctuates words with expressive movements of his hands. "The Trust is dedicated to the eradication of evil and the safety of mankind. It's not all…money and politics. It's centuries and *centuries* of people joining together and fighting the good fight. A sacred charge. There are places like this all over." He motions out at the sweeping vista, trying to illustrate the scope of their influence.

Harry gnaws her lip. "Doesn't seem like it was such a great culture to be raised in."

"That's…" He winces, scrubbing a hand through his hair. "My situation was…a special case." He takes a fortifying breath before looking up at Harry. "I've got some ideas on how to make that better. For the next Chosen."

She doesn't blink. "Still not quite ready for that

conversation."

Ravi nods. Nate shifts next to him, leaning in a little closer.

"But yeah," she continues. "This has been good to see. Educational. Are we all heading back to the jet, or do you feel like teleporting instead, Val?"

Val shrugs, seemingly indifferent.

"I quite like flying," Constance chirps. "I know not how you all behave so cavalierly at soaring through the air like the very birds themselves. I shall never grow tired of it."

Harry grins. "Yeah, that's because you've only been on private G5 airplanes, doll. Being crammed in economy is a whole other story."

"It seems this modern age makes every wondrous thing an uncomfortable mundanity."

"Preach, sister."

Nate leans back on his hands. The sunset catches in his hair, picking out threads of gold. "Crazy to think that if we hadn't been here, there'd be tons of demons busting out of here in a couple days."

"It is good work," Val declares. "I enjoy battle, but a bloodless victory is no bad thing."

The breeze kicks up for only a brief moment, bringing with it the lush scent of green. Harry scrapes strands of hair from her damp neck, piling it all up into her bun. "So, most of The Trust doesn't know about the Chosen? Just the old families?"

"Not these days, no. Since the consortium was formed—"

"The *consortium*," Harry groans. "I'm getting sick of hearing about that. Seems like everything used to be pretty cool before those rich assholes got together and started changing things."

An odd pang strikes Ravi's chest.

"What? The rich asshole thing didn't rub you the wrong way, did it?"

"No, no. You just...reminded me of my mom." He clears his throat. "Yeah. The Chosen has been kept secret from all but the inner circle for the last couple centuries. It's supposed to be...safer."

"Safer. Right. You think that's the only reason?"

"I..." He gives the question the consideration it deserves, taking his time. "Confident people," he says with a glance at Nate, "are harder to control. A Chosen with friends and allies to support them isn't as easy to guide as one who's...on their own."

You may want to ask your little friends if they've been keeping any secrets from you, dearest.

And at the one tiptoeing memory of Cayenne's silk-slick voice, others start tumbling forward, one after another, like a shoddily propped cairn of stones beginning to fall.

I'm going to make The Trust what it should be, Ravi had told Cayenne.

You can't, pet, they said. *You can't change it.*

Everything's kind of your fault, cher.

If you'd just trust me, you'd be so much happier.

Nobody can give you what I can.

My beautiful broken boy.

Harry kicks out her legs, elbows propped on the steps behind her. "We're definitely talking about collusion now, right? Someone with access to that boneyard wanted to compromise it, and we can safely assume they had chronomage help. That's twice now that they've known exactly where to strike The Trust to do the most harm. Seems a little tricky for the Pepper to manage on their own. Not impossible, but really fucking hard."

Ravi takes a breath, righting himself, shoulders squaring. "I agree. It supports my aunt's claim about factions. Someone is trying to weaken The Trust from within, create opportunities to gain control."

"What do you think their next move's gonna be?"

"I'm not sure," Ravi hedges.

"C'mon man, you're my general. You know this world. We don't think you're some secret Machiavellian jerk just because you know how to think like one."

Harry is an unerringly good detective, and Ravi is speechless for a second, trying not to puff up with pride. *Her general.*

"Well… If it were me, I'd lay low until I figured out how my enemy was anticipating my moves. Probe into areas I believe to be weak. Try to separate my enemies or set them against each other. See what I could leverage from the shadows. I'd gather up as many allies from opposing factions as I could; everyone who has profited most from the long gap in between Chosen, and anyone who benefits from the uncertainty. And then I'd wait until an opportune moment to strike with overwhelming force."

Harry leans her head so far back it knocks into a stone step. "Fuck, okay. How can we guard against that?"

"I have an idea," he ventures, "but it'll have to be a conversation for the two of us."

"Ah," she says, then grins. "I hate diamonds. I want something pretty and colorful. But no rose gold, I will fucking walk if I see a *whisper* of rose gold. That's some basic bitch shit, miss me with that."

Ears hot, Ravi glances away with an embarrassed snort.

Nate chips in, "It hasn't come up yet, but Harry and I think someone is helping *us* too. Keeping Cayenne's plans from sticking."

"Yeah. I've been chewing on that." Cayenne had taken

down a powerful crime boss who could open magical doors to anywhere. They'd destroyed generations of predatory vampires in one fell swoop to free up their weekend. *I could do so much worse*, Cayenne had said, and Ravi didn't doubt it was true. So why didn't they? Why hadn't they?

Harry gives Nate a significant look, her brows angled. He shrugs back at her, and she asks Ravi, "Any idea who?"

"Not even seers can predict what a chronomage will do, so…no. No idea. Maybe James? But the last time he traveled back to warn us about Lucy, it almost killed him. He's not built for chronal manipulation the way Cayenne is." He sighs. "So, I have no fucking clue."

Val grumbles, "Unseen enemies *and* unseen allies."

"I mislike it as well," Constance agrees. "Mayhaps 'tis the same entity who sent the weapon to Harry, mayhaps not. We possess far more questions than answers."

"We'll figure it out," Nate says with a buoyant confidence that leaves no room for doubt. "We're getting closer all the time."

I feel like it's all going to be torn down, no matter what I do, Ravi had told Nate.

Maybe so, he said. *But I don't think that'll stop you for long, sunshine.*

You're going to do great.

If I can help in my nerdy little way, lemme know.

"Maybe it's Durga." Nate smiles, giving Ravi's shoulder a gentle bump. "Answering some prayers."

Anyone who says love hurts isn't doing it right.

Slowly, Ravi smiles back. "Better late than never."

Chapter Ten

- Ravi -

You at home?

- Nate -

Sure am, having a lazy Saturday. What's up, another job?

- Ravi -

Nope. Can I swing by?

It's my turn to bring "stuff."

- Nate -

Hmm, well I do love stuff. Okay, come over.

Fifteen minutes later, Nate's door opens on his broad, welcoming grin. "Hey man, how've things been—whoa, what's *that?*" Eyes wide behind wire-framed glasses, Nate steps aside.

Without a word, Ravi hefts a large, irregularly shaped bag in his arms, kicks off his shoes, and heads straight for the kitchen. Nate follows close behind. After setting the bag on the table, Ravi reclines against the kitchen counter, arms loosely folded. He can't keep his mouth from crooking into a halfway smile.

"Open it."

Nate eyes the bag, pushing the sleeves of his Henley up over his forearms. Nice arms, the roll of muscles underneath fabric suggesting casual strength. He looks freshly scrubbed, like he'd just stepped out of the shower, fair hair damp in the back. "When you said you were bringing stuff, I was expecting…I don't know. Chicken wings, or something."

"You guessed it, Doc, it's a big bag of loose chicken wings."

Nate laughs. "Only one way to find out, huh?" He rubs his hands together, waggles his brows, and unzips the bag. "What the… Is this…? *Dude.*" Nate pulls out a black carbon fiber compound bow, all sleek lines and coiled power. "This is beautiful." Admiring, he handles the bow, testing its draw.

"Check the arrows." He's pretty proud of that detail.

Grinning ear to ear, Nate lays out the quiver, a full bouquet of arrows fletched in red and white. "Is there more to them than just looking awesome?"

Ravi slides an arrow from the quiver and taps the point against his forefinger. "Meteoric alloy tips. They'll pack an extra punch against creatures weak to any metals, whether it's iron, silver, or anything else. And…" He unzips a side pouch and pulls out a shatterproof vial. "Some basilisk venom. There was a bit left after the monks redrew the glyphs. Dip arrows in it, and you've got a paralytic that will last for days." He sets it on the table with satisfaction. "Thought that since I was at the black market anyway, I might as well do some shopping."

"Ravi… This is way too much."

"I know you're rusty, but I can help you brush up. You'll be a better archer than me in no time. I haven't picked up a bow in years." Admittedly he learned it young, along with the other traditional martial weapons, and archery is a bit like riding a bike. He's likely still good enough to train someone a little.

Nate rubs the back of his neck. "No, I meant this is…*too much*. This all must have been obscenely expensive."

"Nate. There's a diamond corpse in Constance's basement."

"Ha, I guess, yeah, it's just…"

"Besides," Ravi continues with a small smile. "This way you can finally stop jumping in front of monsters with that hockey stick. Keep some distance."

"Oh, I *see*. This is actually a present for *you*, so you don't have to keep pulling my ass out of the fire."

"That's fair," Ravi admits, because it is one hundred percent true, "which is why I brought this too." He digs a small brown bottle out of his pocket and holds it out. "I said I'd bring you some of the sandalwood. Use very sparingly. It's not meant for…blonds."

"Not calibrated for my delicate Caucasian follicles, I gotcha." Nate snickers, unscrewing the cap to take a sniff. "Huh. It smells better on you." He shrugs and sets it on the table. "Still nice though. Thanks. For all of this, Ravi, it's super thoughtful. Thank you."

A slow smile creeps across Ravi's face as he tries to think of something to say. He comes up dry for a moment before settling on, "I've been sleeping better."

"That's great. You look it." Nate rubs his ear, knocking askew the set of his glasses. He curses under his breath and plucks them off his face.

"Why do you do that? Take off your glasses."

"They're just for reading. Also, it's, uh, vanity, I guess."

"They look good."

Nate's blush is written across his fair skin as clear as

day. If there's a deception gene, he must have been born without one. Scrubbing his palms against his jeans, he clears his throat. "You want to maybe watch a movie? I bought you some hard cider instead of restocking the beer, guaranteed gluten-free. If you want."

"I want to kiss you."

Nate goes still, even his chest halting its rise and fall.

"You said you were interested," Ravi says softly.

"I am," Nate says, breathless.

Ravi takes a step closer. "I've still got to be careful. Harry's position is precarious, and mine's even worse." All it will take is one rumor for his social stock to tank, for Trust hopefuls to flood Harry with marriage proposals, for backstabbing and infighting to give their hidden enemies a glaring weak spot to aim for.

"That's okay," Nate says, still standing frozen, as if Ravi were a wild animal who might be scared away into the brush.

Another step closer. "And I'm a lot of work. Even when I'm not…going through whatever all this bullshit is."

Nate edges forward. "Don't know who told you that about yourself, sunshine, but even if it's true, that's okay too."

"And…" Ravi looks away, then wrenches his gaze back to Nate's. "I'm not sure what Cayenne would do if they found out. I don't want to put you in danger."

"Screw them and the clock they rode in on. If you want me, I'm right here."

Ravi touches Nate's cheek, grazing stubble so fine it's nearly invisible under the overhead kitchen light. Nate swallows hard. "You've got to stop doing that, Doc. Running headlong into danger."

"Look. About that. I know I'm just a regular guy here. I don't have superpowers, I can't do magic, and I wasn't trained for battle. But I can't see someone in trouble and not want to help."

Ravi takes Nate's face in both hands and kisses him, a rough surge that puts Nate's back to the counter. A few metal utensils clatter off a shelf behind him.

He lets out a muffled noise of surprise, Nate's hands grasping onto Ravi's shoulders in a desperate bid for balance. There's one brief, stunned second that feels like an eternity, but then Nate pulls him closer, kissing back, the hot slide of his tongue over the seam of Ravi's lips stealing the breath right from his lungs.

"We don't have to," Nate gasps unsteadily against Ravi's mouth. "You don't owe me anything."

Ravi lets his fingers card through Nate's still-damp hair, breathing the bright, clean scent of his soap, like citrus and oakmoss. "This isn't about that."

Nate's hands fist in Ravi's shirt, reeling him closer. "If you need more time… You've been going through a lot…"

"Getting some mixed signals." He leans in and nips Nate's bottom lip.

At the touch of teeth, Nate makes a sound like he's been punched, small and choked. "Yeah, sorry. I've been a rebound bang before, and it was fine, but…you're *you*."

Ravi pulls back. Nate's pupils are blown wide, blue irises darkening to cobalt, his lips invitingly wet and open.

"Nate."

A visible shiver. "Yeah?"

"You think too much."

Any hint of reticence dissolves as Ravi tugs Nate down, matching him beat for beat. He sucks hungrily on Ravi's tongue, his long-fingered hands burning like hot coals at the small of Ravi's back. Then Nate twines a thigh between his and leans in.

The pressure against Ravi's hardening cock hits him like a freight train, heartbeat hammering in his ears. Nate cleaves tight, silently encouraging Ravi to start up a slow roll. Sheer *want* thrills through him, a sudden roar of it— after so long going without feeling like this, so long not *letting* himself feel like this, his desire blazes hot and newly forged.

"Fuck," Ravi hisses. He falls out of the kiss to drop his

forehead to Nate's cheek, hips moving in a wanton grind.

Nate breathes hard, tongue running over kiss-bruised lips. "Please let me take you to bed so I can suck you off."

The plea in Nate's tone is almost enough to set him spiraling. Ravi groans, already too turned on to try to minimize his eagerness, to keep a veneer of cool. He *wants*. He wants, fiercely, a contradictory mess of things. He wants to slide down to his knees to swallow Nate whole; he wants those strong arms around him while he strokes them both off; wants to hold Nate face down and sink teeth into his shoulder while he buries himself hilt-deep inside; wants Nate's gentle voice in his ear as Ravi sinks down onto him; and he can't decide which he wants most. He wants all of it. He wants more, everything.

Ravi nods.

Afternoon light spills in to gild the bedroom, illuminating a potted fig tree by the window and cascading down a stack of colorfully page-marked books on the nightstand. Nate leads Ravi in, fingers interlaced, then kisses his way down Ravi's neck, the sharp drag of stubble a delicious counterpoint to soft lips.

Nate works at Ravi's shirtfront, buttons slipping from his fingers. "Couldn't have worn something without buttons for once?" He ducks in for a quick kiss before fixing his concentration back on the shirt. "Do you even own a T-shirt?"

Ravi gusts a chuckle against Nate's collarbone. "I own a couple."

"Uh-huh. I'll believe it when I see it." Nate finally pops open the last button. He pushes the shirt down Ravi's arms, then exhales shakily, eyes roving. "You're...*gorgeous*." The reverent kiss he drags down Ravi's breastbone feels like the first drink of water after days in the desert, and Ravi gasps, head spinning, letting himself be led backward until the backs of his knees hit the bed, and he sinks down onto the mattress.

Nate grins down at him, dimples flashing, and tears his Henley off over his head. "Still good? This okay?"

"Still good," Ravi breathes. An unexpected scrolling of tattoos decorates the breadth of Nate's upper body. "Impressive amount of ink for an academic."

"Ha! That's what everyone thinks. We bookish types are all secret *freaks*." Laughter bubbles up between their lips as Nate kisses him, guiding him up the bed with the press of his mouth alone, until he has Ravi stretched out over the pillows underneath him. He looks down and licks his lips. "I'll tell you about them later. Right now, I have a pretty dire need to get your dick in my mouth."

Ravi's lungs hitch, his arousal a hot, heady thing scattering higher thoughts to the wind. "Okay," he manages, gaze glued to Nate's mouth. He's already so hard it hurts, and when Nate slides a hand over Ravi's crotch and *squeezes*, need wells up in a desperate, overwhelming rush.

"*Nate*," he pleads, voice gravel. He's not going to last long at all.

"Yeah, sunshine, I got you," Nate croons against Ravi's stomach, tongue tracing the furry trail leading him south. Wasting no time, he unfastens Ravi's pants and tugs down the waistband. His eyes go gratifyingly wide as he wraps a hand around the base of Ravi's cock. "Well, hello," he murmurs, and drags his tongue from root to tip.

Ravi's hips shoot off the bed in a backward arch. Bedcovers creak under his grip, perilously close to tearing. "*Fuck*," he hisses, blood rushing heavy in his ears. Feels like it's been years instead of months since he's been touched. Every inch of his skin feels like it's just grown back after a burn, newly healed nerves sparking hot and eager, barreling his self-control to the ground.

Nate grins and slings a forearm over Ravi's hips, pinning him to the mattress. "Squirmy," he says with obvious approval. His eyes flutter shut as he teases the throbbing crown over his slick lips before taking Ravi into the searing heat of his mouth with an unselfconscious moan.

Choking off a sharp exclamation in Hindi, Ravi digs his heels into the mattress. Good thing Nate's holding him down, because he can't stop the buck of his hips, straining to get more of that perfect silken heat.

Sweat prickles along his scalp, his skin on fire. He gasps a warning. Nate flashes up a warm look, cheeks hollowed, and groans encouragement. The hand not pinning Ravi down slides lower, rolling tight balls along the cradle of Nate's palm, and it's—

Liquid heat floods Ravi's veins, but instead of the pleasure drowning him, pulling him down, it lifts Ravi high, buoyant with it, crashing through one wave of ecstasy after another like the breaking of a dam, riding the swell with fists full of bedding and toes curling tight. Nate stays with him for every drop, the scorching slide of his tongue coaxing out shivers until Ravi collapses, every line of limb gone as loose as unspooled thread.

Kadavule. His *ears* are ringing.

Fighting for breath, he lifts his head to watch Nate plant a trail of soft kisses along the V of his hips. "What can I do? What do you want?"

The look Nate tips up makes air catch in Ravi's throat. "So much," he rasps; eyes glazed, aroused to distraction, his mouth well-used. It's a good look on him.

Ravi rolls up to his knees, pulling Nate with him into a languid, satiated kiss. "Yeah? Tell me."

"I'm easy." Nate nibbles at the hinge of Ravi's jaw.

"You got any preferences?"

"No preferences. Whatever you want, I want to give you."

"*Jesus,*" Nate mumbles into Ravi's shoulder. "I should buy a lottery ticket. Do you like oral?"

"*Yeah,*" Ravi purrs, and pushes him flat. He sets his teeth to the flushed curve of Nate's ear. "You want my mouth?"

Nate moans, going pliant, his legs falling open. "*Yes. Please.*"

There's something compelling about how his scarred hands look against Nate's illustrated skin, making him want to map Nate's body, to thoroughly explore all that enticing geography, marking the cartography of his tattoos; but it'll have to wait. All of Ravi's considerable focus narrows down to a singular goal. Flicking a button, unzipping a fly, cupping Nate's straining erection through cotton underwear, earning a softly uttered curse as he pulls him out and licks a long, slow stripe up. He lingers there a bit, enjoying the weight on his tongue, before testing some techniques, puzzling out what Nate likes best: a tease, a flutter, a spiraling suck.

Nate's fingers are gentle in Ravi's hair. "God, that's good," he groans. "Just like that, sunshine."

Ravi fights back a shy flush, the endearment hitting

him sweet and heavy. He takes Nate to the back of his throat, until his nose brushes Nate's abdomen. Nate keens, thighs trembling with the effort of keeping still. His hand clenches involuntarily, giving Ravi's hair a single sharp tug.

Fuck. Ravi goes molten and boneless, the sweet sting going right through him. He reaches up and curls his fingers tight around Nate's and meets the blue of his eyes. Even someone without the professor's exceptional vision should be able to read that clear of an invitation.

Ravi's mind goes blissfully blank as Nate gets the hint and holds him in place to thrust into his offered throat with the perfect balance of almost-too-much and not-nearly-enough. Nate shouts, every muscle tense and quivering.

"Jesus, *fuck*—"

Ravi swallows, satisfaction curling through him.

Still grabbing his hair by the roots, Nate pulls him up the bed and into a breathless kiss. "Fuckin' hell, Ravi. There anything you're not good at?"

Goosebumps spread across Ravi's skin. He turns his face to the side until he regains some composure, enough to cup Nate's head in his hands and melt into a slow, exploring kiss.

He wants to say something back; maybe that he likes the way Nate kisses, or that he likes the way Nate talks to him, likes how he touches him, how he always asks permission. Every scrap of true pleasure Ravi has ever gotten, he's had to work hard for, but everything about Nate is easy, simple, effortless. Like all this time, all Ravi had to do was ask.

But he's no good with words.

*

"DO YOU THINK we can actually get our pants off now?" Nate murmurs, finding his way back to rational thought after a long, lazy eternity of losing himself in Ravi's lips.

Shucking their remaining clothes gets a little silly, hands tangling in each other's way more often than not, but soon they're both naked, sprawled, and smiling. Nate shifts until Ravi is tucked along his side, slinging an arm across his shoulders.

"I really like you." He's still tingly from the force of his orgasm, but it'd be true even if he wasn't, so Nate says it, tracing a thumb over a thin scar on the back of Ravi's corded triceps.

Ravi is silent for a moment, but Nate can feel a smile smudging into his chest through the pleasant rasp of beard. "Like you too."

"Glad to hear it." He feathers a touch through Ravi's hair, the diffused sunlight catching hints of blue. "The hair-pulling was okay? Seemed like you liked it."

"That…was fine, yeah."

"Uh-huh," Nate says, grinning to himself. *Fine*. Ravi practically melted into a puddle. "We should probably talk a bit. About expectations." Usually, Nate likes to do that *before* getting in bed with a potential lover, to make sure everyone's on the same page. But Ravi's enthusiasm had shut Nate's brain down to the primal essentials—do not pass go, do not collect $200, go directly to blowjob.

"Expectations?"

"Yeah." Nate stretches a little, basking under Ravi's weight. Miles of burnished bronze with dozens of stories illustrated by scars; Nate wants to know all of him, wants to hear every tale. "You're getting married and you're in the closet, so that's my expectations managed."

Nate's been with closeted guys (though that's not his favorite) and also with people in open marriages (which kind of is), so neither prospect bothers him. Thinking as far ahead as the inevitable wedding might be getting a little bit ahead of himself. If Ravi only wants a friends-with-benefits situation, that's…that's okay too. Nate's easy.

But he can't deny he *really* hopes Ravi doesn't want this to be a one-time thing. Either way, he'll still be Ravi's friend, isn't going to make any demands of him. But nevertheless…Nate hopes.

"How about you? Your expectations?"

Ravi smooths a hand over Nate's collarbone, his thumb sweeping across a nipple, which keeps the afterglow kindling nicely. "I don't have any expectations." He sounds slightly baffled, as if no one has ever asked him such a thing before.

"No preferences and no expectations, huh?" he says lightly. A combination that paints a picture of someone used to tiptoeing through encounters, leaving no footprints and staking no claims.

Ravi's thumb pauses. He's quiet for so long that Nate thinks he must be done with conversation, and is ready to let it go and doze for a bit when Ravi asks, his rich tones breathier than normal and threaded with hesitance, "When did you know?"

"Know what?"

"That you were…different."

"Oh." Nate angles his leg under Ravi's knee to encourage him into a more full-bodied snuggle. Ravi gusts a breath in amusement and obliges, throwing a leg over Nate's hips and wriggling in closer. "Hard to say," Nate considers, brushing a knuckle over the shell of Ravi's ear. "My interests are split down the middle. I kind of always knew? There wasn't a defining moment. I had crushes on both girls and boys when I was a kid, didn't really care which was which." It took longer figuring out what he *did* care about;

compassion, integrity, the sort of spark that makes a person unique.

Ravi nods slowly, as if in agreement. He traces the edge of a tattoo, one of the Celtic knotwork ones curving across Nate's ribs, seemingly content to listen instead of talk.

"I was, let's see, fifteen when I had my first girlfriend. Sixteen for my first boyfriend. My parents have always been supportive of us kids. They're great. Even when Naomi went through her ill-advised goth phase."

A moment passes in comfortable silence, Nate trailing figure-eights along Ravi's spine.

"I was sixteen too," Ravi says suddenly.

"Oh yeah? Wanna tell me about him?"

Ravi doesn't speak for so long, Nate wonders if he's fallen asleep. "Age customs are different on this side of the globe." A pretty revealing non-answer. Nate just hopes he wasn't someone in a position of authority, or a teacher.

"You don't have to convince me, my guy. My whole career is based on not judging cultures through a narrow Western lens. I didn't mean to pry."

"It was…good. I don't want you to think that it was…" Ravi exhales, breath soft and warm over Nate's heart. "All the men I saw back then were…nice. Safe. I was careful. It was…" He clears his throat. "I asked Robert out once."

"Ooh, Bobby Hernandez? *Very* nice choice. How'd that

go?"

"He said no."

Grappling with that impossible concept takes Nate a minute. Next time he sees Bobby, he's going to *mercilessly* give him shit for fumbling the opportunity. Honestly, he's having a hard time wrapping his head around it. Bobby seems like an intelligent guy, and he definitely has functional eyes.

"Mind me being curious?"

"I…no. Go ahead."

"How'd you go from silver fox daddy type to the time twink?"

There's a sharp bark of laughter as Ravi lifts his head to stare at Nate. "The time—fuck, Nate." He shakes his head, but he's smiling. Nate grins back, shameless. Making Ravi laugh is as good as getting a trophy. He settles back on Nate's chest and snorts. "*Baap re*, please don't go there with the daddy thing. That's not… I don't have a *type*. I'm used to working with limited options."

Nate can imagine. He pets Ravi's hair, skimming light over the soft skin of his neck. "Wish I could have given you some of mine."

"Yeah. You're lucky."

"I know," Nate says, very aware of his many privileges.

"My options did open up when I was stationed in

London. Found out I like a lot of things. Not everything, but lots."

"Except daddy stuff," Nate laughs.

Again, Ravi snorts. "Yeah, that's not for me."

"Not my thing either, or any teacher-based roleplay. No thanks. Too close to home."

Ravi's touch flows from the knotwork tattoo to one above the jut of Nate's pelvis, a speckled watercolor wolf wrought of fire. "Is this Leto?"

Warmth wells through Nate, that he remembered such a small detail. "No. Well, sort of." He clears his throat and adopts his professorial lecture voice. "The Pact of Fire, a legend from the Sioux Nation, imagines the illustrative history of the domestication of wolves into the modern dog. The legend tells us that during a bitter winter the First Dog bargained with Man to keep her pups safe and fed by the fire, and in doing so her progeny and all their descendants would loyally serve Man as long as they were allowed a space by Man's fire. If ever Man should mistreat Dog, then Man would be cursed with war and strife for all their days." Nate traces over the tattoo fondly with his forefinger. "One of my favorite myths."

"Are all your tattoos myths?" Ravi asks, propping his chin on layered hands. When his eyes catch the light, they are painted almost a deep, dark amber.

"Course they are," Nate says, chest suddenly constricting at the sight before him. "It's kind of my thing. Myths and stories. The ways people explain the universe around them." He slides his thumb across Ravi's cheekbone. An impish glint appears in Ravi's eyes, and he catches Nate's thumb in his mouth. Nate sucks in a breath and bites his lip. He manages to keep his voice steady. "You have any ink I haven't seen yet?"

Ravi shakes his head, dark hair spilling invitingly down over his brows as he lets Nate's thumb slip free from the tempting heat of his mouth. "No. Not allowed to." He shifts his weight to stretch across Nate, peppering kisses to his chest and swiping his tongue over a nipple as he goes. Nate's dick twitches with interest. "Maybe I'll get one anyway," Ravi says with a crooked smile. "I've already ditched the prohibition on alcohol, so why not the tattoo one as well."

Nate jumps as Ravi's teeth graze his throat, breath stuttering. "Mm. Got any ideas what you'll get?"

"I… Maybe." Ravi absently touches a curious set of faded claw-like scars over his solar plexus. "Someday I might."

Both of his hands spread wide over Nate's chest, like he's trying to fit Nate's whole frame in the palm of his hands. Be nice if he could. Amazing hands, beautiful and deadly like Ravi himself. These same hands Nate's personally witnessed taking out monsters with efficient brutality are also capable of remarkable gentleness, caressing him as if he were some precious, breakable thing.

Then Ravi's fingers curl and he scrapes his blunt nails down in a decidedly less-than-gentle manner. Nate bows up with a gasp, electricity sparking through him.

"You trying to seduce me or something, sunshine?"

The predatory gleam in Ravi's half-mast eyes send a shiver up Nate's spine, and he's tugged into a hungry kiss, Ravi's thick length pressing against his hip, gratifyingly hard and ready and *Bobby, you missed your shot, dude.*

Nate's determined not to make the same mistake. He rolls Ravi underneath him and aims down an inviting smirk, pitching his voice rough.

"Wanna go again, gorgeous? How do you want it?"

Cobra-quick, Ravi yanks Nate down by his hair and licks searing hot into his mouth, a surprise strike, and flips Nate beneath him in a smooth, effortless display of martial ability that short-circuits his brain in one second flat.

Nate's got maybe twenty pounds on Ravi, and he just got flipped like a fucking pancake. *Jesus.*

Beard catches on stubble as Ravi mouths along Nate's jaw, then sinks a savage bite into the cords of his neck.

"Oh, fuck," Nate whispers, every drop of blood in his

veins rushing south. Instinctively he tips his head back, surrendering his throat. "Yeah, this definitely works for me. I usually top, but uh, okay, this is yes." Very yes, all the yes.

Ravi pauses, head to the side, scanning Nate as if reading him for clues. "We can do that, if you want. It just seemed like you wanted—"

"Oh, I do, yes, absolutely, good instincts, this is…yeah, good." His body is very on board, so hard he could hammer nails, his legs sprawling wantonly like they have minds of their own. "Wanna come on your cock."

The black of Ravi's pupils expands, his eyes going velvety dark. "Yeah?"

"Hell yeah, my guy. Fuck me already." Nate grins and gives Ravi's cock a few firm strokes. "Supplies are in the nightstand. Help yourself."

Ravi groans, then flashes a scimitar smile. He darts forward to pull Nate's bottom lip between his teeth as he takes the base of Nate's cock in his calloused grip and aligns them both skin-to-skin.

"S'good," Nate mutters, the praise wholly inadequate but all he can currently manage, lending his efforts to tighten the grip, entwining their fingers together. The view alone is spectacular, one he can already tell he's going to vividly recall at inopportune moments, like during lectures or when he's trying to concentrate on a grant proposal.

While Ravi stretches to open the drawer, Nate experiences a hazy second of disbelief. Did he dream this whole thing? Any minute he's going to wake up alone with his dick in his hand.

But the way Ravi licks and nips and scratches down Nate's flanks is a pretty convincing argument for reality, keeping him guessing, soft kisses one second and a harsh bite the next. Nate's normally busy mind quiets under the sensory assault. Christ, Ravi's really got his number. By the time he's properly introduced to Ravi's slick fingers, he has been reduced to a complete, writhing mess, flushed from head to toe, starving for more.

"Ravi—" What started as a plea ends up a challenge. "You gonna show me what you got *today*?"

Ravi gives a silk-throated growl. It's not often a guy over six foot gets folded nearly in goddamn half, but Nate's an immediate fan, helpfully tucking his hands under his thighs as Ravi pushes them up and open. Anticipation kicks his pulse jackhammer fast. It would feel like forever, waiting for Ravi to roll on a condom and thoroughly slick himself over, if Nate wasn't so busy feasting his eyes on the sight. Finally, Ravi presses in, a torturously slow slide, sinking in inch by inch, sweat beading on his temples.

"Jesus." The pleasure is already enough to send Nate's eyes rolling to the back of his head, but it's not nearly enough. He wriggles, trying to speed things along. How the fuck Ravi can stand to be so patient, Nate has no idea. *He's about to lose his mind.*

"C'mon, I'm fine, give it to me, Ravi, please—"

Ravi exhales heavily and licks his lips. His voice is strained. "You sure?"

Nate's voice isn't much better. He clamps his legs around Ravi's waist, pulling him in, driving him deeper. "Wouldn't say it if I didn't mean it."

The knot of Ravi's throat bobs, his eyes burning embers. Lean hips snap forward. Nate throws his head back with a grateful shout.

Then it's kind of a blur for a while, writhing and grasping and bucking, brain off, cock weeping against his stomach, skin on fire with every thrust a fresh splash of kerosene. Nate has to yank Ravi down into a kiss or he's pretty sure he's going to die, enfolding his arms around sweat-sheened shoulders and crashing their mouths together until they have to untangle for air.

"*Muhje vishwas nahi hota tum kitne perfect ho,*" Ravi murmurs, hungry eyes roaming.

The way Ravi looks at him… Christ. All that unwavering focus, all that sleek, compact strength, devoted to fucking Nate senseless… It's driving him crazy, desperation filling up nearly every corner of Nate's awareness, leaving barely any room for his innate curiosity.

He rallies enough to ask, "What's—fuck, right *there*, Jesus—what's that mean?"

Ravi kisses the hollow of his throat, one hand steadily working Nate's cock. He grins, a sudden bright flash of sunlight spilling through clouds. "I'm calling you handsome."

"Look who's fuckin' talking. So good, *yes*, do that *again*—"

And Ravi pistons into Nate with a long, drawn-out grind, downstroke tightening on Nate's leaking cock on every pass. He's going to feel the ghost of this for days, and just the thought alone has Nate perilously close to the precipice.

But he wants Ravi there too, wants to give him back an equal measure of abandon, to do his fair share of the work. So Nate surges up, managing to roll on top while still keeping that perfect cock planted within him, sits back, and rides Ravi for all he's worth.

"*Kadavule*," Ravi breathes, barely audible, fingers digging into the meat of Nate's thigh. He gazes up, eyes wide. His grip on Nate's cock loses its unerring precision as the strokes go sweeter, less calculated. Nate grins. That's more like it.

"Yeah, so good, Ravi, just what I wanted. Fucking perfect."

Ravi makes a low, torn noise in his throat, his expression yearning, as if he's starved for the sight of Nate falling apart—yeah, that look's gonna do it.

Nate comes in a blinding, overwhelming rush, molten heat coursing through him and across Ravi's sleek stomach. Through it, he forces his eyes to stay open, not about to miss the view. Ravi shudders and gasps like he's been waiting for exactly this, like he needs to be claimed and marked, a willing canvas for Nate's pleasure.

Every muscle taut and straining, Ravi arches up, chasing his own climax, and Nate honest-to-God whites out a little bit. When his brain is back online, he's barely keeping himself up on shaky arms, head bowed close over Ravi's.

Wow. And he'd thought Ravi had been gorgeous before. Dark eyes half-lidded with contentment, features compellingly lax, his rough edges all sanded away, wearing a faint smile Nate can't help but echo. He covers the back of Ravi's hands with his own, where they still clamp tight over his hips, and grinds down in a lazy circle. Ravi gasps, gaze snapping to Nate's.

"Did so good," Nate croons, because he's observant, and besides that, he's been around. If he looked up "praise kink" there'd probably be a picture of Ravi underneath.

Ravi's teeth furrow deep into his lower lip, his whole face flushing a richer hue. He looks up at Nate through unreasonably thick lashes, a wordless request.

Who could deny that face? Certainly not Nate, with his delicate himbo heart. He makes an educated guess and kisses the praise into Ravi's lips. "Good boy."

Ravi slams his eyes shut as a full-bodied shiver races through him, and when they open they are nearly bottomless, a little glazed. His hands skate lightly over Nate's gleaming skin, drifting as easily as leaves down a river.

Nate grins, places a kiss on Ravi's temple, and heaves himself off to fetch a washcloth. He stumbles and laughs, legs unsteady as a newborn colt's. He wobbles back, doing his best to clean up Ravi's abs, after taking a moment to commit the sight to memory. Another one that'll stick with him a long, long time.

"We're gonna need a shower," he decides, flopping back down to octopus around Ravi, head slotting under his chin. He's deliciously fucked-out, loose-limbed with endorphins, and in the mood to cuddle.

Ravi looks like he is still floating in whatever fun headspace Nate got him in, so Nate drifts a bit while Ravi silently strokes his shoulders and his sweat-damp hair. It's nice, even nicer than Nate had imagined—and obviously he'd imagined it. Not just the sex, but this part too. The part where he gets to see Ravi without a wall between them. Hell of a view.

"A…a shower would be nice," Ravi eventually says, his octave somewhere near bedrock.

*

THE SHOWER IS intensely pleasurable, a hot balm cascading over him, unknotting Ravi's shoulders for the first time in weeks. He tips his face up into the spray for an indulgent moment before stepping back to make room for Nate, shaking out his wet hair.

"So, are these all from different monster fights?" Nate traces a finger-long jagged line over Ravi's flank as he steps under the water.

"Most of them. Some are from friendly fire."

Nate whips his head around. "Friendly fire," he mutters, blinking water out of his eyes.

Ravi shrugs. "It happens."

"Jesus," Nate grumbles, scrubbing through his hair. "What's that one from?"

"Not friendly fire."

He watches water sheet off Nate's skin, the heat coloring in an enticing blush between tattoos. A full-back black ink tree compliments his proportions, growing from the dip of his spine to the crest of his broad shoulders. Tree roots trail down to a particularly exquisite ass. Ravi palms one firm cheek, pressing his face to the nape of Nate's neck, licking salt from his skin where the shower hasn't yet washed it away.

"Ghoul nest. The hunt went smoothly, until the end. My patrol took out about a dozen before the last one sprang out from behind a corner. Almost got me. It managed to land a slice before I shot it." He pushes his half-hard length up against the swell of Nate's ass.

"Dude, your pillow-talk needs work." Nate turns around with a chuckle. "Well, look at you, sunshine. To be twenty-five again." With a fiendishly arched eyebrow, Nate shoves Ravi against the tiles, teasing him with light, barely there touches.

"Hm, you do have almost a decade on me. You telling me that you can't keep up, Doc?" Ravi clucks his tongue in mock sorrow.

Admittedly, Ravi's libido is ramped higher than normal. He hasn't even been able to touch himself since August, and Nate makes him feel safe—not just in body, but like Ravi is safe even with his own tumultuous thoughts. Nate had mentioned Cayenne in passing and it was…it was *fine*, astonishingly. It hadn't sent Ravi into a spiral of guilt, grief, and betrayal. Just words, with no power to harm.

"You can't goad me, I am very secure in my machismo, thank you very much." Nate laps water from the divot of Ravi's throat as his grip finally, mercifully, tightens. "Don't worry, I got you." He lays a forearm across Ravi's chest, below the collarbone, pinning him firmly to the wall. Ravi looks down at the arm, then back up with a skeptically angled brow.

Nate laughs. "Oh, I'm under no illusions having the size advantage doesn't mean a damn thing. You could still kick my ass into next week. Just thought you might like it." Nate presses a smiling kiss to Ravi's cheek as he jerks him with perfect, rapid strokes.

Ravi tests the restraint, leaning into it. He's enjoyed tying guys up on the rare occasions he's both been asked to *and* had the necessary time and space to do so, but he can't bear it himself. Even if he hadn't gone through all that escape training at the Manhattan branch, the thought of an ambush being sprung while Ravi is bound and helpless brings the sour taste of panic to the back of his tongue.

But being held down like this, when he can easily get out of it whenever he chooses... Instead of trapped, it makes him feel like he's being held secure. Safe.

He relaxes, letting Nate take his full weight, thrusting into a fist deliciously slick with running water.

It doesn't take more than two dozen strokes. He's like a teenager again, barely in control as he comes with a sharp gasp. Nate kisses him through it, his pleased hum almost doing the job as much as his firm touch. As Ravi regains his breath, Nate gives him a sly smile. He lifts his hand and licks a slow, filthy stripe over his messy fingers. Ravi stares; if he hadn't just come, this sight would have done it.

"That take the edge off, gorgeous?"

Ravi nods, palms flat on the shower tiles, not yet trusting himself to speak.

Nate nibbles at his earlobe and whispers, "You're fun."

Not a description ever attributed to Ravi before. He ducks his head to shield a shy smile, turning into the spray of the water to sluice off.

Nate drops a kiss into Ravi's hair and draws back one side of the shower curtain. "Come out when you're ready. I'm going to make us something to eat." Nate gifts him another easy, honest smile, and leaves Ravi to finish up.

Ravi sags against the tiles, allowing himself a private moment to catch his breath, both physically and metaphorically.

Any intimacy Ravi's ever had was won through strategically developed habits borne of necessity. He's used to a long, coded dance of wary seduction; of making sure the other guy is interested, and more importantly, unable to hurt Ravi without hurting himself. Mutually assured destruction.

Then, when that was locked down, Ravi would take everything available while he still could. Get in and get out, before anyone gets caught. Cayenne was…an anomaly. A lot of easily transferable feelings still rattle around unfettered in Ravi's broken heart, and it would be unfair to pin them on…someone else. And unwise. Ravi isn't going to do that again, won't willfully put himself into someone else's crosshairs.

True to his word, Nate obtained some suitable bread since the last time Ravi visited and presents a pair of grilled cheese sandwiches into the bedroom along with a couple of hard ciders.

"I swear I can actually cook something besides dorm food, but this was quick and easy."

"I'm not complaining," Ravi assures him, biting into the melty sandwich with a sharp sound of surprise. "Is this brie? And a little slice of pear? I've never been in a dorm, but I doubt they cook like this."

"Well," Nate admits, cracking open both ciders, "I may have added a *little* bit of flair." He stretches out on his side, plate on the duvet and bottle leaning up against his thigh. His cotton shirt displays a hatch-marked stone tablet with the caption *Gotta Love a Man in Cuneiform!* His sweatpants look well-worn and comfortable, *Memorial University* printed all down the sides. "Hard to impress a guy who no doubt grew up with a personal chef."

Ravi snorts. Like Nate could feel any need to impress

him. He takes another bite, brushing a stray crumb off borrowed plaid flannel pants. "It's really good."

"And you doubted my cooking skills." Nate hands Ravi a drink. "So, you were talking about ghouls. Was that here in Atlanta?"

"No, in the UK. I was nineteen, fresh out of training, and still not used to working with a team. I was advancing ahead without backup. Not the brightest move." The cider is good, dry and tart. "This is pretty nice. The cider. A lot better than beer."

Nate pumps a triumphant fist. "Another one for the 'yes' column. We're really making headway on that list."

Biting down on a smile, Ravi asks, "What about you and your first experience with the supernatural?"

Nate grimaces. "I'll tell you anything you want to know about me, Ravi, but you're not going to like it."

"Nate, every story I've ever told you about myself, you haven't liked."

"Okay, *true*, you've had some rough breaks, but I still want to hear them. I want to learn about you."

Ravi's ears grow warm, and he fixes his gaze down at the empty plate. "Yeah, well. Likewise."

Instead of his usual wide grin, Nate's smile is a sweet, small thing, almost bashful. "Point taken. Okay." He finishes the last bite of his sandwich and takes a slug of cider.

"A few years ago, I moved back to Minnesota after grad school, before I started working here. I'd had a bad break-up and was drowning my sorrows at a local dive. This hot guy bought me a drink. We talked a bit, and he invited me back to his place. I don't usually, uh, cruise, these days, but I was kind of in a shitty place, emotionally speaking, and was feeling reckless. And he was nice. Sweet, kind of. So we went to his place, and were making out pretty hot and heavy, and he asked if he could bite me. You, uh, *may* have noticed I'm a fan"—Nate slips Ravi a wink—"so, I said yes. And then the fangs came out and he bit my wrist."

Ravi sits up very straight.

"I did say you wouldn't like it," Nate says mildly. "It felt…weird. Not bad exactly, but like painful good? Kind of like getting a tattoo. But I'm just… All I could think was, *whoa, holy shit, an actual vampire.* So, I started asking questions."

"Questions? While you're getting *drained*?"

"Yup. Like, is the folktale about vampires having a compulsion to count grains of rice really true? Do cameras work on them? How old is he? Asking what sort of history he's seen, blah blah blah. And he started laughing. Apparently, that had never happened to him before." Nate chuckles, tipping his cider back. "I'm naturally curious, I can't help it. Anyway, after that, we saw each other occasionally and ended up being friends. Miles introduced me to some supernatural contacts and some friendly hunters he knew. I started consulting on things here and there, and that's how I got into it. But I've learned more about the supernatural working with you guys than I have my entire time doing remote consulting. That's fieldwork for ya." He shrugs. "Hence, the tale of how I first faced the world of the weird."

"You went alone into a room with a hungry vampire."

Nate gives Ravi a fond roll of his eyes. "You're so protective, Agent Abhiramnew. I did, and it was fine. I'm here, aren't I?" His cavalier tone is offset by a comforting squeeze on Ravi's wrist. "If it makes a difference, I know better now. I know what signs to look out for."

Ravi scowls, thinking of Nate alone and unguarded with a creature who could easily kill him. But…it's not like Ravi's judgement is any better. He let a murderer fuck him, so who's he to say?

He plucks at the edge of the label of his cider with a fingernail, not meeting Nate's eyes. "And when did you learn to crush a monster's head with a hockey stick?"

Nate grins. "Childhood. That's a transferable skill. We ice-faring folks do not fuck around with our hockey. But before I joined up with you, I'd just been providing research and book-learnin' to monster hunters who needed it, not thwacking anything besides the occasional puck."

Ravi smiles a little, remembering the bookshelf picture of a younger Nate in skates holding up a trophy with his team.

Nate's gaze tracks Ravi's hands as they curl back the edge of the label. "Speaking of book-learnin', I finished my report on demon princes before you texted. I'll drop it off with Constance tomorrow."

"Anything actionable?"

"Listen to you, Secret Agent Man. *Actionable.* So cute. There might be, but it's all magic stuff. More her area of expertise."

"That'll be… She'll be pleased. I know she's really torn up about what she did, bringing Hartnell here. Putting all of us in danger." Ravi looks away, twisting the bottle in his hands.

Nate's face softens. "You okay, sunshine? And don't give me the tired 'I'm fine' line. You can tell me if something is bothering you." He smooths his thumb over Ravi's hand, stilling its restless fidget. "Is it about Miles?"

"No." Ravi sets his bottle aside and laces his fingers around Nate's. "I…I know exactly how Constance feels. I brought trouble to all of you, to The Trust. Put everyone at risk. I'm trying my best to stay ahead of it, but if our luck runs out…I don't know. This is all my fault, and I can't figure out how to fix it."

Nate regards Ravi for a thoughtful moment. "When you were a kid, back when everyone expected you'd grow up to be the next Chosen, were you told about the apocalypse-thwarting part of the deal?"

"Of course."

"So…you were told pretty young that someday it was going to be your sole responsibility to save the world?"

"I… Yes."

"Seems like way too much to put on a kid."

Ravi is silent for a long moment. "It is," he agrees, meeting Nate's eyes.

Nate moves his plate out of the way and scoots closer. He caresses Ravi's wrist. "None of what's going on is your fault, Ravi. You didn't turn The Trust into the bloated oligarchy it is today. You didn't make Cayenne do *any* of the insane bullshit they are doing, did do, or will do. None of it is your fault. You *are* fixing it. It's difficult and takes a long time, but you're doing it anyway." His knuckle traces Ravi's jawline. "It's inspiring. You should be proud of how far you've come with basically no info to go on, and proud of what you're still going to accomplish."

"But I *did* cause it, I—"

"Hey, hey." Nate kneels up and takes Ravi's face in his hands. "You were manip—" He cuts himself off sharply, closing his eyes on a flash of anger. He takes a deep breath and opens them again. *"It's not your fault."* He presses his lips to Ravi's forehead, whether by happenstance or intent right at the point of the third eye where a vermillion *tilak* might mark good luck, or victory, or blessing.

Ravi takes a shaky breath, leaning into the touch. Several beats go by in silence.

"Do you ever think about how insane your life has become?"

"Pretty often, yeah. Though I think our baselines are different."

Ravi ghosts a little laugh before bringing their foreheads together. It helps. Grounds him. "What's the story behind the tree tattoo?"

"Change of subject, huh?"

"Yes, please."

The warm rumble of Nate's chuckle. "Sure thing, sunshine." He steals a quick kiss before stretching out on his stomach, head pillowed on his arms.

Ravi traces the trunk of the tree over Nate's spine. Goosebumps rise in his light-fingered wake.

"Yggdrasil," Nate says, a bit breathlessly. "The World Tree. If you can't tell, I've got a little Scandinavian heritage."

"Nooo."

"Sarcasm, *wow*. Harry's a bad influence on you. Anyway, I originally wanted to get some cool Viking runes, but white supremacists ruined that. People see runes, they think you're some bigoted asshole instead of a history nerd." Nate sighs in frustration. "Fucking white supremacists."

"Truly, their worst offense to date."

Nate cackles a little, aiming a dimpled grin over his shoulder. "You've got a dark sense of humor. You and Harry are going to be such a scary power couple, I love it." He settles back down flat, his voice shifting into the rolling cadence he adopts when telling stories. Ravi could listen to it for hours. "The Norse believed the tree of life connected the different worlds together, and it was inhabited by a myriad of fantastical creatures."

"Is this a squirrel, here?"

"That's Ratatoskr. He runs up and down Yggdrasil, carrying messages."

"And these are…crows? Ravens. Ravens are a Norse thing, right?"

"Correct, gold star for you."

A smile creeps unbidden onto Ravi's face.

"Huginn and Muninn," Nate continues, "Thought and Memory."

"Which one is which?" He traces each black bird one by one, the skin under his touch visibly prickling.

"What, you can't tell? It's so obvious," Nate teases. His shoulders shift slightly under Ravi's feather-light touch, arching up like an affectionate cat. "I got those added on later, after the tree itself, when I got my sister her first tattoo as a graduation present. She got cold feet until I went first."

"Which sister is this?" He's looking forward to hearing another snippet of "exotic normalcy."

"Natalie. The youngest." Warmth carries on the low swell of Nate's voice. "She's studying to be a vet back home. Loves animals."

Ravi stretches out alongside Nate, trying to imagine what it must have been like to grow up the way he had. Family is clearly important to him in a joyful, uncomplicated way that very much isn't the case for Ravi; a thing purely of love and not just duty.

It must be nice.

"It must be hard. Being so far away from your family."

"Sometimes," Nate admits, a husky undercurrent in his voice. He looks at Ravi over the tangled sheets, eyes lambent blue. "We talk a lot, and text often, but yeah. It's not the same."

Ravi can't look away. He wants to stay and hear the story behind every tattoo. But he's probably already overstayed his welcome. Nate doubtless had all sorts of plans Ravi interrupted by inviting himself over. He ought to excuse himself before things get awkward, before Nate says he had a good time but needs to go about his day. Ravi clears his throat, pushing himself up.

But then Nate sits up with him, brushes a soft kiss to Ravi's cheek, and asks, "Hey, wanna spend the night?"

"You're…" Ravi can't help but laugh, warming from the inside out. How is everything with him so *easy?* "Yeah. I'd like that."

Chapter Eleven

DYLAN POKES HIS head into Nate's office. "Dr. Corbin? There's a guy in the quad asking for you."

Nate perks up, setting his lesson plan onto his desk. "Oh, yeah?" Goes without saying that he hopes it's Ravi. Combing a hand through his hair and smoothing his blazer, Nate wonders if Ravi will want to get a meal with him, if they're discreet. Just two colleagues having a friendly meeting. Nate will gladly take an early lunch.

"You've got quite a pep in your step today, Professor," his TA says with a small smile. Nate just grins back. After three years working together, they know each other pretty well. Dylan specializes in ethno-linguistics with a focus on cultural narrative strategy. Somehow a nerdier nerd than even Nate.

"I had a good weekend."

It's the understatement of the century. He's been walking on clouds since Ravi left his bed at the break of Sunday dawn, and followed up with a text later that night, just to be polite.

- Nate -

I don't want to make things weird for you, so just know that if you want any more grilled cheese, I'm happy to oblige. ;-)

*But sometimes once you have grilled cheese, you don't necessarily want another helping, so if you *don't* want more grilled cheese, that's okay too.*

- Ravi -

This is the most tortured metaphor I've ever seen.

- Nate -

LOL

Okay, I had a great time with you, and I'd love to see you again in any capacity you'd be interested in. If that's just as co-monster-hunters, I'd be disappointed but would get over it.

That was true. Probably. Nate's never had trouble with rejection before. Sure, he'd never been rejected by the Platonic ideal of manhood with a heart of gold before, but Nate is nothing if not adaptable. Cool. Chill. Unassuming and un-demanding. If Ravi just needed a safe harbor for one night, Nate's happy to have been there for him. It's not like he's gone against Harry's sage advice and gotten his delicate himbo heart tangled up in an impossible situation.

- Ravi -
I very much enjoyed the grilled cheese.

Nate grins ear to ear, relief washing through him.

- Nate -
It was the thin slice of pear, wasn't it?
- Ravi -
Okay, now the metaphor has gotten away from us completely. Can I see you later this week?

"Walking on Sunshine" starts playing in Nate's head.

- Nate -
For grilled cheese or sex?
- Ravi -
I'm at the Atlanta branch getting my old strike team briefed on your latest demon prince intel, and you just made me laugh at a very inconvenient time.

Now everyone thinks I'm a skinstealer or bodysnatcher.

-Nate-

I'd sure like to snatch that body ;-)

-Ravi-

(laughing emoji) *I can't decide if that was smooth or ridiculous.*

-Nate-

That's my brand! (sunglasses emoji)

So yeah, Nate's still riding high on all that, even after a lackluster response from his morning class. Likely due to the weather; a beautiful autumn day makes students antsy, and even reminding them that they're paying out the nose for this education doesn't help much.

Debating whether to take off his blazer, maybe roll up his shirtsleeves a little to show off his forearms, it occurs to Nate to wonder why Ravi didn't just come up himself. Not like he doesn't know where Nate's office is.

He ambles out of his office and asks, "What did this person look like? The one in the quad." *Please say like a devastatingly handsome GQ model with gorgeous eyes.*

He's aware he might be teetering dangerously close to smitten, here.

Typing furiously, Dylan doesn't look up from his laptop. "Redhead in obscenely tight black jeans and a floral button-up. Parisian accent, but with a curious alternation of long and short vowels." After a pregnant pause, Dylan looks up. "Is…is everything okay, Dr. Corbin? You want me to call security?"

Nate shakes himself out of his frozen stupor, eyes narrowing. "No, I got it. Thanks, Dylan."

He calls Val on his way downstairs. Way better than security.

"Hey, Val. If I don't text you in twenty minutes, assume I need help."

Val doesn't pause, doesn't ask questions. "Very well. We are well-acquainted enough that I can arrive at your side. Will that suffice?"

"Yes," Nate says gratefully. "Thank you."

Val hangs up. As Ravi has stated before, she doesn't do human niceties.

And Nate doesn't do intimidation. Ravi would probably have something laconic to say about running into danger again. Like he's one to talk, the way he flings himself into trouble. If Nate can help ease his burdens even a tiny bit, it's worth trying. If Cayenne has something to say, they can fucking say it, then fuck off.

*

"BONJOUR, NORMCORE!" CAYENNE waves from an insouciant sprawl on a wooden bench, under dappled shade. "What a beautiful day, *non?*" They smile, all charm and innocence.

"Say what you're going to say and then get the fuck out of here. You show up at my place of work again, I won't bother giving you that opportunity a second time. I'll just call Val and tell her to bring her hammer."

Cayenne brings a hand to their chest with an expression of wounded shock. "Why, Professor, such *vitriol*. Where's that laid-back attitude you're so famous for?"

"The fuck do you want, Cayenne?"

Cayenne pulls their outstretched limbs off the bench, as if making room for Nate to join them. Fat fucking chance of that.

"I *really* would have thought you'd be more *relaxed*, Professor. A night spent with *mon beau garçon* always leaves *me* in a *sparkling* mood." Cayenne taps a finger to pursed lips in mock-speculation. "Though perhaps he's less *enthusiastic* with you than he is with me."

Really, it's no surprise Cayenne found out. Stalking is hardly beyond their abilities or outside their pattern of behavior. Nate can think of a dozen retorts off the top of his head including *you gonna chop me up into pieces like Marquette?* but that could implicate Genevieve and put her in danger. He finally settles on, "What are you gonna do, crash a plane with me on it?" He hasn't forgotten there were innocent kids on those planes.

Cayenne scoffs, leaning elbows on their knees. "Please. I've witnessed Ravi's protective instincts first-hand. I'm not going to do a single thing to you. I won't have to." They smirk. "You really think *you* can compare? I certainly don't begrudge him a little stress relief, and you're convenient. When he loses interest in you, I'll still be here." Slim hands spread out wide, expressing an inevitability.

Convenient, for fuck's sake. Nate's determined not to show that one stings, crossing his arms over his chest.

"*That's* what you came here to say?" he laughs, and Cayenne's eyes sharpen. "That you think he's going to take you back because I'm *boring*? Jesus Christ, you need all the therapy."

Laughter rings out in a merry, bell-like peal. "*That* would be amusing.*" Cayenne pushes copper hair out of their eyes. Nate can't deny they picked a pretty package to wrap up all that crazy in when they used that somamancy artifact on themself. So much supernatural lore plays on the motif of shapeshifting, Nate wonders what the correlation— He shakes himself out of his academic reverie. Not the time.

"Speaking of therapy," Cayenne continues with a

small, sly smile, "has *mon tigre* told you where he got all those fetching scars of his?"

His greatest weakness—curiosity. But he won't be so easily baited. "Are you done yet? If that's what you wanted to say, then we're done here."

Cayenne lets slip a frustrated little snarl, casual affect dropping as they sit up straight. "You don't like The Trust either."

"Nope," Nate shrugs. "If I hadn't met Ravi first, and he wasn't so unquestionably good, I would think the whole enterprise is, at best, some bullshit tax dodge for the Skull and Bones crowd, and at worst, straight-up evil masquerading as altruists."

All the agents he's met so far have seemed like good folks, but if Ravi's cold and warlike aunt is an example of what The Trust's upper echelons are like, Nate isn't impressed. It hasn't escaped his attention that she hadn't exactly been a supportive figure in her nephew's life when he desperately needed one.

"*Oui, exactement*! Then our interests are aligned. We should be working toward the same goal."

"Nope. Because unlike you, I believe Ravi when he says he can fix it."

"Ravi is idealistic. I've *been* to the future. I *know* he won't be successful."

"So, everything is written in stone? I thought you changed the future all the time. He could surprise you."

Cayenne sneers. "An overabundance of education does not make you more of an expert on paradox than a real, live time traveler, Professor."

Nate shrugs. "Maybe you're right. It doesn't matter. If Ravi wants to try, I'm going to help him."

"If you truly want to *help* him instead of just *fucking* him you would be… *Non*. It is no use arguing with you." Cayenne's hands flex into pulsing fists before they smooth out over the wooden planks of the bench. It looks like it takes some effort to manage.

"Hey, how about that, there *is* something we agree on."

Cayenne's smirking green eyes rake him over from head to toe. "I suppose you'll do to keep him warm for me. Don't get too attached, *mon pauvre petit*. It's impossible to compete with someone who can offer him a once in a lifetime experience *over* and *over* again." They hold up their tattooed hand, wiggling their fingers with a playful, salacious wink.

It's not smart to goad this lunatic, but Nate can't help himself. "Yeah, I can't do any time wizard sex magic, so I guess the only thing I can offer is a healthy, supportive relationship built on a foundation of mutual trust and honesty instead of one built on murder, lies, and betrayal."

It's a good hit; Cayenne doesn't quite manage to hide a flinch. Then they laugh, careless and amused, stretching their arms overhead as they stand up. "Funny what people call a *relationship* these days. Or maybe you don't want to admit you're just a rebound screw. *Quelle douloureux.* Well, *good talk.* I'd best be going. So much to do." They turn as if to walk away, stop, then lean in close. Nate refuses to shy away, even as they get close enough to touch him, able to throw him forward or back in time and abandon him there if they so please.

"How many sisters do you have again? Four, yes?" It's as casual as an acquaintance might inquire during a friendly chat.

Despite the warm sunlit breeze, Nate goes completely cold, a shiver chasing up his spine.

Cayenne puts a finger to their chin, smiling guilelessly. "Hmm, are you *totally* sure about that number? But of course, silly me. How would you ever know if there used to be more? Maybe a brother or two?"

Nate hands curl into fists so tight his nails are going to leave deep grooves on his palms. They wouldn't. They couldn't. It's just an idle threat. Ravi wouldn't stand for it.

"You're a monster."

"Even worse," Cayenne says silkily, "I'm a monster in

love. Bye-bye, rebound boy." They blow him a kiss and disappear.

*

HARRY CLIMBS INTO Ravi's Escalade in torn jeans and a baggy sweatshirt, sunglasses big enough to cover half her face. "Punctual as always, my dude. *Kyaa chal rahaa hai?*"

He turns to stare at her, though it's doubtful she can make out the expression beyond his own mirrored lenses.

"You're learning Hindi?" Her accent is not the worst he's ever heard.

"Correction, I've been watching a fuckton of Bollywood movies and downloaded Duolingo. That's 'how's it going,' right?"

"Almost. It's 'what's up?' Then I say, *zyaada kuch nahi.*" She rotates a hand at him expectantly. "'Nothing much,'" he translates.

"Nothing much, huh. Nothing new going on with you?"

He looks away and signals into traffic, letting the silence stretch out.

Harry has several effective probing strategies he's seen her use in the field to extract information. Usually a potent mix of charm, innocent questioning, and outright grilling. From her silence, Ravi expects her to be wearing her unimpressed, incisive stare; the one that informs the suspect Harry has already figured out every little detail, so they might as well stop wasting time and come clean. But when he glances over, she's not bothering with that weak, amateur-hour interrogation approach.

Instead, Harry edges toward him with her chin propped on a fist, sunglasses tipped down her nose, eyes wide and soft as a puppy dog's.

Ravi chokes out a surprised laugh. "Don't give me that look."

"Come *oooon*. It's a long drive out to your aunt's country pile. I demand entertainment. Dish. Spill that tea, fam."

"*Bhaad me jao!*"

She swipes into her phone. "Ooh, I don't know that one either, teach me. Can't find it on my translation app."

"It won't have it. It means 'fuck off.'"

She breaks into peals of laughter, head thrown back. "Oh, fuck," she gasps, wiping the corner of her eye. "Is that any way to talk to your sacred avatar whatever?" Grinning, Harry slides her sunglasses back up her nose.

"You're invulnerable, you'll live."

"Sticks and stones, my dude." She shrugs, then wriggles into her seat to get more comfortable. "Remind me why I have to be present for this Grand Gala pre-pro. Padme can just send me the bullet points through you."

"There's probably going to be a fitting."

Harry's big sunglasses make her look like a flummoxed insect. "A what now?"

"A fitting. For your dress."

A beat of perfect silence before Harry bursts into another laughing fit. "Can you *imagine*? Oh, Padme is going to be one unhappy camper." She fights for breath, then glances at Ravi. "Unless there's a compelling, tactical reason I should play dress-up?"

"Clothes tell a story. It's…one of the few narratives about yourself that you can control." He clears his throat. "But wear whatever you want, Harry. The decision is entirely yours."

"Hm. Fair enough." She kicks a boot up on the dash and gives Ravi's slate-blue three-piece an obvious once-over. Hopefully it'll impress his professionalism upon his aunt, a hint that he's ready to take on more responsibilities. Aunt Padme is largely immune to sartorial psychology, but she might still appreciate the messaging.

"I'll consider it." Harry drums her fingers unevenly against her knee. "Has Val talked to you yet?"

Ravi blinks at the non sequitur. "About what?"

Harry shakes her head. "Not my place to say." Her foot bounces on the dash.

They drive for a while in companionable silence,

listening to the low chillhop beat of Ravi's playlist.

"Hey, you wanna talk about getting married?"

Ravi does not crash into the car in front of him. "Uh. Sure. If…if you want."

"I'm ready to have that conversation."

"Okay."

"Are *you* ready?"

How did his mouth get so dry? Did he swallow a handful of sand? "Yeah. Sure."

"Item one!" Harry holds up her index finger in an imperious manner. "Can I ride in on an elephant?"

His own bark of laughter takes him by surprise. "You want an elephant?"

"One movie had the groom arrive by elephant, and I gotta say, I *like* that vibe. Big entrance, you know." Harry gesticulates vividly with her hands.

Ravi relaxes, smiling. Harry isn't Jessika Eaton or Isabella Cattano, or any of the other grasping heiresses who have been clawing at him since he was a kid. Their wedding won't be the life-ending disaster he's dreaded ever since he was old enough to understand what was expected of him. It'll be…something different.

"Item two! I want one of those big, choreographed numbers. I want— Oh, hey, don't suppose you can dance, can you?"

His lips twitch. "Think I'll manage." His wedding might even be *fun*. Something he hadn't imagined possible, not that long ago.

Harry McAllister. Delivering miracles.

"Excellent." She rolls down her window just enough to stick her hand flat out of the window, gliding it along the airflow. "Okay, that's it."

"That's it? Those are your only two caveats? Dancing and an elephant?"

"Yup. I want full Bollywood flair, but apart from that, I'm good."

"Easily done," Ravi says with a low laugh. "There'd be dancing anyway, and the elephant is probably doable." The *baraat* procession is usually for the groom, but fuck it, Harry's the Chosen. Not like Ravi is itching to take center stage.

"Yeah, doable," he decides. "Traditionally there are a lot of steps to a Hindu engagement, but Abhiramnews are used to cultural fusion ceremonies. We've had enough of them over the centuries. Not a big deal to adapt however much you want. The wedding normally takes three days, but we can probably condense into two, if we do your mehndi party after the haldi."

Holding her hands up in front of her face as if picturing them embellished with henna, Harry asks, "You sure? It's your wedding too. If you want all three days of Hindu extravagance, I'm totally down, dude."

"You know me, big fan of being the center of attention," he snorts, then flashes her a quick peripheral smile. "I don't mind. The important thing is that it's official, not that it's extravagant. To be honest, I'm looking forward to seeing you hobnob with the old families. There are going to be a whole lot of dropped monocles and clutched pearls."

"I'm sure they'll be won over after hearing my charming anecdotes about shooting 'possums in the trailer park."

The laugh bursts out unchecked. "Why were... What *for*?"

"Dinner, obviously." She turns an exaggerated, toothy grin in his direction. "Reconsidering your marital choices yet?"

He smirks, shaking his head. "How about your guest list? Any family besides Constance you want to invite?"

Harry is quiet for so long that he glances over. Her hand hangs limp outside the car window, her face turned fully away, though he can make out her reflection in the glass. Her jaw is tight.

"Do you know why I was kicked off the Atlanta CID and had to go private eye?" she eventually asks. "Was that in a dossier or whatever, when you were assigned to contract with us?"

It's an abrupt change of subject. Harry lost her mother

sometime in her teens, Ravi knows. Maybe he shouldn't have asked. "Broad strokes only. At the time, we were more concerned with the powerful time-traveling sorceress who showed up at your door."

Harry snorts. "Broad strokes, sure. What stuff do you know?"

"I know you…" Ravi hedges. "Had a lot of other jobs, first."

Harry's snort transforms into an amused bark. "Boy howdy, did I ever."

"After a brief time in social work—"

"Hey, guess how I fucked that up."

He's unsure how to parse Harry's expression. "How?"

"I punched a guy in the face." Harry gives him an overly sweet smile. "And since the whole social worker creed is about de-escalating violent situations, it was pretty clear I wasn't cut out for it."

"I assume he deserved it."

"Oh, *bruh*, like extremely."

"Well, that's fine then." Ravi shrugs. "Then you went into case work for the District Attorney, right?"

"For like a hot minute. Until—you guessed it!—I punched a guy in the face. The ADA. He…maybe deserved it a little less than the other guy. But I still stand by it."

"Huh. That would explain why your timeline gets a little murky on our end, if nobody wanted to have a political incident publicized. Our intel says you were headhunted from the DA's office by the commander of Criminal Investigations Division and fast-tracked to detective. Youngest ever in the state. Breezed through the Academy and made it through two months of patrol before you were discharged while still on probation for a call that resulted in a fatality. It was flagged by our intel as nonspecific, but possibly supernatural."

He slides a quick assessment her way. Her body language is unusually still, like leaves staying motionless on the branch despite the high wind. She's silent for a long time.

"Wanna guess how I fucked that one up?"

"Did you punch a guy in the face?"

"I blew up a house."

"Whoa. Talk about escalation."

"A man was inside. And before you ask, I'm not totally, completely sure if he deserved it. I was investigating a missing persons case, and he was just some guy on the list of possible persons of interest. The whole thing is kind of…fuzzy. Memory-wise."

"What do you remember?"

"Well," Harry says lightly, "I remembered waltzing

into some kind of fucked-up, shadowy nether realm in the middle of this guy's living room, so obviously I had gone insane." She pulls her hand back inside the car, tipping her head against the seat. "Even after I woke up later in the hospital, post-explosion, my first thought was: *Wow, so this is what it feels like to be crazy.*" She exhales, a single harsh gust. "Now I know that kind of bullshit can happen to people alarmingly often, tripping into Faerie or wherever. But back then? I'd always wondered when it would happen to me. When I'd crack."

She's quiet again as she undoes her hair tie, shaking out dark tangles. "So, all my biological family are certified wackjobs. Tin foil hat wearers, woo-woo conspiracy theorists, people who make Flat Earthers seem reasonable. I'm not exactly prime genetic material, dude. I got an uncle who insists he's been abducted by aliens three dozen times, and a cousin who says she's spiritually married to Bigfoot through the astral plane." She wiggles her fingers in a vaguely mystical way before tying her hair back up. "My mom was…well, I couldn't live with her." Harry picks at invisible lint on her knees. "Dead dad, unstable relatives, so into the foster system I went. Cue the usual foster kid sob stories. Nothing new or interesting to tell on that front."

A few beats pass. Ravi knows this kind of silence well; it's not the kind he's welcome to interrupt.

"Then, when I was older, Mom shaped up. Sobered up. Wanted me back. Wanna hear something fucked-up?" She doesn't wait for Ravi to answer. "When she got the cancer diagnosis, I was *thrilled*. How messed up is that? I just *knew* it was a brain tumor. Finally, a reason why she was such a fucking nutjob. All the shit she pulled when I was growing up, all the fucked-up shit she said? It wasn't really her after all. It was the tumor all along." She flops her head sideways to give him a smile that isn't. "Nope. Bone cancer. Took years. Fuck me, right?"

"Harry…I'm so sorry."

"Eh, whaddya gonna do. You know…" Something resembling a laugh scrapes its way past her teeth. "I really liked how you said that, before. 'Headhunted from the DA's office.' That sounds so much better than I fucked up everything I did, and then even the thing I was great at? Being a detective? I fucked that up too." She spreads both hands out with theatrical flair. "So, into the fun-filled world of the private sector I went! To sneak in bushes catching philanderers and surveilling insurance defrauders."

Ravi gives her a few breaths of space before he adds, "And then someone claiming to be an angel turned up, and a witch spilled out of a time rift from the Dark Ages, and you found out magic is real."

"Ha! Yeah. *Good* times. What a kick in the teeth, that my

family isn't as crazy as I thought. I hate being wrong. It happens so rarely." Her grin is equal parts self-deprecation and simple truth. "Honestly, ghost hunting and all that spooky shit with Val and Constance was a big step up, after regular PI work. Turns out I have a knack for it." She waves her hands over herself like a game show host displaying a quality prize. "Must be that diluted Shaw blood."

"Or, you know. The Chosen thing," Ravi says with a lopsided smile.

"Oh, right, that too." A bitter laugh. "I'm so fucking special."

A burden he was raised to know well. "I get it."

Some tension leaves her. "Yeah. I know you do."

"Harry, you built a name for yourself out of nothing. Only just discovered the supernatural and in a span of months, you had a reputation for helping people, and built such an effective team that the biggest monster-hunting agency in the world took notice and extended their resources to you."

"Aw, fuck, you asshole, I just realized you got me monologuing! That stoic, serious face, *ugh*. People must want to spill their guts to you at the drop of a hat. It's gross, dude." She turns away, forcing a chuckle. "Good for interrogations though. Handy talent."

"So…your guest list is gonna be pretty easy, huh?"

She cackles loudly, her posture loosening further. "Yeah, just put the team on it and leave the rest blank."

"Did you ever find out what it was? The portal you stepped into?"

"Nah. Not sure what caused the explosion either, though I definitely got blamed for it. Sounds like something I'd do, to be honest. Thing was, the guy whose house it was? There was juuuust enough evidence left to hint that he might have been behind those missing persons. Opinion was split down the middle on if I was some kind of hero or just a lucky fuckup."

"Harry. If it helps?"

The set of her mouth stiffens. "Yeah?"

"I don't think aliens *or* Bigfoot are real."

A quick, honest grin flashes before Harry drags the back of her hand across her forehead, a parody of relief. "That's a load off my mind, man. Thanks."

"Any time." He chews his lip a bit before suggesting, "Look in the glove compartment."

Not wasting breath on questions, Harry slides her feet off the dash and opens the hatch. "Okay, do you want this Ruger for something?"

"Not the revolver, that's just a spare. Next to it."

Harry pulls out a red velvet box, quite obviously sized for a ring.

"Oh my god," she deadpans, "this is so sudden."

"Okay, smartass. I can wait and do the whole down-on-one-knee thing you Americans love."

"Don't you threaten me, mister. And I hate to tell you, bud, but you have a gas-guzzling full-size SUV with a gun in the glove compartment. That's as American as it gets. You've gone native." She flips open the box. Her eyes go wide. "What…what is this?"

"You don't like it."

"That's not…" Harry plucks the ring out of its box and holds it up to the light. "I didn't think…" She slips her sunglasses down her nose to get a better look.

The silver stem of a lotus weaves into a fretwork of Irish style knotwork to form the band. The lotus petals hold in their heart an iridescent sunset-colored sphere that catches the sunlight, the surface shimmering like a tiny dancing fire.

It took a while to get it commissioned to his specifications, but Ravi's pleased with the results. "It's a melo melo pearl. Rarest kind in the world. Set in platinum. Should be pretty strong." When she doesn't say anything, he glances over. "You *said* no diamonds."

She punches him in the shoulder.

"*Aiye*, fuck!" He swerves a few inches into the next lane, eliciting a honk from another driver. "You don't like it?"

"You'd have to cut my hand off to get it away from me," she says crisply, sliding the ring onto her finger. "This is *stupid* thoughtful. No backsies." She angles a sly look over the top of her sunglasses. "Nate hit the jackpot with you."

He looks away, traitorous ears going hot as coals.

"C'mon, you don't wanna tell me? Your own fiancée?" Harry wheedles, holding up her left hand.

"That's— I don't kiss and tell."

She grins in triumph. "So, there was kissing."

Ravi turns the music up.

When Harry's laughter trails off, she heaves her boots back up onto the dash. "This might be another delicate topic, but is there any reason to keep up appearances after the wedding?"

Ravi gives this some thought as he takes the exit toward Deal. "I'd assumed you wanted to present a united front. But it's an interesting idea to draw out any hidden enemies. We could pretend to be reluctant about the alliance. Bound to be plenty who assume I'm not thrilled that you've—"

"No, no, no," Harry says with an annoyed cluck of her tongue. "Is there any reason for you to pretend you're straight?"

Ravi opens his mouth but nothing comes out, brain blue-screening for a full half minute. "I... What? Yeah? Yes."

Harry takes off her sunglasses. "*Is* there, though? As long as we 'present a united front,' what the fuck does it matter? If we do the thing, follow the dumb bylaw rules, then who the fuck cares who either of us are banging? You *cannot* convince me that you upper-crust multimillionaire types don't have *arrangements*." She rolls her Rs with an ostentatious posh accent.

"That's…true enough."

"Look, I'm not saying it'll be a *picnic* for you, and I, a mostly straight white chick, one thousand percent don't get to dictate when someone comes out, but…" She claps a hand to Ravi's shoulder. "I'm just saying, maybe you don't have to hide who you are anymore if you don't want to. I want you to be happy, dude. Think about it, is all I'm saying."

He's barely able to manage a "Thanks," which sounds pathetically inadequate as soon as he gives it voice. "You're right. I…I get more out of marrying you than you get out of marrying me." He gets freedom, family, the right to direct his own legacy, the ability to run The Trust the way he knows it should be run. Against all that, Harry getting a nice ring and access to intel seems lacking.

"That wasn't even close to what I was saying, but ah, well. Baby steps. Maybe I'm just planning on divorcing you a year in and taking half your fortune."

He's grateful for her teasing. It's way easier than her supportive sincerity. "Roughly two hundred pounds of diamonds in your great-aunt's basement isn't enough for you, McAllister?"

"I've got expensive tastes, babe," she drawls with a hearty dose of vocal fry. "And maybe marrying me is all an elaborate scam to get your Green Card, how am I to know, huh?" Her face twists in an absurdly aloof sneer that she drops only when Ravi erupts into a short burst of laughter.

"I already have my lawful permanent residence, thank you very much. Fucking hell, Harry." He tries to control the wild grin on his face, but it's not easy. "*Mostly* straight white chick, huh?"

"Well yeah, Charlize Theron exists, so." Harry claps her hands together briskly. "While we're on the subject of seizing empires and making them ours, let's talk kids."

Overcorrecting a turn, Ravi taps the brakes harder than intended. "This whole conversation had to happen now? While I'm driving?"

Harry ignores him, tone all business. "Is there a time frame that we are obligated to hold to? Any deadline for the firstborn?"

Ravi takes a few deep, focusing breaths. "Not officially. The sooner the better."

"In case I bite it."

"Essentially."

"Well, now that I know my genes aren't a complete clusterfuck of kookiness, I'm, you know. Not opposed. I could be a cool mom, I think."

"You'd be a very cool mom." He swallows, a bit taken aback at how soft his voice sounds.

"Obviously, our kids will be absolute smokeshows. I'm a stone cold ten outta ten, and you're not bad either."

Ravi runs the tip of his tongue over dry lips. He's glad they're on the highway. No way he can focus on taking the correct turns right now.

"I...really want to be a good father, Harry."

Harry slams a fist into her breastbone with a hearty *thwock*, like she's trying to unstick a fishbone from her throat. "Jesus tapdancing fuck," she chokes. "My ovaries actually twinged when you said that. Woof, gimme a second to recover from that." She digs into her bag and pulls out a mostly empty bottle of diet soda. It must be old and flat, as it doesn't hiss as she opens it and takes a drink. "Look, I'm not thrilled a kid of mine could go through the same shit you did. I've seen some of your scars. Physical and otherwise."

"They won't."

"Oh?"

"That's the first thing I'm going to change. I promise

you." Harry doesn't answer, so Ravi keeps talking, trying to impart every ounce of his sincerity. "After we get married, we're going to have resources. I'm not just talking about money, I'm talking strike teams and intelligence. Contacts. Networks. Arsenals. The full force of The Trust's influence. But our child..." His heart flips over in his chest, and he has to start again. "*Our* child will have a normal life. Go to school. Make friends. Have choices. Futures. Whether they're Chosen or not, they get to decide what they want to do with their life."

Harry stares directly at him for a long, drawn-out moment, then shrugs. "Okay, I'm in. Let's tell your aunt. Then we'll get The Trust started in the direction you want it, get hitched, and then when we feel like it, we can hit the clinic."

"Yeah?"

"Yeah."

For a heady, giddy second, Ravi has the same sense of wild, unrestrained freedom he has only felt once before — at the lake house, Cayenne promising a whole rewound day of having anything he pleased. Only this wasn't a single day, but every day from here on out. An entire future. A future where Ravi could, just maybe, have everything he'd ever wanted. Even the parts he'd never dared hope for.

"Thank you," he rasps.

Harry makes a flatulent noise with her lips. "Enough of

that, yeesh. Tell me about your sordid affair! Barely engaged and you're already tomcatting around. Men, I tell ya."

He chuckles, then taps a nervous rhythm on the steering wheel. "About that. You don't think…it's unwise?"

"Asking me for relationship advice is even funnier than me wearing a dress." Harry sighs. "I think you deserve something uncomplicated. You don't owe Cayenne anything. People have this belief that the person who broke your heart is the person who should fix it. But let me tell ya, as a PI who's seen a *lot*—and I mean like *wow*, a metric fuckton—of shitty relationships go down in flames: that doesn't happen in real life. Ever. It either ends or it escalates." A muscle jumps in Harry's cheek. "It's fun to romanticize the tragic, wounded asshole, to give them chance after chance, to think 'I can change them,' etcetera, etcetera. Pop culture thrives on the idea. It's almost the basis of the entire romance genre. And it's total. Fucking. *Bullshit*."

Harry fixes Ravi with a penetrating look. "Nate's a good guy. Solid. I'm as suspicious as they come, and even I think he's trustworthy. Plus, he's crazy about you. And if you tell him I told you that, I will deny it and also shoot you in the foot."

Ravi's heartrate jumps. "Crazy about you" is surely another one of Harry's exaggerations, but "trustworthy" is an apt choice of words. Nate's exactly what he appears to be, no artifice, no ulterior motives. After a lifetime navigating the exhausting layers of intrigue and politics Ravi had been born into, Nate is a golden coin among counterfeit bills.

"Anyway," Harry continues, "you can't live in fear of what the Red Menace is gonna do. Like you said, we just gotta keep on keepin' on, right? For the integrity of the new fucking timeline or whatever Dr. Who nonsense—"

She stops abruptly, massaging her forehead.

"You okay?"

"Eh, didn't sleep well. Dumb dreams. Sticking with me, is all."

Ravi gives her a reproachful look over his sunglass frames. "Was it a vision?"

She pulls a face. "No. Maybe. I don't know."

"*Harry.*" Limited prescience has got to be an adjustment for her, but it's part and parcel of the Chosen deal. "Is there going to be an attack? We got a job?"

"No, it was just like…weird team stuff. Muddled. Just dreams, man, let it go."

In a sudden rush of displaced air, Val appears in the backseat, her eyes burning blue fire. "There is a problem."

Adrenaline spiking, Ravi twitches for his gun as he swerves back into his lane. "Does nobody understand that *I am trying to drive here?*"

"Ah, fuck," Harry sighs wearily. She doesn't look surprised in the least. "Pull over."

Chapter Twelve

"IF YOU SAY 'I told you so,' I'm gonna huck your sniper rifle off a cliff."

Ravi puts the car in park and holds his hands up to fend off Harry's accusation.

Val's ashen brows shadow glowing eyes. "I will keep my explanation brief. Time may be a factor. Earlier, Constance called to inform me that if she did not call back in an hour, I should alert the team and go to a particular spot in the woods fully armed."

"And it's been over an hour?" Ravi asks grimly, unclasping his seatbelt.

"No. It has been only a little over five minutes. I did not

like the tone of her voice." The angel takes a breath, pauses, then lets it out. "I took some initiative."

"Atta girl," Harry says, lips hiking in a half smile.

"After assessing the situation, I fetched the professor. He is already with Constance. Will you come? This situation may require a more human touch than I possess."

Harry starts stuffing her things into her bag. "Of course, big gal, with bells on. Why Nate first?"

"He is the most congenial of you."

"Well golly, don't spare our feelings or anything. Let's go."

"What's the situation?" Ravi readies himself for the unpleasant swoop of teleportation as Val clamps a hand on each of their shoulders.

"Constance is summoning a demon."

*

THEY MATERIALIZE IN a wooded glade at the edge of a meadow clearing. A circle has been painted into the center of the clearing, with a complicated mesh of sigils ringed by a profusion of wildflowers. It would otherwise offer quite a picturesque scene if it weren't for the unsettling beam of red light pouring up through sigils, making the surrounding forest look as if it were awash in blood. Thick waves of tangible heat ripple off the painted runes, nearby flora wilting and sizzling. The woods are conspicuously absent of bird calls or insect song.

Dread brings sweat to Ravi's palms. He can't read a lick of magic, but he knows a demon summoning circle as well as any field agent. One of the highest offenses a mage can commit; some of the worst disasters in history had been caused by reckless warlocks calling up demons in hopes of obtaining power, knowledge, or revenge. It rarely went as smoothly as the mage planned.

Constance stands at the edge of the circle with both hands raised and trembling, her usual cheer stripped away. Loose strands of hair escape the braids framing her grimly determined face and curl aloft with the heat. Griswold prowls around her boots like a miniature jungle cat, hackles raised and eyes glowing yellow.

Bathed in red light, Nate inches a step closer to Constance, his posture loose and non-threatening. "—if we can just talk this through first, I promise I'll help you with anything you need, Constance. You know that we care about— Oh, look, the others are here, thank Christ. We're all here now. We want to help you, Constance, we do, so just…close the portal, okay?"

"Speaketh not to me as though I were a mere stripling, Nathan." Constance's throat sounds raw, her speech slipping in and out of archaic diction. She lifts her chin, the light not helping the dark shadows under her eyes. "I know what I am doing."

"Okay, good," Harry breezes, stepping closer to peer at the circle. "Because I have no clue what's going on. What *are* you doing?"

Ravi sidles alongside her, his heart in his throat. "It's a hell portal, Harry." All Constance has to do is call up a being from that plane of existence, or even get sloppy with her concentration, and they're all in very deep shit.

Constance says, "You heard the information broker. We may set a demon to *catch* a demon. My nemesis hath walked free in this land of milk and honey too long, supping on souls while I have been doing *nothing*. Messing about in the future *enjoying* myself while Hartnell murders innocents." Her voice cracks.

The blue flame of Val's eyes has gone violet with hell-light. "We shall find him and end him. But this is not the way."

Constance shakes her head. "None of the information thou all have gathered is of any help. My quarry has gone to ground and eludes my best efforts to hunt him. It is not as easy as it once was, tracking through wealds and over roads. But if I call a rival demon prince and bind it to my service long enough to—"

"And then what, Constance?" demands Ravi. "Let's

say everything goes as planned, which it rarely does. You bind this new demon to obey you and hunt down your old demon. What happens when the binding spell runs out? What bargains will you have to make?"

"I know the risks, witch-hunter. At least Hartnell will be dead," Constance spits.

Nate asks, "Did they have the story about swallowing a spider to catch the fly in your time?"

"*My time*," Constance sneers, an alien look on her friendly face. "What do you know of it? You don't know what it's like to be so unthinkably far away from everything you know, from the people you love. *None* of you truly understand. You all speak of my time as if I should be grateful to be rid of it, but it was my home. I...I miss knowing how things are *done* and how to *dress* and how to *speak*. I miss my *family*." A tear spills down her cheek. At her feet, Griswold sets a paw on the top of her thick leather boot, looking up at her.

Harry steps over the painted lines and brushes the tear away. "What are we, chopped liver?"

Constance coughs a thick-throated laugh, then shakes her head. "I cannot even visit my homestead. The Weir Wood is gone. There is a lake now where my cottage once stood. My brothers and sisters have all been dead for so long that their graveyards no longer remain. Their bones are lost to dust and memory." She stares into the hell portal, unseeing and wistful. "The air used to taste different. There was more birdsong, the forests thicker. The stars are now all in the wrong place. No one remembers how the night used to look."

"I do."

Val flinches as she walks past the crackling heat of the infernal rift but doesn't slow until she stands beside Constance. "I remember how the heavens would wheel overhead, how on clear nights they could cast starlight as brightly as day. I remember much, my friend, and I too have known loss. But this will not bring any of what you have lost back to you."

Constance sags, hands falling to her sides. The portal doesn't flicker or dim the way it might for a less accomplished sorceress.

Ravi keeps his eye fixed on it, alert for anything attempting to sneak out. He's underequipped with only his gun, knuckledusters, and a small flask of holy water. He scans the surrounding trees to gauge the clearance he'd need to fight, for potential tripping hazards and possible improvised weapons, all the while painfully aware that Nate is completely unarmed.

"Mayhaps not. But if it shall keep that accursed demon from slaughtering more folk, it shall be worth any cost.

Another body was found this last fortnight. A bit of flotsam beset by fish for many moons afore she washed up ashore. Another life snuffed out, and I carry the blame."

Harry's shades reflect crimson as she pushes them up her head. "That's awful, Constance, I'm really sorry. How'd you even find that out? It's been tough going tracking his known kills. Fucker keeps changing up his hunting patterns."

Constance waves vaguely to her leather satchel on the ground against a nearby tree trunk. "Bobby sent me a file."

"Thought you called him off the case." Ravi frowns. Oddly, the hairs on the back of his neck stand on end. The hell portal seems clear, so he's not sure what's pinging his instincts.

Nate picks up the satchel and pulls out a thick manila folder. He opens it, immediately blanches, and closes it again. "I could have done without seeing that."

Harry extends her hand. "Gimme." Nate hands it over and she starts sheafing through it, the picture of professionalism. The furrow between her brows deepens.

In the meantime, Val hasn't taken her flaming eyes off Constance. "You would set a demon loose into the world to avenge your cousin. You would send another to enact your vengeance instead of facing your enemy yourself."

Back stiffening, Constance sucks in a sharp sip of

breath. She pulls a thick plait over her shoulder and gives it a reflexive tug. "I…nay, Valiance. I would take the fight to mine nemesis. Control the battlefield. I want him flushed out as pheasants from the brush before the arrows fly. I want him cornered, with no ground to go to, to hound and harass him until he has no spirit left within him to fight."

Her words strike a chord, a fierce little string plucked to resonate deep in Ravi's chest.

Val simply nods. "We will help you."

"This isn't right," Harry declares, looking up from the file. "Rav, check this out. Does The Trust do their reports like this? Because cops and private eyes sure as hell don't."

He peers over her shoulder. Something's off, that's immediately obvious. The pictures are gruesome, camera flash shining off flayed skin, but they're arranged like a scrapbook. The missing persons and autopsy reports look hastily copied, not even stapled together. Like something out of a movie; not a real report but a sensationalist assortment all for show. Sloppy.

"We do *not*."

Constance's face knits in confusion. "To what art thou referring? Thou believe the information to be false?"

"Not exactly." Ravi shares a meaningful glance with Harry. "But there's no way Robert Hernandez sent this to you."

"This was meant to upset you, Constance," Harry says grimly, tucking the folder under her arm. "To provoke you so you'd do something rash. Three guesses who likely orchestrated this little jab."

"That *fucking asshole!*" Nate throws his hands up in the air and stalks a few steps away, back turned. "*Ostie que je suis tanné!*"

Ravi scrubs a hand over his jaw, spirits sinking. "Yeah. That tracks. Constance is the only one who's figured out a way to keep Cayenne from manipulating time. Makes sense they'd want her distracted."

Easy enough to remove her from the equation, they had said, silkily and suggestive, before claiming it wasn't a threat.

"Or killed." A growl underlies Val's resonant voice. "There are endless ways for a demon summoning to go wrong. The summoner can be killed or incapacitated, or even be dragged through the portal themselves."

Constance looks from one face to the other, then down at Griswold. The familiar lashes his tail and hisses, "Vile trickery and deceit! A missive of calumnies and legerdemain! This wretched warlock of time shall meet my claws, mistress, and—"

"Hush, Griswold, my knight." Constance sighs softly. Her fingers twist in a complicated downward succession, as if playing a glissando on invisible harp strings.

Like a switch being flipped, the unearthly red light cuts out, grass blackened and steaming beneath their feet as the hell portal closes. Ravi's coiled tension eases, though he's still holding back a quiet, consuming fury.

Fair enough to strike out at *him*, at The Trust. At least he understands Cayenne's motives there, as warped as they are. But to purposely endanger his team? To taunt Constance with images of her enemy's victims to goad her into exposing herself and others to indescribable danger?

Ravi *seethes*.

At his shoulder, Nate radiates a calm so grounding that Ravi's able to take a series of soothing breaths, to fix his attention back on the present.

"Well." Constance's voice is a bit frail at the edges, and her smile isn't better off. "If that knave intends for me to do a thing, that is a fairly compelling reason to not do it, aye?"

"Aye." Harry pulls Constance into a side-hug, heads together. "We're gonna get him, Constance. I swear it. I'm a divinely mandated demon killer now. Hartnell's going down, the slimy fuck."

"He hides from you because he is a coward," Val says with certainty. "We shall flush him out, and when you slay him, history shall forget him utterly."

Constance gives Val a long, hard look, then nods once

with satisfaction. "A curse worthy of my time."

Behind them a sharp *crack* accompanies a sudden bright flash, illuminating the clearing like lightning. Ravi shoves Nate behind him and spins around, gun leaping to his hand. Val's wings snap out and Harry complains, "Oh, what fucking *now*?"

A man stumbles from nothingness onto the grass, eyes wild. "Stop! Don't do it! It's a trick—oh." He stares at the group and blinks in confusion. "I thought… Sorry, is this the right day?" He pushes up a sleeve to look at one of his watches, as he wears a stack of them in varying styles all up his arm. He taps at one with a carved wooden band.

Ravi tilts up the muzzle of his gun. "James."

James smiles wanly. "Hi." Then his nose starts gushing blood.

Constance tuts and plucks a handful of leaves from a nearby plant. She strides up to James in a no-nonsense manner. "Move thy hands, my fellow. Put this yarrow up thy nostrils. There we are! That shall quell the bleeding." She wipes at his face with a bit of her sleeve.

James slumps, face red, leaves shoved up his nose. He bled last time too, which he attributed to his method of time travel, a technology instead of magic. Much rougher on the body, he'd claimed.

Where Cayenne is all flash and flamboyance, James is

aggressively average. His plain clothing and haircut could easily be at home in most countries anywhere from the '40s to present, and likely will be for decades to come. He has a forgettable face. If someone were trying to relay details to a sketch artist, they might say, "White guy, maybe? Curly hair, I think?"

"To what do we owe this unexpected visit, my good man?" Constance asks as Griswold sniffs at James's pant leg, whiskers pushed far forward.

James averts his eyes, scuffing brown shoes into the grass. "I came to save your life," he mutters.

Harry flaps a dismissive hand, pitching her voice into the particular type of chirpy sarcasm she favors. "Oh, the demon summoning thing? We got that covered, thanks, dude. Guess you zapped back in time for nothing. That's *so* embarrassing."

"'Tis good to see you, however!" Constance grins, hands akimbo. Her dark mood seems banished with the portal, and she tosses some braids over her shoulder. "We have many queries we'd hoped you could answer."

Finally, a chance to get some answers. Cutting through to the most important question, Ravi holsters his gun and steps forward. "Have you been helping us by ruining Cayenne's plans?"

"Oh, no. What are they doing *this* time? I can't keep

track anymore. They're flinging out paradoxes left and right, it's a nightmare. Whatever you're thinking, it's not me. I just keep an eye out for Conssssss—for…*conflict*. I keep an eye out for specific types of conflict." James darts a glance up at Constance and back down to his unremarkable brown shoes.

They all stare at him.

"Oookay," Harry drawls. "Well, cool to see you, dude. Do you know what a shitshow the last year has been for us?"

"It wasn't like this last time I was here!" He throws up his hands in distress, voice stuffy from the leaves crammed up his nose. "The timeline is in shambles. Mapping it has been impossible."

"Yeah, we've been hearing that," Nate pipes up from beside Ravi. "Hey, are you behind the special delivery that showed up on Harry's door?" It's a smart leap of logic. The plain brown package the urumi came in wasn't Cayenne's style, but it certainly was James's.

"A delivery? No? What delivery?" James looks genuinely lost, like a confused puppy. "And how come there isn't a hell portal here spilling out imps and hellhounds?"

Harry briskly snaps her fingers a few times. "Because of the power of friendship, keep up. Glad you're as sick of all the time travel bullshit as we are. So, in your future timeline, there should be an open portal to demon city here?"

James holds up his wrist and taps a watch. He peers closely at a small but complex holographic display that pops up a few inches above his arm.

"That's pretty cool," Nate mutters, his breath warming Ravi's ear. Impressed despite himself, Ravi nods in agreement.

James clicks his tongue as the display winks out. "There *should* have been. I came to stop it. It was going to be this…this whole *thing*." Crestfallen, he finally manages to meet Constance's gaze. "I know I'm nowhere near your level of ability, but I wanted to help."

Constance gives a hearty scoff. "Nonsense! You can trip yourself back and forth through the veil of time itself! Whether thou callest it magic or mechanism, 'tis a thing I cannot manage."

James leans forward in fervent admiration. "Oh, but *no one* has *ever* managed to jump through time as far as you have, natural chronomancer or no! Most time travelers have a hard limit of three centuries *max* before or after their birth. Eight hundred years is insane! It must have taken so much energy."

"Well. I was quite vexed."

"Wow," James breathes, stars practically shining in his

eyes.

Harry stuffs the manila folder into her brimming bag. "James, my dude, you wanna go get a drink and chat while you're here? Promise to only interrogate you a little." James awkwardly chews his lip before he finally nods. "Awesome. Everyone ready to go?"

"Actually," Nate interjects, "something happened at the university that I want to fill Ravi in on, if he has no objections. You can catch us up on—wait, *hold up*. Is that an engagement ring?" He goggles at Harry's hand.

Harry glances down at her ring, infinitely casual. "Oh yeah. It's official. Ravi popped the…the not *question* exactly, but the tactically sound alliance? Yeah, that's been solidified. Something was popped, anyway. Really swept me off my feet. Ah, fuck, we're gonna need to reschedule that meeting with your aunt." She doesn't seem too broken up about it.

"Got it covered. What happened at the university, it's a pressing issue?" Ravi is torn; he'd very much like to spend more one-on-one time with Nate, but he also wants to grill James for anything that could help give the team an edge. Especially if Cayenne is making a play on his teammates. He has to remember to take one breath after another, quashing the sharp swell of his anger.

Nate shifts, discomfited. "It's…no. Personal, not

pressing. I think." Something in his voice gives Ravi pause.

"You guys go," Harry waves. "We got this." She slides an arm over Constance's shoulder and gives Ravi a significant look. Yeah, okay, she's a way better investigator than he is. He can trust that if James has any important info, Harry will extract it with ease. "Val, would you mind escorting the gents?"

"I would not." Without ceremony, Val picks up and dumps Griswold into James's arms, who squeaks as he clumsily juggles the large cat. "I shall teleport you both to Ravi's vehicle."

"Thanks, Val." Nate looks around at the forest clearing. "I have no idea where we are right now."

Val sets her hands to their shoulders and with an unsettling, falling-in-a-dream sensation, they're on the shoulder of the highway, cars whizzing by fast enough to stir their hair. Ravi blinks off the static and sets his hand to the door handle, engaging the auto-unlock.

"Better than a roller coaster," Nate laughs, clapping Val on the arm before moving to the passenger door.

"Thanks," Ravi tells her, and is about to open the door when two meaty hands settle on his shoulders. "Val?"

"I wish to speak with you tomorrow morning."

"I… Okay, yeah. What's going on?"

"You need not be alarmed. I merely have…" She stops

as if uncertain, closing her eyes, and it's the most *human* expression Ravi has ever seen on her. For a moment, she appears to be simply a tall, well-muscled woman with an ash-white ponytail, not like an ancient being of light and righteous fury given flesh. Then her eyes flash back open, glowing like white-hot pearls. "I have information to volunteer."

"Okay." He's curious but doesn't want to push. Val isn't naturally forthcoming, to put it mildly.

Her smile is a barely-there tick of her lips. "Good. Dress casually." She whisks away with the sound of fluttering feathers.

Once Ravi is steering the Escalade back into traffic, he asks Nate, "Where to?"

"You hungry?"

"I could eat."

"There's a cool '50s style diner around here. We could do breakfast for dinner."

"I know the one. It's close by." Ravi glances at the clock. "I've got to check in with my aunt. Do you mind?"

"Not at all, my guy, do your work stuff. I promise not to eavesdrop on your super-secret Trust business."

Ravi snorts and slips a bud in his ear while he cues up the call.

Padme picks up immediately, cutting the first ring in half. "Ravi?"

"Yes, ma'am."

"I have never known you to be late." Her throaty voice has a strictly controlled edge, carefully emotionless. "I am sure there is some overwhelmingly pressing reason you and the Chosen have been delayed."

"There was a minor emergency. It's handled. We're going to have to reschedule."

"I see," comes Padme's permafrost drawl. "I suppose I have no choice but to bend to your wishes." An affronted sniff.

Ravi pauses. "The engagement is official."

Nate shifts in his seat, propping his head up on his fist and gazing out the window.

Her frost melts into rare, genuine warmth. "*Khushkhabri*. Excellent. This is—" She clears her throat. "This is good news, agent. And it could not come at a better time. The Katarajus and even the Prestons have been rattling their sabers about our bloodline's obvious unsuitability to bear Durga's favor, and this…hmm."

He raises his eyebrows and waits. His aunt interrupts herself even more rarely than Val does.

"This affords us an opportunity. We shall make the announcement at the Gala. In one move, we shall solidify the new Chosen's place in The Trust and our family's rightful place alongside her. *Your* place."

"Yes, ma'am." Always a safe bet when he's not sure how she wants him to answer.

"Then there is much to do. A multitude of preparations to oversee."

"Harry wants to ride in on an elephant."

Nate snorts, then quickly covers his mouth with his hand. Ravi shoots him a small, sly grin.

Padme is silent, and Ravi holds his breath, bracing for a tirade about tradition and seemliness and who-knows-what-else.

"Nephew, your betrothed can ride in on *my* back if it will secure this wedding."

Ravi blinks. "I, ah. Don't think that will be necessary."

"No? We shall stick with the elephant, then? As you wish." Padme sniffs again, this time a swift expression of pleasure. "Good hunting, Ravi." The line goes dead.

Ravi removes the earbud. "I think she's pleased."

"How can you tell? If your aunt smiled, her face would crack like an egg."

Ravi chuckles. After a long moment of silence, he looks over to find Nate watching him intently. "What?"

"You're really handsome, you know that?"

The unexpected compliment sends a flush to his cheeks. He tears his eyes away to concentrate on the road.

Nate grins. "Your dick has been in me, but you blush at

that. It's cute."

Heat flares up under Ravi's skin, the vivid memory of the slick warmth of Nate's body crystal clear in his mind.

He coughs. "Want to tell me what happened at work, or do you want to wait until we get to the diner?"

Nate's smile fades a fraction. "I think it's best on a full stomach. Or at least when we're not in a moving vehicle."

"Sure." Ravi takes the exit and changes the subject. "I feel for Constance."

"Yeah, me too. She's integrating amazingly well, but sometimes communication is still an issue. Her values are different than modern ones. I could tell I wasn't convincing her to shut the portal down. Really glad you and Harry showed up when you did."

"I didn't do anything," Ravi protests with a guilty pang. The situation could have gone real ugly, real fast. The standard operating protocol for hell portals can be summed up in two words: Avoid them.

"Yes, you did. You made us all feel safer just by being there." Bracing his hands on the center console, Nate leans over and plants a quick kiss to Ravi's cheek, almost at the corner of his mouth. "It's nice knowing a guy who can kick an imp in half."

Despite his rising blush from the kiss, Ravi splutters a laugh. "I've never *kicked an imp in half*."

Nate raises up a single finger. "You've never kicked an imp in half *yet*. I believe in you."

Biting down on a smile, Ravi pulls into the parking lot of the silver-shining retro diner. By habit he parks far back from the entrance, in a shady spot away from other cars. "You're ridiculous, you know that?"

"Guilty as charged."

The restaurant is the perfect amount of busy. No one near enough to eavesdrop, but enough ambient conversation buzzing to foil any listening devices. Ravi picks a table that'll allow him to keep his back to the wall and still maintain a view of the whole diner.

"You're like a meerkat. Always on alert."

Ravi's shoulders tense. "I can't turn it off," he mutters into the tabletop.

Nate smiles over his menu. "That was in no way a criticism, my guy. Meerkats are alert *and* adorable. You be your badass secret agent self."

A little twist of pleasure curls in Ravi's gut. "Want to tell me what happened earlier?"

"Yeah. Okay." Nate gnaws on his lower lip, teeth leaving a furrow Ravi wants to trace with his tongue. "Look, Ravi. I'm not going to hide things from you. You've had enough people lying to you and keeping secrets. I'm always going to be upfront with you, okay?"

Ravi straightens at Nate's lack of levity. "Okay."

"Cayenne came to the quad at my school. Wanted to have a little chat with me."

Instantly Ravi is hyperaware of his surroundings, pulse hiking high. "You're okay? What happened? What did they do?" There's no telling what a spurned time assassin might do if they had the whim and motivation. *Fuck*, he should have insisted on more wards, somehow secured places of work too.

"They said some nasty shit, but that's it. And they know. About us sleeping together."

Ravi can't breathe for a moment. "They said that?"

"Yeah. But they said it didn't matter, so, I guess that's good? They didn't Donnie Darko me, so that's something."

"Donnie who?"

"Sorry, pop culture reference." Nate reflexively reaches his hands over the table, then draws them back with a furtive glance around. "I'm fine. They were salty about it, but not violent."

Ravi wishes they weren't in public so Nate could have touched him. "Fuck. An attempt to provoke Constance. And another to put pressure on you." He scrubs a hand over his jawbone. "Prodding for vulnerabilities. Seeing how the team can be weakened. It's a sound strategy."

"Surprising, really," Nate says dryly, "considering

they're not known for their superior strategic skills."

"Yeah. Fuck, I'm sorry. I didn't want this to spill over on you. *Fuck*," he hisses, sinking low in the booth. "Anything could have happened to you, and there's *nothing* I could have done…"

The waitress finally comes over with a carafe of coffee. While she pours, Ravi broods. Who's next on Cayenne's To Fuck With list? Val? Harry? They've been lucky so far, but Cayenne only has to be lucky once. All of Ravi's training is for nothing when there's no way to prepare. No way to defend. He's fighting blind, stumbling around in the dark. Useless.

I would take the fight to mine nemesis, Constance had said, all rage and vengeance. *Control the battlefield. Flushed out as pheasants from the brush.*

Surprise me. Blindside me. I will always have an advantage unless you take it away from me.

And as simple as opening his eyes, Ravi has a plan.

It…could work.

"Ravi?"

"Hm?"

Nate indicates the waitress waiting impatiently at his side. "I said, you ready to order?"

Holstering his plan into the back of his mind, Ravi forcibly drags himself to the present. "Sorry." He orders, and when the waitress leaves, he asks, "But you're okay?"

"Yeah, sunshine, I'm fine. I'd rather it be me than you, to be frank. I just wanted you to know what happened. And if you want the others to know too, that's up to you. It's your decision."

"A warning can't go amiss. I'll let Harry and Val know they might be next." He'll text them tonight. Forewarned is forearmed.

With an angry snort, Nate looks away. "If we're lucky they'll try Val." He rubs the back of his neck with a sigh. "And here I was hoping I'd get to take you on a date without any gloom and doom."

Ravi pauses mid-sip of his coffee. "Is this a date, then?"

A slow smile tugs at Nate's cheeks. He's got nice dimples, Ravi notices, and not for the first time. "It could be. I should have sprung for somewhere less tacky, huh?"

Ravi takes in the metal-paneled walls, the red vinyl curves of the diner stools, the little rotating pie case lit up with neon. "I actually love this kind of thing."

"What kind of thing? Kitschy?"

"*Kitschy*," Ravi repeats, lingering over syllables he so rarely gets to use. "No, I mean classic Americana."

Nate smiles, leaning his chin on his hands. His eyes are very blue. "What do you like about it?"

"It's exotic."

Nate laughs. "Fair."

The food comes out quickly. Bacon and a big pile of pancakes for Nate, and one plain egg white omelet with a side of fruit for Ravi.

As they dig in, Nate pours syrup and notes, "You're not very food motivated, are you?"

"Not especially." His shoulders tense of their own volition, ready for an argument, or to be harangued into ordering extra.

But Nate just nods. "You've got a favorite food though, right?"

"Of course." Ravi can't remember if anyone's ever asked him that before. "Keralan coconut prawn."

"Ooh." Nate crunches bacon. "Sounds tasty. Your family is from Chennai?"

"The outskirts. For the last couple centuries, yeah."

"Yeah, no big deal, a few centuries."

"Constance has a point. Everything here only dates back so far."

"They don't call it the New World for nothing," Nate chuckles, dipping his bacon in syrup. "So did you jet out to Kerala special just for the coconut shrimp?"

"No," Ravi scoffs, taking a perfunctory bite of the omelet. "Occasional business took me there."

Nate looks up with avid interest. "I sense a story."

"I'm not good at stories."

"Well, that's patently ridiculous. Voice like yours, I'd listen to anything you want to tell me."

"My stories just end up depressing people."

"Try me."

"Fine." Ravi puts down his coffee and leans back in the booth, arms crossed. "So, my first time in Kerala, this standard-level monster was attacking a town. I was sent for field training. My very first monster hunt. The strike team leader was like, 'Okay, kid, this thing is fairly straightforward, just needs to take a lot of damage and it'll go down. No fancy weaknesses or anything. We'll get it warmed up, and you can take it down.'"

Ravi pushes his hair back off his forehead. He'd been so eager to finally put all his training to use. He'd wanted to prove himself. To tell his mom he held his own.

"So, they're fighting it, the strike team, but I was *really* excited about my first hunt, because I was fifteen and an idiot, so I kept trying to jump in. Because that's going to be my job someday, right? I wanted to learn.

"But every time I tried to engage, one of the squad leaped into the fray, and I'm just thinking… What the fuck is up with this team? Crazy reckless. Keep making dumb mistakes, leaving themselves open for attack. Bizarre tactics for a straightforward mission and such an experienced team of field agents."

Nate watches him with wide eyes. "So, what happened?"

"I found out later that this poor team's *real* objective was to keep me alive. The monster stuff was just to get me blooded. Pretty sure my aunt gave them a shovel talk beforehand; 'Not one hair on his head,' kind of thing. So, every time I tried to engage, the agents were all having heart attacks, trying to jump between me and the monster until it was sufficiently weakened. Anyway, I did manage to wedge myself in there and get in some good hits. Barely avoided taking some damage. The team leader was livid, but we took the thing down. And then as soon as the monster was dead, the leader looked over at his team and said, 'I'm fucking retiring.'"

Nate bursts out laughing and clamps a hand over his mouth.

Gratified, Ravi smirks.

"Okay," Nate says with mirth, "both funny *and* horrifying, like all the best myths. See, you're great at stories." His eyes sparkle as he lays an arm across the table. His hand rests almost but not quite on Ravi's side, close enough to touch. "Thanks for telling it to me."

Fingers twitching with the suppressed desire to take Nate's hand, Ravi shrugs, willing the blood warming his ears to disperse.

"Why a strike team? Why not with your mom and uncle?"

"Ah." Ravi slices up his omelet with the edge of a fork. "They were off… Where were they that time? I want to say Madagascar? Some kind of ooze in the trees. A rot coming in from another plane of reality, or something like that. Sounds about right." He chases a forkful of eggs around his plate. "Anyway, that's why I first went to Kerala. Not exactly for the cuisine, or the black sand beaches."

"You know, I bet Val could pop over and grab you some fresh coconut shrimp if you asked her. Chances are good she's been there before."

"Seems like misappropriation of angel."

"Yeah, I suppose. Guess I'll just have to learn the recipe and make you some. I'll add it to the list with poutine," Nate promises, smiling.

The sweetness of the offer takes Ravi off-guard. He bites down on a return grin and warns, "It's spicy."

"Eh, I'll suffer through." Nate winks. His expression shifts minutely. "I meant to say earlier, congratulations."

"For what?"

Nate rolls his eyes. "For getting engaged, dude."

"Oh, yeah. Right." Despite himself, Ravi laughs, spearing a chunk of melon. "Thanks."

"I think it's cool how the two of you are taking a shitty situation and making it work for you. You're taking an unfair system and working it to get what you want. It's inspiring."

"I...thanks." Ravi clears his throat. "When we get enough say over how the system works, we can change it into a different system. A fair system. And we will."

Nate beams. "See? Inspiring."

It's Ravi's turn to roll his eyes. "There are a lot of changes I want to make. Changes I *will* make."

"Is there a reason you keep doing that, my guy?" With his fork Nate gestures to the tense line of Ravi's posture, the way he's tilted up his chin in challenge. "If I'm doing something that upsets you, let me know and we can talk about it."

Ravi jerks his head back, flat-footed. "You're not...no. It's..." The realization hits him like lead in his gut, and he grinds the heels of his hands into his eyes. "I keep expecting a fight," he scoffs at himself, sourness twisting in his stomach. "Shouting and arguing and...and then make-up sex," he finishes with a barren, derisive laugh, unable to meet Nate's gaze.

He had been all too willing to overlook how often he and Cayenne fought when they were together, assuming it was part and parcel of falling in love. The cost of any relationship, surely. How was he to know different? All those arguments and fights were surely just proof of their passion. A cycle he'd evidently grown so accustomed to, a part of him expects it even still. But now, like a veil removed from his memory, each instance of friction is starkly illuminated. How could he have been so fucking naïve? Had he been so starved for any affection he was willing to put up with constant antagonism?

"We can skip the fighting and just have the sex."

Nate finishes a bite of pancake, licking the syrup from his fork. Ravi watches the path of his tongue, the train of his thoughts completely derailed. He attempts to dig through the wreckage but can't salvage a single surviving brain cell.

Nate grins, eyes roving over Ravi as if he's thinking about shoving his pancakes off the table and trying a bite of Ravi instead. "You ever gotten a handjob in the back of that semi-truck you drive around?"

Ravi's throat clicks as he swallows. "No one's ever talked to me the way you do."

Nate's manner softens. "Too much?"

Ravi takes a long breath, locking their gaze. "No."

A rakish grin spreads slow and warm over Nate's handsome face. "Good to know."

"You're very…forthright."

"I'm a forthright kind of guy."

Ravi huffs a low laugh. "I've noticed. I've never met anyone like you."

A flush blossoms at the edge of Nate's collar and creeps up his neck. "Sure you have," he says incredulously.

"I really haven't."

Nate bites his lower lip before asking, "So, any plans after this?"

Ravi doesn't look away, vision tunneling on white teeth catching at the softness of Nate's lip. "The rest of my schedule today has been unexpectedly freed up." He watches color bloom even higher on Nate's cheeks, vividly remembering how it took over the whole of Nate's body like a rush of fever, how good it looked against white bed sheets. Greatly daring, Ravi slides his foot under the table until his shoe presses close to Nate's.

Nate breathes out shakily, his foot pressing back. "Sometimes you get this predatory look that makes it very hard to think clearly."

"Do I?" Ravi tips his head to the side with a small, toothy smile.

"You're still doing it," Nate protests weakly.

"How would you prefer I look at you?"

"Maybe under some mood lighting."

Nate requests the check from the waitress with a polite gesture. As he does, his socked foot suddenly slides up

Ravi's inseam. Ravi jumps in surprise, silverware clattering. His face blazes hot until the wicked little smirk Nate gives him sends his blood rushing south.

"*Nate*," Ravi hisses, eyes darting around the diner.

"Hm?" Nate sets his chin on both hands, eyes round and innocent. "Something wrong, sunshine?" Then, softer, "This okay?"

"You—" Ravi exhales sharply, swallows, then offers, "My car windows are tinted."

"I've noticed." Nate's eyes glitter. "How are the shocks?"

With a breathless laugh, Ravi scoots forward in the booth, mindlessly chasing sensation. The ball of Nate's foot finds Ravi's growing arousal against his thigh and *presses*. Ravi fights the impulse to shut his eyes, to let his head fall back against the vinyl.

"*Ah*. They're, um. Fine?"

"So, no one is gonna be coming a-knockin'?" Nate teases, passing his credit card to the waitress as she swings by. Ravi freezes statue-still until she leaves, his fingers clenched so tightly around the edge of the table that he might leave dents in the laminate.

"My treat," Nate says magnanimously. "You're a cheap date, anyway." His toes wriggle.

Ravi gulps, rallying to find a response that isn't just

wordless moaning. "If…if I'd have known you'd be buying, I would have ordered the lobster."

It feels like a victory when Nate cracks up, dimples playing at the corners of his smile.

*

IN THE BACK of the Escalade, cursing under his breath with impatience, Ravi fumbles at Nate's belt while Nate is similarly occupied trying to remove Ravi's double-breasted waistcoat. Maybe he's got a point about all the buttons.

Ravi's jacket and tie have already been strewn over the headrest with his shoulder holster. They hadn't made much headway on Nate's blazer, only shoved it partway off broad shoulders, the fabric straining. Pausing his sartorial labors, Nate drags Ravi down to seal their lips together in a hungry kiss that he doesn't break until the need for air becomes a pressing concern. Even then he just surges right back in, as if he could survive solely on oxygen he gleans from Ravi's lungs.

"Wanna feel you," Nate gasps into Ravi's mouth, the words more felt than heard as he finally manages to wrench the last waistcoat button loose. He yanks it down Ravi's arms and blindly tosses it in the right direction. "Ravi—"

"Nathaniel." It's a promise sketched in breath that Ravi aims into the shell of a very pink ear. His hands are busy sneaking up Nate's untucked shirt. Bare chest ripples under his touch, skin blazing hot.

A full-body shiver rolls through Nate. "*Fuck,*" escapes in an airless hiss, his eyes glazed and darkening with arousal.

A perfect opportunity to press his advantage. Ravi tugs the belt from the loops, unzips the fly, and pulls Nate out, already flushed and throbbing in his hand. It's a heady sensation, the naked want in Nate's voice, the open, boneless sprawl of his body, the way he keens and pushes up into Ravi's fist. Every line of his solid frame is an invitation, begging Ravi to take.

Ravi straddles Nate's hips. "To answer your earlier question: no, I have not," he growls, pulling down his zipper and guiding Nate's hand to his rampant cock in one smooth motion.

Nate grins, tongue flicking out to wet kiss-bruised lips. He wraps his fingers tight, thumbing back the hood and stroking with an easy confidence that makes Ravi short of breath.

"No time like the present," Nate laughs, cheeks ruddy, sweat beading on his forehead. He looks like he was made for this, for laughing and kissing and sharing pleasure in the backseats of other people's cars.

Ravi fists a hand into the disordered blond tousle and

jerks back, baring Nate's pale throat, and after running his tongue up from clavicle to chin, sinks his teeth in. Nate stops breathing, his grip on Ravi's cock convulsing.

"This okay?" Ravi murmurs against Nate's fluttering pulse, against the reddened imprint of his teeth. "You like this?"

Nate's voice shakes. "Babe, your instincts are *top* fucking *notch*, I like it a *lot*."

Babe hits Ravi hard, breath faltering as his stomach flips over, warmth rolling rich and sweet as golden honey. A mess of words gets tangled up in his throat, a Gordian knot he slices through with a small cough. A little hoarse the first syllable or two, Ravi pulls himself together enough to say, "Yeah? You'd tell me if it's too much?"

Head lolling loose against the backrest, Nate aims up a dazed smile. "Yuh-huh." He matches a sure stroke of his hand with a thrust of his hips, and his lashes fall before he forces his eyes open. "Right. Words. I can do sentences." Even as Ravi watches, his pupils swallow all but a thin blue ring of iris. "M'not a small guy, so the way you can just manhandle me any way you like is kind-of-very-extremely-the-hottest-thing. That's new for me. Getting me off like crazy, babe."

Heat prickles up Ravi's spine, a fresh match of desire striking each nerve afire. Dragging his tongue across the rasp of stubbled jaw before biting again, he nearly gets a mouthful of shirt collar in his haste and has to suppress the sudden savage desire to tear every stitch of Nate's clothing right off him. Ravi leans back a few inches, trying to think clearly, but that's impossible with Nate's long, clever hands driving every ounce of reason right out of his skull.

"Is this—ah, *haan*, that's— Nate. Whatever you want." It's an offer, a declaration. A plea.

"I just want *you*," Nate gasps, sincerity punctuated by the reflexive twist of his thumb.

One of Ravi's oldest weaknesses. Being wanted, needing to please. But Nate isn't asking for anything Ravi isn't already willing to give; demanding nothing other than to enjoy himself, to take what's freely offered. Ravi swallows against an unexpected swell of emotion, galloping heart loud in his ears.

He crushes their mouths into desperate, devouring kisses, into open-mouthed gasps and muffled groans, hands interlocking to press their glistening cocks into exquisite alignment. Hips rocking, they match each other stroke for stroke, and Ravi's skin feels too tight, like he might split at the seams, all of him pouring out in a heedless, liquid rush.

The reins of his control slip, and he goes harder, faster, more aggressive. He catches an earlobe between his teeth and bites down, growling a wordless demand. Nate yelps in surprise, squirming deliciously under the press of Ravi's weight.

"I haven't been able to stop thinking about how good it was to fuck you," Ravi grates, the truth spilling out of him like it can't stand being trapped behind his tongue any longer.

"Ravi, *Jesus Christ*—" Nate shudders underneath him, slicking their hands with pulse after scorching pulse. Nate goes lax for only a moment, skin pebbling on his well-nibbled neck. After sucking in a juddering breath, Nate surges up and claims Ravi's mouth, snarling his free hand up into Ravi's hair. He keeps an effusive stream of praise pressed against Ravi's lips.

"That's it, babe, so fucking good, you're *perfect*…"

The wave of Ravi's pleasure crests and crashes over him in a blinding, blissful rush, knocking the breath out of his lungs. Every muscle in his body tightens, quivering through every pulse, before they all loosen in tandem, and he collapses into Nate's arms in a languid drape.

Murmuring gently, Nate guides him into a slow, sweet kiss. "We…did not think this through," he eventually says with a breathless chuckle, cupping Ravi's cheek.

Ravi hums an inquiry, not enough brain cells regained yet for speech. The car is very hot, humid, and he'll have to drive with the windows down to banish the thick aroma of sex.

"We made a mess. You know, last time I had sex in a car, I think I barely had my driver's license. Christ, you make me feel like a teenager." Nate looks Ravi over and winces. "Shit, your suit. Sorry."

"I'll buy a new one," Ravi mumbles, not moving an inch. He always has a few changes of clothes in duffels stashed in the trunk. Hunts often get messy.

"Course you will," Nate chuckles, then buries his nose in Ravi's hairline. "How do you always smell so good?"

Instead of answering, Ravi pulls his hand up to his mouth and runs his tongue cat-like over the back of his striped knuckles.

Heat sparks anew in Nate's eyes. "You wanna go back to my place? Spend the night? Please tell me you're driving us to my place."

"Like I said"—Ravi grins, wide and unchecked—"my schedule is clear."

Chapter Thirteen

"BREAKFAST?"

"Sure, thanks," Ravi says at the peak of a push-up. "Something light?"

Nate watches him from the bed, elbow crooked and head propped. Hair wild, and color still high in his cheeks from their lazy dawn tumble. "I've got everything to make mango lassi. Lotsa protein in that."

Ravi finishes his set and sweeps a hand through his hair with a smile. "Sounds great." It's crazy that Nate has bothered stocking his pantry with things he knows Ravi likes. There's barely anything personal in his *own* apartment, but the fact there's a place in Nate's kitchen solely for him, is…it's a lot to absorb.

He stretches over the bed to push Nate back against the pillows. The sight puts him in mind of nineteenth century paintings of odalisques, all peach and gold in the early-morning light, languorous against ivory sheets.

"This is a good look on you," he murmurs, scattering kisses to Nate's chest, lingering over a tattoo of an Irish harp, and another of a constellation of stars tracing the outline of a bear.

"Mm. What is?" Nate trails his hands from Ravi's shoulders down his spine, leaving goosebumps in their wake. "Incredibly well-fucked?"

Ravi nips at Nate's collarbone, making him twitch. "That's one way of putting it."

"Okay, give me another way," Nate challenges.

"Hm. *Sundar*," Ravi suggests, tipping up a smile. "*Aakarshak. Séduisant. Mozzafiato.*"

"Mozza-what? Did you call me a cheese?"

Ravi rolls onto his side with a deep laugh, somehow feeling light and unburdened despite the weight of his troubles. Amazing how Nate keeps doing that, taking Ravi's shadows and effortlessly turning them into light.

"It's Italian for breathtaking."

Nate bites down on his lip, then grins wide. "You're showing off. Just so you know, I fully support that one hundred percent."

Ravi grins back, running his fingertips through the sparse hairs on Nate's thigh. His legs, with that well-hewn hockey player tone, are worth some extra attention. "I have two skill sets. The first is hitting things, and the second is asking in different languages, 'Where's the thing you need me to hit?'"

Nate cups Ravi's face in his hands. "I can think of plenty more than two, sunshine." They slide easily into a series of kisses, warm lips and wandering hands soon unraveling any intentions of getting up.

Ravi regretfully pulls back before they get too carried away again. "Val's picking me up soon."

Val is so indifferent to human relationships he doubts she'd even notice if she caught him and Nate in a clinch, much less care, but even the thought makes Ravi want to throw his clothes on as soon as possible.

"Cockblocked by an angel." Nate sighs and heaves himself out of bed. He pulls on some shorts. "You get first dibs on the shower. I'll start some coffee." But instead, Nate stops in the doorway and looks back at Ravi for a long stretch of time, lips curving into a half-moon smile.

Feeling Nate's admiration as if it were a tangible thing, Ravi plays into it a bit, stretching and flexing for his audience. Nate's smile only grows softer and more heartfelt instead of heated, his eyes shining brighter. No one has ever looked at Ravi in quite the same way before; he can't even put a name to the expression.

"What?" he asks, suddenly shy.

Nate doesn't speak for a moment, throat bobbing, then he breaks into a broad, easy smile.

"You're cheese too."

*

NATE PUTS WHAT he claims is pure Ontario lavender honey in the blender with the yogurt, and it's very likely the best lassi Ravi's ever had.

"I can't believe it," Nate says in false shock, giving him a once-over. "A *T-shirt*. Are you okay? Is it painful?"

"Laugh it up, Doc." Ravi rolls his eyes. He finishes his coffee and rinses out the mug. "I told you I owned some."

"My guy, you know it doesn't count as a T-shirt if it costs over a hundred dollars, right?"

That's news to Ravi. He avoids the question. "Jeans too, see? Very common man."

"Uh-huh," Nate says knowingly, arms crossed as he leans against the fridge. "That's exactly what you bring to mind. Common."

In a sudden rustle of unseen feathers, Val appears a yard away from Ravi. He jumps but refrains from snatching up a blade off the knife block.

"We've talked about knocking first, Val," Nate says mildly.

Val inclines her head. "Apologies." She raps a fist on the table thrice.

Nate's eyes narrow. "Are you fucking with us? I can never tell if your 'I'm so alien and clueless' thing is legit or just a hilarious angel gag."

"Often the ways of heaven are unknowable." She looks to Ravi. "Your clothes are acceptable. Though you may wish to bring a jacket." She's eschewed her usual gym clothes for a white long-sleeved jacket worn over a long skirt. A silk scarf twines around her neck.

Ravi nods, grabbing a moto jacket from his duffel along with his shoulder holster.

"Firearms will not be necessary."

He shoots her an incredulous look.

"Should battle become inevitable, you and I are both lethal enough on our own."

True enough. Reluctantly he zips the duffel back up, 9mm inside. Ravi trusts Val, but she's got a divine maul she can summon up with a mere thought. Going into an unknown situation unarmed and unprepared makes Ravi edgy.

Nate waves, smiling brightly. "You two have fun on

your mysterious adventure! Call me if you run into any weird monsters you need me to identify."

A desire hits Ravi strong and sudden, unaccountably difficult to resist for such a simple thing: he wants to kiss Nate goodbye.

Val takes his shoulder and in a breath the apartment swoops away from underfoot.

Blinking away the disorientation, Ravi is confronted by an endless golden expanse, tall grasses swaying over hills for as far as he can see. The cool wind whips past them with a soughing sigh, low-hanging clouds overhead puckered like ostrich leather. The placement of the sun behind the clouds confuses Ravi briefly before he realizes they're no longer in North America; Val must have taken them somewhere where it is afternoon instead of morning.

"Val." Ravi turns around. Nothing but grass stretching for miles and miles, until it meets faint, far-off blue mountains. "Where are we?"

Valiance gazes westward. Strands of hair almost the same color as the clouds fly out of her ponytail across her burning ice-blue eyes. "These are the steppes of Mongolia."

"And…why are we in Mongolia?"

"Because this is where the urumi was delivered to Zhen Zi-Qi, four hundred and sixty years ago."

Individually each word makes sense, but all lined up

together in a sentence Ravi is utterly lost. "Zhen Zi-Qi…my ancestor?"

"Yes."

"You…" Ravi stares at her. Val's abilities have limits. She can only teleport to people she's familiar with, or to places she has already visited. "You've been here before."

"Yes."

"Are you saying… What *exactly* are you saying, Val?"

Her gaze has all the calm of a bodhisattva carved into sandstone. "Harry is not the first Chosen of Durga I have stood beside. I was here with Zhen. This was where Naimanzuunnadintsetseg's eagle brought him the urumi, passing the destiny of your bloodline to him at the age of twenty."

Stunned, Ravi takes a step back, reciting facts by rote. "That's…that's Eight Hundred Precious Flowers, the falconer. One of Zhen's comrades-in-arms. She… Val. I don't—"

"We three met the jiangshi shortly after, the vampire who joined up with Zhen's cause. We traveled far and wide, slaying many great evils before Zhen fell." Val brushes ash-gray hair from her eyes and puts on her sunglasses. "Perhaps I should have eased into this revelation."

"*Perhaps you should have!*" Ravi throws up his hands and has a difficult time wrangling his voice back down to a reasonable volume. "I don't understand. I get that you've had different bodies before, been in different times. But that you knew *my* ancestor—"

"I have known all of the Chosen Ones not born Abhiramnews."

Ravi's jaw hangs open. *"Kya? Par tum…* You…" He slips into the refuge of Hindi. "Why haven't you said anything about this sooner? When Harry got the urumi? And if you say because 'nobody asked,' I *swear*—" He covers his face, taking long measured breaths before pulling himself together enough to speak. "I'm sorry. I don't…"

Val slips her scarf off her neck and pulls it over her hair, tucking it around her face. She answers in the same tongue as naturally as a native speaker. "Your reaction is understandable. Brace yourself."

"For wha—"

Val touches his arm, and with another rush of wind the plains wink away to be replaced by a busy outdoor market, throngs of milling people fortunately not noticing the pair appearing out of nowhere, sandwiched between a large stand of women's bangles and a spinning rack of colorful fabric.

The momentum causes Ravi to sway slightly in place as he gets his bearings. The aroma of spices, incense, and sizzling street food is immediately familiar, though a quick glance around at the local clothing tells him he's likelier to be somewhere in Kashmir or Pakistan than in India.

Val releases his arm. "This is where Nayab bint Mukhtar was approached by *Shraddha*, as The Trust was known in those days, though then it was only a loose confederation of like-minded people intent on stopping evil. How it's grown," she says, the way one would remark on the size of a friend's child. "Nayab was a commoner of no renown when Durga Chose her, a daughter of Caspian traders, and your family welcomed her with open arms."

"That's… In 554. You were here too?"

"I…met Nayab later. She showed me this spot." Val shifts, which he's never seen her do before. "Nayab didn't have the training your family is raised with, or any of the advantages which graces your bloodline. She was a girl of fourteen with no knowledge of the destiny that would be thrust upon her. But she did have me, to help bear the weight."

People pass by, talking, laughing, engaging in commerce.

"Does my aunt know about this?" Ravi asks hoarsely. "Is this another secret I wasn't in on?"

"No, Ravi. No one knew except the Chosen themselves. This incarnation is the first where I have not kept my true nature hidden." She holds out a hand. "Are you ready?"

Ravi hesitates only a moment, then switches back to English as he gives Val his hand. "William Harbridge?"

"Indeed," Val says, and they're away again, carried on the celestial breeze until Ravi's feet touch down on polished parquet flooring. It's easier this time to shake off the strangeness of teleportation, blinking away static.

They're surrounded by familiar Old-World opulence, a baroque foyer Ravi knows well from several formal Trust events. Harbridge Manor outside London. On the left is his favorite credenza, a huge Regency era monstrosity that casts a conveniently large shadow. He'd often stood in that shadow during the endlessly dull parties he was forced to attend, trying to blend in with the wallpaper. More than once that credenza helped Ravi avoid a long-winded blathering from some old white guy—almost universally one of the Prestons—boasting of their family's ancestral prowess at slaying monsters or bragging about their beloved family heirlooms. Bits of statuary torn off Indian temples, tea chests of ivory taken from Indian elephants.

Ravi's very fond of that credenza.

The faint rumble of low voices carries from an adjacent room.

"Val," Ravi hisses in alarm. "There are wards and defenses here for intruders. We can't be here." Later he'll have to suggest the Harbridges update their wards to account for teleportation.

"I shall be brief, then." Val strides to the base of the grand staircase, not modulating her voice or gait in the slightest. Ravi winces; she's not cut out for stealth. "The widow of the previous Chosen accompanied the Director of The Trust and performed the ceremony right here, to give William Harbridge the sword. He was twelve."

Footsteps click down from the long hallway. Val rejoins Ravi and whisks him once more around the globe.

This time he blinks hard, shaking off the staticky buzz. Val must be tiring, her teleporting less smooth. They stand high on a balcony, ivy spilling in a riot over iron fretwork railings. The view is unmistakably the red sandstone of Jaipur, Amber Palace looming proud across Maota Lake. The weather is fine, sun shining, the arid breeze playing with Ravi's hair. Almost winter; Sharad Ritu, a proper season. It feels good on his skin.

Val guides Ravi to a pink lacquered bistro table and waves at a chair. He plunks down, belatedly glancing around for possible threats and finding none. A secure spot with excellent lines of sight. Val takes a seat across from him, slipping the scarf from her head back into a fashionable knot at her throat. A kettle on the table steams with fresh coffee.

Val slides him an empty cup. "I thought you might

welcome some refreshment."

"Yeah, it's very thoughtful, but *what the hell*, Val?"

"You must have questions."

"*Yeah.*"

"Ask."

The funny thing is, Ravi doesn't know where to start. His thoughts are a complete jumble and he grasps until he finds the most important thread to follow. "Did you know all along about Harry? Before the urumi came to her?"

"No. I was surprised, as well." Val sits with her hands flat and unmoving on the table, posture unnaturally perfect. "I knew someone was fated to be Chosen, though I did not know it would be her. I had wondered if I had been found unworthy of guardianship, for my failures."

"What failures?"

"They all died, Ravi." The faintest of changes comes over Val's voice, like a far-off bird fluttering a broken wing. "Nayab, Zi-Qi, and William all died alone, because I had already fallen in battle protecting them."

Ravi stares at her, a distant pain under his breastbone.

Her head slants minutely to one side. "You are wondering if I have ever met Durga."

Frowning, Ravi turns his profile quickly away out to the skyline. "You can read minds, now?"

"No. But I have been asked similar questions before, by

those whose curiosity you carry."

Ravi holds his breath. "Well, have you?"

"I have not."

He exhales in considerable relief. He's pretty sure he doesn't want to hear what any of the nine manifestations of his family's patron goddess has to say about him. Carrying the weight of his aunt's disappointment is bad enough.

He crosses his arms over his chest, then drops them, then sets them on the table. Suddenly he's grateful for the coffee, if only to have something to do with his hands. He pours himself a cup, trying to focus on what's important. His personal issues are definitely not.

"Tactically, what can we do to help Harry? To make her situation more survivable? You must have…wisdom from the ages, right?"

"My strategic skills are best suited for the immediacy of the battlefield, but I believe our greatest strength lies in Harry's support system. Nayab had personal allies and comrades-in-arms, as did Zhen. Neither of them had The Trust as it exists now, as a powerful organization of wealth and influence. William did, but he did not have a personal team. That had long fallen out of favor for the Chosen. He just had me."

"So, Harry has the allies *and* the resources. That's good. That means we're doing something new, something that hasn't been tried before. That's hopeful." Harry is going to die of old age, comfortably in bed and surrounded by loved ones, if Ravi has anything to say about it. *We're eternal optimists*, Harry would snark.

"What were they like?" he bursts out, a boyish exclamation he immediately wishes he could reel back.

Val doesn't even pause. "Courageous. Determined. Strong."

Not quite what Ravi had hoped for, though he doesn't know what else he expected to hear. He takes a sip of coffee without tasting it. "I didn't give my real name when we first met. When did you figure out I was related to them?"

"I knew the very instant we met that you were an Abhiramnew, and a direct descendant of the Chosen line."

"It's the cheekbones, isn't it," he huffs sarcastically.

"No." Ravi's reflection is stretched and strange in the dark glass of Val's sunglasses. "William had an unassailable sense of purpose, and an iron dedication to it. Zhen was a wanderer, never happy unless he was moving, and would throw himself into battle without regard for his own well-being if innocent lives were at stake. Nayab was a guarded woman, but underneath she had a hidden spark of humor, and she loved those close to her with unmatched fierceness.

"Before Harry, out of nearly ninety generations of Chosen, I have only known three. But I can easily see that the best of them live on in you."

Ravi's eyes burn. He drags in a shaky breath and presses his knuckles over his mouth. He looks out over the landscape for a long, long time. Val sits with him in contented silence.

When he drags himself back together, Ravi clears his throat and wraps both hands around the warm cup. "Okay. So. Why you? Why an angel instead of—wait, *are* you an angel?"

"I am a soldier. Harry may try to instill a greater sense of autonomy in me, and I do not fault her for it. She is used to superiors who are flawed, as mortals are. Mine are not. I am Valiance." She shrugs, a tiny shift of her muscled shoulders. "I am my purpose. I guard the divergent Chosen's steps so that when the world needs them, when only they can turn the tide of evil, they stand ready. Whatever name or guise I must wear to do this is immaterial. Here and now, *angel* is a good enough moniker. For Nayab I was a *malaikah*, and for Zhen I was a heavenly champion of Zhong Kui. All are correct."

"Nate would love to hear this," Ravi mutters, rubbing the bridge of his nose.

"But I was not always such." Val's fingers convulse on the table, a swift clench of knuckles. She glares at her hands until they again still.

"You weren't…always a soldier?"

"No. I would like to tell you a story about Nayab bint Mukhtar."

Eagerly, he leans forward. "Yes! We have records, but there are so many gaps. I'd love to hear…" He clears his throat. "Yes, please."

"Nayab was hunting demons," Val begins, "that plagued the region through a small, unstable breach into the hells. She had been Chosen for mere months, still unsure of herself and unskilled with weapons. Nevertheless, she did what was needful, picking off demons one by one through cunning and subterfuge. One demon, a small and unimportant thing of Hunger, snuck through the rift to feed on scraps left from the greater demon's slaughter. This demon was a wretched, carrion thing, seeking only the abattoir." Val's lip curls slightly. Rapt, Ravi listens. "It was not long before it ran afoul of Nayab, and the two battled. But just as Nayab was about to land the killing blow, she stopped."

Ravi waits, but Val seems committed to the dramatic pause. "Why?"

"She claimed she 'had a feeling,'" Val says with the faintest of smiles. "In that moment of weakness, the demon should have killed her. But it didn't. Demon and demon-killer both stayed their hands, in an unspoken armistice."

Ravi's eyes widen. "Val…"

"Nayab spoke to the demon," Val forges on, lifting her chin. "She made a bargain to let the demon live if it would help her close the rift. The demon agreed. An uncertain truce." She pauses again, looking out over the rosy city. "The demon kept its word. It helped Nayab get all the way to the triumvirate of devils that had breached the Veil, and helped her slay them, all but the last. The last devil had Nayab at his feet and would have killed her then and there, but for the demon's intervention. The demon took the blow meant for her."

Ravi's mouth works soundlessly for a moment. "Why?"

"I do not know. The demon…had a feeling." Valiance takes a long, even breath. "I do not have memories from that life, any more than vague, distant images."

Ravi stares.

"Mortals like to make much of angels who fall," she says, "but rarely care to think about demons who rise. You'd think humans would speak of nothing else, if only for the wickedest among them to claim they should have infinite chances to reform." Val's hands twitch again. "I have been reticent to tell you of this."

"I…can appreciate why." Ravi feels a little like he caught an uppercut in the boxing ring, his bell rung. "You sacrificed yourself. And the gods, or…the powers-that-be, decided to make you a guardian for the other unconventional Chosen?"

"No. I chose that purpose myself."

Ravi's head begins to clear. He smiles crookedly. "You wanted to change your nature. To be better than you were."

"Do not think that demons are redeemable as a rule," Val says sternly. "Any who stay their hand to offer it to a demon will get that hand ripped off. Nayab was special. I chose to return to be by her side, and to do the same for any irregular Chosen who would come after her. None of them were truly prepared, as you were from birth, to be the one person in the world who could thwart the end of it. A heavy weight. I am honored beyond words that I have still been deemed worthy to help carry it."

"I'm sorry," Ravi finally says, after a long pause.

"For what?"

"I'm sorry they fell when you couldn't be there with them."

She gazes at Ravi placidly through her dark glasses. Then a single tear trails from under the frames and rolls down her face. Val touches her cheek and regards her wet fingers for several breaths.

"This body feels grief," she says, as calm as a smooth pond on a breezeless day. "Though burdened by responsibility, your ancestors were selfless and dedicated. They all believed in their purpose, in The Trust, and worked hard to build a lasting foundation. They would be proud of you, Chosen or not."

That hits far harder than learning Val used to be a demon. Ravi blinks rapidly, unable to speak. Finally, he manages in a dry leaf rattle, "Thank you."

They sit in companionable silence for a time, watching the flow of people below, listening to the sounds of the city. A radio set in a nearby open window plays some oldies. A vendor across the street cooks up fragrant batches of pyaaz kachori.

Ravi clears his throat. "I've been meaning to tell you. I, uh. I told my aunt we were an item."

One of Val's white eyebrows climbs upwards.

"She thought… I wanted to divert her suspicions. I'm sorry. I shouldn't have."

"Will continuing that deception aid you in some way?"

He's touched by the implied offer. "I…" He makes a face. "I'm tired, Val. Of deception. Not for the job, not tradecraft in general, but…I'm so fucking tired of lying about…"

"About who you are."

He hesitates, then nods.

"I did not know who she was fated to be, but when Harry was confronted with the evidence of my celestial origins, I did not attempt to conceal the truth. Perhaps I had grown weary of the artifice, as well. I did not anticipate how good it would feel to not have to pretend anymore. To stretch my wings."

Ravi considers this over the dregs of his coffee. "You know, Val, back there with Constance, you weren't so bad at the human touch, yourself. I don't think you needed the rest of us at all."

She smiles, though a shade rueful. "Being a human is very difficult."

"Tell me about it."

*

IT'S BEEN A while since he's visited the lake house himself, though he knows Harry and Constance swap kappa-feeding duty every other week. He's had no reason to go back since that extended July day with Cayenne. Until now, Ravi hadn't been sure he could ever face it again.

Even walking to the backyard brings back an unwelcome wash of memories. The basketball hoop in the driveway. The grassy stretch by the lake where he'd poured himself heart and all into Cayenne, where they murmured his name and whispered that they loved him. Where they offered to spar with him, showing instead of telling how ruthless they could be—*would* be. He remembers their face as they examined his blackened eye. Not apologetic, but with resignation. Like hurting him was an inevitability they wouldn't even try to avoid.

Ravi forces himself to tread past the spot. At the edge of the manicured lawn, he pries up a small garden statue. Underneath, a tightly lidded plastic container is halfway buried into the dirt, and inside that a brilliantly scarlet phone with its charging cable.

Ten minutes later, Ravi sends a text.

- Ravi -

I need to see you.

- Cayenne -

Mon cher, what a SURPRISE! I want to see you too. I do, however, feel that it's in my BEST interests to ask if your DE-LIGHTFUL friends are going to be there as well? Perhaps lying in wait in the bushes?

- Ravi -

Just me.

- Cayenne -

Then the question is, WHY do you want to see me, beautiful boy? You were VERY clear about never wanting to be graced with my scintillating presence again LAST time we spoke. Something about throwing a phone into a lake?

How can such a good liar be so bad at bluffing?

- Ravi -
Please.

The response takes an eternity to come.

- Cayenne -
Where
- Ravi -
Apartment on Peachtree. It's clean. No surveillance. One hour.

He follows up with the address and quells a rising tangle of nerves. It's in motion now. He can't avoid the consequences of his actions any longer. He has to face them head-on. Do the job in front of him. No turning back.

- Cayenne -
Your monster will be waiting for you.

Chapter Fourteen

HE DRESSES FOR the occasion. Stylish white chinos paired with a sharp, richly textured charcoal houndstooth jacket over a deeply V-necked sable T-shirt that—as Nate had suspected—cost well over a hundred dollars. He's aiming for effortlessly elegant, breaking a few fashion rules with style, and Ravi's always had excellent aim. Cayenne will appreciate it.

Even so carefully attired, he feels naked being unarmed. Heart tripping a mad drumbeat in his ribcage, Ravi approaches the apartment. He tries the knob: unlocked. Before going in, he rests his forehead against the door. One last chance to change his mind. To think of any other way.

Finally, Ravi squares his shoulders, lifts his chin, and walks in.

He hears them before he sees them; their soft, indrawn breath. Their shape silhouetted against the far doorway. Ravi flips on the light.

A vision in sheer black silk and crimson leather, Cayenne has painted their eyes in purples and grays—monsoon colors. Tight leather pants hug every curve and angle, juxtaposed by the billowing midnight cuffs of their shirt, and overtop is a stunningly fitted corset that outlines their slender frame to perfection. Copper hair uncharacteristically slicked back, letting their sharp-edged bone structure take center stage. They look him up and down with a dangerous, bladed smirk.

Ravi's never seen anyone more beautiful in his life.

"Well," Cayenne begins, tone sultry. They stop, throat visibly jumping as they swallow. A little of their artful pose slips. "Alone at last, *oui?*"

Ravi walks toward them slowly, hands non-threatening at his sides. "Cayenne," he says, desire lacing the edges of his anger, a thin, reedy undercurrent of want.

Their verdant eyes widen, but Cayenne doesn't move away as Ravi nears. "Well, *mon amour*, here I am," they say with hands spread wide. "See what an obedient little pepper I—"

They gasp as he crosses the last bit of distance in a quick, skillful dart, their hands rising for their tattoo. But Ravi makes no other sudden moves, stopping only inches away. The scent of their spiced cologne hits his nose, intoxicatingly thick. Cayenne lets their hands fall as they stare up at him with lips parted, moon-pale and eyes wide.

Ravi slides a brazen palm over the leather of their scarlet corset and rests it at the cinch of their narrow waist. Cayenne's breath skips.

"Cay," he husks, voice low. "You said it would be fun to be a member of our little team. Now's your chance."

They shiver, even through an incredulous roll of their eyes. "Oh, of *course*," Cayenne laughs. "I just throw in my lot with your *merry* little band, help you fix your terrible Trust, and no one will object? Why do I *doubt* that, I wonder?" Their hand rests, seemingly absently, over where Ravi's jacket normally conceals his gun and finds nothing but his ribs, moving with unsteady breaths. Cayenne's eyebrows fly up. "Besides," they continue, a little crease appearing on their forehead, "you're the hero, not me, darling."

"It can be like it was between us."

Cayenne jolts under his hand as if he's struck them, their elegant fingers curling on his lapels. Their tongue sweeps out in a quick pink flash and their gaze flicks from

Ravi's eyes to his lips. "I… *Quoi?* Do you…" They drag in a ragged breath. "Do you mean that?"

Ravi leans in closer, close enough for his breath to brush their ear. "I mean it."

The laugh Cayenne digs up is a small, broken thing. They set a hand to the bare skin framed by the sharp neckline of Ravi's shirt, the touch branding hot on his chest. "I really *am* a monster. I've taught an honest man to lie."

"I'm a monster-hunting secret agent in a world that doesn't believe in the supernatural. I've spent my whole life hiding who I really am. I've always been a good liar, Cayenne."

"Hmm. Maybe so," they murmur, eyes bottomless emerald and lined with kohl.

"This is an interesting look," Ravi says, voice acquiring a deep burr as he splays his fingers wide over their corset. It feels warm and taut under his hand, almost like living skin.

"Oh, *this* old thing? Do you like it?"

"I do," he confesses.

Cayenne smiles, the tip of their tongue touching their teeth. "I thought I'd really *lean* into the whole villain aesthetic, since you were so adamant of my clichéd role in our little disagreement."

"'Little disagreement'?" *Careful. Keep your shit together.*

Like dropping a costume, Cayenne trades their arch tone in for sincerity. "Listen to me, Ravi. I know you *think* you want to take over The Trust, want to lead it, but you *can't*. Please listen, for once. *You can't do it*. I'm *trying* to do what's best for you." They cluck their tongue in annoyance. "If you'd stop being so *stubborn*, The Trust would already be rubble. We could be together. *Really* together, not whatever video game team-up fantasy you've devised here to offer me. It would all be *over* already, and it'd be *perfect*."

They take his face between their hands, smoky eyelids catching pinpricks of light like mica dust. "I *knew* you'd come back to me, my beautiful, broken boy. We were hurt in so many of the same ways, we *understand* each other the way no one else possibly could. There's no one else in the world for either of us. I understand that strange times call for stranger bedfellows. I don't hold that against you." They smirk and step closer, the heat of their breath on Ravi's lips. He wishes they would kiss him already.

"Can I ask you a question?"

Cayenne sweeps both thumbs over the planes of his jaw. "*Oui*."

"Why this body? This face?" Ravi walks forward, steering Cayenne until their back hits the wall. He cages them in with his body, hands on either side of their head, and tilts his head to one side, letting his hair tumble into his eyes.

"When you got the idol."

As their shoulders press flat, Cayenne breathes out unsteadily, pulse ticking in their throat. "You saw what I looked like before."

"I did. Why change?"

A pleased smile, genuine and without artifice, takes over their face. "You're so *silly*, darling. I had the opportunity to look how I've always wanted to look. How could I not take it?" They drape their arms over his shoulders and trail their fingers up into his hair. His skin prickles under the brush of their nails. "Who wouldn't do such a thing? Well. Perhaps you, *mon beau.* Can't improve on perfection, can you?"

They grin dazzlingly wide. Cayenne treats the wall as if it were the finest feather mattress, reclining back with their hips canted forward so they very nearly fall flush with Ravi's. "And if I'm being *honest,* which will be a fun little irony, I also did it because of you. If I'd have known you had no objections to my original body, *frightfully* dull as it was, I might have left well enough alone. Using that damn idol *hurt,* the fucking thing. Believe me, I am *not* keen to repeat that particular trick, as fun as it would be to shift around the gender spectrum."

Ravi drifts closer, only inches apart. "You didn't need to change yourself. To get me to want you."

He slides the pad of his thumb over Cayenne's full lower lip, tugs it lightly down. Cayenne's pupils expand, green swallowed by black. Their tongue darts out to wet reddened lips, brushing his thumb.

"Ravi," they whisper. "Please."

Ravi crowds in and kisses them, fisting both hands in their hair to hold them still for the demanding press of his mouth. Cayenne melts against him with a gasp, tonguing at the seam of his lips.

After far too long, Ravi pulls back, and Cayanne grins triumphantly, licking their lips. "*C'est ça, mon coeur*, no need to be nervous. See? No tricks. Just us." They push away from the wall and hold up their hands, waggling their fingers.

Then Cayenne blinks, swaying in place.

Ravi waits.

Cayenne takes a step and stumbles, features knotting in confusion. Then their eyes fly open wide. They press a hand to their lips. "Oh, *well done*," they exclaim, bracing themself on his chest, and their knees give out. Ravi catches them by the arm and holds them upright.

Nix venom is even rarer than basilisk—rarer now that Ravi had ensured the world has one less nix in it, though Calvin Guinto hadn't known that detail when he'd sold Ravi the few precious drops of poison. Hardly a week ago,

Ravi had been utterly, steadfastly certain he would never ever use the stuff, intent on consigning even the memory of the best way to trap a chronomancer into oblivion, to ensure The Trust would never capture Cayenne and set the whole cycle spinning.

But he'd bought it anyway. *Guess all the tutoring on strategy and precaution had been too ingrained to shake off.* Ravi spits on his jacket sleeve, scrubbing at his lips until only the barrier compound remains.

Looks like he's a good liar *and* a good secret agent, after all.

Sagging in his arms, Cayenne snarls a weak laugh. "I'm truly impressed, my *ravageur*." Under their honesty peeks a flash of betrayal, fury underlying their words as bones jut through dried skin.

Ravi holds himself steady against it, against his own self-loathing. This is the price he has to pay. A sacrifice of himself, his ideals and morals. Small things, really, when weighed against stopping the next apocalypse.

Already slow and sluggish, Cayenne tries to squirm away, ducking low under Ravi's arm. Easy enough to counter, spinning them around and goose-necking an arm behind their back. He pulls a metal cuff from inside his jacket pocket and secures it with a snap around one narrow wrist.

"Darling, if you wanted me in handcuffs, all you had to

do was say so," Cayenne slurs. They lean their body against his, then explode into movement, twisting and clawing and spitting like a wildcat. A brief struggle only; they're disoriented and likely hallucinating, going for Ravi's vulnerable spots with open savagery.

Ravi takes a few hits and scratches with only a mild grunt, dragging Cayenne to the small kitchenette. He maneuvers them down to the floor and attaches the handcuff's mate to the heavy frame of the fridge.

Cayenne laughs, tilting up a disturbing grin while Ravi pulls out a second set of cuffs. "You know, it's funny, *mon amour.*"

"What is?"

They lick their poisoned lips again, as if relishing the taste of his treachery. "It's going to be so *gratifying* for me when everything's finally done, my pet. When you're all *mine* again." Their head lolls back against the fridge door. Their focus fades in and out, disorientation battling with lucidity. "Such extra fun to have my way with you when you won't even remember this little scuffle. It won't have happened for you. I'll have to handcuff *you,* my sweet, won't that be *très amusant?* Oh, *mon tigre,* how deliciously duplicitous of you. Guess I *have* taught you a thing or two. My good, *noble* knight, so honest and true. See, we *are* perfect for each other."

Ravi tries not to flinch.

"You know what, my *ravageur*? I'm not sorry for any of it. I'll do it all again harder next time. Family just holds you back. You should be *thanking* me. I did you a *favor*."

Ravi cuffs Cayenne's other arm to the opposite side of the heavy fridge despite their attempts to wriggle free, leaving no chance for them to manipulate their tattoo. Won't matter much when the venom fades enough for Cayenne to slip their consciousness back to their past self, but that should be hours off. Hopefully not until morning.

"What are you going to do with me now, hero? Hmm? Call up your avenging angel? Lock me up and throw away the key? Planning to *gun me down*, my love?"

Ravi steps back, impassive, giving nothing away. Cayenne grins before fading into some hallucination, muttering in a soup of languages while peering into nothing. Ravi reaches into his pocket and slips on the black titanium ring. The memory wipe has been pre-set to erase everything from the present all the way back to before the future-Trust took Cayenne into captivity, well before they swore revenge.

The most difficult part of planning this strategy had been mapping out Cayenne's timeline, figuring out how many months before their meeting in Chicago would need to be forgotten. But Cayenne has dropped enough little hints along the way for Ravi to piece together. He's no intel agent, but he can follow a trail as well as any hunter.

All the ring needs is to be set spinning while pointing at Cayenne. A dangerously easy weapon to wield. *A black bit of magic,* Constance had proclaimed.

Surely this is something like mercy—even a kindness—erasing the memory of being taken prisoner, of being…tortured. Undoubtedly Cayenne will be confused about the lost time, but they'd have no reason not to go back to living their carefree, hedonistic life, tripping through the timeline as they please. Memories reset to before they knew about The Trust, or the Abhiramnews, or the team: before Ravi. They wouldn't remember meeting him. Loving him. Betraying him.

That's mercy, isn't it?

It will only take a moment. He can't be indecisive. Cayenne threatens to topple everything his ancestors worked for, everything centuries of sacrifice has built. This is for his legacy. For his friends. His future. Intentionally or not, Ravi started this mess. It's up to him to finish it. It doesn't matter that this is someone he used to love, the only person who's ever loved him. It doesn't matter that it's dark magic, the very thing he's sworn to guard against. Don't the ends justify the means?

He hears the echo of his aunt. *Do you imagine that we are above using any means to keep the world safe?*

He's come this far. No backing down.

Is this what his ancestors would have wanted for him? Would they still be proud of him?

How do you stand?

Unflinching.

He lowers his arm. "Fuck," he hisses, furious with himself.

Blearily, Cayenne blinks up. "'*Allo, beau gosse! D'où viens-tu?*" Then they shake their head as if clearing cobwebs. "Ah, did it work, then?"

"Did…what work?"

"Wiping out The Trust, my sexy samosa!" Their pupils are tiny black pinpricks. "It's a crazy plan, but *c'est la vie, non?* Talk about strange bedfellows. Besides, if it goes sideways, I can just rewind and try again. *Pas de mal.*" They look down at their bound wrists with a perplexed frown. "Did I do something fun last night?"

Ravi's attention laser-focuses in. "What is this crazy plan?"

They pull weakly at the cuffs, muttering in French. He crouches down in front of them and cups their chin in his hand, making them meet his eyes. "Cayenne. *What are you planning?*"

"Cayenne? *Un voyage en ville? Nous étions récemment.*" Then they blink, lucidity crystallizing again for a moment.

Suddenly Cayenne arches backward with a shocked, pained gasp, mouth and eyes open wide, tearing out of Ravi's gentle touch and convulsing hard against the fridge.

Heart in his throat, Ravi shields the back of their skull with his hand, keeping them upright. Has he misjudged the venom? What has he done?

Panting, Cayenne looks at him, hair at their temples rust-dark with sweat. Their slow smile is an agonized rictus, a terrible thing to behold. "Isn't…that…*interesting*," they choke out with difficulty, then crane their neck to snatch a glimpse at Ravi's wristwatch. Then as suddenly as a marionette with its strings cut, they droop in his arms with a gasp of relief. "That was bracing," Cayenne says with a fragile laugh, shaking like a leaf.

A terrible suspicion begins to take shape. Ravi pulls away. Despite their clammy pallor, their drugged gaze, and their wrists restrained, the grin Cayenne wears is one of undisguised triumph.

Then Ravi hears the screams.

He whips around. Outside the apartment window orange light flickers, and far off in the distance, sirens begin to wail.

"*What did you do?*"

"What *will* I do, my sweet." Cayenne grins, visibly keeping the drug at bay and hanging on to consciousness tooth and nail. "No idea, but no doubt something *very* villainous, knowing me. I'll bet you can still save some innocent bystanders if you act quickly." They settle in against the fridge door, stretching their long legs out on the linoleum with one ankle kicked up over the other, looking for all the world like there's no place they'd rather be. Cayenne winks. "Better run, hero. I'll be seeing you."

*

RAVI LIMPS HIS way into Constance's shop. Griswold, fur standing on end as he bounds down the stairs to confront the intruder, takes one look at him and yowls, "Mistress! Thine companion has met an injurious calamity and needs thy healing!"

"Thanks, Griz," Ravi mutters, throwing himself into a nearby chair as the sound of boots comes clomping down the wooden stairs.

"God's blood, Ravi!" Immediately, Constance is on him, hands gentle at his jawbone as she inspects him head to toe. "What happened?" She kneels and pushes up the burned tatters of his trousers, everything below the knee now more ash than fabric. She prods at his raw shins. "Myrtle and arnica," she calls over her shoulder, and Griswold darts off like a shot.

"Fought a hellhound," he says shortly then sags into

the chair, exhaustion finally catching up with him.

She stares at him while her hands busily unravel gauze and uncork bottles. "Oh, is that all? Hardly a busy night, then." She holds out her hand as Griswold trots up and drops a few sprigs of plants in her palm.

"Saved some people," he says morosely, as if that could make up for his actions putting those people in danger in the first place. Stupid. How could he have thought that he, just a guy with good aim, could outmaneuver someone who had destroyed dozens of ancient vampires on a *whim*? Fucking hubris, pure and simple. He coughs, lungs still smoky.

"Whyever did you not call for any of us?" Constance demands, sweeping hair out of her face before attending to the plethora of scratches and burns on Ravi's wrists and hands, spreading on a green paste.

He sighs with relief as the pain fades. Having his hands impaired makes him less effective in a fight, hampering his reaction time. "Thank you."

"Save your bloody thanks and answer my question, witch-hunter."

He looks away. "I tried the same thing you did."

She kneels up to carefully pluck out wooden splinters embedded in his cheek. "You shall have to be more specific."

"I tried to control the battlefield. Meet my enemy on

even ground."

Her hands pause for a beat before she continues, pressing a soaked square of gauze against his face. He ignores the sting. "Thou attempted to take on the time wizard by thyself?"

"I did."

She adopts a matronly tone. "And how did that go?"

"Not well."

"You shock me, my good fellow." She guides him to hold the gauze in place while she fixes her attention back to his legs. "Breath of hellhound?" When he nods, Constance drums her fingers against her chin in thought before slapping together a few ingredients from her satchel. "How did that red-capped whitlow get a hold of a hellhound?"

"That's…an excellent question. Could have found reports of one either in history or the future and just tossed it through time."

"Aye, that could be." Constance concentrates on her work for a few minutes, drawing a cleansing cloth over raw skin. Ravi tries to keep still. "So, your endeavor to face thine nemesis went about as well as mine."

"Worse."

"True! But the only reason my situation did not go utterly tits-up is because the team came and helped me." She angles up a stern brow. "I should have asked for help from the start, and so should you. We are as the many twigs."

Ravi wonders if he'd struck his head harder than he thought. "Twigs?"

"If you try to snap a twig, this is done easily. If you try to snap many twigs all held together, they do not even bend."

"Ah, an idiom. These days we say, 'united we stand, divided we fall.'"

"Oh. Yes, that is much catchier." She gestures to Griswold, and he moves to her side and sits primly with his striped tail wrapped around his front paws. Constance sets one hand on his head while the other hovers over Ravi's wounds. Griswold's yellow eyes close, his loud purr filling the space. A warm energy tingles outward from Constance's fingers and into Ravi's leg. "Do you wish to tell me what happened?"

Ravi hesitates, then sighs. "I set a trap. Had them cornered. I had the opportunity to…to take them out of the fight." Constance's eyes snap up to his. "Not *kill* them," he says quickly, queasy at the mere thought. Even with everything on the line, he couldn't ever bring himself to commit violence against Cayenne.

Fuck, they'd really picked the perfect mark with him.

"I…I couldn't do it. I didn't take the shot. They got the better of me. At some point in their future, they come back and set a hellhound loose in the apartment across the street to draw me away." He drops the gauze to rake a hand through his hair, dislodging flakes of char. "When I came back, of course they'd escaped."

He's not sure how Cayenne managed to snap the hand-cuff chains on their own while drugged on nix venom, but as Constance has pointed out, there were any number of ways a chronomage could accomplish nearly anything.

Constance hums sympathy, moving her magical ministrations to his other leg. "There is one other great difference between your enemy and mine. I never loved that wretched demon—repulsive, even the thought—and would feel no conflict of heart should he perish."

Shoulders slumping, Ravi whispers hoarsely, "Yeah."

Constance sits back on her haunches and gives Griswold a hearty scratch around the ears before he trots off. She eyes her work with satisfaction. "Thou shalt be unmarked in another few moments, save for some singed hair. I hath channeled a fair bit of healing magics into you, and thou art a quick healer by nature." She gathers up bits of cloth and recaps jars before standing up with a brisk clap of her hands. "Now, then. Are we in imminent danger of retaliation, do you think?"

It takes a moment to drag his scattered thoughts together, forcing them to fall into orderly ranks. "I don't think so. If I were them, I'd go off and lick my wounds while planning a large, decisive strike at the most advantageous possible moment."

"Then we shall be on our guard and be ready for anything." Constance sits on a nearby chair and smiles at him. "Nothing has changed then, really."

He smiles wanly back.

Her pleasant smile fades to concern. "How are you doing with all this?"

"I'm fine."

Constance rolls her eyes so emphatically her eyelashes flutter. "Oh aye, of course, *fine*. Fine must mean something different than it did in my time."

He runs tentative fingers over his cheek, finding no remaining abrasions. "Thanks, Constance. For the healing."

She brushes off his gratitude with a wave and a smile. "A witch must always be helpful." The words have the weight of an oft-repeated phrase.

"What's that from?"

Her hazel eyes slide off him as her smile fades. "Lessons learned at my parents' knees."

Ravi rubs soot from his lapels in vain, only managing to work it deeper into the houndstooth pattern. "Lessons on how to be a witch?"

"Of a sort." Constance tips her head back against her

chair until she's gazing up at the ceiling and recites, "A witch must always be helpful. A witch is unarmed without a smile. A witch must always have a knife handy and hidden. A witch must always keep her boots on."

No reason for that last one unless a witch had to always be ready to run. "Lessons on how to *survive* being a witch."

She turns toward him in surprise. "Aye. Yes. I admit I had not expected you to see the truth of it."

"Not too different from some things my tutors have said," Ravi sighs, suddenly wearier than he can ever remember being. He wishes he were in bed; preferably Nate's bed, which is softer and has the added bonus of Nate being in it.

He attempts a sympathetic smile and is glad when Constance returns it. It's not her usual broad, disarming grin, but something smaller and more delicate. Maybe it's even the real thing. "Did you and Harry learn anything useful from James?"

Constance perks up. "Indeed we did! I discovered he is quite enamored of me."

"Uh, yeah. Already knew that."

"You did?" Constance goggles at him. "'Twas a surprise to me. Anyroad, I spent a very pleasant night tumbling him into a state of near stupor. He is quite interesting when you scratch the surface. Eager to please. Takes direction well."

Ravi's ears blaze hot. "Constance!"

"What? He can't be in our time overmuch or it causes some-such 'causality problems.' A beneficial situation for me, I don't mind telling you. I had a merry time, but I can't abide lovers who are constantly underfoot, demanding the whole of my attention. I'm a busy witch with diverse interests."

Ravi coughs into his fist. "Hey, uh. Harry had…a talk with you, right? About…" he fights through embarrassment to mumble, "about safe sex?"

"Hm? Oh, aye! Worry not, 'twas quite safe. I only fell off once."

Mortified, Ravi pinches the bridge of his nose, grappling for a change of subject. "Did you learn anything useful *to the team?*"

"Oh, oh. Also, yes. He's nothing to do with abetting or ruining Cayenne's plots. They are acquaintances at best, from vastly different eras, only meeting when it suits Cayenne's rare whim. Likewise, he is ignorant of the circumstances surrounding the urumi, only vaguely aware of the Chosen and The Trust beyond knowing to stay off their — the whatsit. Thingy. *Radar*, that's the word. Harry was able to extract a great deal from the man he did not realize he let slip. My niece is very clever," she says with pride.

"Extremely," Ravi agrees. "So, it's still a mystery who sent Harry that package." The only useful information they've obtained is that they still don't have any useful information. He sighs. "Is James going to stick around and help us out?"

"He's already left, back to his far-flung time. He's much more mindful of changing things, this time traveler. He almost stepped on an anthill, and I swear I saw him spring out with sweat."

"Great, so he's no help. Is there *anything* we can use?"

"Only an interesting time travel fact, perhaps. It seems those who manipulate the timeline will still carry the memory of the no-longer-viable timeline. James said otherwise, time travelers would continue making the same loop over and over, endlessly trying to achieve an impossible goal, wearing a hole in space and time. He said something about a 'probability matrix' imploding."

"Doesn't sound ideal."

"Exceedingly so, it would seem. He also called Cayenne 'that selfish chaos gremlin,' which I found rather amusing."

"Not exactly helpful to us."

Constance shrugs, idly playing the end of a braid against her palm like a paintbrush. "Sadly, we still fight in shadow. But take heart, mine friend. It takes but a single spark, and the darkness is no more."

After a moment, Ravi returns her encouraging smile. "Yeah."

"Speaking of sparks," she says slyly. "What flame is kindling between you and our favorite man of letters?"

"That's…" Heat floods his cheeks. "Nate and I are… spending some time together, yes."

Constance leans over to pat his arm. "Excellent. You're good for each other."

"Look, it's not… I'm not ready to…"

"Harken to me, Ravi. Nathan is a good person, through and through. Kind. Compassionate. Gallant. And, it must be said, very fair of form."

"I…know all that."

"Well, then. Should you cleave to him, your swain would sooner throw himself off a parapet than hurt you."

He shoots her a glare. "Would you stop matchmaking? It is what it is. Pretty sure being fresh out of a bad break-up isn't the best time to start thinking about…*cleaving*. I'm not looking for more."

Constance considers him for a long moment. "You're not allowing yourself to *hope* for more. There is a difference."

Ravi looks down at his hands, brushing soot from what's left of his jacket cuffs. "I thought you didn't believe in 'having lovers underfoot.'"

"For *myself*, certainly, mine heart is as open as the sky. But you, nephew-to-be, are the most prime exemplar of a One-Man Guy that I have ever beheld." She leans in with a conspiratorial whisper, "Don't tell him I said so, but so is Nathan."

Ravi shakes his head. "But…Nate dates a lot of people."

"Stars above, Ravi, he hasn't dated a single solitary soul since the day he met *you*."

"What?"

"I tell ye true. We converse over poker nights. A terrible bluffer, you know. A flirt the fellow is indeed, but he's 'been too busy to get involved with anyone' for quite some time." Constance briefly adopts a gruff, masculine imitation that is nowhere near the real thing. "A keen observer would note it happens to coincide perfectly with your meeting. *Surely* just coincidence. Far be it for me to insinuate that you owe anyone your interest merely because they give you theirs, but it is as I said: he would sooner drink hemlock than cause you pain."

Ravi gnaws at his lower lip, eyes locked on his healing hands.

He wonders bleakly what knowing Cayenne has done to him; made him both reckless and ruthless, someone he barely recognizes. Is this what love is supposed to be like?

A thing that blinds you, scorches you, warps your own morals, drives you into a constant string of bad decisions until you are left with only the worst version of yourself?

"Do you think," he rasps, throat dry, "that's a better basis for a relationship than mutually assured destruction?"

Constance gives Ravi a slow, stunned blink. "It could hardly be worse, could it?"

Chapter Fifteen

MASSIVE LIVE OAKS, dripping with Spanish moss, cast down dappled sunshine on the groomed rows below. The whirring of fall insects creates a pleasant, steady drone that muffles distant sound, making the archery range feel more secluded. There's a faint, cool crispness to the air, especially under the shade of the trees.

The mossy oaks give each shooting lane the illusion of privacy. Ravi walks past several groups of game-hunters and hipsters, all engaged in archery or axe-throwing parties, before he finds Nate's lane.

"There he is," Nate calls out with a grin, hopping down from a picnic table. "Fancy meeting you here." He's dressed for movement in a workout tee and olive drab cargos. A colorful hint of tattooed knotwork peeks past the hem of one short sleeve. No doubt early November in Georgia is practically shorts season for him, whereas Ravi in his long-sleeve merino sweater is on the verge of needing another layer.

"Sorry I'm late. I had to dig around the armory at the Atlanta branch for a normal, non-enchanted bow." Ravi unzips the bag and removes some equipment, setting a quiver of arrows on the picnic table next to Nate's sleek carbon bow.

"You're pretty much right on time. No worries, man." Nate glances around for onlookers and steps closer, on the verge of platonic distance. In the dappled sunlight his eyes are an arresting shade of cornflower blue. "Missed you."

Warmth curls in Ravi's stomach and spreads slowly outward. "Good thing we're here to work on your aim."

"Funny guy. Well, go easy on me. I haven't picked up a bow in a while."

"Then let's start with you showing me what you remember." Ravi steps to the side to allow Nate room to work.

Nate picks up his equipment and straps on the wrist guard. "Yeah, not like you standing there is going to give me performance anxiety at all."

"I can look away, but that kind of defeats the purpose

of having this refresher course."

Nate shakes out both arms, loosening up. "My idea of a refresher was brushing up on mythological archers earlier today. Probably not super helpful, huh?"

"You never know. Like what, Robin Hood?"

"Though Robin Hood is a fictional character in folklore, he's likely a conflation of several real people of the era. I teach a unit on cynosuric folk heroes wherein Robin Hood features heavily." He tests the draw before readying his posture. "I was more interested in mythological figures. Skadi, Artemis, Agilaz, aaand I'm going to stop before I launch into a lecture." Nate's neck goes a little pink. "Lots of archer heroes in Indian literature, aren't there?"

Ravi watches Nate's stance with a critical eye. "Tons. Our histories and epics are full of them. Sri Ram, Arjuna, Pradyumna. It's one of the traditional weapons I was taught early on after basic footwork. Bow and arrow, sword and shield, spear. Stuff like that."

"So cool." Nate nocks an arrow and takes a shot. It barely misses the printed target, just off the largest ring into the blank space. Nice power though, the arrow lodging deeply into the straw. "Eh, well. Coulda been worse, right?"

Nate looks *really* good with a bow in his hands. The way his features firm with concentration, the play of his muscular arms as he draws back... Ravi shakes off the distraction and hooks his sunglasses over his collar. "Good start. There are a couple of things… Can I show you?"

"Absolutely."

Ravi slides up behind Nate. "Okay. Start upright. Feet ninety degrees to the target. Yeah, perfect." He slides a hand down Nate's arm, from the edge of the knotwork tattoo on the taut rise of his bicep all the way down to his bare wrist. "Your grip is already good. Very important, a good grip."

The flush on Nate's neck deepens. "You're making this suggestive on purpose."

Ravi *tsks*, as if mortally offended. "Get your mind out of the gutter, Doc. This is how the pros do it. Next is finger position."

Dropping the bow to his side, Nate laughs out loud. "*Dude*, c'mon."

Ravi has to bite down hard to keep from laughing. He guides Nate's arms back up to nock the arrow. "All right, draw back." He backs off, giving Nate space. As the bowstring bends, Ravi sets a hand between Nate's shoulder blades and gently corrects, "Don't use your biceps. Pull with your back."

Nate nods, adjusting easily.

"There you go," Ravi breathes, and steps away to watch. He looks good, solid. "Maintain your position after you fire. Don't fall out of stance until you see your arrow hit."

The arrow flies true and lands with a satisfying *thunk* into the heart of the bullseye. A perfect shot.

"Nice," Ravi says with a nod.

"Holy shit." Nate stares at the target, then swings around. "Holy shit! You're a *really* good teacher."

Coming from a professor, that hits harder. Ravi shakes his head, ears warm. "Doubtful. You're a natural. You just needed a reminder. Like riding a bike."

Wide-eyed, Nate turns back at the bullseye. "Must be a fluke. I'm gonna go again." He's clearly taken Ravi's direction to heart. His position is good, elbow dropped, sighting down the shaft with focused intent.

He'd suspected Nate would take well to the bow. Practically built for archery. He looks...*very* good. Ravi swallows.

Thunk. The arrow hits again in the center, a whisper away from the last.

"Whaaaat," Nate hisses in a forceful whisper. "No way!"

Ravi can't help but grin. "Nice shot. Like I said, a natural."

Nate keeps looking back and forth between the target and Ravi. "See, among normal people, this would be an unreal accomplishment. Jumping around, cheering, getting silly with it. Figures that martial prowess is just another day at the office for you."

"I *said* nice shot."

Nate laughs, then fully faces the target with his hands proudly akimbo. "I know shooting at a moving target is a whole other ballpark, but this feels pretty great. I'll keep practicing." He slides the bow crosswise over his chest and bumps shoulders with Ravi. "Okay then, tough guy, let's see what you got. Show me how the pros do it."

Ravi rolls his eyes and gathers up his longbow, eschewing the quiver in favor of tossing a few arrows point-down into the ground in front of him. "Literally haven't fired a bow since I was sixteen, so don't get your hopes up." He limbers up his shoulders, rocks his neck side to side, and squares up.

Ravi sights down the arrow on an inhale. His archery tutor had been a leathery, rawboned woman from one of the Nagaland tribes. Instinctively, he straightens his posture at the phantom memory of her hooking a bow around his ankle to correct his stance. *You are not the eyes and arms that direct the arrow,* she would harp. *You are the arrow, the breeze that guides it, the target the arrow seeks. Dhyana, child. Fix your mind solely on your goal.*

He empties his lungs and fires.

The arrow misses the mark completely, landing

halfway to the fletching into the blank space off the outer ring; a much poorer shot than Nate's first had been. Ravi grunts, his neck burning as he draws back another arrow. His second shot is even worse, nearly off the straw entirely.

"Are you trying to make me look good? My ego can handle it if you split my arrow in half or something badass like that, you know."

Ravi drops his arms, glaring at the target. Even this, he can't do right. His throat feels tight.

Nate's gaze sharpens. He steps a bit closer, posture going aggressively casual. "Hey, my guy, you know what's coming, right? The great North American question! So: how are you?" He flashes his boundless, easy grin.

Several heartbeats pass before Ravi can muster up an answer. "I'm…I'm *not* fine."

Nate's eyes widen for a split second. "Okay. *Okay*. You wanna sit and talk, maybe?" He motions toward the picnic table.

Ravi stares at the table. Then tosses the longbow onto the grass and sits.

Nate sits across from him, chin propped in his hand, and gives Ravi an encouraging smile. "So, what's up?"

"I saw Cayenne again."

Nate's mouth twists up like he's taken a bite of a whole lemon. "What did they want this time?"

"Actually," Ravi says, strained, "I arranged the meeting."

Nate presses his lips together. "Okay. You don't have to tell me anything if you don't want to. I'm not trying to pry. But can I ask why?"

Ravi looks down, tracing the grain of the table with a nail. "I drugged them, trapped them, and then tried to wipe their memory with that dark magic ring we confiscated from the black marketeer. It…didn't work out."

Nate stares.

Ravi takes some long, even breaths, bracing himself for castigation. For judgement. For whatever is coming next. He deserves it.

Nate rests his hand atop Ravi's. "I'm so sorry, Ravi."

"You're… *Why?*"

Nate strokes the back of Ravi's knuckles lightly with his thumb. "You loved them. When you care for someone, that doesn't just go away. Even when they hurt you." His touch tightens into a squeeze, the warmth solid and grounding. "I'm sorry you went through that. Are you okay?"

"Don't be *sorry* for me!" A sudden spike of anger fizzles and dies just as quickly as it flares. "I was going to do this terrible… I almost did it. I was *so close*."

"But you didn't," Nate says firmly, still holding Ravi's hand. "And if you had, it would have been to protect others.

You're a good person, Ravi."

"I'm… *Fuck*." Ravi pulls his arm back to cradle his forehead in both hands. "You must be so sick of this. Of me always being such a wreck."

"Don't do that. You're not a wreck. You're going through an unbelievable amount of pressure. You're *human*."

Ravi swallows thickly, eyes locked on the wooden table. "You don't think…you don't think I'm broken?"

A pause. Nate's voice drops into a low scrape. "Did *they* tell you that?"

Ravi doesn't answer, and Nate inhales and exhales steadily for a full ten seconds.

"Ravi." Ravi doesn't look up until Nate takes both his hands in his own, enfolding them like a bird in a nest. "You're not broken. You're the strongest person I've ever met. You're *kintsugi*."

"I'm what?"

"It's a Japanese custom I talk about in class. Sometimes when pottery breaks, instead of throwing it away, the cracks are sealed with gold. Then the piece is repaired without obscuring its history. The break makes the piece even more beautiful than it was before; just another chapter in its story." Nate's gaze doesn't waver. "You've been knocked down so many times, Ravi, and you keep getting up. I've never seen anything like it. I keep telling you, it's inspiring. You're a revelation, my guy."

Ravi stares at Nate for a long moment. "I really like you," he accuses.

"That's…good?"

"It's not," Ravi insists, fingers entwining through Nate's. "I should be more guarded than ever. After… I should be distrustful of everyone, keeping my head down and not…not holding hands in a *park,* and you just make it…" He glances away with a huff. "I should be *terrified* of trying to be with anyone else, but you're just… You make it so easy. You're like armor-piercing rounds. You cut right through my defenses."

Both dimples make an appearance, framing Nate's smile. "Wow. I've had better compliments, but not many."

"You're just so…so perfect, it's—"

"Whoa, whoa," Nate protests, holding up his hands. "I am *far* from perfect, Ravi."

Ravi rolls his eyes and holds up a fist, extending a finger with each subsequent point. "Dreamboat professor. Supportive family. Emotionally healthy. Natural archer." He pauses before adding a new one on his thumb. "Great in bed."

Nate snorts, palming the back of his neck. "I mean, you're a badass ninja warrior and I'm a bookish nerd with glamour muscles, so if we're talking about perfection, here…"

"That's ridiculous. First of all, none of my training was *ninja related*."

"But you're so light on your feet."

"That's just…agility and stealth training."

"Do you hear yourself? How is that not ninja-related?"

"This conversation has gotten completely away from me." As he stretches out his legs under the table, Ravi's foot knocks something with the clink of ceramic.

"Oh, yeah, sorry, I was going to surprise you with this later as a thank-you-for-the-archery-lesson present, but…" Nate reaches under the table to pull up a small cactus in a colorful planter. He unceremoniously hands it to Ravi.

"This…" Ravi squints. "A sand dollar cactus?"

"I'm impressed! You know your cacti."

"Yeah, some guy keeps giving the things to me, so I've had to brush up on my botany." It's a very handsome little cactus. Ravi admires it, turning the planter. "She looks like a Chloe," he decides; one of his favorite video game characters of Indian heritage.

Saying nothing, Nate gazes at him with a faint, distant smile.

"What?" Self-conscious, Ravi puts Chloe down.

Nate pillows his cheek in his palm, voice going a little

dreamy. "I'm just having a hard time believing that you're the same stone-faced guy I first met. Wondering how I ever kept my hands off you. You're something else, sunshine."

Somewhere behind Ravi's breastbone, embers kick up into a warm, flickering glow.

"Feeling better?" Nate asks softly.

Incredibly, he does. Somehow Nate keeps chasing away all of Ravi's shadows, leaving him light and unbound. He shakes his head in disbelief. "How do you *do* that?"

"Just the power of heart, my guy," Nate laughs, standing up and retrieving Ravi's bow. "I gotta do something useful in this crew of superheroes besides getting all the coffee orders right. Now, c'mon." He offers the bow with a wink. "Show me some ninja moves."

After that, Ravi's aim shows marked improvement, causing Nate to whoop congratulations and work through his own quiver in a near-perfect run. Continuing for a while, they work up a light sweat until the sun lowers enough for Nate to suggest that it might be too dark to safely continue practicing.

"Too dark, huh?" It's barely late afternoon.

"Yup. Definitely. Might accidentally shoot our feet. Better not risk it." Nate grins as he leans a hip against the picnic table. "We should probably go back to my place."

In the interest of safety, Ravi agrees.

*

NATE KISSES HIM as if he's trying to condense a whole lifetime of missed make-out sessions into the space of an hour. Every time they part for air, Nate murmurs some sweet little snippet of admiration before pressing into another eternal, devouring kiss.

"You are so unbelievably hot," Nate gasps, each syllable an open-mouthed caress to Ravi's bared throat. Ravi squirms a little against the overstuffed sofa cushions, flustered and fighting the instinct to hide his face. "Just look at these lithe muscles." Nate lands a playful nip to the meat of Ravi's shoulder. "Like a panther or something. So strong."

Ravi goes still.

Nate immediately pulls back. "Something wrong?"

"No, no, it's not—"

Ravi's breath catches. He's *tired* of being strong. Of being resilient. Tired of being praised for how well he takes a hit. For once, he wants to trust someone and not regret it later.

Maybe this time he can.

He's not even sure what he's going to say until the words start coming, halting and tripping as they go. "Would it…would it be okay if I wasn't? Strong. For a little while."

Nate's searching gaze strips right through skin, as if he could read the words printed on Ravi's innermost heart.

"Of course, it is, sunshine. I got you." He cups Ravi's chin and pulls him into a sweet, rich kiss that goes on and on until Ravi forgets anything else exists beyond lips and breath. "Here's what's going to happen," Nate murmurs in a low, confident croon while he slides a hand up into Ravi's hair. "We're going to take a shower. And while we're in there, I'm going to lick you open and get you ready to take my cock."

Ravi gasps sharply, heartbeat stuttering.

Nate knots his fingers just hard enough to be on the right side of painful. "I'm going to take my time. Make a *buffet* out of you until your legs give out. Then I'm gonna carry you to my bed, and I'm going to fuck you until you come while I'm still buried inside you." He licks a long stripe up Ravi's throat and chuckles. "Your pulse is just *racing*. That for me, babe?"

All his words have dried up like a puddle in deepest summer. Ravi swallows.

Nate's grin grows wider, his eyes so glazed with simmering arousal they look like polished lapis. His grip on Ravi's hair gentles, bringing their foreheads to touch. "You wanna be a good boy for me, sunshine?"

A bullseye bolt strikes through Ravi with perfect aim,

the shaft quivering with impact. His dick is already so hard against Nate's thigh that it *aches*.

"Use your words, Ravi." Nate's eyes dance as he patiently waits.

"Yes," Ravi whispers, muscles going hot and lax as molten honey.

Nate smiles so broadly his eyes crinkle at the corners. "You sure?"

"*Yes.*"

"Good. Wanna take care of you," Nate murmurs, swooping in to suck Ravi's lower lip between his teeth. Ravi twitches at the unexpected bite, mind quickly emptying of any thoughts more complex than *this* and *yes* and *more*.

In the shower, Ravi can barely keep his balance even before Nate turns him to the wall to press him against the tiles. "Stay just like that," Nate murmurs in his ear, then tongues his way down Ravi's spine, tracing each vertebra with the barest hint of teeth. Ravi shivers, the cascade of hot water doing nothing to stop the rise of gooseflesh, and does as he's told.

When Nate sinks to his knees, he gives an appreciative little groan that sends Ravi's heartbeat into high gear. He lets himself be positioned, lets Nate pull back his hips, and braces his forearms against the wall, dimly aware that he's quivering with anticipation.

The first ghost of Nate's breath threatens to undo him already. Ravi scrabbles fingernails against tile as if grasping for the last scraps of his self-control. At the hot, slick drag of Nate's tongue, Ravi stops breathing entirely.

Nate drops a sharp bite to Ravi's cheek, jumpstarting his lungs back up again. "That's it," Nate murmurs, "I want you nice and relaxed." A broad lick sends Ravi up onto his toes, stars bursting behind his eyelids. Mindlessly he presses back, body yielding, giving all his weight to the wall.

"Yeah, doing good, babe." Then, holding Ravi tight, Nate really sets to work.

Head buried in the crook of his elbow, Ravi can't gather enough oxygen, half out of his head from the slick, hot pleasure of it. His desire is already at its peak, lightheaded with the speed of his arousal, and Nate's barely gotten started. Thumbs slotted into the grooves of Ravi's hipbones as if they were carved to fit there, Nate sets an undulating rhythm that knocks the air out of Ravi as soon as he can get any down his throat. He tries not to melt into a useless puddle at the bottom of the tub.

Then Nate groans, his stubble dragging, reverberations carried by lips and tongue, and the last vestiges of Ravi's composure utterly shatters.

"*Otha,*" he pants, a vulgarity his tutors would have

been shocked he picked up. His cock aches, begging for attention, but he ignores it in favor of pushing back and pleading for more.

"Sorry, babe, I don't speak that," Nate chuckles. "Do you need me to stop?"

"Don't you dare," Ravi hisses, wanting nothing more than to get that clever mouth back where it had been taking him apart. The tiles echo the words back at him oddly, and he realizes he's spoken entirely in a jumble of Tamil and Hindi. "*Fuck.*"

Nate laughs low and warm against Ravi's skin. "I'm going to take that as a compliment."

A few intense minutes later, Nate turns the water off and gives Ravi a quick head-to-toe rubdown with an oversized towel. "Give me a second to brush my teeth. Then I'll get you to bed, gorgeous."

Ravi catches a glimpse of himself in the steam-edged mirror, hair a damp, disordered mess, eyes impossibly dark. He already looks like he's been tumbled for hours, thighs visibly trembling like he'd fall over without the shower tiles to lean against. He's not sure he wouldn't.

Next thing he knows, Nate presses into a demanding, minty embrace as he nibbles a line from the corner of Ravi's mouth to the cut of his jaw. "Mm. *That* was fun. Hop up. Legs around my waist."

True to his word, he carries Ravi from the bathroom to his bed, using his larger size and glamour muscles to full advantage. He lays Ravi down on the covers with care, as if he were precious cargo, easing into a sweet, unhurried kiss. Ravi squirms, in no mood to take it slow. He grinds up against Nate, a note of pure impatience escaping his throat.

"Easy, sunshine, I got you." After a quick supply stop at the nightstand, Nate looks down at Ravi writhing and wanton on his bed, and his Adam's apple bobs hard. "Christ. Wish you could see what I see right now."

He pushes Ravi's thighs wide and settles between them. He glides both palms over Ravi in wide sweeping arcs, all the way from knees to collarbone, then skating across shoulders to trail down to the tips of Ravi's fingers. Instead of a ravenous, all-consuming burn, a scorching thing quick to flare out, Nate's touch is the steady, sustaining heat of sunlight, incandescent and enduring. Under his hands Ravi feels like a new-grown thing, a green shoot in fresh-tilled earth, unfurling up into golden light.

"How did I get so lucky?" Nate breathes, eyes locked on Ravi's. "You're so beautiful, and I don't just mean your looks. I've never wanted anyone this much."

The onslaught of open admiration is far too much to bear. Face burning, Ravi growls, throwing his head back into the pillows. "You don't have to—you don't need to say that, you can just…"

"I know I don't have to. I want to." Nate pushes a slick, seeking hand past Ravi's balls. "Why not? You like it, don't you?"

Ravi exhales shakily, chest heaving. He digs the heels of his hands against his eyes. "I like it too much."

"No such thing. You're just going to have to get used to being lavished with praise," Nate teases, even as he rolls on a condom and hikes Ravi's leg up over his forearm.

"You going to talk, or are you going to fuck me?" Ravi's eyes nearly cross as Nate rubs his slick cock against him in a purposeful tease, his want rapidly turning into *need*.

"Guess I'll have to do both. What a hardship." Nate grins, and presses into Ravi with a slow, steady push. "Jesus," he mutters when Ravi takes him to the hilt, eyes fluttering shut.

Ravi sighs in relief, the welcome stretch bringing a sheen of sweat to his skin and a shiver to his limbs, and then it's *good*; so good that he gasps, pulse racing so fast he can feel it thrumming at the base of his tongue. He takes two healthy handfuls of Nate's round ass to draw him closer, and distantly realizes he's muttering something—babbling, really—all of Ravi's languages shaking around like dice in a cup and whatever comes tumbling out is a random, polyglot mess.

Nate presses his forehead to Ravi's, his breath coming hot and fast. "Fuck, you're so tight. You okay?"

A feeling too big to name drums against Ravi's ribcage, a fierce greedy thing. All he wants is more; the sweet-salt taste of Nate's skin, the bright earthen scent of his soap still clinging to flushed skin, the soothing spill of his voice. Ravi wants more of him everywhere, wants to be brimming full with Nate lighting up his veins.

"*Yes*," is the best translation he can muster, the single syllable an artless growl into the heat of Nate's mouth. He wraps a leg around Nate's waist, taking him deeper, moving their bodies in tandem.

The way Nate smiles while kissing him might be his new favorite thing.

"You're pulling the sheets off the bed, babe."

It's more observation than chastisement, so Ravi ignores him and keeps grabbing, his hands everywhere, mussing the covers, Nate's hair. Every thrust sends a new shock of pleasure shuddering through him, a relentless onslaught heightened by the sweet croon of Nate's voice in his ear; *that's it, babe, you feel so good, is that what you needed?* Ravi kicks his heels into the mattress, digs them into the small of Nate's back, grinding down to wantonly fuck himself on Nate's cock, wild with abandon.

"Fucking *hell*, Ravi." Nate tries to hold on, keeping Ravi

from writhing clear out of the bed. He leans back on his haunches, panting heavily. Ravi reaches out with a desperate keen as they separate, empty and wanting. "Just a sec, don't worry, sunshine." Tucking his arms under Ravi's thighs, Nate heaves him up and over with a grunt, flipping Ravi onto his hands and knees.

Ravi's head spins. He gathers great fistfuls of sheets when Nate eases back inside to start fucking him in earnest, working up a rhythm that shocks the breath out of him on every deep drive. Nate pulls his hips back hard enough to make his teeth rattle, moans Ravi's name, and it's *perfect*.

Ravi twists around, snapping up on his knees to yank Nate by his hair into a fierce, biting kiss.

Nate gasps into it, "Christ, you're flexible."

"Martial arts," Ravi rasps, grinning.

Nate breathes out in a tremulous rush, butting his temple against Ravi's. "I love your smile," he murmurs hot in Ravi's ear, then wraps strong arms around his middle to bear him down flat onto the mattress, his cock landing each stroke right where it sends fireworks shooting up Ravi's spine to explode in colorful bursts behind his eyes. "You feel *incredible*, babe. Gonna come for me?"

"Nathaniel—"

Nate moans again, more desperately, his thrusts going rough and demanding and exquisite. "*Fuck*, Ravi, so fucking *good*, that's it, such a good boy for me—"

And Ravi is completely, utterly gone, the blazing thread of ecstasy wound so tightly around him it can only snap, and he's in freefall, coming against the sheets so hard his vision blurs. Full-throated, he cries out his pleasure with words he's not sure are any recognizable language at all. He clenches tight, needing to drag Nate over that blinding precipice with him, to join him in that ecstatic headlong tumble.

Nate follows a spare second later, the press of his teeth to Ravi's shoulder drawing forth aftershocks nearly as intense as the climax itself. Ravi would be happy to buck into it, if he weren't a pliant, boneless mess, Nate's praise still buzzing through him in a soft electric hum.

It takes a full minute just to catch their breath.

"Wow," Nate says into Ravi's skin, trembling. "Any more enthusiastic and I'll be dead."

Ravi manages an inquiring noise, limp as a noodle.

Nate gusts a breathless laugh. "Don't worry about it. How you doin'?"

"I'm…this *is* English?" Ravi's only half-joking.

Nate drags Ravi's earlobe through his teeth. "That's English, you got it, gorgeous."

"Then I'm doing pretty good," Ravi rumbles in exhausted amusement. He throbs pleasantly, and stretches out his toes, luxuriating in the afterglow while he basks under the warmth of Nate's weight.

"*Very* good," Nate husks into his ear. "S'just what I wanted. Such a good boy." He nuzzles Ravi's neck, stroking damp hair out of his eyes.

Goose bumps prickle up all over Ravi's arms. He presses his forehead into the strewn covers, hiding his burning face. After a few blissful minutes, Nate rolls upright with a series of lingering kisses to Ravi's spine and a regretful sigh. One eye open, Ravi watches as Nate tosses the condom and stretches to his full height, absurdly long with his arms outstretched. Ravi could climb him like a tree.

"Be right back. Gonna clean up, get a new comforter. Get you some water?"

Ravi couldn't care less about cleaning up. He wants Nate back in bed, craves the closeness of his skin, the enticing warmth of him. He snakes out an arm and holds Nate by the wrist.

"I'll just be a minute, babe. Half that."

With a grunt of protest, Ravi hooks the back of Nate's knee and tightens his grip on his wrist, deftly yanking Nate off his feet and tumbling him back into bed. Nate bounces with a surprised yelp. He laughs as Ravi crawls over him to sprawl across his tattooed chest, pinning him in place.

"That's cheating," Nate chuckles, nevertheless giving up and accepting his lot as an illustrated human pillow. "No fair using your superior ninja tactics."

Ravi pushes his face into the center of Nate's chest, where his scent is thickest. He feels a little drunk. Must be endorphins. "S'not ninja tactics, it's Krav Maga."

"That's just Jewish ninjas."

Ravi can't remember the last time he laughed like this, so loud and long that his cheeks hurt. "You're…completely ridiculous." He rolls onto his back, head fitting neatly into the hollow below Nate's clavicle as they drape into a comfortable tangle of limbs.

Ravi is almost about to drop off when Nate says, "Can I ask you something?"

"Hm?"

Nate caresses Ravi's arm, tracing a few scars. "What are all these big changes you're going to make? With The Trust, I mean. You said at the diner you were going to make changes, when you get more say over things. I know you're gonna fix things, naturally, but I've never heard any specifics."

Surprised, Ravi twists to meet Nate's eyes. "You really want to know?"

"Yeah, my guy, you said you have big plans. And, you know, you don't have to tell me, it's not really my business. It's just, I have a hard time seeing it the way you do. I wanna… I want to see it from your perspective. But if you don't want to tell me, that's—"

"No, I…want to." Ravi bites down on a little smile. "No one's ever asked me, before. Harry did, sort of, but that was more focused on…well."

"Your kids and stuff?"

Ravi breathes out, idly tracing the line of a tattoo down Nate's flank. "Yeah. That's a lot of it, the changes. About the Chosen. How things will be different for them from here on out. But The Trust itself is…a bigger question." Ravi takes a moment to marshal his thoughts. "You ever been in a jungle?"

"Uh, like a real jungle? I did a trek in Costa Rica once. A guided tour thing. Soooo, no."

"Okay. So, in some South Asian forests, you can be in the middle of nowhere, and suddenly step onto an ancient road you didn't know was there, hidden under moss and tree roots. Leftover from some ruined city or something. Only a few stones sticking up out of the undergrowth, but you know that somewhere under your feet, there's a trail to follow. It's…it's been a lot like that."

Nate twines his fingers through Ravi's, listening with obvious interest.

Ravi chews his lip for a moment. "I'm not sure where to start, it's all kind of…" He waves a hand in the air as if trying to herd the uncooperative ideas into a sensible formation. "Bits and pieces."

"That's okay," Nate says, threading his leg through Ravi's. "I start a lot of lesson plans like that. I sit down and type out a bunch of amorphous ideas, then restructure them later."

"Yeah? Okay." Ravi sweeps a hand through the rat's nest of his hair, but trying to get it in some semblance of order is a lost cause he quickly gives up on. "The occult black market is a concern. The Trust always struggled to stay ahead of it. But after seeing some of what Guinto had on offer, and knowing Cayenne still has a bunch of Bhagavati artifacts out there…I've been thinking about it a lot lately."

"Gonna shut it down?"

He looks sidelong at Nate and a smirk tugs the corner of Ravi's mouth into a brief, crooked slant. "Nope. I'm going to run it."

"Huh?"

Ravi lets his grin widen. "There's always going to be a black market, that's unavoidable. In a few spots around the globe, Trust presence is basically nonexistent, and that's always where the darkest magic stuff ends up going to auction, where the really dangerous brokers are. Hotbeds of criminal gangs who use supernatural means to gain wealth and power. So, I've been thinking: what if a really nasty gang shows up in one of these spots and takes over? Or even better, two or three gangs? And they form an uneasy truce to make the place a safe haven from Trust interference, encouraging the majority of the world's illicit occult trade to go through them?"

Jaw agape, Nate sits up, dislodging Ravi. "Are you saying you're going to set up *puppet crime gangs* to regulate the flow of black-market goods?"

"Yeah." Ravi settles back into the tangled mess of bedding. He stretches, relishing his body's faint, languid soreness. He's glad for it, wanting to keep a reminder of Nate with him even when they're apart. "That way we can snap up the worst of the worst and know who in the underworld has the less dangerous stuff we let slip through. Assuming I can find suitable agents. Good at deep cover." His smile fades as he's struck with sudden apprehension at how Nate will take the idea. Maybe it's too manipulative, too underhanded. "What do you think?"

"Are you kidding? That's the *coolest* shit I have *ever* heard. I think it's brilliant."

Ravi ducks his head, ears warming. "It's just sound strategy."

"Ha! Just some shadowy cabal of secret undercover Leonardo DiCaprios infiltrating the magical black market. No big deal. Jesus Christ, I am *so* on board with this, dude."

Nate flops back down on his side next to Ravi, beaming. "Can't wait to hear what else you got."

Ravi tries not to glow with pleasure. "The only reason Cayenne was so easily able to steal a whole mess of dangerous artifacts is because the old families hoard them. I want to make sure that the irredeemably dangerous items get destroyed, and the useful ones get allocated to agents for use in the field. Could save a lot of lives. That's going to have to be a whole process with tons of checks and balances. But there's no point keeping magic items out of the wrong hands if we aren't the *right* hands."

"System of checks and balances, also good stuff, though somewhat less exciting than the whole undercover gangster thing."

"They can't all be hits."

Nate's radiant grin warms Ravi from toe to tip. "I dunno, man, I'd say you're two for two so far. I'm going to have to blow you after all this exposition."

"W...what?"

"Yeah, turns out when a hot guy says a bunch of smart, competent things, the nearest himbo has to step up and deliver fellatio. Sorry, I don't make the rules." Nate pairs a helpless shrug with a wicked grin. "Keep talking."

Had Ravi been talking? "I... You're...very distracting."

"My bad."

"'Himbo' is a new one for me."

"Eh, it's like a buff hot guy who's nice, but not too bright."

"But you're…"

"It's tongue-in-cheek, speaking of fellatio." Nate grins and winks. "Where were we? Right. I can't imagine any big-wigs will be jazzed to give up their good magic shit."

It takes considerable effort to drag his attention away from Nate's mouth and back to the topic at hand. "Yeah. That's…gonna be the tricky part. Anything involving the consortium. High-level stuff I don't have intel for. I know more than most because of my mom, but…yeah. Not enough." He sighs. "The problem is that most of the families aren't directly involved in the *work* anymore. They've relied on the Chosen to challenge supernatural threats. Every generation, fewer and fewer Trust kids go into fieldwork, or even intelligence. So now there's this big divide between the people who keep the secrets and make the decisions, and the people who are affected by them. Those of us fighting the fight."

"So, li'l Callum Harbridge is an anomaly?"

"Very much so. The Harbridges are more active than most. Their firstborn, Eleanor, died a few years ago in the line of duty in Nepal to a horde of *kawa cha.*"

"Damn. Skeleton cannibal monsters. That's rough."

"I liked her," Ravi says, wistful. "Good with a sword. We'd spar. She was a bit older than me or else she'd have been the obvious choice for my, uh, betrothed." He clears his throat. "The Katarajus are always training, but almost never deign to become actual agents. One of the Eaton siblings does intel out of the Monterey branch, but apart from her and Callum, none of the younger generations of the leading families have any real idea what it's like out there for Trust operatives."

"*You* do, my guy. That divide doesn't sound like a great formula for long-lasting success."

"Yeah. The situation with the families is going to be…difficult. It would be even without this rogue faction stuff going on."

"But the whole of the Trust was set up around *your* family, right? Don't the Abhiramnews get some significant sway?"

"We do. But for eight years we've been subject to rumors that we're not suitable to carry the legacy anymore. Longer back, really. When I wasn't Chosen, a fair amount of people blamed my mom."

For having a bastard, he doesn't say.

"A fair amount of people are complete pricks," Nate huffs, clearly hearing it anyway, squeezing Ravi's shoulder. "Man, these other families sound like assholes."

"There's definitely some in there. But mostly decent people too. No family got to join without proving themselves worthy at some point."

"So, how does a family join The Trust? Not in antiquity, but nowadays. Is there a sign-up sheet?"

"Thinking about adding the Corbins to the roster, Doc?"

"Oh God, no," Nate blurts fervently, then tries to backpedal. "Not that it wouldn't be, uh, an honor?"

Still smiling, Ravi waves a hand. "It's okay, I get it. I wasn't being serious."

Nate relaxes. "Not sure we'd be a great fit anyway. I mean, yeah, my family's going to love you, but I'm not super eager to have the whole 'monsters are real' talk with them just yet, you know?"

Ravi pushes up on his elbows to stare at Nate. "Wait. What did you say?"

Abruptly Nate freezes like a deer in the headlights, eyes wide. He runs a hand over his mouth, stubble rasping. Then he drops his shoulders with a sigh that straddles the line between resigned and determined.

"I said my family is going to love you."

Ravi keeps staring.

"Look, I'm not saying…you know, *now*. But…someday?" He locks eyes with Ravi and takes a deep breath, hand fisting in the sheets. "I would like that. If you met them. A lot."

Ravi cannot stop staring. "You…want me to meet your family?" That's hard enough to wrap his head around, but the real question is, "You want your family to meet *me*?"

Nate's nervous smile melts soft at the edges. "Well, of course, my guy, who wouldn't want to meet you? And my family is pretty cool. My sisters can be *a lot*, but you'd like them. You'll see."

Of course, Nate says. As if meeting the family weren't some outlandish, remarkable thing that Ravi had always assumed—had always *known*—was meant for other people. People who weren't him.

He'd learned early in life not to think about his future. Planning was for battles, to survive the next fight. What good was it to imagine what *could* be when his future had been thoroughly mapped out, his fate already written before he'd even been born?

Ravi had done it anyway, of course. One more small, invisible rebellion; like developing his aptitude for guns, or the way he'd dress, or drinking coffee instead of tea, or sneaking off the family estate to get a taste of what it would be like to be someone else for a few hours.

In his younger years, Ravi had never planned for something like this, never even imagined someone like

Nathaniel. His open optimism, his fearless honesty. Ravi's younger self would have dismissed the idea as far too unrealistic.

Of course, my guy.

"Am I?" he says, barely a whisper, heart a humming-bird.

"Yeah, they're easy to get along with. You'll—"

"No, not that. Am I...am I *your guy*?"

Nate's eyes go so wide that Ravi can see the whites all around the clear sky of his irises. A flush rises over his throat like the first blush of sunrise. Nate sucks in a breath before letting it out all in a rush.

"Asking the big questions today. Okay. Okay. I know this is new for you. *Us*." He gestures between them evocatively, then swallows with an audible click. "But it's not new for me. You need to know I'm not going to make any demands of you, Ravi. Ever. I like you a lot, but I'm your friend first. So, if this is just...convenient for you, just passing the time or whatever, I'll respect that." He licks his lips, though his gaze stays level. "But there's more on offer, if you want it."

Ravi looks at Nate. Really *looks*; at his apprehensive posture, the heavy pulse in his throat, the steel determination lying underneath the surface. The affable, amiable manner he wears is suddenly so obvious as another type of armor, just a different kind of wall than Ravi's own, that he's ashamed it took him this long to recognize it.

His own walls are a crumbling ruin around him. Taken down not by any siege attack or battering ram, but by the gentle erosion of friendship, kindness, and cactus.

"How long did you say is the average amount of time to get over a bad breakup? In that study you were talking about."

A glimmer of hope sparks in Nate's eyes, the whole of his face lighting up, so arrestingly beautiful that Ravi can't bring himself to look away. "Three months and eleven days."

Ravi offers a tentative smile, reaching out a hand. "Ask me again in a month."

Chapter Sixteen

HIS AUNT'S OFFICE is a panopticon of weapons, tapestries, and various curios. All four walls are covered in such an assortment of oddities that it's difficult to keep any attention fixed on the massive desk taking center stage in the room. It's a favored technique of hers to note where wandering eyes are drawn to. Something of a psychological profile, to see what visitors find most deserving of their attention.

Even knowing this, Ravi is not immune. While he waits, he stands before a mounted display of crossed blades. Two long talwars, curved and sleek, the swords well-worn but still regularly polished.

"Nirav's," Padme clips shortly, entering the room as silently as the smoke her voice resembles. Her hands are clasped behind her back as she strides up to him, adorned in a Persian-styled suit in dark sapphire blue, a long silver dupatta draped across one shoulder.

"Kind of you to find the time to meet. Sit. There is much to discuss." She sweeps past and takes her place behind the desk. "I suppose your betrothed had more pressing matters to attend to than the ceremonial unveiling of her existence to the organization dedicated to her service?"

Ravi lets the criticism roll off his back; it's barely even a stab, merely a testing slash of the blade through the air. "These were Uncle Nirav's?"

His aunt folds her hands together atop her desk. "Yes, yes. He used them in the field rather extensively for a time."

In Ravi's memories, his uncle had favored dual *kukris* or *katars*, weapons that let him get up close and personal, all the better to shield his sister's back. He must have wielded these before Ravi's time. He leans in for a closer look. "This here…" He sets a finger lightly aside a notch near the tip of the blade. "Hit bone, looks like."

She waves her hand peremptorily. "Hence why he retired them. Sit. Tea?"

He walks to the desk but doesn't take the low-slung, narrow seat across from her. To her clear indignation, he picks up one of her many polo trophies and turns it over in his hands. A golden statue of a woman astride a polo pony. The engraving reads *Ladies Cup Championship Winner* with a year dating back decades before Ravi's birth. Like the swords, it is well-polished.

He keeps his head down when he speaks, as if addressing the trophy. "I'll take coffee. I don't drink tea. Why didn't you tell me about the inter-branch rankings?"

Padme leans back in her plush chair, slanting a perfect brow. "You are referring to those little spreadsheets Intelligence mocks up to score the field agents? Of course you drink tea. It's the family Nilgiri."

He replaces her trophy, shifting it minutely until it's settled into its exact place. "Yes. I learned about it in Manhattan. Evidently, I'm the best agent by any measure. And I don't drink tea."

Padme snorts with derision, which Ravi expects, but the words that follow are decidedly a surprise. "Of course, you are the best. You're an Abhiramnew."

Though it sets him almost six inches below her, he finally takes a seat in the little chair, posture flawless. "You could have told me."

She sniffs in reproach. "Did another agent want you to sign their yearbook? I didn't realize you needed accolades to merely perform your job to expected standards. There is no reason to rest on your laurels simply because you are a decent enough shot. We should always strive to be better."

Ravi knows his aunt very, very well; likely better than anyone save her late husband. He's made a lifelong study of her every sniff, every micro-expression, the slightest change of her tone. She's gearing up for a lecture, likely one about responsibilities, one Ravi's been subjected to over a dozen times.

So, he parries. "How's Rivaan?"

His aunt's brows twitch at this breach in protocol. They haven't engaged in small talk in…maybe ever? "The same," she says.

"And your grandchildren? They're also well?"

Padme looks at him as if he's grown a second head. Her son Rivaan, over a decade older than Ravi, lives in New Delhi with his wife and their two children. They're not entrenched with the inner workings of The Trust, only peripherally involved in a financial and political capacity, which suits them just fine. Ravi hasn't seen his cousin in years. Visiting always makes him feel like he's living in a strange, foreign country with no concept of the language or customs. Ravi, the odd quiet cousin, always falling short of the family's expectations.

"They are," Padme finally responds. "Shall we also remark upon the weather? How did you find the traffic on the way here?" She drops her saccharine affectation and scowls. "If it suits you, agent, there's a great deal of work to be done and very little time to do it in. Let us speak plainly."

"It would be a rare novelty to have a frank discussion with you, Aunt."

She sniffs in scant amusement. "While you've been playing with your angel and your...*fiancée*, I've been keeping the old families from eating one another. Though admittedly, it wouldn't hurt the Katarajus to have a few bites taken off." She exhales, wearing her weariness and determination like fine jewelry. A few inky strands of her hair hang uncharacteristically free from her tight chignon, concealer barely visible underneath her eyes. "Of course, the seers have been less than useless. They used to pay for themselves with peace of mind, but I'm considering tossing them all out of their palatial suites and replacing them with a coin to flip, for all the help they have been." She taps her nails on the desk once, decisively. "First order of business. Is Harry pregnant yet?"

Ravi keeps himself carefully still. "No, ma'am. That's going to wait until after the wedding."

"Oh, is it? How fortunate that the forces of evil are polite enough to adhere to your family planning schedule. Please do not tell me you have been emotionally compromised by the angel. If you *must* continue your dalliance,

Miss McAllister seems to be a pragmatic sort, as long as you are discreet."

Ravi's ears burn. On the list of conversations he's never wanted to have with his aunt, this nears the top. But he couldn't ask for a better segue into the first and most daunting of the issues he wants to broach with her today. He steels himself.

"I am not involved with Val."

At least Padme also looks as if she'd rather gnaw off her own arm than talk about her nephew's romantic exploits. "Very well, if that affair is ended, then there is no issue."

A trickle of sweat rolls down Ravi's back. "I've never been involved with Val. Or any woman."

Padme's eyes narrow as she ripostes, "Ravi, if you are implying that your reticence to secure your legacy is because you are a virgin, that would stretch my credulity rather thin, I believe you'll find."

"No, ma'am." His skin goes cool and clammy, palms damp on his knees even through the wool suit. "I'm gay," he says out loud for the first time in his life.

The sky doesn't fall. The earth doesn't swallow him up. The only thing that happens is his aunt disengages the bout with a sniff of disdain and a roll of her eyes.

"I don't see the point to this ploy, nephew, but I'm not amused."

He doesn't answer, letting his walls drop low enough for her to plainly see his nervousness, his trepidation, his sincerity.

Her expression goes abruptly blank. "Nonsense. I would know."

"With all due respect, *Mausi*"—he's rarely called her that since he was a child, *mother's sister*—"you don't know a single real thing about me."

"Ridiculous," she claims, her shoulders set like a hawk poised to dive. "I raised you."

"You hired people to raise me. But let's say you're right, that you know me. What's my favorite color?"

As if struck, Padme reels back. "This is absurd, Ravi. You are not—"

"Yellow. Like marigolds. What am I allergic to?"

"Gluten," she snaps with triumph.

"Cats. Gluten is a mild intolerance."

"I knew that," she counters with a glare. "None of that is of any consequence. Are you seriously griping that you weren't paid enough attention as a child? You had the best training available from the most skilled warriors and tacticians that could be bought, and you're upset I don't know your favorite color?"

"I was a child. It would have been nice to be asked."

"And what would be the point?" She slams a fist down

onto the desk, eyes flashing. Ravi jerks back, pulse kicking fast. Padme shuts her eyes and composes herself. When she opens them, she doesn't look at Ravi. Instead, her gaze is drawn to her little brother's battle-worn *talwars* on the wall. "Would it have been *advantageous* to get to know you? A child I was raising to die?"

Breath snags in Ravi's lungs.

Padme lifts her chin with the cool poise usually reserved for statues of *ranis* and freedom fighters. "But then Tanvi died, and the mantle passed you by. Not slated for an early grave, after all. Turns out you take after me; unworthy of Durga's favor, but good enough to do the grunt work. The inglorious work. After that day, my sole priority has been keeping you alive while not letting your training go to waste. A delicate balance, I'm sure you'll agree.

"So," she says, smoothing her sleeves. "Yellow. Cats. Homosexual." Padme regards Ravi in inscrutable silence long enough for him to start mentally mapping the exits. "I am impressed you've managed to mislead me for this long, nephew. Congratulations. You must be very proud of yourself."

It's a far better reception than Ravi imagined he'd get. He'd half expected disgust or being outright disowned. But Abhiramnews are nothing if not adaptable, and like it or not, his aunt can't scrape up another heir.

"Years of intensive training and centuries of selective breeding. I was bound to get something right eventually."

Padme smiles sharply. "This does illuminate matters with that French chronomancer."

He can't help it: he flinches.

"Ah," she says with cold satisfaction, the tap of her fingers like securing the final piece of a puzzle in place. "And the unsatisfactory level of detail in your reports, as well. Are you still seeing him?"

"*No.*" Ravi's shoulders hunch, nausea draining a pallor to his cheeks. "They were... We're not..." He should have been prepared for this, for the tumult of emotion her interrogation would stir up. Maybe he's raw from spilling his most deeply held secret, from peeling back his armor to let her have a glimpse of who he is underneath. He runs a hand over his face, shakily trying to brick up his defenses.

She always could read him if he wasn't careful, as easily as she could cut a page out of a book. Padme's spine goes stiff, her eyes as cold and focused as a steel blade. "He—*they*—hurt you. I remember quite well how willing they were to kill me, Ravi. One doesn't easily forget hands at your throat."

"I... That was *before*...and also *after*—"

She holds up a hand, curbing the disordered tumble of his words, her expression a storm cloud. "Before they knew you, but after you knew them?"

He swallows. "Yes."

"How interesting." Padme clips each syllable dangerously short.

"You *can't*," he rasps desperately. "You can't do anything to them. If you do, they will—"

"Yes, yes, the whole future-torture scenario. Which until this very moment I found patently absurd." Padme's mouth twists unpleasantly. "Why would I resort to such draconian methods when there are far more effective ways to secure the loyalty of a powerful mage? But I see I have a reason to be vindictive after all." She gestures a hand toward Ravi, her seething anger flashing at the surface for just a moment.

Her quiet fury is more comforting than Ravi would have expected it to be. For the first time, it occurs to him to wonder who he got his protective tendencies from. It certainly wasn't Tanvi. "Aunt…"

Exhaling harshly, she waves the hand as if shooing away an insect. "Your concern is unnecessary. After our last discussion, I have already taken steps to ensure that the chronomage will not be taken captive."

"You…have?"

"Yes," she says icily, annoyed at having to repeat herself. "I've devised a strategy I think you'll agree will work."

"What did you—wait, more importantly, *why*? You said I was behaving like a child. Not willing to get my hands dirty."

"Yes, your idealism is no doubt charming," Padme drawls, "but while we may strive for ideals, we have to live in reality. Of course, there are the rare times of dire need when the harsher methods are necessary. We're on a holy mission to save the world from monsters, Ravi. We've routed countless apocalypses. True good is willing to sacrifice a bit of its own morality if those actions benefit the greater good. If a little light waterboarding is all that prevents the end of the world, I say get a bucket."

Ravi stares at his aunt, belly roiling.

Padme rolls her eyes. "*That being said*, The Trust as it exists now does not employ torture by any definition, Ravi. I'm sure you're imagining bamboo shoots and iron maidens, or whatever nonsense you have seen on television. The truth is physical and psychological abuse simply isn't effective. While we do have methods for dealing with dangerous individuals, I can say definitively that whatever future the chronomage hails from, if those methods can be labeled as outright torture, then that is not The Trust that I run."

She laces her hands together. "Seers can only do so much. I do not know the future. It's possible that the current course of things can become so thoroughly derailed to the point where The Trust of the future is unrecognizable from what it is now. Perhaps a different Director, a different family running the show? A different me, even, one who would allow herself to be relegated to wet works." She utters the words with scathing disdain, the way some field agents talk of being assigned to archives. "Or, and I believe this option to be even more likely, the chronomancer was exaggerating the severity of their capture." She shrugs. "Perhaps we shall never know."

Ravi eyes her for a long moment, detecting no signs of falsehood. "What's this strategy you've devised?"

"I've foregone the usual approval process and directly appointed you as the next Director of The Trust. The others will scream nepotism, but they were always going to complain of that regardless, when I retired. Consider the lack of consortium hearings you would have otherwise had to attend a gift to ease the transition."

Ravi stares at her.

She continues mildly, "Clearly you have strong feelings about several issues you think I have neglected to address. If you can find a better way forward without using the same measures I have had to, then I congratulate you on your resourcefulness. And if not, well." She gives him a thin, scalpel smile. "Then it will be on you to live with the consequences."

Forcing him to make any ugly decisions for himself instead of just following the path already laid out. A double-edged test. Reassuringly familiar.

The realization hits Ravi hard. Cayenne wouldn't be tortured by The Trust, not if Ravi was in charge of it. A huge weight lifts from his shoulders, the relief dizzying. But…what about paradox? If he's changed his future, then his past should have been changed too. Or perhaps this is what Cayenne had always meant when they told him that their past couldn't be changed. Being tethered to the time-line. Maybe the past could be changed, but what did it matter if the memories remained?

Still. "I'm your successor?"

With a disbelieving cluck of her tongue, Padme throws up her hands in an unusually demonstrative show of frustration. "I would have thought that by now this should be blindingly obvious. It was *always* my plan to put The Trust in your hands, from the moment it was clear you weren't to be the next Chosen."

"I…I didn't know."

"Of course not, I've been intentionally veiling it from you."

"Why?" he snaps. Why would she choose the nephew who had never measured up to take her place? The cause of her greatest disappointments?

Padme's dark gaze doesn't waver. "You were always an obedient child. Eager to please. Which is ideal in a Chosen"—Harry being described as "obedient" makes Ravi stifle a snort—"but a Director has to make difficult choices. Has to be willing to stand firm against the consortium, if need be. To disagree with the other families despite the grief it may cause you. To mete out unpopular decisions down to the branches. You have always dutifully followed any orders I set. Until recently, I didn't think you had any real spine to you off the battlefield whatsoever."

Honestly, it's one of the better compliments she's ever paid him. Tendons tense in Ravi's jaw. "Is that why you sent me off to Israel? So I'd grow a backbone?"

Her stern expression wavers like a mirage over sand. "That... No."

In short, economical motions Padme rises from her chair, goes to the cabinet, and pours herself a neat whisky. She dips her finger into the liquor and flicks a drop over her shoulder in an archaic ritual offering to their ancestors. "Would you like one? Doubtless you've partaken before, since you don't appear to be overly concerned with rules and customs."

"I'll take a brandy, if you have one."

"Of course, I do." Padme hands him a cut glass snifter and returns to her seat. "It was supposed to be a surprise.

The sniper training. You'd asked for more focus on your marksmanship. Your instructors agreed, so arrangements were made with our contacts in Mossad well before my siblings went on that mission to Guangzhou." She pauses to sip her whisky. "Matters changed when the urumi was lost."

Feelings he'd thought long buried rise, climbing up fierce and hot into his throat. Grief and anger and shame, welling up like old blood from a picked scab. "Ten months, Aunt. I was seventeen, my mother was dead, the entire course of my life had been derailed, and I was there alone for *ten months*. Barely a week after the funeral and you shipped me off to live with strangers. I didn't hear a word from you for *nearly a year*." Ravi takes a measured breath, smoothing a hand over his close-cropped beard in an attempt to keep a scrap of his dignity intact, when all he wants to do is slam his hand down and demand that she give him a satisfactory answer.

"When you finally did call, it was to assign me to a field post in London with two days to pack my bags. That was it. That's all you had for me? After *abandoning* me?"

Padme stares into her glass as if it were a crystal ball. When she eventually speaks, her voice is hollow. "Sometimes looking at you is like a dagger in my heart. To be faced with that failure all over again."

This time he doesn't even try to hide his pained flinch. He would have preferred it if she'd stabbed him with one of the blades adorning the wall. "You exiled me so you wouldn't have to be reminded of my failure."

She looks up with an irritated sniff. "Not *yours*, Ravi. Mine." Padme wraps her fingers around the tumbler, tracing the grooved edges of the design. "Durga found me wanting, I've long come to grips with that. But for Her to pass you by as well? Unthinkable. What better path could there possibly be for you? Who better to carry the urumi?" She puts the glass to her lips and takes a long pull, nearly draining the liquor in one go. "I raised you to be hard. Resilient. To be self-sufficient. To be *better* than the Chosen before you. I kept you at arm's length, honed you sharp, didn't learn your favorite color, and for what? For no reason at all, as it turned out."

Avoiding his gaze, Padme crosses her arms loosely at the elbows, her head tipped back against her chair. Her gunpowder voice deepens even further as if the words are forcibly dragged from her throat by barbed hooks. "Perhaps it was…ill done of me."

It's the most apology he's ever witnessed her give anyone before.

Strangely, unbelievably, Ravi feels better.

His aunt sets the glass aside and slides open a drawer.

"But mortals plan and the gods laugh. So. Let us talk Director to Director." With some difficulty, she pulls up a thick stack of bulging folders onto the desk and tosses him a file.

He catches it. "What's this?"

"You have already been to the South Asian Ossuary. There are five more like it around the globe. All the information is there." She slaps down another stack of files. "These are all the black sites in operation. They function to detain dangerous entities until trials can be held." More files. "Here's a précis on the trials; and here's a summary of what holdings and responsibilities each of the families in the consortium maintains, and here's a list of mundane law enforcement, hospitals, and other such institutions we regularly work with worldwide. Anything else you'd like to see?" Her voice is crisp, brows raised.

Ravi realizes he's looking at the abundance of information the way a kid might look at a stack of presents. "I… This is…"

"A good start, I'm sure you'll agree. The tip of the iceberg. Once you are wed, you'll have access to even more. Give it a thorough look. If you think you can improve upon all your predecessors' collective centuries of experience, do let me know, nephew. *Apni khichdi khud pakaana.*" A turn of phrase he's never heard from her before; *cook your own porridge.* Go your own way.

Despite her sarcastic tone, this is truly meant as a gift. "Thank you, Aunt."

"Yes, well. Thank you for sharing some secrets of your own." Hesitantly at first, then with increasing confidence, she reaches over and pats his hand. "I am not insensible to how…difficult it must have been. But you are obviously discreet, which is as it should be. To be perfectly frank, I would not take the news as well as I am if you were not marrying Miss McAllister and securing the Abhiramnew legacy despite your predilections." Her gaze sharpens, hands again folded before her. "Which you are, to be clear?"

He braces himself. The other vital issue he'd been planning on unveiling. The most important. "Only on one condition."

"*Condition*? There are no conditions. This is not a negotiation."

Ravi keeps his head held high. "I have served The Trust to the best of my abilities—and they are considerable abilities—without faltering. I have never once strayed in my devotion to the cause we serve, and I have never asked you for anything, not once. But there is a condition, and it is not negotiable." He plants his hands flat on her desk. "*No more child soldiers.*"

"Child sol— Is that how you see it?"

"Frame it however you like. But my children, and their

children, and their children's children will *not* be subject to the methods that you and I were both raised with. I'm going to be the last."

She stares at him for a protracted moment, expressionless. "Ravi. Our line is unique. Our mandate, divine. The demands placed upon us are unyielding. Coddling the future Chosen puts the entire world in jeopardy."

He runs a finger along the edge of the brandy snifter. "You say 'our line,' but it's mine really, isn't it?"

Her eyes freeze over as he strikes a palpable hit, but Ravi strides ahead regardless. This is about the future of his family. In this, he's fearless.

"The line of succession is direct. An unbroken chain. From the very first Chosen all the way to Tanvi, through me, and to the next. Even when there's been the rare gap generation, it's only ever gone through the Chosen's children. Not siblings. Not cousins. Your grandchildren will never be Chosen. Mine will." Ravi holds her gaze, unwavering. "I used to think that made me chattel. But it makes me valuable, doesn't it?"

His aunt's lip curls. "It is true you have a bargaining chip I cannot match. But you are being willfully naive. We are Abhiramnews. We've been fighting the forces of darkness long before any of the other families began to meddle. It was a task given to us, nephew, and yes, it calls for sacrifice."

"Sacrifice is a concept I am intimately familiar with, Aunt, I don't need you to explain it. I will *not* bring children into the world only to take all their choices away from them."

"You are barely twenty-five, practically a child your-self. You've hardly begun to understand the kind of sacri-fices that will be required of you. The kind I've had to make over the years."

"I see. I'm a child when I disagree with you, but old enough to fight in the field? Getting shot, mauled, bitten, scarred." He places a hand over his solar plexus, over the old marks left by his uncle's *bagh nakh*. "Old enough to be married off and *bred*?"

Padme looks away, conceding another hit. "Touché," she mutters. "What are your conditions, exactly?"

"No serious combat training until they are Chosen or they turn eighteen. Whichever comes first. They will have no knowledge of their destiny until it becomes necessary for them to know it. And they go to school."

He can give them that. A normal life. There's no way to avoid teaching them about the supernatural entirely, in the interests of safety, but Ravi can ensure that any child of his won't be alone in it. That the legacy he'll leave them will be something they can be proud of.

Padme barks out a short laugh. "I don't even know where to start with this lunacy. Why would you be so eager to reject the traditions that have worked for—let me remind you, nephew—over a thousand years?"

"Because it's a mistake!" He's never raised his voice to his aunt before. Her eyes widen. "Isolated people are weak. Vulnerable. You can prepare someone their whole life for battle, to face down any sort of evil. But if they feel alone, they're easy prey for the first person who comes along with a smile and a promise."

Blood drains from Padme's face, and she looks at Ravi like she's seeing him for the first time, a small spark of that fierce protectiveness in her eyes. He barrels on ahead, not wanting to hear any questions, needing to stay on task. He's good at that; doing the job in front of him. And this is important, far more important than himself.

"Any child I have is going to be surrounded by people who support them. Love them. And they'll be stronger for it. They'll fight that much harder. Saving the world is one thing, that's a duty. Saving what you love though? That's a need." Ravi stands up to lean his hands on his aunt's desk. "And they won't be told the cruel truth that you and I lived with, that we were fated for glory and righteousness and an early death. How is a child supposed to live with that burden? And if they're never Chosen? Then they won't suffer the knowledge that they weren't good enough for it."

He takes a handful of long, even breaths. "We have an international agency of the best monster-hunters on the planet at our beck and call. If they can't protect, support, and defend the Chosen, why do we even have them?"

As he speaks, Padme's face shifts from withering scorn into true thoughtfulness. "That may be the most words I have ever heard you speak at once."

He snorts and takes a fortifying gulp of brandy.

"That's a forty-year-old *eau*-de-vie you are mangling." His aunt crosses her arms under her chest. "The Chosen is in agreement with you?"

He nods curtly.

"Hm." She tips her head back again, calculating. "You raise a compelling argument. One I'd be willing to discuss more fully when it becomes relevant. But this whole issue is a moot point if The Trust collapses in on itself. The in-fighting has gotten to a critical point. Rumors abound that the only possible way the Eatons and the Bhagavatis could have been targeted was from another family. And the old alliances only work if we, as an organization, live up to our name."

"Do you have an idea who's behind it?"

Padme's mouth twists up as if her answer tastes foul. "None. Someone very comfortable moving from the shadows. Which, unfortunately, does not implicate either the Prestons or the Katarajus, much as I'd be delighted to winnow them out. Though both families take every opportunity to question my authority, they are unfailingly brash and outspoken about it."

Ravi perches on her desk and mirrors her pose, arms across his chest. "I think we can expect an attack on the Gala."

"Based on what evidence?"

"No evidence," he admits. "Based on…suspicions. A hunch."

To his surprise, she doesn't reject his statement out of hand. She knits her brow, tapping her fingernails. "A hunch. How likely do you consider this eventuality?"

"Pretty likely. It will be a large gathering of high-level Trust personages all in one place." He presses his lips together and forges ahead. "I think someone or possibly a group of someones are colluding with the chronomancer to take us down from within. And if I were them, that's when I'd wait to strike."

Padme's expression goes flat. "Perhaps you should keep that possibility in mind next time you carry on an affair with one of the most dangerous entities alive?" Then she sighs, shoulders sinking. "In your defense, it is not as if I ever adequately prepared you for…silk work. Attacks of the…the heart." She clears her throat and ascends to her feet in an elegant rise. "Very well. We will move up the timetable and set up extra defenses. The Gala will take place next week. I trust you will procure something suitable for your betrothed to wear, since we will have to forgo some of the usual spectacle."

Ravi automatically stands with her. "Next week? I… Yes, I can do that. The whole team will be attending."

"Yes, I had assumed, considering how adamantly Miss McAllister laid claim to all of you at the airport. Every precaution will be taken to forestall any moves against us, now we know to expect them. *Jiski lathi uski bhains,*" she says with satisfaction. *Who has the stick has the buffalo.* Her expression flickers, then firms. "Harry knows?"

"About my suspicions?"

"About your orientation, obviously."

"Oh. Right. Yes. She knows."

"A common gumshoe figures it out before a seasoned spymaster. Embarrassing."

"To be fair," Ravi offers with a slight smile, "I've been intentionally veiling it from you."

Padme barks a laugh. "There's an English idiom about acorns and trees that might be applicable here." She brushes his shoulder with her fingertips. "I would like to…talk, sometime. Not for business. To…correct the gaps in my knowledge. If you wouldn't find such a thing too disagreeable." She fixes her attention on adjusting the lay of her dupatta, though it looks perfect to his eyes. "Perhaps over coffee. Not tea."

"I think I'd like that very much, *Mausi*." Ravi pauses, then bends at the waist to brush her feet with his hands. She stiffens in surprise. Another custom they haven't engaged in for many years. She relaxes and touches the top of his head, her hand briefly resting in his hair.

After he rises, she smiles so swiftly that if Ravi had blinked, he would have missed it entirely. "So would I, *bhanja*."

Chapter Seventeen

"I'M GOING TO throw up." Harry enunciates each syllable as she yanks at her metallic satin shirt, trying to pull the edges closed. Since it's so deeply cut that her décolletage is displayed right down to the navel, her attempts are very much in vain. "This was a bad idea. Why didn't I just wear a stupid fucking dress? Why did I listen to you and go rogue? I just had to pick this 'Fuck off, I'm the Chosen and I'll wear a sexy lady-suit if I want to' thing? Fuck, I can't remember a single fucking word of Hindi, what the *fuck* have I been doing?"

"You're not going to throw up, and you don't have to speak any Hindi." Ravi steps up and adjusts the flowing strip of necktie under her golden collar. "And you look great. Stop freaking out."

In fact, Harry looks like a model, the outfit she chose evoking the suggestion of a classic suit while delivering a louche, undone air of ease and confidence. The wet look black of her jacket glimmers in the light, and her dark hair is clipped back sleek over one ear while the rest piles over the other side in loose waves that brush her shoulder.

"Who's freaking out?" Harry bats his hands away. "What's to freak out about? Just some white trash snapping up both the favor of The Trust's patron goddess *and* their most eligible bachelor slash heir apparent in one night! It's all very cool and chill and in no way is Durga going to strike me dead with fucking lightning or something the second I step in there." The whites of her eyes widen around blue-green irises, voice edging into a high, panicked squeak.

Ravi places both hands on her shoulders. "*McAllister.* Stand up straight. Shoulders back. Head high. Pretend like you own the place. Don't let them see they get to you."

Harry closes her eyes and takes a breath. She calms, nodding once, spine lengthening. "Yeah. Okay. You're right. Is that how you get through all these formal things?"

Ravi smiles ruefully. "Pretty much. Sometimes I'd pick a stretch of wallpaper and try to camouflage into it. Not going to be an option tonight."

"Yeah. Yeah. Look. Rav." Harry adjusts her ring, nibbles her bottom lip, then says in a rush, "I have no idea what I'm doing, I'm a complete disaster, this whole thing is a huge mistake—"

"Harry…"

She grabs his wrists, shaking her head insistently. "No, look, it's absolutely absurd that I'm some magical Chosen warrior thing, it's somebody's idea of a prank or some shit, and Durga's probably furious with my pasty ass, and—"

"*Harry*. You're not a mistake."

She goes still, her eyes snapping to his.

"It's not absurd. You're a natural leader. Look…I've been raised since birth to be in your place."

"I know, dude, you think that doesn't tear me up?"

"No," he cuts in quickly, "that's not what I'm saying. What I'm saying is, I would follow you anywhere you lead, Harry." Her lips part as she stares up at him. "*I* think you're good enough to be in that place. Who would know better? Durga doesn't Choose wrong."

A hollow laugh. "I don't believe that."

"Okay, then *I* don't choose wrong." He smiles crookedly. "This is my world, my legacy, my family's sword, and I think you should have it." Cayenne stole the urumi away from Ravi's bloodline and hid it far away in the future, but even so, despite the vast distance of time, it still came to

Harry. Someone pretty important must think she's right for the job. "I have faith in you. I've got your back, Harry."

Harry stares at him. She sniffs hard and grabs Ravi in a full, clinging hug. "I'm not great at letting people into my personal space," she mutters into his shoulder.

"Me neither," he says, linking his hands around her back.

"But we're doing this anyway."

An amused huff. "Yes, we are." Ravi hates these formal events worse than she does, hates being the center of attention. Knowing that his best friend is going to be there beside him is a huge relief.

Her body swells in his arms with a deep, bolstering breath. "Okay. Okay. We can do this. Fuck, I need a drink. Tell me I don't need a drink."

"You don't need a drink. I'm going to be with you the whole time. The whole team is with you. A powerful witch, a brilliant professor, and your own personal guardian angel. We got this."

He wishes the rest of the team were here now, but they'll be inside the party awaiting the Chosen's entrance as she sweeps in, consort on her arm. McAllister's monster-fighting crew, forged in the fires of many a battle, now facing down their greatest challenge yet: black-tie required.

"Yeah. I know." Harry gently pulls away. "I might still

throw up though."

She *is* a little paler than usual. "Go splash some water on your face."

"But my smokey eye with the cut crease," she grumbles, nevertheless heading toward the bathroom, shooting a resolute smile over her shoulder.

He smiles back until she disappears around the corner, then goes to the living room to wait. The empty, sumptuous suite is quiet enough that he can hear the rising wind brushing the leaves of the potted plants outside against the balcony doors.

As Ravi waits, he smooths the lay of his jacket, likewise second-guessing his sartorial choices now there's no going back. He'd chosen the suit both to compliment the feminine cut of Harry's, and to distinguish himself from all the other standard black tuxedos that would be at the Gala. His tuxedo is one in name only, boasting bolder lines and a mandarin collar with gold embellishments capping the corners. Contrasting gold trim angles across the shoulders to emphasize the breadth of his torso. Even his shoes have gold-capped toes. Standing together, the pair of them are going to look sensational.

"Tactical pageantry," as Harry had put it, before giving him a pair of tiger-head cufflinks. "Symbols are important."

The wind picks up, the gathering cloud cover sketching

the Atlanta skyline in obsidian. Absently wondering if it will rain, Ravi glances out beyond the glass doors only to see the unexpected red glow of a lit cigarette. Fair skin brightens against the stark night sky as Cayenne takes a long drag.

Ravi's heart stops. Frozen in place, he watches them warily. His hand flexes on instinct toward his absent firearm; the suit is too well-fitted for a gun. But Cayenne doesn't make any other moves, seemingly satisfied with having arranged themself into a dramatic tableau for him to find.

He sets his jaw and joins Cayenne on the balcony. They barely turn from their relaxed lean on the railing as he slides the door shut behind him. The scent of ozone is thick, the air charged with lightning.

"*Bonsoir, mon chéri.*" Cayenne turns back to the city and takes another drag of the cigarette.

"You smoke now?"

Cayenne purrs a silky laugh, elbows bracing back against the railing in a long, insouciant lean. "Only when I'm in a time period where it would be suspicious to *not* be smoking, my sweet." They flick ash over the edge to be carried away on the restive breeze. "Before you were born, darling. But you have to admit, the look of it creates quite a film noir ambiance, does it not?"

Ravi rests his arms on the railing, carefully staying out of easy reach. "What do you want, Cayenne?"

They snort, something between a laugh and a sob. "The question I have lived my life by." They contemplate the cigarette between their fingers before dropping it off the edge, eyes following the path of the glowing cherry as it falls.

Ravi in turn watches them, the way someone expecting sharks watches dark water. "That could fall on someone," he says mildly.

"It hardly matters now, does it?" Cayenne presses the heels of their palms into their eye sockets. They drop their hands and turn to him, green eyes plaintive with urgency. "Don't go through with this, Ravi. You don't have to go in there."

"What happened the last time we saw each other?"

Cayenne grins in a sudden bright flash. "Ah, *clever*, my love. You want to know how *linear* my narrative is, compared to yours? You think I should be angrier about you luring me into your ineffective little trap, *oui?*"

That *is* what Ravi had been thinking; he'd thought maybe this was a Cayenne who'd skipped ahead from the path, unaware of Ravi's attempted betrayal. Their calm, almost resigned demeanor makes no sense otherwise.

"Aren't you?"

They flap a dismissive hand. "No, *mon tigre.* I am many

things, but not a hypocrite." They make a little face, eyes rolling. "Okay, yes, a hypocrite too, but *in this case*, I can't complain too much. No matter what else I do, I'm still the same selfish asshole who caused the grisly deaths of your two closest guardians even when I had the chance to undo it. A bit of payback is honestly *reassuring*. I don't think I'll ever manage to drag you down to my level, but it *is* nice to know that heroic luster of yours can get a *little* tarnished."

Cayenne pushes themself upright and holds out a beseeching hand. "Don't go in there. You don't have to go through with this farce. Come away with me, Ravi."

"Cayenne…"

"*I'm doing you a favor!*" they yell, hands raised. The line of their posture goes tense, their movements jerky. Ravi tenses, adrenaline tart on his tongue, readying for an attack. "Are you so fucking *proud* that you can't… *Ugh*, this is so *typical*. You're making *so much* more work for me." They push a hand into their hair. "Look. I'm sorry. But this…this party, this engagement, it's… *Don't go.*"

Ravi moves into reach, standing with his feet firmly planted under him. A challenge. "Why? Tell me what's going to happen in there."

"Nothing at all, darling, if everything goes to plan. Truly. Some dancing, perhaps." A slow, sultry smirk spreads as Cayenne slides an appraising look up and down

Ravi's frame. "This is quite the ensemble. Flashier than I'd expected. *J'adore, tu êtes délicieuse.*"

"Cayenne…"

They bite their lip so hard it goes white. "Why can't you see that The Trust is broken?" they whisper, like they're continuing a conversation Ravi can't remember having. "Why can't I *ever* make you see that, no matter how many times I try?"

They're rewinding him. The knowledge makes him feel sick. Helpless. Bound and unarmed. Nevertheless, he keeps his eyes locked on theirs. "You liked me best when I was broken."

A breath punches its way out of Cayenne, and they sag against the balcony railing. "*Merde.* Mark that down for yet another thing I should have never told you. It is a *long* list."

Unnervingly candid, for Cayenne. Like they don't think anything they say is going to matter.

"I'm not going with you. I have to do this. I *want* to."

"I know, Ravi." They suck in a shuddering breath, setting their shoulders as if bracing for a fall. "I just want you to be happy. That's what I've always wanted."

Ravi remembers the soft play of their hair through his hands, ardent words brushing his lips as they murmured praise and adoration into him. All those relived days the pair of them spent together in a tumult of wild, reckless freedom. The nights Ravi spent yearning for them after. And he remembers the day it all came crashing down.

Despite everything, Ravi doesn't doubt that they want him to be happy. One of the few truths Cayenne has always woven into their patchwork of lies. He offers softly, "If that's really what you want…I think I can be. Happy."

"Without me." Cayenne's voice bristles like dry stalks on barren fields. They sink down until their chin rests on arms folded over the railing's edge. "That's not going to work for me, my beloved. You're *it*. The one thing in my life I've ever wanted to keep. The only thing I haven't run away from, that I haven't left a smoking ruin. The only person who I've ever let know me. *C'est que je n'ai jamais aimé avant, et que je n'aimerai plus jamais.* I can't…I can't," they croak, the angry wind whipping their hair across their brow. A distant roll of thunder haunts the horizon.

Ravi licks his lips. "Please don't take everything I've worked for away from me."

"Ravi…"

"It's not just me you'll be affecting. It's…it's the team, and so many more people beyond counting. I'm going to be the next Director. I can do so much good there, Cay. Changing that isn't just taking it away from me, it's taking it away from the *whole world*."

Cayenne's eyes harden, brittle as flint. They reach for

him, and Ravi allows it, fearing they're on the knife's edge of doing something irreversible, going as still as he would before a rearing cobra as Cayenne strokes along the arch of Ravi's cheek.

"The whole world can burn. We'll build something better from the ashes. You *have* to trust me, Ravi. I know I've given you no reason to do so. But next time, I will." They let their hand drop limply to their side with a bright, bleak smile, terrible with self-loathing. "I'm a chronomancer, darling, which means I get to make the same mistakes *over* and *over* again and never have to learn a thing." They take a step back from him, lightning briefly shrouding them in white. "Enjoy the Gala, *mon amour*. Be happy, tonight." Their tattoo flashes and they're gone.

Harry finds him out there. How long after, he's not sure.

"Hey, there you are. Getting some fresh air?"

Ravi continues staring out into the night. "Just talked to Cayenne."

Harry groans, unknowingly taking the place Cayenne had just been occupying. She steps up onto the bottom rung and leans way over the railing, looking down the many stories without any evidence of discomfort. "Oof, that sucks. You need a magical restraining order. You good?"

"Good is such a relative term."

She joins him in a brief, biting laugh. "Ain't that the truth. They say anything useful? My 'visions' have been a muddled mess. We got a clue what kind of hell they're going to drop on us tonight?"

"Again, useful is relative," he sighs, finger-combing his windswept hair back into place. "They made it sound like they're not going to do anything. They said to enjoy the Gala. Have a dance."

Gears turn behind Harry's eyes. "How kind of them. Giving us a calm before the storm?"

"Maybe."

"Maybe we'll be lucky and our mysterious benefactor will keep any shenanigans at bay."

Ravi snorts. "I'm going to be on high alert for any attacks anyway."

Harry smirks as a loud peal of thunder cracks overhead, the air heavy with the promise of downpour.

"Speaking of storms," he adds, offering his arm. Harry lays her hand on it, the fiery pearl of her engagement ring prominent on her slim hand. "Ready?"

She lifts her chin. "Let's make some history."

*

ONCE IN THE penthouse elevator, Harry takes out the enchanted key Padme had given her and inspects it closely.

"It's indicative of how weird my life has gotten that I'm actually disappointed this magic key looks so normal." Without waiting for a response, she inserts the key and turns it. The elevator shifts, and a strange but brief disorientation washes over them, tingling from scalp to toes as the elevator begins to rise. "I guess going up when we're already at the penthouse is kind of cool," Harry concedes. "Hey. Rav."

"Yeah?"

"Thanks. For back there. Pretty good pep talk."

"That's what generals are for."

"I got your back too, you know that?"

"I know." He hesitates, then leans in to give her a quick kiss on the cheek.

Harry punches him lightly in the shoulder. "Save it for the wedding night, stud." They both try and fail to stifle their laughter as the elevator doors slide open.

"Ah, hark, our worries were unwarranted, mine friends! They are in excellent spirits," Constance remarks to Nate and Val. Constance is adorned in uncharacteristically witchy fashion, hugged by a midnight dress, iridescent black feathers trailing up over the high collar, contrasting with a plunging neckline that shows off her significant assets. Gilded ribbons weave through her upswept hair, and she's traded in her usual leather satchel for a tiny golden handbag. When she moves, Ravi spots her sturdy boots peeking from under the hem of her gown.

"*Ayyyy*, there's my squad!" Harry steps out, arms wide. "Thought you were supposed to be in there already?"

"Ravi's aunt suggested we trail in after you," Val says, muscular arms crossed over her chest. Ash-white hair braided up into a crown, she wears gold-hued sunglasses and a slinky, black-sequined strapless number with a thin golden hem tracing the slit up to the thigh. Stiletto heels adding to her already imposing height, Val looks literally dressed to kill.

"Hell, yeah, an entourage," Harry exclaims, exuding confidence and ease. If Ravi hadn't been privileged to witness her earlier uncertainty with his own eyes, he would have doubted she'd ever experienced a moment of trepidation in her life. "I've always wanted one of those."

"Can I just say"—Nate gives Harry and Ravi an appreciative sweep of his eyes—"that you both look incredible?" He follows this with a wink aimed solely for Ravi to catch.

He's one to talk. The way Nate fills out a fitted tuxedo makes Ravi's brain completely short out. All broad shoulders, narrow waist, and charming smile, Nate wouldn't be out of place in a Hollywood movie, especially with the gold accents on his bow tie and pocket square. Ravi admires him so openly that Nate flushes red, looking away with a pleased cough into his fist.

"That's us! Your prom royalty." Harry sketches a mocking bow. "We all clean up pretty good."

"A witch-hunter's ball." Constance sets her hands on her hips, features bright with mingled nerves and excitement. "And bold as brass, we are just going to swan into the thick of it."

"Fear not, mistress! I shall guard thee most attentively, lest any of yon knaves think to accost thee." The ringing, strident voice seems to emerge out of nowhere. Constance sheepishly twists her hands in front of her, smiling innocence.

Harry presses her knuckles hard into her lips, then removes them just long enough to say, "You brought Griswold."

"I've made him invisible," Constance answers with practiced breeziness, the hem of her dress fluttering as an unseen shape presses against it. "Mine familiar is most canny and shall not be underfoot. No harm done!"

Harry taps her foot a couple of times, then throws up her hands in an expansive shrug. "An invisible talking cat is literally the least of my worries tonight. Knock yourself out, Griz."

A faint, pleased purr emits from near Constance's feet.

Ravi rolls his head side to side as if loosening up before a fight. "Val, you've got a lock on our weapons cache?" If the situation gets out of hand, Val alone will be able to arm the team with a quick teleport out and back.

"I do. What form do we expect tonight's threat will take?"

Using the intel he'd received from his aunt along with his own experiences, Ravi already briefed everyone on the basics, marking all the attendant families and the handful of Branch Directors high up enough to get an invite into The Trust's inner workings. "New intel says that there might not be any threats," he says, his doubt audible. "Apart from the standard, run-of-the-mill, feeding frenzy of sharks that is high society."

"Aw," Nate mock-pouts. "No fun monster fights. Just *hors d'oeuvres* and awkward mingling. Sorry, Val."

"Regardless, we should remain vigilant."

Harry nods emphatically. "Oh, *yeah*, my dudes, obviously. I want everyone on highest alert. And be polite to these folks, but don't be *too* polite. We're making a statement here. New sheriff in town." She jerks both thumbs back at herself with a cocky grin. "Let's hobnob and mingle but keep an eye on one another's backs. We're trying to suss out who's got designs on snatching the reins away from Ravi's fam. Eyes peeled for anything fishy."

"There will be fish?" Griswold pipes up.

Constance sets both hands to the sides of her intricate

updo as if worried it might topple over. "My niece, do you wish a dramatic entrance? I believe I can assist in that regard."

"Hell yeah, do it, doll." Harry links her arm through Ravi's and heads toward the double doors. "Everyone ready to rock and roll?"

Ravi looks around at Nate, hoping his smile is more reassuring than nervous. Nate answers with a broad, sunny grin, accompanied by an encouraging thumbs-up, to all appearances ready to dive into unknown danger once again. How can Ravi do any less? His shoulders straighten, and he takes a deep breath. As ready as he'll ever be.

At Harry's signal, Constance mutters a spell that sends the doors flying open, and they all stride into the Gala.

Though his aunt bemoaned the necessity of paring down the rushed Gala from a white tie event to a less formal black tie, Ravi can't discern any other evidence of corners being cut or expense being spared. Looks like dozens of other formal soirees he's attended—crystal chandeliers dotting a vaulted ceiling and full-length windows looking out over the city skyline. An expansive ballroom edged with a band of conversational nooks by clever use of floral partitions. A sea of black suits and gowns glittering with gems, the monochromatic throng here and there enhanced by the odd colorful sari or salwar kameez.

One significant detail makes this Gala different: not one single server weaves through the crowd with trays of refreshments. Instead of caterers, a massive buffet table along the south wall showcases a central multi-tiered champagne fountain flanked by two intricate ice sculptures of rearing tigers. No live musicians line the dance floor, instead replaced by a speaker system subtly hidden among decorative pillars and bouquets. No doubt one of the tightened security measures to limit potential infiltrators, in addition to the enchanted keys, overlapping layers of counter-spells and anti-hexes laid everywhere, and the high-tech scanners at every point of entry.

Steeling himself against the onslaught of eyes turned their way, Ravi assesses the crowd for immediate dangers and threats. Mostly familiar faces, all composed into polite, restrained surprise with a few notable exceptions of shock, admiration, or disapproval. He's a little impressed at the turnout. Despite the short notice, he expected a fair showing from Bhagavatis, Katarajus, Prestons, Harbridges, Cattanos, and Eatons. But he can also pick out several faces from other families, desi and non-desi alike. Even one or two of the nearly died-out Portuguese family tottering around on canes.

Nothing sets off any alarm bells. Not yet.

Padme approaches the team in an elegant high-collared

gown, steady on impossibly high heels and with a flute of champagne in hand. She locks eyes with Ravi for an instant of silent communication, and he relaxes even further. No signs of infiltration or attack on her end either.

His aunt draws herself up, and the crowd goes utterly silent and attentive. She places her palms together and gives Harry an exactingly correct formal bow of respect. Padme doesn't raise her throaty voice, but nevertheless it rings out clearly.

"*Namaskaar*, Chosen One, and welcome to you and yours. For too long, we of The Trust have been bereft of our Chosen. A sword without our blade. It is with great honor that we formally welcome you into our fold. May you be as a bright beacon, standing unflinching before the darkness."

She turns to face the crowd and declares with a sweep of her hand, "I present you with your Chosen: Angharad McAllister, her fiancé Ravi Abhiramnew, and her comrades-in-arms." Padme raises her drink. The crowd raise theirs as well in a solemn, silent salute. She lowers her champagne flute and begins to applaud. The other Trustees follow suit with varying degrees of enthusiasm. Ravi can discern the tiny victorious slant of his aunt's brows. Engagement announced, saluted, and cemented. She'll be thrilled.

Next to him, Harry clears her throat, and another expectant hush falls over the Gala as the sea of faces wait on tenterhooks for their Chosen's first official words.

Harry waves. "Hi! Thanks. It's just Harry. Ooh, champagne." And she leans into Ravi and steers him toward the south wall, the team close on her heels. The crowd parts for them, murmuring in a low, shocked buzz, soon dispersing into smaller conversational rings.

Harry murmurs, "How was that?"

"Perfect," he whispers back, biting back a wild grin.

"Stars and saints!" Constance stops stock-still in her tracks.

"What?" Ravi's eyes dart frantically, scanning for danger. Val likewise stands alert at Harry's shoulder, her fingers spread as if waiting for orders to summon her massive maul.

"Hath ye e'er beheld anything so uncommon fair in all of thine days?" Constance dreamily drifts away from the group, weaving past a knot of older mustachioed gentleman until she reaches the extravagant buffet table. Standing before the heaped table with all the solemnity of a pilgrim throwing herself at the foot of a sacred reliquary, Constance opens her golden handbag and starts dropping delicacies into it. Far more shrimps and pineapple wedges go into the little bag than it should be able to contain, almost as many as get popped into Constance's mouth. Nearby, a few elegant ladies in saris stare at her in aghast disbelief.

Harry snorts with mirth, loosening her grip on Ravi's arm. "This is gonna be a fun evening. I can already tell."

Nate snags a couple of glasses and tips them to the flowing champagne pouring from the fountain. He hands the first to Harry and the second to Ravi. "Lots of mixed reactions from the crowd."

Ravi murmurs agreement, taking an absent sip of champagne while scanning the crowd. "Judging emotions is one of your strengths. Keep an eye out for anything suspicious?"

"Course I will. You two want me to mingle? Looks like there are some folks waiting to talk to Harry."

Harry glances back over her shoulder. "Yeah, good idea. Hey look, it's little baby Callum. Must be the Harbridge clan."

"Get ready. You're about to be very popular, Harry."

Ravi isn't kidding. As Constance and Nate spread out and strike up conversations, Harry and Ravi are at the center of a slow, shifting maelstrom of introductions. The Harbridges are effusive with both their thanks for being saved, and congratulations on the engagement. They're halfway through an offer to visit their manor on holiday when an imposing older man wearing a monocle pushes to the forefront. He possesses both a surfeit of casual arrogance and exceedingly bushy eyebrows.

"Hrm, so you are the latest Chosen. Charmed, I'm sure." He regards Ravi with cool indifference. "Abhiramnew."

Harry turns to Ravi, not bothering to lower her voice. "Who's Eyebrows here?"

The man visibly bristles. He's an impressive bristler.

Ravi utterly adores this woman. "Sir Alisdair Preston. Head of his family."

"I didn't think you were being literal about the monocles. Yikes." She turns back to Preston with an upbeat smile. "Yep, that's me, the Chosen! I see you already know my dashing bit of arm candy here. This dame behind me with the killer gams is Val. She's an angel."

Preston manages to look down his nose at all of them, even the looming Valkyrie that is Valiance. "Hrm. We've been apprised of this angel situation. It would appear the powers-that-be have decided you require divine intervention to successfully execute your duties as our Chosen."

The champagne flute cracks neatly in two in Val's hand, and blue-white flame licks out past the frames of her sunglasses. Preston takes a step back, jowls blanching.

"My apologies," Val intones. "I often do not know my own strength." She shoves the dripping pieces of glass to Preston, giving him no choice but to reach out to take them lest he get covered in champagne. "Be careful that you do not cut yourself."

Harry claps Preston on the shoulder in clear dismissal. "Thanks awfully for throwing that away for us, Al, bless your heart. You're doing a great service for the Chosen. *Such a pleasure to meet you.*"

Blinking, Preston drifts away like a rudderless ship.

Elation bubbles under Ravi's skin, finding its way into a barely bitten back grin. "Okay. That was pretty great."

"You can knock down the next one who starts getting all snippy." Harry's eyes are bright, color high in her cheeks. "Go nuts, dude. They can try to stick a knife in me, but guess what? I'm fucking invulnerable. Nice assist, Val."

Val nods, but her gaze drifts toward a knot of chatting Harbridges.

"Do you want to go talk to them?" Ravi asks gently.

The angel's stance shifts. "I would not leave Harry unprotected."

Harry bumps her shoulder into Val's. "Aww, big gal. I'm good. I've got Ravi, I've got my urumi, and we'll still be in the same ballroom. If I need you to be somewhere, I'll text you. Go ahead."

Val turns an inquiring look to Ravi. Solemnly, he vows, "I'll protect her with my life."

Harry rolls her eyes. "Can you warrior types take it down a notch? Look, there's Ikshana over there. If something were going to go down, you think a seer would be standing around eating…little tartlets, it looks like? Mini quiches? I love me a mini quiche."

Ravi twists his head, peering over the crowd. "They let a seer be in the same place as the heads of the consortium *and* the Chosen?"

"Yeah, that's sloppy. Something to fix when you're running this gig, huh?"

"Another one for the list," he sighs wearily, then looks back up at Val. "Seriously. Go ahead and tell them you knew William. I'm sure they'd love to talk to you."

Indecisiveness is not an expression any of them are used to seeing Val wear. It only lasts a moment before she nods, glancing at Harry one last time to check. Harry again rolls her eyes with a fond smile and shoos her away. They both watch Val make her way over to the family. "Our little angel, going out there and making friends," Harry says with a fake sniffle.

Ravi snorts a laugh. Movement stirs in his peripheral vision, and he quickly gets very serious again. "Heads up. Katarajus. Very old family. Traditionalists. They're constantly trying to prove they are worthy to be Chosen instead of the Abhiramnews, but that hasn't been working out for them for the past few centuries. They're less than thrilled about that."

"Ah, douchebags. Gotcha." Harry plasters on another bright, American grin as a cluster of stern-faced men approach them.

"Chosen." The first to speak is Jihan, unsurprisingly. The man loves the sound of his own voice. "Ravi."

"She prefers Harry," Ravi tells him with a bland smile. It's surreal to think that before too long, he's going to be this guy's boss. He can afford to be gracious. "Harry, this is Jihan Kataraju. Eldest son of his family. He was a field agent for a time." Not a very successful one, despite extensive martial training. Couldn't take orders. Couldn't work with a team. Cared more about his own glory than helping people.

Jihan inclines his head a small fraction. "An honor to finally meet you. Congratulations on your engagement. How comforting that you're going to marry before having your heir."

Okay, maybe graciousness isn't on the table after all.

Jihan lifts a single brow in inquiry. "May we take this as a favorable sign that you are committed to a return to tradition?"

Well. Harry said he should take the next one. "What tradition is that, Jihan? You being a complete prick at every opportunity?"

Harry's face splits into a broad, delighted grin.

The corner of Jihan's eye twitches, and in Hindi he mutters *sotto voce*, "Since when did you learn to speak, mulligatawny?" He switches back to English with a painfully tight smile. "What interesting choices in attire. Surely not your usual style, Miss McAllister. I do hope your betrothed hasn't pressured you into wearing it. He always did have quite the talent for overly conspicuous apparel."

Ravi levels a smile at Jihan, likely for the first time in history. "I could have dressed down and tried to blend in. But what would have been the point? People were always watching me no matter what I did. I must admit, Jihan, I've always admired one thing about you."

"Oh?"

"That your plainness must allow you a peaceful anonymity."

Harry gives a heavy, unladylike snort.

Jihan glowers. "Arrogant as any Abhiramnew, I see."

Ravi turns to Harry, giving Jihan his shoulder. "Speaking of arrogance. Jihan lost a cricket match once, and he threw such a fit about it that the families had to institute a ban on the kids playing it anymore."

Picking up on his tone, Harry nods in mock sympathy. "Well, kids can be little shits."

"He was nineteen."

Harry presses her fingers over her lips, suppressing a

full laugh. "Mm. Mm. Interesting. Say, you happen to have any more fun stories?"

"Dozens."

Jihan splutters, his shoulders rising. The back row of Katarajus begins to shift, murmuring protests as Constance barrels right through the knot of them, elbowing a few out of her way as she goes. On her bent arm she leads a tiny, wizened woman wearing a luxurious sari through the middle of the Katarajus and right up to Harry.

"A thousand pardons, my good fellows! Harry, I have simply the most delightful lady to introduce you to!" Constance grins down at the elderly woman. "This is the matriarch of the Bhagavati clan. We've been having such an enjoyable conversation about the myriad applications of saltpeter within magical remedies."

Ravi dips into a respectful bow. "*Pranaam*, Mihika-ji."

"*Baap re*, you've grown, child." Mihika Bhagavati looks up at Ravi crankily, as if his height is a personal annoyance. Her hand snakes out and snatches his shirt sleeve. She pinches a cufflink between a gnarled thumb and forefinger. "Tigers, eh?" Though ancient, her eyes are still eagle-sharp. "Subtle. And this is your bride-to-be?"

"A genuine pleasure to meet you, ma'am." Harry extends her hand. Mihika bats it away. Several gasps sound out from onlookers in the ensuing silence. Ravi goes very still as Mihika steps right up to Harry. The old woman raises herself up on her tiptoes, mere inches away from Harry, and peers straight into her eyes with a narrow, piercing glare.

Harry, for her part, blinks once in surprise, but returns the stare.

A long, long moment passes with the breath stuck in Ravi's throat. Mihika Bhagavati is one of the oldest and most respected members of the consortium. Her opinion carries enormous weight, especially with the Indian families. Jihan looks downright gleeful.

Ten seconds pass like an ice age.

"Acceptable," Mihika declares, dropping back onto her heels and turning her back. She takes Constance's arm again. "Now, let's go feed more canapés to your invisible cat." They amble off together, chatting amiably.

All the Katarajus look as though they just swallowed live scorpions. Jihan, scowling, performs the smallest, least heartfelt bow on Earth, and fades back into the crowd.

"Uh." Harry blinks again. "Why did that feel like a bigger deal than your aunt's welcome?"

"It was," Ravi murmurs, shocked and delighted. "That was a ringing endorsement from the most powerful sorceress in The Trust."

A surreptitious glance around places all their allies and double-checks for trouble. Val is surrounded by a throng of

Harbridges, a small smile on her face. Nate appears to have made some friends, which is no surprise. He's incredibly easy to like. Ravi wishes he were over there too, listening to Nate relate some amusing anecdote.

Aunt Padme catches Ravi's eye from across the room. She tips her glass with a barely concealed smirk, indicating she'd witnessed the whole affair. He returns one of his own and turns back to Harry. "No one is going to dare gainsay Mihika Bhagavati. I think we can safely assume no more barbed comments."

"That's almost a shame," Harry says, "I was having fun. Nate is going to be so bummed he missed you being catty. What was that Jihan called you? Mull-something?"

So, she'd caught that. "Mulligatawny."

"Oh my god, what a prick. I can't believe he called you that. The nerve. That's so offensive. Mulligatawny. Unbelievable."

He gives her a look. "You don't know what mulligatawny is."

"Not even a little. By his tone, I'm going to guess a really horrible slur."

"It's soup," Ravi says.

"It's…what?"

"It's a British influenced South Indian dish with a lot of variable ingredients."

Harry's eyes narrow. "So, it *is* a slur."

Ravi sighs. "Jihan has a talent for making anything into an insult."

"Joke's on him, our talent is saving the fucking day and looking great doing it." She takes his arm again and winds through the crowd toward a slim figure in white. "Speaking of, we should say hi to our fashion-forward future-seeing buddy."

Ikshana smiles as they approach, setting aside their plate. "Hello, Chosen. Hello, Scion." They've eschewed the standard dress code for a pure white tuxedo, platinum hair sheeting down straight and loose. Ravi has to admire the commitment to their aesthetic. "I wish to express my admiration of how you handled that potential situation in Borobudur. Neatly done."

Using Ravi like a wall, Harry leans an elbow against him as she kicks one ankle out over the other. "Happy to help. Thanks for the tip."

"And congratulations are in order."

"Oh, yeah. I guess it's not every day a girl gets a debutante ball and an engagement party all in one."

"Ah, indeed, there is that," Ikshana says serenely in their smooth, Icelandic lilt. "However, I was speaking to you, Ravi."

Ravi straightens without dislodging Harry from her

nonchalant perch. "Me?"

"Word is you are to be the next Director. It is a sound choice. We see many favorable possibilities as a result."

Harry claps Ravi on the back. "Hell, yeah, it's sound as fuck. My dude here's gonna whip this whole mess into shape. And we, who? Are you doing a royal 'we' these days?"

"No. We seers. There are a few of us here tonight. I can introduce you later, if you wish."

Ravi frowns. "Weren't there objections to having so many seers in one place? It's a security risk."

"There were many, in fact. But an equal number argued that it would be worth the risk to have us present as an early warning system. The vote was split down the middle, and the tie had to be broken by a Branch Director."

"Branch Directors don't get votes."

"Usually true, but in this case, enough of the families agreed to hear Mason's opinion. He's been very active lately. There's some who say he's aiming for a position in the consortium, when he starts a family."

Harry purses her lips together. "Javier Mason, I know that name. That's the guy who runs the Manhattan branch, right?"

"Yeah," Ravi says. "He's supposed to be a cool guy. Very dedicated. Rumor has it he killed a yeti bare-handed.

I've always wanted to meet him. Is he here?"

"I believe so. I can't say where he is now, I haven't seen him for some time," Ikshana says. "The night is still young."

"Any predictions for it?" Harry asks. "I'll be honest, we're half expecting to get jumped any second, so if you could set our minds at rest, I sure would appreciate it."

"Of course. We've been checking periodically, but all seems well enou—" Ikshana's already pale eyes flash pure white for a brief moment, then they very slowly look over their shoulder toward the buffet table.

Ravi's pulse kicks into high gear, scanning for threats, but the only thing of note in that direction is Constance talking animatedly with a flock of Bhagavati women.

"What is it? What do you see?"

For the first time since Ravi has met Ikshana, he gets to see that aloof, otherworldly demeanor crack. "Um. Nothing."

"Nothing?" Harry quirks a brow. "No attacks incoming?"

Ikshana keeps staring straight at Constance as if unable to tear their eyes away. "Uh. No. I don't know. I don't see one currently." Against the backdrop of their porcelain pallor, two red spots appear high on their cheeks. It's…a *blush*, Ravi realizes.

He shares an incredulous look with Harry. "Do you

want to go talk to Constance?"

Ikshana goes even redder. "I foresee that…talking…is one very likely possibility, yes."

Harry's other eyebrow joins its twin, rising nearly to her hairline. "*Well*, Ravi and I were gonna go dance anyway, right?" She elbows him in the ribs.

"We were? Oh! Yeah."

"So, you should definitely go say hello." Harry shoves Ikshana in the direction of the smiling witch. "She's weird, you're weird, it'll be great. Be prepared to have holy water sprinkled on you."

The seer gives Harry an affronted look which quickly melts into sheepishness. "If that is the Chosen's wish." Ikshana clasps their hands in front of their chest and dips into a bow before they approach the buffet table. They fidget with their vest a bit, adjusting an ivory bow tie.

Ravi laughs under his breath and nudges Harry's shoulder. "Harry McAllister. Private eye. Monster hunter. Chosen One. Matchmaker."

"Right? I'm getting everyone laid around here." She links their elbows. "I was not kidding about that dance, by the by. C'mon."

Chapter Eighteen

THIS EARLY, THE dance floor is sparsely attended, so when Ravi leads Harry out onto it—or more accurately, when Harry allows herself to be led—they are one of only a handful of dancers. He glances around before he can rein in his nerves. Eyes from all corners, scrutinizing their every move. He takes a deep, steadying breath. Music swells up from the speakers. He extends a hand, and with an exaggerated curtsey, Harry takes it.

Ravi leads them in a simple waltz, the usual ballroom fare. This seems to suit Harry just fine, as she's mostly using the pretense of dancing to case the room over his shoulder. Ravi does likewise, again finding Nate looking so exceedingly fine in his tuxedo, laughing with one of the younger Preston siblings. He's got a smile that makes everyone else's look dull and lifeless by comparison.

"Still all clear?"

"Seems like it," he says on the downbeat, snapping his attention back to Harry.

"Thank *fuck* for that." She rests a hand on his shoulder and leans in, dancing close. "You look thinky. What's up?"

He nibbles his lip. "I've been thinking about what you said. I think you're right."

"Gonna have to be more specific. I'm always right."

"I'm thinking about…how you were *right*. About before. There's nothing they can do. If the worst our detractors can do is lob some mild insults our way, then…they're *toothless*. If they had anything real to use against us, they would have made nice to hide their true intentions. Not bothered with petty insults." He chews on this a little more, the implications setting a fresh zing of nervousness in his stomach. "I'm thinking…we're following the bylaws, so…"

Harry grins, no doubt already seeing where he's going with this. "So?"

"So maybe we *do* get to do whatever we want."

"Maybe?"

"Okay, not just maybe." With a sudden sidestep he leads her into a spin. She laughs and moves through it.

Ravi swallows, glancing past Harry. Nate's already watching him, the wistful admiration in his expression making Ravi's chest tighten. "And I've been wasting time playing by the rules."

"You should do it," Harry says softly, squeezing his shoulder.

"Do what?"

"Don't kid a kidder. You want to ask him to dance."

"I… Yeah. I do."

Harry leans up to kiss his cheek. "Do it, you dummy."

Ravi ducks his head, embarrassed at the shy flutter that has set up shop behind his ribs. "But this is your day, Harry. I can't. It'll steal focus—"

"Can't steal what's freely given." She sways to a stop, placing both hands on his shoulders. "Honestly, Rav, take *one* thing for yourself once in a while, geez. You have my blessing. If anyone asks, I'll insinuate we're in a hip, modern polyamorous triad thing. *Really* give these stuffed shirts something to gossip about." She winks outrageously.

Clocking movement on their flank, Ravi picks Harry up by her waist and spins her to his other side, disguising it as a dance move, before setting her back down on her feet. She swallows a little squawk of surprise, but otherwise keeps her cool. Ravi turns to the unfamiliar man approaching with a wary glare.

Very tall and very handsome, a man with a mane of sorrel hair silvered prematurely at the temples places a hand over his chest, giving them each a polite bow. "Sorry, didn't mean to alarm you. I just wanted to introduce myself. And hopefully ask if I might be so bold as to request the next dance, It's-just-Harry McAllister?" He smiles widely at Harry.

Astonishingly, Harry's pulse quickens in her wrist under Ravi's steadying touch. *Very* interesting. But whether she likes him or not, certain rituals of betrothal have to be upheld.

"Ravi Abhiramnew." He offers a hand. The man is mid-to-late thirties, appears unarmed, though he carries himself like he knows how to throw a punch. Not nearly as polished as most of the other Trusties here. Rugged, a little sun-worn, the back of his hands scarred. His tux is brand new, off-the-rack but well-tailored, and his handshake firm and steady.

"It's a pleasure. Javier Mason."

Harry shakes his hand. "Harry McAllister, but everyone knows that. I'm old news."

Mason's smile is slow and sincere. "Not to me. I just arrived. I understand I have you and your team to thank for saving my branch from certain interdimensional doom."

"You know, I heard the same rumor." She favors him

with a sardonic smile, fiddling at the clipped-back section of her hair.

Ravi glances askance at Harry. Neither of them has spontaneously developed telepathy, but it hardly makes a difference.

You want to dance with this guy?

Duh. Scoot.

He hides a smile. "You've accumulated a few rumors yourself, Mason. Is that thing about the yeti true?"

Javier laughs richly. "That's a long story."

"I'm sure Harry would be delighted to hear it." There's no sign of Constance, but Val is only a few yards away. Plus, Harry is armed. Safe enough to leave her side for a short while. Besides, Ravi wants badly to talk to Nate. "I'm going to sit out the next dance, I think. Can I trust you to keep my fiancée entertained?" He narrows his gaze, just a fraction. A clear warning, though politely issued, like any good consort should.

Mason catches it and readily relinquishes eye contact, his tone deferential. "It would be my honor. If I may?" He holds out a hand to Harry with a peculiar flourish to his wrist that Ravi recognizes but can't place. Seems like Mason enjoys a bit of showmanship.

"Sure, I don't mind," Harry says coolly, as if she's doing Mason a favor, and takes his hand. Surreptitiously, she winks at Ravi. "See you later, honeybunny."

Striding off the dance floor to make a beeline toward Nate, Ravi catches a glimpse of a sour face aimed his way. Jessika Eaton. When she realizes she's been caught looking, she tosses her hair and turns her back.

Perhaps there's an opportunity in disguise. A chance to right a wrong.

Ravi catches up to Nate as the professor leaves one group to start mingling with another. "Hey," he says as he steps up, so as not to startle.

Nate turns around, his bright party smile shifting into something deeper, more sincere. "Hey! How's everything going?"

"Good. Really good."

Nate exhales in relief. He pitches his voice low so as not to be overheard. "Thank Christ. Or whoever. And you're okay? I know parties aren't your thing."

"To say the least." Ravi's mouth tugs into a crooked smile. "But this one is better because you're here."

Nate clears his throat, then glances around with a casual nod. "Yeah, having the team at your back is probably a nice change from the norm."

"It is," Ravi agrees, taking a small step closer. "But I wasn't talking about the team."

Nate's eyes go wide, a blush rising above his collar.

A pleased smile touches his lips before he takes a long quaff of champagne to cover it. "I'm trying to be good, here. Supportive teammate. Doing whatever you two need me to do, which includes keeping my eyes where they should be."

"Oh, yeah? Thought I saw you looking before."

"Well, yeah. You guys looked amazing out there, everyone was getting an eyeful. Don't think Harry stepped on your feet once, that's a bonus."

Ravi bites his lip and takes a breath. "Actually, that's... Can I introduce you to someone?"

"Sure. Is it someone terrifying? You're acting a little off."

"Yeah. I mean, no, she's not terrifying. I just—" Ravi closes his eyes briefly to collect himself, then stands up straight with renewed confidence. "I want to introduce you to the woman I was supposed to get engaged to."

"Oh! Yeah, okay." Nate falls into step beside Ravi as they weave their way toward Jessika. "You want me to, what? Lay on the charm, smooth her ruffled feathers about Harry?"

"Not exactly. Just be yourself."

"No problem. Don't really know how to *not* be myself, to be honest."

"I've noticed." Ravi slides a warm, wide smile over his

shoulder, and Nate's step hitches.

Jessika glares sidelong at Ravi as they approach, pointedly ignoring them in favor of her conversation with an older Cattano brother.

"Jessika."

She stretches out a pause to the limits of socially acceptable politeness before she faces him, flicking a dismissive glance Nate's way. He detects a hint of curiosity before she schools it away.

"Why, Ravi, I'm surprised you're still here. Seeing as how you get so easily bored." The Cattano carefully backs away, looking for all the world like a man avoiding ground he knows is covered in landmines. "Congratulations on your engagement. I hope you'll be very happy together." Sincerity is buried under Jessika's arch tone, Ravi notes with interest.

"I'd hoped we'd get a moment to talk." He glances at Nate, silently appealing to him to wait a moment. "I wanted to apologize for my behavior when we had dinner. You have every right to despise me."

She looks taken aback, quickly masking it with a very Padme-like sniff. "I *do* have every right. You were just awful to me."

"I know. I'm not going to make excuses for myself. But I want you to know that I am sorry."

She squints at him suspiciously, then looks over toward where Harry is still mid-dance with Mason. "I suppose...I suppose you had a reason to put me off. Were you two an item before she was Chosen?"

"Ah. No. You're not...completely wrong though. I did have a reason." Ravi pulls Nate over by his elbow. Nate shoots him a surprised, puzzled look. "May I introduce you to Dr. Nate Corbin?" And feeling like he's stepping off a cliff blindfolded, Ravi lays his hand on Nate's forearm and keeps it there.

Clearly confused, Jessika nods at Nate before she notices Ravi's hand. Her brows fly upward. "Oh. *Oh.*" She stares blankly at Ravi. "Oh."

He swallows another quaver of nerves, glancing at Nate to gauge his comfort level. Nate's expression is...strange. His gaze is locked on Ravi, but not in affront or alarm. More like the rest of the room has disappeared, and Ravi's the only thing worth looking at.

"So..." Jessika lays a hand over her throat. "Sorry, this is a surprise, to say the least. I mean, it's *fine*, don't get me wrong. Okay. Wow. Was this...a new...revelation?"

"No."

"Well, this sheds light on some things. When we were kids, I thought...I thought maybe you were trying to play us girls off each other, making us compete for you. Thought maybe you got a kick out of it."

He doesn't bother disguising his distaste. "*No.*"

"No, I can see that. Well." Jessika blinks a few times, then purses her lips together as she looks back toward Harry. "And everything is…" She's clearly uncertain how to finish her sentence.

"Yeah, it is."

"Huh." She watches as Harry finishes dancing with Mason and heads off with him to the champagne fountain. Her pretty face flickers with calculations before she turns back to Ravi, smiling wryly. "Nicely played, sugar."

He huffs a laugh, sliding his elbow through Nate's. "Thanks." He keeps his attention on the conversation, though he knows there must be dozens of eyes upon him, picking apart his every move and hint of emotion. In India, two male friends linking arms isn't remarkable, but the Western families are going to be wagging tongues for sure. "At dinner, you mentioned bringing The Trust into the modern era. I'm interested in hearing more about your ideas."

Jessika's smile is delighted and sincere. "You should be. They're great ideas. And now that the Eaton name has been cleared of those ridiculous charges, I'll be in a much better position to implement them." She tosses long hair over her shoulder and levels a very white smile at Nate. "It has just been a delight to meet you, Dr. Corbin. A little ray of sun-shine in this stuffy party."

"Yeah," says Nate distantly, sparing her a tiny fraction of his attention away from Ravi. "It has been that."

"I should apologize too," she says to Ravi with a wince. "I said some pretty unkind things to you."

"I was being a massive prick. It's understandable."

"You're a darn good actor, sugar. You know, it's too bad we couldn't be more honest with each other back when we were kids. I think we could have been friends."

Ravi gives her a broad smile. "Maybe we can make up for lost time."

Jessika goes a bit pink under her tan, then gives Nate a significant arch of her thin brows. Nate just grins widely, cinching his arm a little tighter around Ravi's.

"You have my number?"

"I'll call you," Ravi promises, "and thanks, Jessika."

"Thank *you*, sugar." Her smile shifts into a wicked curve. "Isabella's going to be madder than a wet hen. Just for that alone, consider my forgiveness granted." She smooths her dress over her hips and saunters off.

Ravi breathes out. "Sorry. I should have…I should have warned you. Or asked permission."

"Don't worry about it, my guy." Nate appears slightly dazed, like he's floating with his feet unbound from the floor. He looks down at their linked arms. "So… Isn't this going to make things difficult for you? For Harry?"

"It's a tactically sound strategy, honestly," Ravi admits, having given it a fair amount of thought. "Anyone gunning for us will jump on the opportunity to discredit us. This way, we can predict exactly how they'll come at us. Try to draw them out."

Nate snorts, shaking his head. "Always working the angles," he says fondly. "Very smart."

"Nah," Ravi says, ears warm. "I'm just a guy with a gun."

"*Pfft*. And Constance is just a simple peasant girl, and Val's just a CrossFit enthusiast. You're not 'just' anything, Ravi Abhiramnew. But…the engagement. Are you sure Harry—"

"Nate." Ravi gently disentangles arms to step in front of Nate. "Harry's given her blessing. Besides, she's bulletproof. Maybe I am too." With a courtly bow, Ravi extends his hand palm up, letting his smile shine through unfettered and free. "Nathaniel. Will you dance with me?"

Throat bobbing, Nate whispers, "Are you sure?"

"I'm sure."

"And here you always go on about *me* jumping headlong into trouble." Grinning, Nate takes Ravi's hand and follows him to the dance floor. Ravi draws him out to the middle, not paying the slightest attention to who he's brushing past, the whispers that rise around them.

"You should lead," Nate murmurs, casting a worried glance around. "Better optics. So they don't think…"

"Nate, I couldn't care less about optics or what any of them think." Ravi hates being the center of attention, of being watched and judged and found wanting…but somehow, right now none of that bothers him. Let them stare. He'll give them something worth looking at. He pulls Nate's right hand up onto his shoulder and places their palms together. "But I *will* lead." He grasps Nate's waist tightly and reels him in close.

Nate gasps, focusing in on Ravi completely. "Oh, yeah?"

"Mm-hm." Ravi places his feet with precision, as if he were in ready stance for a fencing bout. "Got a secret for you."

The last vestiges of apprehension melting, Nate smiles at him, golden and glowing. "I do love secrets."

Ravi leans in so his lips barely brush Nate's ear. "I'm a *very* good dancer." Then he grins, and on the swell of the music guides Nate into a lively Viennese waltz. Nate laughs with surprise, following along. After a few steps, he's got the rhythm of it, and they carve out a section of the dance floor just for them.

"Aren't you full of surprises, sunshine." Nate's face is flushed and vibrant, and Ravi doesn't want to look at anything else.

"I try." He steps them around another couple, letting his feet follow the music. "This is a thing my mom and her brother taught me. Dancing."

"Really?" Nate brightens, as if Ravi sharing this with him was a cherished gift. It occurs to Ravi that he's never once told Nate about a happy memory from his childhood. He's got a few.

"They dropped in on a ballroom lesson when I was about eleven. They watched for less than a minute before insisting that the tutor was doing it all wrong. They sent her away and started teaching me themselves."

He'd stood on his Uncle Nirav's feet to learn the steps. His mother had looked so beautiful when she laughed. She did it so rarely.

Ravi shifts Nate into a faster style, the movements a little snappier, the steps closer. "Including the tango. Think you can keep up?"

"Nope, but I'm thrilled to be along for the ride." But Nate matches Ravi's moves without issue, some inner synchronicity at work keeping them in perfect step. After a few turns Ravi moves them into the wide, sweeping steps of a bolero, chests so close a sideways hand wouldn't fit between them.

Delighted, Nate laughs, holding on tight. "This is really brave of you, Ravi."

Ravi tips his head back to meet Nate's eyes. A brace of butterflies is set free behind his heart, wings fluttering with every breath he takes. "I think she would have liked you. My mom."

Nate nearly misses a step. Ravi quickly compensates with a half-turn. "I…" Nate flushes and can't seem to look away from Ravi's face. "You think?"

"Yeah. She hated artifice. Fake smiles, fake people. You're…you're real. Honest." He snags his lip between his teeth for a moment before continuing. "Do you remember that night I came over to your place a total wreck?"

"The time we slept on the couch? Vividly."

"Do you remember what you told me?" He slows them down into a close, simple sway, their surroundings falling away, music fading, as if they'd danced their way through an unseen portal into a private vignette of space, the whole of the universe nothing but the two of them holding each other close.

"Remind me," Nate says in a tiptoeing hush.

"You told me that anyone who said love hurts isn't doing it right." Ravi takes a deep breath, steadying himself. "I know this is new, between us. I've got no idea what I'm doing. But…I want to…do it right. With you."

The words leave his chest and Ravi is lighter, cutting away an iron shackle he hadn't realized was there, a burden he hadn't known he was carrying. For a moment he's light-headed, weightless, finding his footing.

Nate sucks in a shuddering breath and presses their foreheads together. "Ravi. I want that too."

"Yeah?"

"Yeah. I want to be with you, Ravi. To build something lasting. I've wanted that for a while, but I needed you to have time to decide if you wanted it too. Needed you to be sure of me."

Relief and joy wash through Ravi so fast he would swear it's shining from his pores, bubbling up headier than champagne. "I'm sure. I don't need another month to know that."

He swings Nate out into an open hip twist. Nate laughs at the unexpected move, and when Ravi reels him back, he sets both hands on Ravi's shoulders, grinning bright and vibrant and happy. They move together, heedless of observers, matching steps in perfect time. Daring a puckish wink, Ravi takes Nate's hands and twirls him into a spin, arm extended.

Strangely, it feels like he misses a step, like the whole room jumps between one blink and the next. When Ravi pulls his arm back in, his dance partner spins in to bump right into his chest.

Cayenne looks up at Ravi with a smile.

Chapter Nineteen

IT FEELS AS if Ravi's head has been stuffed near to bursting with dry cotton, his stomach churning. But it quickly passes. Cayenne looks lovely, their fox-red hair falling around gold-lined eyes.

This is… Is this what he had been doing? Ravi remembers dancing, he'd definitely been dancing. But for some reason he remembers dancing with…Dr. Corbin? Why would he have been doing that?

I want to try that with you.

Ravi stops in his tracks, pulling Cayenne to a halt with him. His skull *throbs*, nearly unbearable.

"*Mon amour*, are you all right? You look pale, and that's

saying something." Cayenne pushes a hand through the hair fallen over Ravi's forehead, their features soft with concern. "Too much champagne? Come, let's take a breather. We've dazzled this dull little crowd enough for one gala, don't you think?" They wink, pulling Ravi by the hand off the dance floor. He follows, nausea sending a cold sweat to his palms.

"What... How did you get here?" But no, Cayenne had been waiting for him, resplendent in their luxe black suit with its bright-gold lapels, following Harry and the rest into the Gala. Ravi had been so happy to see them.

Cayenne gives him a strange look. "The elevator? Remember the magic key? Darling, you *are* feeling all right? Are you still nervous about all *them*?" They flip a hand dismissively at the partygoers. "I told you, my hot cup of chai, if anyone raises a fuss, I'll just spin us back like that" —they snap their fingers—"and we can take care of it any *number* of ways."

A glance around only creates further confusion; it's as if he's seeing the same image twice, overlaid like two photo negatives laid on top of another. There are more hostile faces than there should be: more Katarajus, only a couple of sullen Bhagavatis, no Eatons, no Harbridges.

Why would he expect to see any Harbridges? The whole family died in a freak plane crash back in August.

The Trust is still reeling from the loss.

Ravi catches sight of Harry by the south wall, engaged in conversation with Javier Mason. No sign of Val or Constance. No Ikshana. His aunt stands alone in a corner, her expression darker than the storm now beating raindrops against the windows.

But he *remembers* only a few minutes ago catching a glimpse of her from over Nate's shoulder. He remembers how she shook her head with exasperation, even as her lips hinted at a smile. Likely an enigmatic expression to anyone who hasn't made a lifelong study of her little tells, but it stuck in Ravi's mind as a clear gesture of support. He could have *sworn* he saw it.

But now his aunt looks like she's on her fifth glass of champagne, her under-eyes dark and drawn. People avoid her like she's a pariah. And Ravi had been dancing with Cayenne, of course.

Things don't make sense. He's dizzy, unsure what day it even is. Ravi peers around, leaning into Cayenne to steady himself. "Where's Nate?"

Cayenne tilts their head to the side. For one brief instant, their worry shifts into nervous suspicion before it's swept away. "Hmm? Oh, the professor is over there with our fearless leader, *mon chéri*, no worries."

And true enough, Harry has left Javier and stands

across from Nate with her arms folded tightly against her ribs. Nate nods as she speaks, uncharacteristically serious. He notices Ravi looking, half-smiles in greeting, and nudges Harry. Harry cranes her neck and twiddles her fingers as a substitute for a wave from under her elbow, not uncrossing her arms. Cayenne waves back with gusto, then slides an arm through Ravi's to guide him to a quieter corner.

A lot of disapproving eyes follow in their wake, an overwhelming profusion of them. The weight of it is oppressive, of all that judging regard. It wasn't like this a few minutes ago. Was it? Ravi's head pounds.

"Here, darling, it's a bit cooler over here." Cayenne rests against a windowpane, the storm outside beating against the glass. "That was *fun*. Seeing all those shocked little faces. *Quelle amusant*." Their eyes sparkle like faceted gems. "Worth it, *non*? Aren't you glad you let me convince you, sweetheart? Not as enjoyable as our dance in the Seychelles, but still a delight." They wink and slide their hand up his sleeve.

"Cayenne…" Ravi blinks, vision still not quite right. All the lights have haloes. Was his champagne spiked? He's never been truly, thoroughly drunk before. Maybe it's supposed to be like this? "Were…were we on a balcony earlier?"

For a millisecond, Cayenne goes stiff before loosening

into a casual slouch. "A balcony? I don't believe so, *mon coeur.*"

"You had a cigarette? And…" Ravi rubs his brow, trying hard to remember, but it's like trying to pick up buttered marbles. "And you asked me to…not go to this Gala. You…" A flash of clarity comes back, and he turns a sharp glare on them. "You *rewound* me. After you promised not to, you— Wait…you—" A niggling memory nips at his heels like a persistent hound. "There was…an airport?"

A chase. A fight. His face smashing into a metal pole, leaning up against a choking arm to kiss the strangely unfamiliar face that was somehow still Cayenne. It doesn't make sense. Ravi's stomach lurches.

Cayenne stares at him blankly for a long moment.

"Fuck," they finally bark, knocking their skull back hard enough to make the glass shake in its frame. "You remember the old timeline. *Bordel de merde*, fuck me sideways, of *course* you do. You *never* make *anything* easy, do you, my pet?" They rake both hands through their hair with a growl of frustration. "I've spun you back and forth too many times. You're *resistant*. I've tethered you to your original thread. Of *course*, I fucking did. *Ugh.*"

Cayenne takes a deep breath, one of the trained sniper breaths they've picked up from him. "This is fine. It's not going to last. The current timeline will assert itself in your brain before too long. It *is* going to be okay, my love. *Je promets.*" They smile reassuringly, reaching out for his hand.

Ravi jerks back, pulse acid-thick on his tongue. "*This isn't okay*, Cayenne, this is…" There aren't words in any language he knows for what this is. Nausea rises in him so strongly Ravi has to pinwheel a hand to prop himself upright against the windowpane over Cayenne's shoulder. Lightning flashes and thunder rumbles through the glass under his palm.

With a soothing murmur, Cayenne places cool hands on either side of his face. "Ravi. Listen to me. It's going to be okay. We're together, aren't we? Like we should be. It'll just take some time for you to adapt." They smooth their thumbs over his temples.

Ravi stares at Cayenne, at his beautiful, dangerous monsoon, and sees two versions. One who told him enough truths to keep him in the dark, and one who spun enough lies to show him their true colors.

Half of him picks through his original memories with horror and disbelief over what that old version of Ravi knows about Cayenne. The other half tries and fails not to delve into the new memories. His rewound self only knew a thrilling whirlwind of romance with no shadows to darken it, no ugly past with its debts to pay. Ravi's skull is splitting in two, memories fractured, heart flayed.

"How…did you go back that far? Isn't that…" Cayenne can only send their consciousness back so far, though Ravi has never gotten a straight answer on how far that potentially was.

"Trust me, I've worked everything out. It's been an absolute *nightmare*, sweetheart, you can't even *imagine*. So much work, the things I had to agree to! Things kept going wrong even this second time around, *so* frustrating. I *barely* managed to remove the Harbridges, and to get all those Eatons arrested. And you would not *believe* how crafty that old Bhagavati witch was. Well, maybe you would." They chuckle, patting him on the wrist. "But it's fine now. All the dominos are set up, and before too long, just one little *push*, and there we go." They snap their fingers. "True freedom, as I promised, dearest."

Ravi swallows thickly. "Why are you even telling me this?" Realization hits him, and he closes his eyes. Pain lances through him, a spear straight through his heart. "You're just going to spin me back again."

"*Oui*, when your memories even out correctly. It should be no trouble at all to take us back to the dance floor. Smooth as silk, darling." They dart forward to plant a playful kiss on the tip of Ravi's nose before he can recoil away. "Never fear, you'll only remember the good things. It's my gift to you, *mon trésor*. I've done much, *much* better this time around." A slow, saucy smile spreads across their perfect face. "There were even a few *nights* where I've improved upon my, hmm, *techniques*, let's say. No one else can give you what *I* can give you, but even so! Practice makes perfect, after all, and we've had *plenty* of practice together. I know you remember. They were *very* memorable nights."

Ravi lets his head sink down, nearly pressing their foreheads together as he swallows against bile. He does remember. Every single moment. And he also remembers knowing everything Cayenne has done, all the kaleidoscope of ways they've hurt him, hurt others; and Ravi remembers *not* knowing too, right alongside it. Blissful ignorance.

"How is it," he hisses, pushing himself upright with difficulty, "that you have *no concept* of how horrific that is. You've erased the last few months of my life."

Cayenne smiles fondly. "You're so dramatic, darling. It's not erased, it's *fixed*. Let's not forget, you were ready to meddle with my memories, yes? Isn't that what that ring of yours was meant to do? A couple of overwritten months is nothing. Besides," they say with a touch of ice, "not like there was anything worth keeping there, anyway."

There was... Wasn't there something?

There's more on offer, if you want it.

Sand is slipping through Ravi's fingers, his memories turning to dust and blowing away. He clenches his jaw, trying to hang on with sheer force of will, but this isn't a situation he can punch his way out of. He's fucking useless here.

You're not broken. You're the strongest person I've ever met. You're kintsugi.

"But…I'm going to be…*was* going to be the next Director. You won't be…you *haven't been* kept captive."

"True." Cayenne idly picks at a fuzz on their lapel. "But unlike you, my sexy samosa, I remember all my alternate timelines, though in varying degrees of clarity. So, *oui*, it didn't happen in the old timeline because you fixed that—very sweet, by the way, my knight in *shining* armor—but in *this* one it did. You and the others never went to the airport, never found out about where I came from or what I did there, so you never told your bitch aunt to not capture me." Shyly, Cayenne ducks their head, full lower lip caught in their teeth. "It's usually *very* dull, going back and reliving a long span of time. But this time, it was nearly all spent with *you*. Getting to know each other again. Falling for you twice. It seems like I can never get enough of you, my love." Smiling sweetly, they trace a slim finger along the line of his jaw, down over his rabbiting pulse.

"I… But Harry's memories? From the urumi. My mother, my uncle…" The twins died in an accidental explosion. He *knows* that. Cayenne killed them. He knows that too. The urumi was mysteriously lost. Cayenne stole the urumi. Conflicting knowledge collides together behind Ravi's eyes with all the force of a car crash.

"Ooh, oh, yes! I'm actually very proud of this. All I had to do was have someone tell my past self, before I left the airport and went to that demon cult factory thing, to use the idol to disguise myself *before* your mother spotted me! Easy! Unfortunately, then I had to use that ghastly thing twice, but! *This* time I remembered to fix all my freckles, so!" They grin proudly, chin high. "Clever, yes, my love?"

"You… Who did you get to tell your past self? James?"

"*Pfff* hahaha, no!" Cayenne's shoulders shake with mirth. "Don't worry about that, darling, it'll all be worked out." They flick a hand carelessly, as if Ravi's concerns were a fly to be shooed away.

Near frantic, Ravi tries to think, yanking at his hair roots. "Where's Constance? And Val?" Either of them will be likeliest to be able to help, even if he's not making sense to them, babbling about lost memories. Constance can keep Cayenne from rewinding Ravi back in time. Maybe give him more opportunities to figure out a plan. He doesn't know how long he can hang on to his splintered memories, and worse, isn't even sure what memories he's losing any-more.

"You don't remember that one? Ah, alas. While I was

away this week, Glinda got impatient with her demon hunt and opened a little portal to Hell. Too bad she was so angry; that's what got her zapped into the future in the first place. Such a *temper*." They grin, adjusting the lay of Ravi's shirt, smoothing wrinkles. "Anyway, long story short, right now she should be tromping around Hell with Mistress Angelique, trying to find their way out. But even angels can't teleport out of Hell. So, you see? I've thought of *everything*. No one to undo all my hard work, sweetheart."

"But…that never happened." His rapidly dissolving memories diverge at nearly every point, but on this one they agree. Constance hadn't finished that spell to summon up a demon. The team talked her down before it had taken. James had even shown up in both sets of memories, squawking about paradox. In Ravi's newer memories, surging strong to the forefront, Cayenne hadn't been there; gone on one of their frequent trips away, only a couple of days ago.

Cayenne blinks. "*Quoi?*" They rub their forehead, wincing. "*Mais bon sang, qu'est-ce qui se passe?* Why do I have two memor— *Where is Constance?*" They go ramrod straight, eyes wide and alarmed.

"She went into the party before us. With Harry and the rest. You don't remember?" It had been Cayenne's idea to go separately, to "make a memorable entrance, *mon tigre.*"

Oddly Ravi remembers this right alongside going in at Harry's side. Why would Ravi go in arm-in-arm with her? It's *her* Gala. Something about a ring? He can't quite recall, the thought dangling just out of reach.

Cayenne's face twists in rage. "That's *impossible*." They scan the room, using Ravi's shoulder to hop up onto their tiptoes for a better view. "*Non, non*, this could ruin every-thing. Where the *fuck* did she go?" They turn to Ravi with a moue of displeasure, voice rising as they pull at their copper hair. "This is—How do you keep doing this? How are you *still* managing to fuck up my plans? Manhattan. Venice. Borobudur. Monterey. All of it, even on my second try, I couldn't get *any* of it to work!"

Try as he might, Ravi can't remember anything signifi-cant happening in Venice or Monterey in either timeline.

"I had to *actually* get a *shovel* and dig that damn skele-ton up myself. Manual labor, darling, *me!* And for what? It didn't even *work*! How?" Cayenne stamps a foot, drawing some attention from Trusties they soundly ignore. "I know it's not that limp-dick, James. He wouldn't *dare* do anything not on the 'prime timestream' and I would *feel* the quantum fuckery if it were ye olde Good Witch herself. I can't *believe* this!" They grab Ravi's arm and start dragging him toward where Nate and Harry are still deep in conversation. "It's not my fault I had to seek other options, is it? To find a way to go back such a huge span of time, to start from practically scratch. *Putain l'enfer*."

"To…to go back in time so you could lie to me better," Ravi whispers in a pained hush.

Cayenne stops mid-stride, setting a hand under Ravi's chin. "Ah, sweetheart. I want you to be happy. And you were *much* happier this time. See, I told you if you listen to me, I'll take care of you. Once I fix this little hiccup, we can be happy *together*." They bring his hand up to their lips and press a passionate kiss to his pale knuckles. "You and me, ever after. We can finally be free."

"You…you call this *freedom*, Cayenne?" Caught like a hapless fly in whatever web they choose to spin. Ravi thinks about twisting out of their grip, about all the martial skills he could employ, but what would be the point? They'd just rewind again and again and *again* until they get what they want. Despair wells up in his throat like tar. "Fuck, you really did it this time. You got yourself on the team."

"*Eh bien*, turns out it wasn't as fun as I thought it would be." Cayenne shrugs, skirting around a throng of frowning Brits. "But you're worth the effort, *mon amour*. Don't worry. It's going to be okay. We just have to make sure the two of them don't see each other."

"The two of…who?" His headache is beginning to fade. A bad sign. Sand slipping through the hourglass.

Where is Val? Normally she towers over the crowd, but the angel is nowhere to be seen. She was talking with the Harbridges. Who were all dead. Why had she wanted to talk to them? He *can't remember*.

"How's your memory, sweetheart? Things settling, yet?" Cayenne rubs an encouraging circle between Ravi's shoulder blades.

"My memory? Is…is something wrong?"

"Ah," Cayenne says with satisfaction. "Almost there. Delightfully malleable, those neurons. Let's not say anything too troubling for our friends, *oui*? Or I'll just have to skip us back again, which sounds *so* boring. We're trying to find Constance, darling, let's focus on that, hmm?"

Finding Constance. Yeah. That sounds right.

Ravi playfully teases, "You, focused? I'll believe it when I see it."

Cayenne casts a wide grin back over their shoulder. It's always gratifying to have made them smile, the sight warming Ravi right down to his toes.

Fuck, wait, that's not…that's not *him*. Or it *is*, but it's…

He's forgetting. The new timeline erasing the old. Ravi swallows hard, his breathing fast and shallow as they approach Nate and Harry's relatively secluded position, camped out behind the champagne fountain by the door to the unstaffed kitchen.

Cayenne pulls Ravi forward, leaning on his arm. "*Bonsoir, mes amis*, anyone know where Glinda has squirreled herself away?"

"Glad you two are enjoying yourselves," Harry says with bright, upbeat sarcasm. "While you were shocking the upper crust, I've been fending off marriage proposals left and right. Most of them obviously despise me even while they were asking, so, ya know, that's been super fun."

"I'm surprised you didn't say yes to that Javier guy. He's pretty dishy." Nate grins, nudging Harry with his elbow.

Ravi stares at Nate while something claws at the inside of his skull, trying to get out. Looking at Nate is weirdly unsettling, makes the world tilt sideways. As if Ravi were underwater but didn't realize it until he tried to breach the surface and hit a solid sheet of ice. He can't breathe.

Harry's arms are still crossed tight across her chest. "Nah, he acted like a normal person and didn't ask, because he actually seems sane, unlike everyone else here. I have no idea where Constance is, but it looks like she had the right idea and ditched this shindig. Agent guy, I know you were hoping this would fix things, but even with all the help we've given The Trust, I'm not sure this gala is moving the needle in my favor."

"You okay, Secret Agent Man?" Nate asks, frowning.

"You look weird."

Ravi is drowning and doesn't know why. He opens his mouth, no idea what to say.

"So complimentary, Professor," Cayenne interjects sweetly. "With charm like that, one has to wonder why you are woefully single. Has *anyone* seen Constance? Where was she last, and how long ago?" They cast a nervous glance about, then freeze like a startled hare. "Oh, *merde.*"

Javier Mason waves at Harry and begins walking over.

"Ooh," Nate gasps theatrically, giving Harry another nudge. "Spoke too soon, Harry. I think I see him holding a ring box."

"Hilarious. You're lucky I didn't bring any quarters, Doc." She steps to the side to greet Mason with a nonchalant nod. "Back so soon?"

"Couldn't stay away," Mason answers with a charming smile. He glances at the rest of the team. "Everyone enjoying the party?"

Cayenne smiles, but their grip on Ravi's arm tenses like a wound wire, the pulse visibly racing in their throat. He squeezes their arm, not sure what's wrong but offering comfort, nonetheless.

A loud hiss rises from ground level. Harry's pant leg moves as if of its own volition. She jumps. "Fuck, Griz, ouch! What?"

"Something smells most foul," comes a feline growl.

"*Le chat*." Cayenne's eyes fly wide. "Fuck, fuck, *fuck*, where did she—"

The nearby door to the kitchen bangs open, spilling out both Constance and Ikshana in a disorderly tumble. Cayenne quickly skips back, putting Ravi's body between them.

Ikshana doesn't look so lofty and disaffected right now, with their ivory complexion splotched and ruddy, long hair mussed into big tufts as if it had been grabbed in handfuls. Belatedly noticing them all, Ikshana snaps out of a smiling daze, cheeks flaring scarlet. The seer draws themself up very straight to smooth their askew jacket, inclines their head in polite acknowledgement, and walks away like their heels were on fire.

Constance, less rumpled but also quite flushed, adjusts her skirt with one hand and stuffs industrial-sized containers of peppercorns and saffron into her little handbag with the other. She grins brightly. "Ah! Hail to thee, mine companions! I hope you have been finding this party as diverting as I have. Pray, did anyone feel anything strange a few moments ago? Like a great shifting, or a turning, perhaps?"

"*You*," Mason growls like a thrown dagger. The sheer, unnatural hatred in his eyes sends the hair on the back of Ravi's neck prickling.

"Are you fucking *kidding me*," Cayenne groans, eyes

rolling heavenward. "My luck today, *c'est incroyablement mauvais.*"

Four people scattered among the crowd cry out and fall to their knees, Ikshana among them, to a growing susurrus of concern. Ravi tenses, swallowing nausea, hand twitching for his absent gun. Harry takes a step toward the fallen, then hesitates, looking back to the team. The only ones who haven't turned toward the uproar are Constance and Mason, locked in an antagonistic stare-down.

Nate's gaze wavers between them. "The fuck is going on?"

Little cracks creep through the parquet floor around Constance's feet, splintering against some unseen force. She ignores everything but Mason.

"What say you we leave these future folk to their fine revelries and settle our score face-to-face, thou craven worm?"

Harry's eyes snap open wide. Her hand flies to her pocket as Mason's face twists into a mocking smile, and he bows with that same archaic flourish of the wrist that Ravi has only ever seen before from Constance.

Mason's American affectation slips. "Alas, beldam, thou hast not the cunning to catch me even now. I've made a wiser choice of allies than you. Though I must admit this ruse has grown wearying. Such a pleasure to see you here,

Shaw, and not trapped in a little pocket of Hell waiting for my return." The demon rolls his shoulders as if shrugging off an ill-fitting coat, mannerisms changing entirely. "This does change matters, chronomage," Hartnell says with a narrow glare at Cayenne. "Our timetable has moved up."

Ravi stiffens and moves to block Cayenne from the demon. He spares a second to scan the room for Val. Without her, no one but Harry can arm themselves. Ravi is more than willing to put his fists to the test, but he doubts there's much he can do to slow down a demon prince.

Harry heaves a loud, exasperated sigh. "Wow, the one guy I was kinda into is a demon. Honestly? Not such a surprise with my dating record." The urumi unfurls from her pocket in a shimmering, deadly waterfall. "Pep, care to explain what he's talking about? What timetable?"

Cayenne ignores her, clinging tightly to Ravi. "This wasn't the *deal*," they snarl around him at Hartnell.

Hartnell sneers. "You speak to *me* of keeping our bargain? Your continual incompetence led to this, time wizard, despite all the wisdom and power I have been kind enough to grant you. I was supposed to have a resurrected demon army by now, and this filthy Trust was supposed to be in tatters. Yet *somehow*, with all the near-infinite power of time travel at your command, you still managed to fuck it all up."

"Go fuck yourself," Cayenne spits defiance at the

demon prince. "Like you would have been able to slip into what's-his-name's life without my help."

"You…" Constance's face contorts with betrayal. "You *helped* him?"

"This…has to be a mistake," Ravi rasps. "Cay, what's going on?" Why does he feel like he's been torn in half and inexpertly sewn together? He's not sure why, but he looks to Nate. Somehow, Nate feels like a safe harbor, a fixed point Ravi can trust even though the world is spinning wildly around him.

Cayenne pats Ravi's arm. "Hush, darling. This wasn't the *deal*, demon."

"A demon, lying? You shock me." Hartnell grins toothily. "I jest. Never fear, time wizard. Your lover shall remain untouched and whole." He waves dismissively in Ravi's direction, then leers at Harry. "It wouldn't have taken much to bed *you*. Some Chosen demon-slayer you are. Durga must be so embarrassed."

"Don't flatter yourself. I think it's high time we fuck up this slut-shaming demon prick, anyone else?" Harry shifts into a fighting stance, urumi poised to strike. Ravi follows suit, waiting on Harry's word. Constance's fingers move at her sides as if plucking invisible threads, the air taking on the faint loamy aroma of old woods, of dark earth and decay.

Hartnell laughs and spreads his arms wide, opening himself for an attack. "Yes, strike at me, Angharad. Show all these good folks what a paragon of sanity and sobriety you are. How well their goddess has chosen! Attacking an upstanding member of their community. Most of them already think your mere existence marks the end of their *noble* institution."

Harry hesitates, doubt flickering across her face. The urumi hangs limp.

"And you've been helping them along, haven't you?" Ravi husks, holding his throbbing forehead. "Whispering from the shadows." He doesn't have any weapons, but maybe he can buy Constance a little more time for whatever spell she's planning.

"Look what you've done," Cayenne pouts. "You've upset my beautiful boy! Darlings, this is all building up to *quite* a dramatic finish, I'm sure, but I think I'm just going to take a mulligan on this whole fucking mess." They lift their hand.

Before Cayenne can touch their tattoo, a piercing yowl cuts through the drone of the crowd. Hartnell reels back, long scratches raking across his face. He screams, hands flying up to grapple with something nobody else can see.

"Avaunt, villain! Taste mine fearsome talons, thou vile scourge!"

With a furious snarl, Hartnell flings Griswold away from him. The cat hits hard, flickering out of invisibility. He limps as he pushes himself up to his paws, wobbling unsteadily.

The cracks in the floor split wide with the sound of breaking bones. "You hit my cat," Constance growls. Her hands curl around air.

For a split second, Hartnell's eyes widen in alarm, but then he grins, blood dripping down his face. "T'would appear the chase is back on, mine nemesis. See you in Hell!" He taps a finger to his forelock in a mocking salute and disappears.

"*Fuck!*" Constance screams with frustration, magic sheeting off her in useless sparks at her feet.

"The Devil!" Ikshana cries out loudly and clearly, attended to by a handful of concerned partygoers. Their head lolls back, eyes pure white. "The Tower! The Hanged Man!"

"A trifle bloody late for that prediction, methinks," Constance snarls, turning a dark glare on Cayenne. "*What hast thou done?*"

Cayenne rolls their eyes hugely. "*Ugh!* This is all wrong. Fine! I'll rewind."

Feral and fierce, Constance bares her teeth. "And allow him to escape again? Don't you *dare*—"

And nearly at the same time as Cayenne sets a hand to

their clock tattoo, Constance lunges forward, her hands still sparking with unspent magic, and grabs Cayenne's wrist.

Chapter Twenty

BELIEVE ME, CAYENNE once said, *you do not want to see what happens when Constance and I get in close proximity.* Later, they'd told Ravi that what happens is the timestream gets very messily fucked.

Apparently, what that means is Ravi gets flipped inside out, shattered into a million pieces, stretched paper thin, then the next second completely restored and set back on his feet, blood rushing through his ears louder than a crashing waterfall.

Blinking, he looks around. He's not even sure *who* he is for a second, much less where, but then it all comes rushing back. All of it. Even the memories he'd started losing his grip on, to his enormous relief. Ravi *remembers*.

And he's fucking furious.

A storm still rages outside. The agony of his headache has disappeared, and the crippling nausea with it. He looks for Nate. The relief at seeing him still standing nearby, alive and unscathed, is so all-consuming that Ravi can't help but grin. Nate smiles back, wan but supportive.

The Harbridges and Eatons are still around, as is Mihika Bhagavati and her entourage. The seers are yet recovering from their fit, by the looks of things. Ravi isn't sure what that means, but he doubts it's good. Both Constance and Cayenne have jumped back away from each other, Constance shaking her hand with a pained wince.

"Mon Dieu, qu'est-ce que tu croyais?" Cayenne pants heavily, rubbing their wrist as if it had been scorched. "You completely fucked everything! *Months* of work for *nothing*, you *plouc*. You've collapsed the timeline back on itself. You could have collapsed *reality itself*, you idiot! You have no idea how danger—"

Ravi twists around and grabs Cayenne's hands, trapping them up in the small of their back in a secure control hold.

"You *selfish asshole*," he fumes, "you were going to make me forget everything?"

Making a deal with a demon to go back further in time,

helping that demon gain power in The Trust, all so Cayenne could try again to seduce Ravi without him ever learning about their true nature? Ravi can barely *think* for how unspeakably angry he is. He'd thought there were still some lines Cayenne wouldn't cross, ways of taking advantage of him even they would balk at.

"Oh, *merde*," Cayenne grumbles, sagging into Ravi's grip. "You were going to do the same, dearest."

"It's not *remotely* the same."

"So, I'm going to fucking find and kill a demon, if nobody minds," Harry declares, urumi in hand.

"Let's," Ravi agrees with feeling. "Where's Val?"

As if this was an answered prayer, Val snaps into being at Harry's shoulder with the sound of fluttering feathers, sunglasses gone.

"Harry," she says, a hint of relief hiding behind her implacable tone. "There you are. I have received word from my superiors. A dire event is about to—" She stops to glare at Cayenne, her face cast in white-blue light from her suddenly flaring eyes. "What is this chronomage doing here?"

"Where have *you* been?" The urumi blades slither metallically as Harry throws up her hands. "Constance's demon was here and I was dancing with him! Chronojerk had us in some bullshit timeline, I think? I'm fuzzy on that."

"They did," Ravi growls.

Harry cocks her head at him. "You okay, Rav? This is *supremely* fucked up. I remember being there, but not exactly what happened in it."

"Be grateful you don't," he hisses, practically in Cayenne's ear. They huff in annoyance, shifting into a nonchalant lean against his chest.

The flame of Val's eyes flickers with distress. "A demon, here? You texted me that you had urgent need for me back at your apartment. I would never knowingly leave your side—"

"No, I didn't!"

"Fucking…" Nate shakes his head in disgust, his fists clenched so tightly they tremble. "Tricked again."

"Wasn't me," Cayenne says with a Gallic shrug. "I thought she was trapped in Hell with the witch."

Suddenly Nate swings forward with a right hook aimed straight at Cayenne's face. Automatically, Ravi pulls back out of range, dragging Cayenne with him as the punch whiffs harmlessly by. Not only does he suspect Nate would regret this impulse later, but the last thing Ravi wants is for Nate to draw Cayenne's ire. They don't believe in turning the other cheek.

"You evil *fuck*!" Nate spits out, moving himself out of the temptation of striking range. "How could you do this to Ravi? Don't you *care* about him?"

"Ooh, yes, *lecture* me, Professor. Is that what you like about him, my sweet? I can see the appeal," Cayenne says with a derisive laugh, resting their head back on Ravi's shoulder.

"I've had it up to fucking *here* with this time travel *bullshit*," Harry storms. "Where'd that fucking demon go, Cayenne? Don't you motherfuck me on this. I want the truth."

"I shall rend this demon in *twain*." Constance picks up Griswold and sets him hissing on her shoulder, his striped tail puffed out like a sheaf of wheat.

Cayenne sighs. "As irritating as it's going to be taking yet another stab at this, you know what they say." They duck and twist their arms. Ravi curses and grasps tighter, but Cayenne slows time, simply there one second and not there the next, spinning just out of his reach. They turn back with a sharp smile, reaching for their tattoo. "Third time's the charm."

The ground rumbles. A line of crimson light shines up from the floor in a curving, spidering arch. Cayenne stumbles, glancing around in confusion. The scarlet line swiftly creeps out under the feet of the increasingly unsettled crowd until it marks a glowing sanguine circle taking up the center of the massive ballroom. Jagged, cramped runes and arcane shapes scratch themselves into being along the circle. Red light pours up from the ground, and with it rises a growing swell of unearthly heat.

"They're backwards," Constance whispers, eyes wide. "The runes. They're being drawn from the other side."

Ravi aligns his shoulders into a firm line. The knot of his reeling emotions levels out in the face of imminent battle.

"*Asura*," he calls out to the crowd, to his aunt. Demons. The first of their foes. Durga's ancient enemies, the ones The Trust had been made to stand vigilant against. Ravi wishes more of the consortium were seasoned fighters. This is likely to be bloody.

"Val," Harry says calmly. "Weapons, please."

Without hesitation, Val winks out, bamfing back with a bulging bag Nate rushes to take. While he throws a quiver of arrows over his shoulder, Val's maul appears in her hands. She hefts it, her mouth set in a grim line.

Meanwhile, Ravi circles around Cayenne on the balls of his feet, watching them warily, keeping his team behind him. Cayenne looks up from the incipient hell portal with a calculating purse of their lips. They catch Ravi's eyes and smile.

"Right! The timetable has moved *up*, I see what he meant now." They take in the crowd, now shouting and milling at the edges of the glowing circle, and tap a finger to their chin.

Mihika Bhagavati takes charge in leading a cabal of other casters into some kind of counter-spell. Padme shouts directives to anyone who looks able to fight.

"*Eh bien.* Maybe I can still make things work in this timeline. You'll be fine, sweetheart. That was the deal. You're not allowed to die before I'm done with you." Cayenne blows Ravi a kiss.

The portal finally splits open with a deafening rumbling roar that shatters the windows. Glass blasts out into the sky as the storm rages in, rain and wind flooding the ballroom as a swarm of leathery-winged imps pour up from the portal with ear-piercing shrieks.

Cayenne disappears only to reappear at Mihika Bhagavati's side, and in the next breath they easily fling her through the nearest window, then disappear again. Ravi lurches forward, but it's done; she's already gone, plummeting to her death. There are cries of dismay as magic fizzles in the remaining spell-casters' hands, the counter-spell failing.

Ravi spins, trying to spot Cayenne, but a cloud of baboon-sized imps crash through the champagne fountain in a deluge of glass, liquid sizzling as it runs over the brightly glowing runes. A few imps snatch up people from the crowd standing too near the shattered windows and take them screaming over the edge. Ravi leaps toward the nearest one, a woman wriggling in the long, curved claws of the shrilly giggling imp pulling her into the air. He's too far away—he's not going to make it.

A red and white fletched arrow neatly clips the imp out of the air before it can carry its victim out past the shattered windows.

"Ravi!" Nate lowers his bow and tosses over the weapons bag. Ravi catches it.

Large talons clasp the edge of the open portal a few yards away, and a hellhound clambers up from the stygian depths, snarling through thick ropes of saliva dripping from impossibly wide jaws. It looks nearly identical to the one Ravi had fought before; a warped, skeletal humanoid hideously walking on all fours, face elongated on a vaguely canine skull. This hellhound wears a thorny chain around its neck and, crawling up behind it, a lesser demon holds the leash in one hand. The other wields a wickedly curved sword.

The demon lifts its many-horned head, grins tusklike teeth, and raises the sword with a roar, sounding a thunderous call to battle. A cacophony of howls and war cries spill upwards from below.

More incoming. Many, many more.

Harry's voice rings out clarion clear. "Val, Ravi, and me on the front line. Nate and Constance, you got range. Stay behind us. Val, reserve as much of your strength as you can. We gotta hold out for as long as possible." The urumi flashes, cutting a handful of squealing imps out of the sky in one blow.

Val's wings snap out wide. She spins her maul in an arc, catching a wiry hellhound in the skull as it scrabbles up from the rim. "Agreed. I shall teleport sparingly."

"I don't have infinite arrows," Nate calls out, shooting another imp down while Constance slaps together some dust and a handful of brambles. At her feet, Griswold hisses ferociously as a wall of thorns rises from the ground, slowing the demons' advance.

Ravi looks at his Glock, then up at the leashed hellhound fast approaching, flame curling through its jagged fangs.

Between battling demons straight from the pits of hell and dancing with Nate in front of the entire Trust, the dancing had been by far the more terrifying undertaking. And Ravi had emerged from that unscathed.

He drops his gun and slides it away, polymer skittering over hardwood until the backstrap bumps against Nate's shoe. Ravi flicks his cuffs straight. He walks directly toward the hellhound.

Harry screams, "What the *fuck* are you doing, Rav?" Nate's desperate shout echoes behind her.

"Getting something that doesn't run out of bullets." The hellhound yanks against its chain, eager to attack. Grinning with bloodthirsty glee, the demon gives the hellhound enough slack to leap.

It lunges. Jaws snap inches from Ravi's face. The beast lands on all fours, shaking its head in confusion.

Ravi waits, breath held, standing firm.

It growls and goes for another bite, jaws opening far wider than physics should allow. Again, its teeth close on nothing, and the worst that happens is the unholy heat of its breath makes Ravi's eyes water. The hellhound cocks its head with a whine.

Ravi gives it a lupine grin. "Untouched and whole, huh? That was the deal."

He springs into motion, slamming a foot into the hellhound's face, cartilage grinding under his shoe, to launch himself right up into the demon's reach. The demon rears back its sword, snarling through a jagged grin.

Ravi *really* hopes he's right about this.

At the zenith of the sword's arc, the demon's sinewy arm locks in place. It roars with frustration, straining as if stuck on flypaper.

Oh, this is going to be fun.

He digs a jab into the demon's fleshy wrist tendons, following with a hammer fist that wrenches the sword free. He tosses it up, catches the hilt, and with a single well-placed strike severs the demon's head from its shoulders. The body crumples, lifeless, and the head rolls, protruding eyes bugged even wider with astonishment, almost cartoonish.

Twisting into a serpentine *chuvadu*, Ravi pins the hellhound straight through the spine, the blade going deeper than expected all the way into the wooden floor. This sword cuts through bone easily as hot butter. Useful. He wrenches the blade free, both bodies already smoldering into bare skeletons.

Ravi rejoins the team, who've shifted around to shield the majority of the crowd, each of them embroiled in a well-orchestrated multi-staged resistance; Nate and Constance whittling demons' defenses down before they even get close enough for Harry and Val to cut them down.

"Cool sword," Harry laughs wildly, her hair flying. One of her sleeves is torn at the elbow, but her skin is whole and unblemished. "Did that dumbass demon prick make it so we've got *two* invulnerable assholes on our side?"

"You're really okay?" Nate adds with a worried frown, Ravi's gun tucked into his cummerbund.

"Told you I'm bulletproof," Ravi jokes. He swings the demon sword overhead, slicing the wings off an imp as it dives toward Constance. It crashes to the floor with a screech, writhing in a puddle of oily blood on the floor until

Val finishes it off with her stiletto heel, her eyes flaring holy blue.

He likes this sword. It's surprisingly light and well-balanced, for its shape. Ravi resolves to keep it when this is all over.

More demons in all different sizes and shapes pour up from the portal like scum bubbling over a sewage drain, a varied assortment of horrors. Some look nearly human, most emphatically do not. A few lead or drag hellhounds on spiked leashes, while others keep smaller enslaved devils on chains instead. Most are armed only with talons and teeth.

It's a flood of enemies—far more than they can keep separate from the crowd. Ravi resigns himself to inevitable casualties, especially if Cayenne is sneaking around picking off key members of The Trust.

"Constance, can you close this?" Harry leaps up a big demon's double-bearded axe to slice its head off, then jumps back lightly to the ground. Even as he cuts through a few more swooping imps, Ravi indulges in a moment of pride. The two of them practiced that move together a few weeks ago.

"Nay. Not without…" The witch hesitates, as a thickly thorned vine sprouts at her feet, creaking as it grows to the size of a tree in less than a second. The vine wraps around several hellhounds just as they open their maws to unleash scorching hot breath on Val, then lifts them up and pitches them shrieking back down through the portal.

"Now's not the time to hold things back, Constance!" Nate snaps off three arrows in quick succession, each one finding its mark buried in another demon's heart. Ravi wishes he could stop and take video; it's incredibly fucking hot.

Hissing and spitting, Griswold blinds a hellhound with a claw swipe before circling back to Constance. Mushrooms erupt from the living skin of the enemies nearest her, blooming over them like a sped-up time lapse until they each slump down lifelessly in a sea of withered husks wearing a rippling coat of fungus.

"'Tis not my casting. I cannot shut the way without a great deal of power. Blood would do it, but t'would take more than any one of us can spare."

"How much do you need?"

Ravi's never been happier to hear his aunt's gunpowder rasp.

Padme cuts through a pair of imps with a slash of a *gupti*, which she must have concealed as a walking cane somewhere close at hand. Flanking her on one side, Callum Harbridge wields a small, concealable pistol, and on her other side, Jihan Kataraju has turned a table leg into a glass-encrusted club.

Callum breaks off to guard Ikshana, plugging a few demons as he goes. Though his eyes are wide with fear, Ravi marks the steadiness of his hands, the accuracy of his shots. The kid's going to go far.

Jihan slams his club into a hellhound's open mouth and kicks the creature back into the hell portal. "It wasn't supposed to be like this," he says bleakly, eyes haunted.

"How was it supposed to go, Jihan my dude?" Harry whips the urumi into a slavering demon so thin as to resemble a reddened skeleton. The multiple blades leave a series of long cuts so deep and hairline-thin it's not until the demon's next heartbeat that blood wells into the wounds. "Your boy Mason promise you a nice, big piece of the pie?"

"He said we could make changes. Defend tradition."

Nocking another arrow, Nate snorts. "Which is it, make changes or defend tradition? You can't have both."

"Sure, you can, if you're a huge fucking hypocrite." Harry slams her shoulder into a grotesque, lumpy demon, knocking it into Nate's sight line for it to be sniped cleanly through the throat with a red-and-white fletched arrow.

"Nice shot!" Ravi yells, grabbing the whip-like tail of an imp and swinging it into a hulking mace-wielding demon. The imp shrieks, clawing at the demon's eyes, and the resulting chaos gives Val the chance to smash the demon's knees out from under it. She rears back her maul and mashes its head into a gooey puddle. Demonic gore splashes into her fiery eyes and hisses as it burns away. Wings spread, Valiance grins, looking like something a very particular type of guy would airbrush on the side of his van.

"Aw, thanks, sunshine. Better than a hockey stick, right?" Without hesitation Nate sends another arrow into a demon's shoulder as it leaps free of the portal, any nerves he might have had swept aside by intense concentration.

Practically made for archery. He could watch Nate all day.

Callum shoots an imp through the wing and pushes a still-reeling Ikshana into cover behind an overturned table. "I really liked your dance," Callum blurts, reddens, then turns to shoot another swooping imp.

"Do you usually let your team waste time with banter, McAllister?" Padme cuts in. "The ice sculptures have been made with holy water."

"Ah." Val perks up. She teleports on top of the buffet table and slams the head of her maul through one of the massive translucent tigers. Splinters of ice rain down.

Imps fall from the air with hideous screeches, fighting with each other to get out of the way. Hellhounds and devils recoil, demons howling as their feet steam and bubble when they step on the fast-melting holy ice.

Taking advantage of the distraction, Ravi ducks in to dispatch as many of the horde as he can. He weaves easily through enemy ranks, none of them able to land a single hit on him. A dance of its own, the ebb and flow of advance and parry, keeping his steps swift and sure as asura after asura falls before him, each one snarling with impotent rage until he cuts the breath from their throats.

"Nice!" shouts Harry, kicking ice into a demon's face. "Any other dope security measures I really should have been apprised of?"

"The ones I haven't kept to myself have all been dismantled," Padme says acidly, joining Jihan to exterminate a brace of grounded imps.

"I didn't know," the man bleats, a vein ticking in his forehead even as he bashes imps into paste with his improvised club. "We wanted to make things better."

"Then you can bleed for the witch," Padme snarls, her posture even now as imperious as a queen's. She winds her way to Ravi as he clears a space by felling a pair of collared devils and their goading master with a savage chain of efficient strikes. "You're unharmed, *bhanja*?"

Every atom of him sharp and thrumming, Ravi nods as he whirls around in a tight circle, on high alert for more demons. Or worse, Cayenne.

Constance instructs Jihan to kneel in front of her and

hands him a small silver knife She points at glowing runes. Blood already drips from her fingertips, a deep slice through her palm.

Harry yells, "Constance, we can't spare you weakening. Keep your blood on the inside, dollface!"

Constance's chin juts stubbornly. "My demon, my fault. Hartnell's presence here is of my doing, time wizard's meddling or no. I'll not let others bleed for my mistakes and stay whole myself."

Val smashes the second sculpture into icy shrapnel, then sweeps into the mess of screaming demons to take them down in wide violent swathes, all the while wearing a joyful, animated grin.

It's almost unsporting, how demon after demon falls before Ravi's agile advance. Each one dies with a comically frustrated look on its hideous face when it discovers it's unable to strike back at him.

Despite everything, Ravi feels at peace, a deep sense of connection to everyone who came before him, to all the men and women who lived and fought and died, who just like him, had hopes and dreams and struggles, had family they wanted to protect.

Chosen or no, he's always been meant for this.

A massive cadaver-gray hand emerges from the portal, looming up high enough to cast a shadow before it slams down onto the ground and cracks the floor into splinters. Heaving its gargantuan bulk up over the edge, the demon is as tall as two Vals, nearly brushing the vaulted ceiling with a pair of twisted horns. It growls like boulders rolling downhill. Gripping an entire dead hellhound in a meaty fist, it wields the corpse like a club, smacking it threateningly against the ground. Ravi has to take a step back to get the whole creature in his field of vision.

"Big boy," Nate says with a slightly hysterical laugh. His arrow lodges deep into the demon's cheek, right below one pure-black eye. The demon doesn't appear to notice, looking around and sniffing. Nate reaches for another arrow and grabs only air, his quiver empty. He swears in Québécois and draws Ravi's gun.

"Do the spell!" Harry leaves Constance and joins Ravi's side, Val following close behind. "Thoughts?"

Ravi takes a flicker-fast assessment of the chaotic battlefield. Enemies everywhere. People dying. "Buy her time to finish the spell."

"Exactly what I was thinking, look at us on the same wavelength and shit. Doc, cover her!"

Nate nods and tips over the buffet table, shielding Constance and Jihan from direct view of the crimson circle as he takes position behind it. Ravi jerks his chin at his aunt, who nods and joins Nate on the defensive line.

The demon's nostrils flare wide as it swings its massive head toward them. Ravi steps in front of Harry, shifting his sword into a backward grip along the length of his forearm.

"Dude, you're not a human shield," Harry tells him. Behind her, Val's wings spread wide.

Balanced in that particular state of battle-calm and savage elation he only experiences in the heat of a good fight, Ravi says, "I kind of am, right now. None of these demons can hurt me. We can use that to our advantage."

Sure enough, the massive demon swings its makeshift corpse club down on them quicker than something that size should be able to move, but the blow stops as if halted by an invisible wall inches away from Ravi's skull. The demon snarls in confused rage. Ravi slashes his blade into its vulnerable armpit, while Val wends sideways to slam her maul into its ribs with a sickeningly loud crunch.

Ligaments snap as Ravi digs the sword in, widening the wound. Demon blood rains down on them. Coughing at the foulness, Harry leans around Ravi and flicks the multi-bladed urumi over the demon's wrist, nearly slicing its hand off. It roars, dropping the hellhound's body, hand clinging to the knob of wrist bones by only a few tendons and scraps of skin.

"You know what I've been thinking?" Harry asks as calmly as if she were having a stroll through a garden instead of kicking aside a dead hellhound that rapidly disintegrates into smoldering embers. Val teleports to the other side of the demon and smashes the back of its knee, staggering the behemoth forward into their ready blades.

Ravi huffs a laugh, leaning in with feet braced to try to pierce the thick cartilage over the demon's heart with the point of his sword. "What's that?"

Harry ducks the demon's wildly thrown fist as she strikes at its eyes, catching one in a savage rake that leaves the creature blinded and roaring. "You must give the best head in the *world,* dude. I can't think of why else your ex would go through all this trouble."

Ravi sputters a laugh. "You're such a romantic, McAllister." The demon's heart is too well protected by a tangle of gristle, so he switches tactics and goes low, opening as many holes in the demon's body as he can manage.

Synchronizing her strikes, Harry goes high, puncturing the demon's throat. "Hey, which one of us banged his way into an apocalypse? I'm just saying."

Falling to its knees, the demon gurgles through bubbles of blood. It manages a backward swing that throws Val off. She skids over melting ice and shards of glass, perilously close to the portal's edge.

Ravi bisects an imp as it dive-bombs Harry, clearing her path for the demon's jugular. "This isn't an apocalypse,

Harry."

"Yeah, yeah," she says as she cleaves the flexible blades of the urumi through the giant demon's neck, releasing a great gout of thick, foul-smelling blood. "Just a Tuesday."

They back away as the demon lurches forward, lifeless even before it hits the ground with thunderous impact.

The hordes of hell pause, giving the trio a wide berth as they stand over the smoldering corpse. A few heartbeats to catch their breath. Ravi's blood sings, alive and exhilarated with battle. He instantly seeks out Nate, with his rumpled tuxedo and disheveled hair. In this moment, Ravi wants nothing more than to stalk over, push Nate to his knees, and take him right there on the floor.

Nate's already watching him, so he catches Ravi's look and immediately flushes up to his eyebrows. *Later*, he mouths, and the weight of the promise, of his utter certainty that there *will* be a later, tips Ravi's heart into wild, reckless flight.

"Just there, if thou please," Constance instructs Jihan, and together they dribble blood onto another set of runes. The markings hiss as the blood falls, the air acrid with the stink of copper. Jihan leans on Constance, unsteady on his feet. "Aye, that's the last, my good fellow. This is going to hurt *quite* a bit," she says apologetically.

Keeping one hand on the back of Jihan's neck,

Constance stretches the other outward over the edge of the portal, the sanguine light painting her ink-stained hand stark red. With one finger she traces the shape of a circle, then clenches her hand into a tight fist. Jihan crumples to his knees with a pained hiss.

Bloody light flutters like a candle about to go out, and the remaining imps shriek in one deafening voice. Most dive back into the hell portal, while the rest scatter from the room through the broken windows out into the night sky, heedless of the raging storm. Any demons and hellhounds close enough to retreat do so, slipping back into the circle to their own realm. Stragglers will be easy enough to mop up by surviving members of The Trust. Or so Ravi hopes.

The air wavers like a mirage over a desert, and the portal winks out completely. The lines and runes all go dark, the massive hole now simply scorched, broken floor. A few late demons scratch at the floorboards until Harry dispatches them with practiced flicks of her wrist.

"I've gotta admit," she says, all tousled hair in a torn gold and black suit, "I've actually been to worse parties."

Ravi scans the room. No telltale flash of red hair, no sign of Cayenne anywhere. He pads over to Constance, cleaning greasy blood off his sword with his sleeve. "Stay sharp," he says grimly. "Cayenne will be back. Can you still do that spell to keep them from jumping time?"

"Oh, aye. Or I shall after a little something to top up mine mystical well." Constance pulls an alarmingly green spotted mushroom from her handbag and tucks it into her cheek. Her pupils expand into black pools as Griswold twines stiff-legged and hissing around her feet. "The last Shaw stands ready for anything."

"The sky is on fire," Ikshana calls out softly, as if in wonder. Ravi extends a hand to pull an exhausted Jihan to his feet while Callum fires a shot into a lingering hellhound that Padme finishes off with a stab of her *gupti*.

Val shakes torn links of spiked chains off her maul while the storm still lashes through the shattered windows. "Harry."

"One sec, big gal." Harry stalks toward Jihan. Ravi gives her space; she looks furious, and if there's one thing Harry doesn't need his help on, it's making her displeasure known.

Instead, he sidles up to Nate with a crooked grin. "Mighty fine shooting, Doc."

Nate scoffs, blue eyes bright. "Nah. Well, with the bow, yes. I had a good teacher, and I've been practicing. But this?" He offers up Ravi's gun. "Your record's still secure, tough guy."

Ravi snorts, shifting the sword to his other shoulder to take the gun. An imp frantically wheels around a battered chandelier until he picks it off with a single shot, the body ash and bone before it even hits the ground. With that, the clip is spent, so Ravi tosses the gun aside.

"Ravi…" Nate moves close, a line of concern drawn between his eyes. "Are you okay? Not the fight, I saw how that went down. Incredibly distracting, by the by, like dangerous levels of sexy. Jesus Christ. But I mean before that. What Cayenne did."

Ravi draws in a long breath. Before he can answer, Val's voice rings out loud and bell-like, her white wings still unfurled.

"Harry."

Harry looks back mid-yell, her hands upraised. "Yes?"

"It is not over."

The team all straighten up, share glances, and reconvene. "I'm listening," Harry says, eyes hard as flint.

"After I was lured away from your side"—Val's eyes flash, incandescent with fury—"I was urgently called to the celestial plane. The war in Hell—"

The ground shifts, the skyscraper shivering under their feet. When Ravi catches his balance, he realizes the storm has gone quiet and still, like a great indrawn breath before a scream.

At the edge of the building, glass crunching underfoot, they all stand side by side looking out over the city with dawning horror. Red lights ooze up. First in one spot, then another, then more and more and more until all of Atlanta is bathed in a bloody glow.

Val hisses, her wings arching back. "The war in Hell is spilling onto Earth."

Hollowly, Constance says, "He's been a busy little prince."

Hell portals are opening up all over the city. All over the world? No way to know. Twisted shapes wing up into the sky, shrieks and howls ringing out among the honking of car alarms and the screaming of sirens.

"Harry," Ravi says softly, his shoulder brushing hers.

Harry's knuckles go white and bloodless on the urumi. She looks at him with a terrible crooked grin.

"Now, *that's* what I call an apocalypse."

Chapter Twenty-One

"JESUS FUCKING CHRIST," Nate rasps thickly, sliding a palm to the small of Ravi's back. "This is… What do we do? How do we stop it?"

"Great question, Doc," Harry says. "Like maybe Constance sends me to Hell and I stab that motherfucking demon in the face?"

Constance shakes her head, still staring out at the city as screams ring out in an increasingly steady cacophony. She picks up Griswold and hugs him tight to her chest. "Would that even end something of this magnitude? I know not. I cannot do such a thing."

"You did before!"

"That was a *summoning!*" Constance blinks rapidly, fighting tears. "Pulling a thing through in our world, not the other way round. 'Tis leagues of difference."

"I don't know, reverse the polarity or something!" Harry stares out at the chaotic vista, hand clenched in her hair like she might rip it all out.

"Harry, this isn't *Star Trek.*" Nate scrambles for his phone, and bites down hard on his lip as he stares in horror at the screen. "Oh, God. My family—*everyone's* families. What do we do?" The look Nate turns to him holds such agony that Ravi feels it as if it were a stray bullet.

Sword in hand, Ravi turns and surveys the aftermath, considering the tools they have available. Bodies everywhere. People he's known his whole life lying strewn among fallen crystal chandeliers and the bone-shard embers of dead demons. Padme and Jihan lead some survivors to pick through the carnage, helping the wounded. Ravi presses his lips into a tight line. They've got only a handful of able-bodied fighters, but at least one surviving seer.

Ravi heads toward Ikshana, still guarded by Callum, shaky but alert. He might be the only adult Harbridge left now. Ravi didn't see any other survivors.

So many dead. More down in the city every second he wastes. Civilians with no idea what's going on or how to combat the threat. There will be time to mourn later. Now,

Ravi does the job that's in front of him.

"Ikshana, we need your vision. Are you—"

Cayenne appears next to Callum, fiery hair windblown. "A seer *would* be helpful, wouldn't it?"

Callum jumps in alarm, turning quickly, but Cayenne slips under the young agent's arm, plucks the gun out of his hands with a practiced twist, and tosses it over their shoulder.

"*Mon Dieu*, would you look at this one!" Cayenne gives Ravi a cute, scrunched-up grin even as they hook an ankle around the back of Callum's knee and smoothly pull him off his feet. "He's like a little *you*. That's *adorable*. I can't possibly kill him." Quick as a mongoose, they snag Callum by his collar and the two disappear, only for Cayenne to pop back alone a mere split second later, Callum lost somewhere in time.

Cayenne approaches Ikshana. The seer leans heavily against the wall while holding their skull in both hands, as if the weight of it is too much to bear. "*You*, however—oh, that hair, darling, *j'adore*. Such a shame."

"Cayenne, no!" Ravi dashes forward, but as quick as he is, he's not faster than someone able to control time.

Unsurprisingly, Cayenne pauses instead of vanishing the instant the seer's wrist is in their grip. They've always loved having the last word. "Don't worry, *mon tigre*, I'll be back to take you somewhere safe where we can wait out all this unpleasantness. I'll be seeing you." They wink.

Val snaps into being behind Cayenne, throwing her muscular arms around their middle to pluck them up off the ground. "He said *no*."

Cayenne wriggles eel-like in her grasp, but her implacable grip doesn't loosen in the slightest. "Oooh, harder, *maman*," they manage through breathless lungs. "We're not on a speeding train *this* time, I think you'll find." Cayenne curls their fingers around Val's forearms and they both wink out of existence. Ravi skids to a halt where they had just been, spitting curses until he runs out of Hindi and has to borrow from Tamil.

Harry calls out, "Constance, you ready?"

"Aye," Constance answers resolutely, her hands poised at shoulder height.

Cayenne reappears alone some distance away, almost where the portal had been vomiting out demons, a few feet midair above the floor. They land lightly and spin on their heel with some leftover momentum.

"*Putain de merde*," they laugh, brushing grass from their jacket, "those Confederates *really* don't like surprises. Good thing she's got wings, no? That should keep her busy for a few hundred yea—"

Constance raises her hands, slams her fists together,

and tears them apart.

Ravi braces for the overpowering lurch, but Constance has had ample time to refine her work since the airport. Instead of wrenching them all back in time, a ring of green seedlings springs up around Cayenne's feet and grows before their eyes, each plant starting from a tiny sprout and stretching into a full-grown flower before it withers and dies, only to rise up again as that little sprout. The pace quickens faster and faster until the flowers seem to be a flickering zoetrope, and a translucent field oozes up from the ground and closes over Cayenne like a bell jar. Staggering as if the wind has gotten knocked out of them, Cayenne bends over with hands braced on their knees.

"Stay," Constance says with tremendous satisfaction. She moves to check on Ikshana, sliding a hand over their pale cheek with a murmur of concern.

Harry sighs, raking bedraggled hair out of her face as she approaches the circle of flowers. She pulls herself to her full height and looks Cayenne up and down, sucking on her teeth.

"Normally, the way we do things on this team is we toss back and forth some gallows humor when the shit really hits the fan. Keep things light, keep our spirits up. But I'm really not feeling it right now, so I'm gonna get straight to the point. You bring back my ass-kicking angel, and then you rewind this whole goddamn fucking apocalypse back to the pregame show. And you do it right. Fucking. Now."

Standing shakily, Cayenne looks at Harry sidelong through their foxy mop. "An interesting proposal, Angharad. If I say no?"

Her hand convulses tight on her urumi. "We make you."

They dissolve into peals of laughter. "Oh *fuck*, that's a good one. There is *nothing* you can say or do that will make me your obedient little servant, Angharad. You can't kill me if you want to have *any* hope of undoing this whole Hell-on-Earth thing, and even if you *noble* hero types could bring yourselves to threaten me with torture, *believe* me, I've survived far worse than anything you could think up." Cayenne's fingers slide through their hair, and Ravi notes the intentional slope their shoulders carve, painting a tableau of someone small and defenseless, in need of protection. "I'd learned to survive just about anything before I even lost my baby teeth, sweetheart."

Harry snorts scornfully. "Boo-fuckin'-hoo, you had a shitty childhood. Guess what, Red? Ravi's was no picnic either, and I can *one hundred percent* guarantee you mine was as bad or worse than yours. And I didn't come out of it a murdering, narcissistic psychopath who keeps torturing the one person I claim matters to me. You *are* going to help us.

My job is to end apocalypses. I didn't sign up for it, and I'm extremely underqualified for it, but *fuck* me if I'm not gonna do it. You can reverse this. So, you're going to get on board, one way or another."

"Hmm," Cayenne pretends to consider, running a finger over their lip. "Go jump in a portal yourself, Chosen One. I wouldn't place high odds on your survival, but that's what you types are picked for anyway, isn't it? Both cannon fodder and sacrificial lambs." Their green-glass gaze softens as it slides to Ravi, their pose shifting into something less confrontational. "Who'd be next in line, darling? Can't be you, *oui?* If it is, I'll go back, put that fucking sword on a *rocket*, and send it to *space* this time."

"It can't be me," Ravi breathes, realization cresting over him like dawn. "It never could have been." He drops the demon sword with a clatter to grasp Harry by her upper arms. "Harry! I know how to fix it."

She blinks, then inspects him shrewdly. "I'm not going to like this, am I?"

"You are not." He spares Nate an apologetic, lopsided smile. Then he straightens, shoulders back, utterly sure of himself. "You have to kill me."

A beat of heavy silence.

"Uh," Harry starts, "what now?" Then she glances down at the urumi, opening her hand so its hilt lies in the flat of her palm. He can practically see her putting the pieces together.

Nate says, "Whoa, now, what are you talking about?"

Harry slides her speculation from the urumi to Cayenne, whose hands drop from their insolent cross over their chest into an artless posture of bafflement. She locks eyes with Ravi.

"It's a big, big gamble, dude."

He knew she'd get it. "What do we have to lose at this point?"

"Doth anyone care to explain?" Constance pipes up from her ministrations over the dazed seer.

Harry doesn't look away from Ravi. "What if it doesn't work?"

He gives her a shrug and a crooked smile. "Punarjanma. Maybe in my next life I'll be luckier."

Nate inhales sharply, and Ravi releases Harry's shoulders. At some point during the fight Nate had discarded the tuxedo jacket, his bow tie undone, white sleeves rolled up past his elbows. An angry red mark from the snap of the bowstring mars his left wrist.

"Ravi, no." Nate steps near, voice breaking. Ravi runs a thumb lightly over that welted wrist, drawing Nate closer, and lays a cool palm over the heated skin to soothe the burn. Nate bites down on his lip so hard it's a wonder it doesn't bleed.

In their cage, Cayenne scoffs, "Whatever lunacy you're planning, it won't work. I've run across several necromancers throughout the years. You think there's *any* possibility that I won't find a way to keep you safe and alive, *mon amour*? Whatever moronic martyr routine you're devising, it's pointless." They flick their gaze back and forth between him and Harry, pointedly ignoring Nate.

Reflexively Nate rubs at his own breastbone, pained lines around his eyes. "The urumi is one of the few ways to kill someone so necromancy can't bring them back."

"*Quoi?* No, no, what the *fuck* are you—" Cayenne surges forward but the forcefield acts like a solid wall. They stumble back, hissing.

Ravi nods slowly, eyes on Nate. "Only the urumi can do it. No type of magic can bring me back from that. Except one." Probably. There's no real way of knowing if even time travel will be effective. As Harry said, it's a gamble.

Nate winces, hand still rubbing his chest as if to stem a spilling wound. Ravi takes it, stilling the restless movement to cradle both of Nate's hands between his own. The breath escapes Nate's lungs in a hoarse rush. "And the urumi can never harm the Chosen who wields it," he grates, fingers closing tight over Ravi's.

"Fortuitous," Constance hums. She pushes back her

hair, dark braids fallen and tangled into a Pictish crest. "I hath long since ceased believing in such a thing as coincidence."

Harry rubs a palm over her face, further smudging her makeup. "You need a minute?"

"Please," Ravi answers with a grateful sideways bob of his head, not bothering to anglicize the very Indian gesture. Harry beckons to Constance, and together the ladies form a wall as best they can, blocking Nate and Ravi from view.

Nate shakes his head, chewing his lip nearly bloody. "This... Ravi. I see what you're trying to do, but there has to be something else, some other—"

Ravi takes Nate's face between his hands and kisses him. Nate gasps sharply against his lips, then melts into the embrace, clutching desperately at Ravi's torn shirt.

"Nathaniel. You're the kindest, most generous soul I have ever met. You make me feel like...like there's whole chapters of myself I've only turned the pages to because of you. One smile from you is better than a hundred from anybody else." Ravi's pulse thuds painfully in his chest, as if his heart were too big for his ribcage to contain. "I should have said yes. When you asked if it was a date, back when I wanted to take you shooting. I'm so sorry I—"

"Don't," Nate whispers, head bowing to rest their brows together. "You don't have to apologize for anything."

He pulls back just far enough to meet Ravi's eyes, a core of resolve settling in to banish fear. "If this is what you think is best, I'm…I'm with you."

"Do you trust me, *jaan*?"

"Course I do. What's…what's *jaan* mean?"

Ravi cups Nate's cheek in his hand, thumb grazing golden stubble where Nate's dimples hide, and sends up a prayer he'll get to see them again. "I'll tell you on the other side."

It's almost impossible to step away, his touch lingering until Nate gives him a small, supportive nod.

Ravi walks as close to Cayenne as the spell circle allows. At his feet, petals unfurl and wither in strobe-like flashes.

Cayenne gives him an unimpressed roll of their eyes. "I suppose that saccharine display was for my benefit," they drawl. "Teaching me a lesson?"

"Cayenne." Ravi keeps his voice steady. A mingled riot of destruction and terror rises up from the city, an unsettling backdrop. "Do this for me. Undo this and help us stop this apocalypse, and we'll be even. All debts repaid."

Cayenne crosses their arms over their chest, lifting their chin to a haughty angle. "You expect me to fall for this, *mon beau?* Threatening me with this ludicrous ploy is, what? Supposed to make me fall to my knees and promise to be a good little pepper? To bring back your angel, to serve up the head of that demon? You want me *tamed,* is that it?"

"No. That ship has sailed. That ship has *sunk.* I can't trust any promise you make. You've broken every one you've ever made me." Ravi shuts his eyes tight for a heartbeat. Dredging the next words up from underground is one of the hardest things he's ever done, every syllable gravel and dry soil. "Do you truly love me? Do you honestly want me to be happy?"

Cayenne clasps both hands over their heart, nothing but emerald earnestness and fervent fact. "Yes, Ravi, *bien sûr! Mille fois oui,* if you believe only *one* thing, you must believe that."

"I do," Ravi whispers, "that's why I know you're going to do the right thing."

Cayenne presses their palms to the barrier. "Darling. This isn't going to work. Just *come with me,* leave this wreck behind you. You expect me to believe that you'd rather *die* than—" Cayenne looks as though they've been struck across the face, like the floor just shattered out from under them.

So, they do get it, after all. Ravi crooks into a rueful smile. "If you don't think I'd rather die than let you hurt people, Cay, then you never really knew me at all."

Their fingers form panicked claws against the barrier.

"This is another trick," they insist. "It's… I can't take this many back, anyway. Not all of you, not without ages to set it up. It wouldn't even work."

"Constance will help." Ravi glances back over his shoulder. "It'll work, right?"

Constance has one arm around Harry's waist and the other slung across Nate's back, all three heads bowed together. She looks up with a startled blink.

"Ah…yes?" Her attention drifts, lips shaping silent calculations. "With enough will, we may. I think."

Cayenne slams a futile kick into the translucent partition. "Ravi, you goddamn selfless, noble *idiot*, don't you fucking *dare* do this to me! You aren't allowed to die until *I* am done with you, you can't—" They clap a hand over their mouth, tears brimming.

Ravi reaches out. He places his palm opposite theirs, only a thin shield of magic between their hands.

Cayenne subsides, going as still as an animal in a snare. They're so beautiful, even still—wild with fury, destruction all around them. Ravi leans close, the tumble of his hair brushing the barrier. He wants to tell them a hundred things—a mad, contradictory tangle of words that stick under his tongue. Maybe someday Ravi will be able to unknot it all: rage, betrayal, guilt, sorrow, grief, regret, even gratitude.

Without the storm, nothing new would ever grow.

"Looks like you get to be a hero, after all, Cay."

Cayenne pounds a furious fist against the barrier, snarling. "You're all *crazy*, this isn't fair, this is…this is… Angharad McAllister, don't you *fucking* dare! Anyone who helps him, who hurts a *fucking* hair on his head, I will destroy *everything* you've *ever* loved! I will *salt the fucking earth!*"

"I'm ready," he tells Harry.

Something bumps Ravi's leg. Griswold's yellow eyes shine up. "Thou shalt travel far, valorous one, across the very veil of death itself!" His striped tail twists into an approving loop. "May fortune favor us, that thou shalt not be lost beyond reach for ever and always."

"Thanks, Griz. Hey…can I pet you? I never have before." Allergies are currently the least of Ravi's concerns.

Griswold stretches into a long, lean line, forepaws on Ravi's knees. "A fine final request, indeed!" He quakes with a mighty purr as Ravi scratches behind tufted lynx-like ears. His fur is even softer than it looks.

When Ravi straightens, Constance offers him a watery smile and the hilt of the demon sword. "No warrior should face death without blade in hand."

The sword is a very welcome weight, and Ravi takes it with gratitude. "Can you imagine the look on Hartnell's face when we go back and know who he really is?"

Constance's tremulous smile spreads into a savage grin. "Vengeance hath been ages coming. The wretched slime shall not wriggle free this time." She glances over at Nate, standing aside with his shoulders hunched and his fingers pressed over his mouth. "I'll keep our favored scholar under mine eye, nephew-to-be. Give him a shoulder, should he need it."

"Thank you, Constance." Ravi fights the need to go to Nate and offer comfort, but he's drawn this out long enough. He wonders briefly what Val would say, but he's fairly certain she'd suggest they hurry up and get it over with.

He gives Harry a nod.

She shakes herself like a wet dog and demands, "Nobody watch this, okay? I mean it."

After making sure the other two have their backs turned, she glances around at the scattered upturned tables and points at the clearest spot of the floor. "Your aunt's going to kill me," she says matter-of-factly. Cayenne's frantic yelling is already drawing attention from the other side of the ruined gala, surely bringing the surviving Trust members over before too long.

"Sorry."

Harry snorts a graceless laugh. "Yeah, you should be

apologizing to me." She lets the urumi unfurl from her hand. Its beauty strikes him, many rivers pouring out from one central source. No matter what happens next, no matter what fruits his actions may yield, in this moment Ravi feels *whole*; a pure, clean clarity of purpose, as true to his nature as it is the urumi's nature to be sharp.

"Rav, listen. Between you and me, are you *sure* about this? There isn't *any* other way to..." She stops and digs thumb and forefinger into the inside corners of her eyes. "No, I get it. Being a private eye *and* social worker means I've seen obsessive, predatory relationships play out a hundred times, and there's depressingly few ways they end." Harry attempts a smile. It's almost convincing. "This should send a pretty clear message. But if it doesn't work, I'm going to be absolutely furious with you. I'll call off the wedding, even. I'm serious."

"Completely fair." Ravi squares his shoulders, sword at his side. Unflinching. "And Harry? Thank you."

Her throat moves a few times before she rasps, "Yeah, well. Love ya, you big jerk."

As last words to hear before dying go, it's not the worst sentiment to go out on.

Chapter Twenty-Two

SO, NATE'S HAD better days.

To be fair, today definitely had its highlights. The crowning jewel was the part where the guy he's been steadily falling head-over-heels for came out in truly theatrical fashion to his entire secret society, all the while taking Nate along for the ride. Yeah, that had been something else, even if Nate can only remember half of it before the timeline got fuzzy and broken. Ravi had been incredible, leading Nate on the dance floor like an honest-to-goodness storybook prince, flashing that unguarded sunshine smile he's only ever seen while in the tangle of bed sheets.

Nate focuses on that image, of Ravi handsome and

happy in his gold-trimmed suit, instead of the current alternative, which is Ravi being dead, just over there, not too far from where they'd been dancing. Unmistakably dead, while literal demons ravage the earth, God-knows-what happening to all of Nate's friends and family and the rest of the world and…

Yeah. He's had better days.

Nate keeps his eyes averted even as he approaches Harry. She switches the urumi back into its disguised form and shoves the coin in her trouser pocket as if she can't stand to touch it. He reaches out to give her a hug.

She stiff-arms him away, lips drawn tight and pale over clenched teeth. "Nobody be nice to me right now," she barks out in an unmistakable order.

Wiping the sympathy from his expression, Nate steps back, palms out. His sister Nicolette is the same way. Able to soldier on through any hardship right up until the point that someone shows her the barest hint of kindness, then she crumples. Is Nicki even alive right now? Nate keeps his attention fixed in the here and now with considerable effort. "You got it, boss." He tries to lick some moisture across desert-dry lips, forcibly keeping his eyes off…off the body.

Constance makes a dissatisfied sound in her throat. "Griswold, my knight. Watch over him. 'Tis…unseemly, to leave him with only a sword for his vigil."

"Aye, mistress. T'would be mine honor." Griswold curls up on Ravi's chest, tail twining around his paws. His yellow eyes glow, keeping watch. Holding vigil.

Strangely, it is better. More seemly.

Nate takes a shaky breath before asking Harry, "What do you need?"

Instead of answering him, Harry wheels around and stalks toward Cayenne, gritting out over her shoulder, "Constance, do whatever you need to get ready for the spell."

"Ah, would that I could, my niece."

A small retinue of Trust members advances on them, makeshift weapons brandished. Constance takes a step back, her eyes darting toward exits.

The look on Ravi's aunt's face is not something Nate ever wants to see again. Pure, glacial murder. He hurries to step in front of Constance with his hands up, happy to provide a human buffer to any witch-hunter ire. "It's okay, there's a plan. I know this looks bad, but it's temporary."

Not slowing, Padme snarls with rage, *"Get out of my way."*

Before Nate can respond, Harry stops in her tracks and spins to face the mob. "Stand the fuck down, Director. Like the Doc said, this is temporary. But not if you charge in and fuck everything up the way The Trust has been doing for the last however many decades. Your nephew, *my fiancé*, has a solid plan and we are sticking. The fuck. To it. Back off and let me do my job." Clearly expecting obedience, Harry turns away and continues toward Cayenne.

Padme glares at Nate, then swings her gaze to the trapped chronomage. She drags in a breath, hands tight on the hilt of a long, thin sword, then looks at the body. The abject loss hits Nate like a gut punch, her face drawn into old, familiar grief.

Nate knows how she feels. He's trying like hell not to think about it.

"Trust him," he says softly.

Padme's stare pierces into Nate. She looks like she's aged decades in mere minutes. "Do what you need to do," she grits out, and directs the rest of the survivors to set up a perimeter at the shattered windows.

Winged shadows darken the skies, some of them far too big to be mere imps. Nate's busy mind wonders briefly about their chances at being attacked by harpies and other types of flying hellbeast. Maybe he'll find time to write an article on demon biodiversity when this is done.

Harry prods at the ring encircling Cayenne with the toe of her shoe. "Okay, Red. Time of truth."

Facing away, Cayenne slumps, arms wrapped tight around their ribs and hair fallen over their eyes. They don't move to acknowledge her.

"Hey. You gonna fix this, or are you going to let him stay dead?"

They flinch. "You already have your blade in my jugular, Harry. There's no need to slice any deeper."

"Look at me." Harry waits until they finally do. "I'm going to tell Constance to take this circle down. What happens after that is up to you."

Constance's mouth curls up in doubt, but she pulls a small, forked twig from the depths of her tangled hair and snaps it in two. The plants surrounding Cayenne explode into fulsome blooms before all shifting into wispy seed puffs that drift like dandelions in autumn, no longer withering and growing in an endless loop.

With bated breath, they all watch Cayenne, poised for anything. Cayenne casts their gaze up toward the ceiling, pulls in a shaky breath, and disappears.

Nate stares in shock. "That *fucking*—"

"Wait," Harry sighs. Sure enough, she's barely done speaking when a short distance away, high up near the ceiling, a confusion of limbs and feathers pop into the air.

Valiance spreads her wings out to catch herself before she tumbles to the ground. Cayenne is less graceful, spilling onto their knees with a muttered curse. Val's ashen hair has fallen from its braid. She's got her maul in one hand, and gripped tight in the other is… Nate blinks. A cannonball. Smoking slightly.

Well, that's likely to have caused some confused Civil War witness accounts he resolves to look up later.

After seeing Harry, Val droops her wings with relief. She gives her surroundings an appraising sweep, from the dark shadows flying outside the windows to the gently wafting seeds. The instant her gaze catches on the cat crouched protectively on Ravi's still form, her fiery eyes flare azure with flame, wings bristling anew. The handle of her maul creaks in her grip, and she draws herself up to her full height, which in heels puts her well above Nate.

"Whoa! Hey, easy, big gal." Harry waves her hands over her head like she's trying to flag down a plane. "Eyes on me. Time travel bullshit soon incoming to fix all this."

Val's face twitches with a cavalcade of emotions too swift for Nate to parse. Her voice resonates more than usual. "Hear my vow. Once this is over, chronomancer, should you ever cross my path again, you will not survive the encounter."

"*Je t'entends parfaitement,*" Cayenne says dully, getting to their feet. They look over to Constance. "I need…I need chalk. Candles. And something to portion out the chronal energy. I usually use pocket watches. Clocks."

Nate appreciates Constance's capable, professional

demeanor as she promptly digs out some chalk from her bottomless handbag. It's comforting to think that somebody here knows what the fuck they're doing.

She tosses the chalk over. "Metaphorical representations, aye. I understand the theory."

"You okay?"

Nate jumps at the sudden words spoken softly at his shoulder. "Jesus, Harry, wear a bell or something."

She gives him one of those stretched-lip humorless smiles strangers give each other in cramped elevators. "Sorry." Val is a silent sentinel at her side, wing feathers bristled high. All the three of them can do is watch as Constance assists Cayenne in tracing a large circle on the ground. Around the...the body.

"Doc... Nate. You okay?"

"Nope. Are *you*?"

"Nope."

"I should have taken your advice."

"Obviously. What advice is that?"

He has to swallow around the lump in his throat half a dozen times before he can answer. "I got my delicate himbo heart all tangled up in an impossible situation."

Harry's smile becomes several shades more genuine as she squeezes Nate's shoulder. "Didn't look so impossible from where I was standing, my dude."

A terrible screech cuts through the air as an imp finds its way into the room, wings slashing through the air as it hovers, calling more of its brethren with loud cries. Val whips the cannonball at it like a fastball pitch. With a sickening crack and a cut-off wail, the imp sails off through the night into obscurity.

"More will follow," the angel states. "I can keep them at bay."

"You're a peach. Enjoy the dance, big gal."

Val hefts her maul, then she's off over the heads of the Trust survivors, bludgeoning imps, and other horrors that approach the windows with a roar of righteous fury.

Harry claps Nate on the back. "Come on. Let's see what we two normies can do to help."

As they approach, Cayenne has an armful of men's watches they pick through one by one, rubbing each watch between their fingers before stacking them all on one slender wrist. Probably best not to ask where they all came from.

"This isn't going to work," Cayenne says while shooting a glare at Constance, no lilting affectation to their speech. The Parisian accent sounds a little off, vowels sliding into a strange patois. "I wasn't exaggerating about that. I've never taken more than one back with me in a single go. It's likely impossible. And despite you picking up a few tricks, Glinda, you are *no* chronomage."

Constance traverses the chalk circle with careful, intentional steps of her clunky boots. "And *you* are no witch. You have never before done magic with a proper practitioner, so you have no way of knowing what the impossibilities are. Any spell may be enhanced by enough willful minds bent upon it, and this room has nothing *but* willful minds within. Nathan, stand here if you would? Across from Harry."

Cayenne mutters darkly under their breath, tosses a watch to Harry, then turns to Nate.

Nate can't stand the sight of them. He has to count to ten just to unclench his fists from immutable knots at his sides.

"I took your suggestion." Cayenne pulls a watch off their wrist and holds it out to him.

"You *really* shouldn't talk to me," Nate manages through clenched teeth, taking the watch and slipping it on.

He receives an annoyed roll of the eyes. Jesus, doesn't this asshole have a single ounce of self-preservation? Does being the only constant in a universe they can control make Cayenne utterly incapable of seeing others as real people, unable to even conceive why Nate might be furious?

"I would have thought a professor would be more pleased that a humble student has taken his advice."

"The only thing I've ever suggested was for you to fuck off. And to get therapy."

"Ah. Well, you also mentioned that a good relationship should be built on trust and support. Something like that, anyway." They glance toward the…the middle of the circle that Nate is avoiding looking at, and they shudder before pulling themself back together. "So, I took your advice, and tried that. I wanted to thank you for it."

Nate can't believe what he's hearing, can barely absorb the implication. "I said *honesty* too."

"Well," they say with false brightness, "two out of three isn't bad, *oui?* I was making it work. It was going so well."

Where to even start with that? Jesus. "After Ravi told you he wanted you out of his life, you went back in time to take that decision away from him. Do you understand what that— No, you know what? *Fuck you,* Cayenne. Whatever you're hoping to get out of this conversation, you're not getting it. We're not tools for your personal journey to self-actualization. *Just bring him back,*" he finishes, voice scratching and broken by the final word.

They gnaw their bottom lip. "Tell him—"

"Oh, fuck *off,* I'm not telling him anything for you."

Cayenne huffs a frustrated breath. "You're very difficult to talk to."

"You mean I'm difficult to manipulate."

They open their mouth, then close it. A nettled, defeated smile finds its way onto their face. "That is what I mean," Cayenne nods, with something almost like respect. "Take good—"

Nate snarls, "I swear to every pantheon that exists, Cayenne, if you dare insinuate that you are graciously *allowing* him to see other people, you better make your next stop to the best dentist in history. You have *no right*."

Cayenne swallows hard, eyes downcast. They press their lips together and slouch away. They fling a watch at Constance.

"Here. Gather your willful minds, then."

Harry fiddles with the pearl of her ring. "How many people do you need, Constance?"

Constance bobs her head from one side to the other, as if weighing options, then ducks as Val soars overhead, grappling a howling multi-winged creature that looks like five different beasts crammed into one form. Nate has *no* idea what that one is. Some type of chimeric demon? After Val slams it into the wall a few times, it's hard to tell from what's left. Ugh. Maybe he should give vegetarianism a go.

"Methinks the more the better," Constance decides, guiding Ikshana into place next to her. They cling to her arm for a moment before straightening with a bleary wince.

Harry joins Padme on the defensive line. "We're going to need people to work the spell to jump back in time before this all goes down. It's likely that anyone not involved with the spell will forget what happened in the future once we're in the past—yeah, I know, grammar and time travel do *not* mix—so I want you, Jihan, and anyone else you pick to lend your…energies. Auras. Whatever."

Padme disengages from her vigil at the window, leaving a handful of fighters slashing at any imps that dare draw close enough. Her striking face is devoid of expression, demeanor carefully controlled. "Ones whose accounts will be trusted by the consortium heads who have been slain in this branching of time, I gather. It shall be done, Chosen. You will need your angel, no doubt. Everyone not assisting with the spell will hold firm the perimeter."

In short order, the circle is ringed by lit candles and a handful of people, each with their own chronally charged watch around their wrists. Val soon joins them, folding her wings away and catching the watch Harry tosses at her.

"What do we need to do?" Harry's gaze falls on Griswold, on where he lays, and her jawline goes stiff.

Planting her feet wide, Constance stretches out her hands with fingers faintly waving as if trailing through running water. "I shall guide our entwined wills toward the time wizard, but the *intent* is the important thing. Focus singularly on the intent to go back, to unravel the stream of time. Hammer thy will against the anvil of the world, that together we may forge our intent into being."

"And they call *me* dramatic," Cayenne mutters. They hug themself tight, fingertips digging into their forearms. They near Ravi's body with steps so slow and labored it's as if they move through a mire of mud.

Harry watches Cayenne with what Nate likes to call her detective face: tough, incisive, brooking no nonsense. "Seems like we're slinging a lot of power your way with no real way for us to control how you're directing it, Red. Be a prime time to fuck us over and go wherever you want."

Cayenne doesn't deign to look at her, folding down to their knees besides Ravi. "It certainly would be, wouldn't it." Blinking rapidly, Cayenne sucks in a lungful of air and places a hand on Ravi's wrist.

Nate tries to do as Constance instructed and focus his intent, to think about the time stream, of undoing the demon apocalypse, but it's no good. All he can think about is seeing Ravi's eyes open again. Deep, rich, velvety brown, so thickly lashed that when Nate had first met Ravi, he thought for a second the guy was wearing eyeliner. Prettiest eyes Nate's ever seen in his life.

All he can think about is Ravi laughing at some dumb joke Nate's made, how every time he looked at Nate like he couldn't quite believe it, like Nate was a gift Ravi never expected to receive. Nate can't think of anything beyond seeing Ravi's hard-won smile, a locked door full of hidden light that only comes spilling out when you find the key.

"*C'est prêt,*" Cayenne says thickly. "Ready."

Constance's voice cuts across like a blade of warning, "No one touches Hartnell. The demon is *mine.*" At their feet, candleflame flares up bright.

Cayenne cups Ravi's face, tears streaming down their cheeks. Before the first one rolls off their chin and falls, the world shifts.

The watch on Nate's wrist goes ice cold, almost painfully so, but that discomfort is nothing compared to the wrenching tug in the pit of his stomach. His guts have been dragged along ahead of him, the rest of his body rushing to catch up, careening through a formless void. His head reels, dizzier than he can ever remember being since he was a kid spinning on a tire swing.

It spins and spins, then Nate's spun as far out as he can go, arm extended and music swelling. Dizziness fades. A hand tugs him back, and Nate follows, stepping in time with the music, ending up chest to chest with Ravi. Ravi, grinning and gorgeous and gloriously alive.

Ravi blinks a few times, taking in their surroundings. Good thing somebody is, because all Nate can do is watch him, only peripherally aware of the dance floor and all its spectators. Ravi's lips curve into a wide, crooked grin.

"I guess it worked, huh?"

*

NATE SMILES SO brightly it occludes the storm outside, outshining even the chandeliers overhead. He grabs Ravi's collar and tugs him into a colliding kiss, deep and true and full of promise.

"Please don't do anything like that ever again," Nate breathes against his lips.

Ravi frames Nate's face in his hands. "I don't intend to. I'll apologize properly later. First, we have a demon to slay." Reluctantly, he pulls back, only to startle at the sudden, baffling sound of applause.

Hard to say where it originated; perhaps from Callum and the other Harbridges, or from Jessika nudging the other Eatons into it, a ring of enthusiastic applause surrounds Ravi and Nate. People he'd never have expected to do so are clapping, smiling, toasting. Even Jihan Kataraju joins in after a roll of his eyes, to the apparent disbelief of his brothers.

Robert Hernandez once told Ravi, *Just goes to show you, there's probably love all around you that you're just not seeing.*

Ravi's ears are hot coals. Swallowing a smile, he takes Nate's hand and leads him off the dance floor to find the rest of the team. Nate follows, playing to the crowd with a shameless wink and irreverent salute. "We certainly slayed the audience."

Weaving through suits and gowns that graciously part before them, Ravi halts for a moment. "Damn."

"What? What is it?"

"Sorry, nothing important. Just a shame that demon sword didn't come back with me." He spots Val, and once they lock eyes, she jerks her chin toward the kitchen door behind the champagne fountain, so Ravi diverts their path to converge with hers.

Nate snorts a laugh, squeezing Ravi's hand. "Tell ya what, sunshine, I'll get you a cool sword for Diwali. Hey, d'you think Constance and Ikshana got zapped back to mid-bang?"

Ravi barks out a laugh before clapping a palm over his mouth. "*Baap re*, Nate!"

"Sorry, sorry. Serious demon-killing, apocalypse-averting time." Nate schools his expression into mock severity. It lasts all of two seconds before dissolving into another brilliant smile. "I'm just so happy you're okay."

As he looks up at Nate, Ravi's heart feels like a falcon ready to soar. Before he can respond, a hand clamps down on Ravi's shoulder and spins him around. Instinctively he squares up, prepared to fend off the attack, but finds himself instead accosted in a rib-crushing hug, blinking down at the blue-black crown of his aunt's head.

"You foolish, *reckless* boy!" After a frozen second,

Padme pushes herself upright, spine straightening. "It was exceedingly unwise to leave all our fates up to the unpredictable whims of someone so dangerous, Ravi. When Mason has been dealt with, we are going to discuss acceptable measures of risk."

"I...I'm sorry to have worried you, *Mausi*."

Her sniff is a little watery. "Yes, well. *Oont ke muh mein jeera*." A cumin seed in the mouth of a camel; his apology is grossly insufficient.

He keeps to the task at hand. "Eyes on Mason? On Harry?"

Padme lifts her chin, brisk and businesslike. "Indeed. She's keeping him busy. Only a handful of us here remember what happened or shall still be to happen. The Trust stands ready to support the Chosen and her team in any way she deems fit."

Ravi gathers his aunt in his arms. She goes stiff for an instant, but then tucks her head under his chin and squeezes him back. When they part, she doesn't meet his eyes. Instead, Padme glares at Nate with all the intensity of an eagle diving down on its quivering prey.

"And you, Professor Corbin. We are going to have a talk about your intentions with my nephew."

"Yeah, that'll be nice," Nate answers easily, leaning his shoulder into Ravi's. "Dinner at my place? I'll cook."

This marks the third time in his entire life that Ravi has seen his aunt on her back foot. There's only an extended pause and a twitch of her brows, but to Ravi it's clear as day that she's as impressed with Nate's lack of fear as she is surprised. Ravi barely smothers a besotted grin.

"I suppose a nice Indian boy wasn't good enough for you, *bhanja*? I look forward to that dinner," she sniffs, then gracefully turns on her heel.

They arrive at the rendezvous with no further delays. Val, arms crossed, waits beside the door to the kitchen, as calm and implacable as ever.

"A bold move," she says by way of greeting. "An invigorating battle. I am relieved that we shall doubtless fight together in many more to come, Ravi Abhiramnew."

"Uh oh, full name," Nate warns. "In my household, that always meant you were going to be read the riot act."

"This is not untrue," Val agrees, eyes briefly flashing.

Ravi clears his throat, eager to steer the conversation off himself. "Where's Constance?"

"Within the kitchen. It appears she has deemed concluding her sexual congress with the seer to be of equal or greater importance than defeating her nemesis."

"Living her best life," Nate says fondly. He startles a little, looking down at his ankle. "Oh, right, invisible cat. Hey, Griswold, nice to not see you."

Griswold's strident voice emits from ankle-height. "Didst thou all witness how I laid tooth and claw to yon demon cur?"

"A valiant attack," Val nods. "I am currently keeping the demon in my sights, do not fear. I'd be at Harry's side now, if it wouldn't tip off the demon and send it into hiding."

The door opens and a bright-eyed Constance sidles out. She grins. "Here again to spy, thou vexing little voyeurs?"

"*No,*" Ravi protests, flushing dark, but Constance just laughs merrily and taps him on the nose.

"I jest. You will have to tell me later what it was like being dead! Did you meet the Wandering Lady?"

"Don't remember it. How's Ikshana? Unharmed?"

The suggestion in Constance's wicked smile is enough to make Ravi blush anew. "*Quite* well, I should think. Give the poor dear a moment to recover. Where is that cowardly churl of a demon?"

"Harry's got him occupied." Nate jerks a thumb over his shoulder. "You're gonna have to tell me about this Wandering Lady thing later, that's a new one to me."

"Isn't 'later' a beautiful word?" Constance leans down to pet the presumably arched spine of her unseen cat. "Ravi. How are you faring? A harrowing eve for us all, but you have borne the brunt of it."

The alternate memories aren't gone; more like faded, distant enough that it feels a little like a dream, or like it happened to someone else. Photographs with the color drained from them.

"I'm okay," Ravi assures her. "Let's kill your demon."

"Aye! Valiance, have you any angelic knowledge of weapons that will rend a demon prince asunder? Preferably one that you could bring hence to my hand. Or mayhaps I could borrow thine maul? All those tomes, all that research and studying, and I have not yet uncovered what Hartnell's weakness be."

"I would lend you my maul, but it would not be a holy weapon in your hand. Likewise, only the Chosen can wield the urumi as anything more than a simple blade."

"Harry can just slip the urumi into his pocket or something," Nate chimes. Everyone stares at him. "According to Turkish accounts from the ninth century, the then-Chosen was able to take down a minor deity after it *swallowed* the noodle sword, and when the Chosen—"

"Vrishin," Ravi adds, easily envisioning Nate poring over old books, glasses sliding down his nose.

"Vrishin Abhiramnew, that's the guy, thanks, babe. So, Vrishin trapped this rampaging blood god in a river and it just up and *drowned*. Now, there's enough data out there about that type of supernatural being to suggest it should not be drownable. So! What can we conclude?" Nate raises a single professorial finger in the air, both eyebrows echoing the gesture. "If just touching the urumi can weaken an actual god enough to kill it with a little thing like lack of oxygen, I'd say your chances are excellent that a demon prince won't fare any better."

Val claps Constance between the shoulder blades, nearly pitching her forward. "Excellent news. Your cousin may be avenged by your own hand. Choose your weapon, my friend."

Constance's eyes sparkle.

*

RAVI TEXTS HARRY a brief sketch of the plan, and she sends back a thumbs-up. He walks with Nate, their shoulders brushing. As they pass partygoers, he receives tiny, somber nods from the handful of Trusties who remember the other timeline, all standing ready to follow his lead.

"You doing okay, sunshine?"

"Yeah. I'm good." Ravi flashes a smile. "I'm glad we got to finish our dance."

Nate's dimples make an appearance. "Me too. Though you still haven't told me what *jaan* means."

"Oh." Ravi clears his throat. Sudden nerves flutter up in his belly in a way they hadn't a second ago, when he'd merely been ready to face down an archdemon. "It's Hindi. Or Urdu. Both. Lots of desi people use a variation of it."

"If you don't want to tell me…"

"No, I…I do." Ravi pulse quickens. "It can be used casually like English uses *babe, honey, sweetheart*. Things like that. Direct translation is *love* or *life*. It's, um. It's *usually* used informally to refer to a girlfriend or boyfriend."

Nate's eyes widen, a rosy flush creeping up his cheeks. "Usually?"

Ravi gazes into Nate's eyes, earth meeting sky. "It grows with intimacy. Over time, the meaning can become more literal. It's a word that does a lot of heavy lifting."

"*Jaan.*" Nate rolls the word on his tongue. "I like it." His fingers brush Ravi's hand.

"The pair of you are so saccharine sweet thou shalt melt in a rainstorm," comes Constance's amused voice behind them.

Nate chuckles. "Hush, you. I'm trying to get swept off my feet, here."

"I'll sweep you anywhere you like after this demon is dead." Ravi is certain his ears have gone floridly dark.

"Why, Agent Abhiramnew! Whatever will your fiancée say?" Nate teases warmly.

"Probably, 'hell yeah, get some.'"

"Oh my God, she would." Nate wrangles his laughter

under control as they circle a decorative pillar.

In an alcove surrounded by potted ferns, Harry and Mason stand closely in conversation, Harry laying a hand on his elbow. The demon smiles, handsome and confident, solely focused on Harry's attentions.

Ravi resolves to look into recovering Javier Mason's body, if Hartnell left any of it. The man's a hero of The Trust and deserves full honors.

"Oh, hi, guys!" Harry gives the pair of them a cheerful wave. She smiles too brightly, swaying as if she's overindulged on champagne. Or perhaps drunk too much from the small stainless-steel flask she furtively hands back to Mason.

Mason plasters a big, polite smile on his rugged face, tucking the flask inside a breast pocket. "I've been keeping your charming bride-to-be entertained, as requested."

While he's distracted, Harry drops her tipsy affectation and slips the coin-shaped urumi into Mason's tuxedo pocket. She keeps one hand wrapped around his elbow.

"Kind of you," Ravi says with a smile of his own. It feels more like a baring of teeth, but it seems to be good enough to keep Mason none the wiser.

"Have you been introduced to Nate?" Harry asks. "Javier Mason, this is Professor Nathaniel Corbin. He keeps us up to speed on monster lore. You know, where to stab stuff, what to stab it with."

"Ah, important work," Mason says with an approving nod and a friendly grin. "I bet your know-how has routed some pretty tough customers."

Harry continues as if Mason hadn't spoken. "And of course, you already know Constance Shaw."

Ravi and Nate part, and Constance drops her invisibility spell, Griswold hissing at her feet, striped tail held high.

"We meet again, Heart's Final Knell," Constance says.

"You!" Hartnell's smile becomes a snarl.

He flinches at the dig of Harry's fingers. Val saunters into view, sunglasses discarded, blue-white flame chiseling her features. The demon's eyes dart wildly as he realizes too late he's been flanked on every side.

"That whoreson time wizard fucked up *again*," he growls, then his face splits into an oily smile. "Surely, we can come to a deal. There's no reason our antagonistic past has to dictate our futures, now does it?"

Constance grins sweetly. "Past, present, or future, there's nowhere you could go where I wouldn't seek to end you, demon."

Something about that rings a little bell for Ravi, a suspicion of a revelation that he shelves to the back of his mind to inspect later.

Constance opens her little gold handbag and pulls out

a leather-wrapped hilt. She continues drawing it forth, past the cross guard and on and on into a long, long blade, until she has gripped in both hands a hefty, gleaming broadsword.

"Do you recognize it, demon? This is the blade my cousin Able forged by his own hand, the very blade he sank into your heart when we had you at long last trapped. The blade you tore from your chest and slew him with." She lifts it aloft, tightening her grip.

"A mere blade against a Prince of Hell?" Hartnell sneers. "It did not kill me then, thou trollop, but by all means, why don't you give it another go? These witch-hunters already have you in their sights. I cannot wait to wear your skin, witch. Go ahead and—"

"Such incessant prattle." Constance rolls her eyes and plunges the broadsword straight through him.

Smugness turns to flabbergasted dismay as Hartnell looks down at his cloven chest, the sword exiting neatly through his back with a wet, grinding hiss. His mouth flaps open, speech trying to form. But Constance twists the blade until its hilt is horizontal, and any last words the demon might have had are lost in a gurgle.

The body crumples backward, sliding off Constance's red-slick broadsword and hitting the ground with a thud. A rising clamor starts up among the nearby crowd. To all appearances, a well-known and highly regarded Branch Director just got stabbed by one of the Chosen's entourage. Harry and the others break off to confront the crowd, and no doubt Ravi will have to help explain the situation in another moment, but for now he hangs back with Constance. It's been a big night for the entire team, to say the least, but especially for the two of them.

"You okay?" he asks, a weather eye on the corpse in case Hartnell prepared any tricks, but looks like the urumi did its job well. Behind them, mingled voices argue and bicker, a loudening din that Harry cuts through with a well-placed counterpoint.

Hackles raised, Griswold spits at the demon, strutting at his mistress's feet. "Fie, churl! To oblivion with thee!"

Constance stares at her fallen foe as the body begins to blacken into ash and bone, bloodied broadsword loose in her hand. "Ravi. Have you heard it said that vengeance is never worth the cost? That revenge is but a hollow and joyless victory?"

"Yeah. Yeah, I've heard that."

She looks up, beaming. "Absolute tosh. I feel better than I have in ages."

Chapter Twenty-Three

THE NEXT FEW weeks are a busy whirlwind of consortium meetings and restructuring committees, but thanks to the vociferous support of all the Trusties who had been present to witness the disaster firsthand, they haven't been met with even a fraction of the pushback Ravi had feared. Jihan Kataraju was one of the first to own up to his responsibility for unknowingly allowing a demon to infiltrate the ranks of The Trust, which went a long way to convincing any of Harry's detractors to publicly throw in their support and vow to mend the rift that has been allowed to fester within the old families.

Ravi doubts the initial swell of goodwill will last

forever, but it's a good start.

"Whatcha doing, babe? Moving around planters?" Nate tucks up behind Ravi to put his chin on his shoulder, pawing sleepily for a steaming mug of coffee. Dawn light pours in through the windows, glinting off the black and chrome of Ravi's kitchen counter.

"Mm-hm." Ravi swaps out one small succulent on the upper level of the counter for a slightly larger one, then rests against the warm bulwark of Nate's frame and takes a sip of black cinnamon coffee. "Just rearranging a little."

Nate hums as he drinks, sliding a hand over Ravi's stomach in a gentle, unhurried caress. "Whuzzat, so they all get an equal amount of sun?" He muffles a yawn against the fall of Ravi's hair.

"Not exactly," Ravi admits. "I think maybe Chloe and Frida don't like being next to each other. Just swapping them out to see if they look any happier after a few days."

Nate's mug meets black quartz with a firm click. "I can't handle how cute you are. I mean, c'mon, dude." He turns Ravi around, plucks away his coffee cup, and slides both hands into Ravi's hair, easing into a series of deep, sweet kisses, murmuring between each one, "A little cacti soap opera, I swear to God. How'm I supposed to deal with that? Weaponized adorability. S'unfair."

Ears warm, Ravi ducks his head, though not enough to

discourage more kissing. "All part of a cunning strategy to keep you invested."

"It's working." The kiss grows more heated. Long fingers sneak under the cottony hem of Ravi's pants before Nate reluctantly pulls back with a frustrated groan. "Dammit, there's no time. I gotta run to my place quick before hitting the campus. Wish I could help you get everything set up, but the start of the school year is always brutal."

Ravi traces a touch up Nate's forearms. "Don't worry about it. Val is going to meet me at the lake house to help out, and Constance is joining in once she wraps up at the magic shop. Should be fine."

"I'll be over as soon as I can. Three at the latest. I promise." Nate hastily gulps down coffee. His untrimmed five-o'clock shadow is noticeably rougher in the morning, more of a seven- or eight-o'clock.

"You know," Ravi wheedles, tipping up off his heels to nip a bite at the stubble's edge, where it meets sensitive throat. "You wouldn't be in such a rush if you kept a go-bag here at my place like I have stashed at yours."

A laugh rumbles in Nate's chest only to stutter at the press of Ravi's teeth. "*Stashed,* so secret agency. It's a drawer, babe, you have a drawer at my place. But you're right, I really should keep some work clothes here. Especially if *someone* is going to keep being such a tempting distraction, making me late. That's you," he adds helpfully, smudging a kiss to Ravi's temple.

Ravi grins. "Well, I'll just have to tempt you later."

Nate's gaze lingers, drinking in the sight of Ravi's unkempt morning visage. "Out of academic curiosity, how quick do you think you can come if I suck your cock right here?"

The breath escapes Ravi's lungs all at once; he'd have to send out a search party to have any chance of getting it back. He props his hands behind him on the counter to keep from swaying.

Nate licks his lips. Just that sight and the promise of more has Ravi half hard already. "Like, under two minutes?" Nate asks, brows raised high. "Because I can definitely spare that."

With a regretful sigh, he reels Nate in for a chaste but heartfelt kiss. "You better go, *jaan*. You deserve to be savored." His voice roughens. "We can satisfy that academic curiosity of yours after the party."

Nate's cheeks go pink. "Sweet talker." He finishes his coffee dregs in another long swallow. "Okay, okay, I'm going."

Before he does, Nate plants a kiss on Ravi's cheek.

"Happy Diwali, sunshine."

*

THERE'S A LOT to be done for the party, and Ravi wants to do it right. Arrange it himself, not rely on event planners and caterers. A small, simple affair. The first on his list of errands is to check his PO Box, then he's got to hit the grocery store, make sure to grab enough cucumbers for the kappa, and meet up with Val to start hanging lights. Considering Diwali is the eponymous Festival of Lights, that job is likely to take a while.

Under the usual assortment of mail, a plain, flat brown package lurks at the bottom of his PO Box. The name and address are printed directly on the white shipping label, no return address included.

Ravi checks the post office from his peripheral vision, assessing possible threats, checking for clear exits. It *could* just be an innocent package. But it's been weeks without so much as a hint of Cayenne, and while Ravi can hope like hell they're going to accept their defeat at the Gala gracefully, his optimism has limits.

Ravi is already used to constantly looking over his shoulder for monsters, to preparing for the worst, always vigilant for danger; so now he's just got to be perennially alert for any signs of his murderous ex too. No big deal.

He stifles a weary sigh and carries the package outside

into the brisk autumn air to a nearby park bench, well away from any bystanders, and opens it. Inside is a tablet of a familiar brand, but the design is thinner than he's used to, the material subtly different. When Ravi flips it over, his heart trips.

A Post-it note reads, *This is your choice. Just yours.* The i's aren't dotted with hearts this time, but the handwriting is unmistakable.

The surface comes to life as he rests his fingers on the glass, powering on immediately. He braces himself for anything—a live video feed, some kind of magic time portal, who the fuck knows—but all the tablet shows is a long list of video files, each one having been filmed with a timestamp minutes after the previous. The first one has been named WATCH_THIS_FIRST!!.mp6.

Harry warned him this might happen. "A hoovering attempt," she called it, "to suck you back in."

Ravi sets the tablet aside and puts his head in his shaking hands. He just wants this to be over. To move on. To not have the worst mistake of his life forever dogging his steps, nipping at his heels, setting snares to catch him unawares. He wants…some modicum of closure.

Fuck it. He hits play.

The first astonishing thing he notices is that they're *older*. Hair long, a few barely perceptible lines around the eyes, a faint dusting of freckles over the bridge of their nose.

"*Bonjour*, Ravi. Um. Hi. So." Cayenne clears their throat, eyes darting away from the camera. "If you're watching this, then you have decided to…to watch this. *Ugh*, sorry. I actually did rehearse this, if you can believe it." They rub a nervous forefinger over one copper eyebrow.

"Okay, so first thing, the tablet's been set up so we can record videos and talk that way. If you want to. I hope you do. But…this isn't about what I hope. James helped me set it up. It involves a lot of *stunningly* boring quantum technobabble I honestly tuned out, but if you record a video on the tablet in *your* time, it'll show up here in *my* time, and I can record one back. It's… I thought it would be better than springing another chalk circle on you and meeting in person. As much as I want to. Don't watch anything out of order, or maybe the tablet explodes? I *really* should have listened better."

Cayenne hesitates, then looks directly into the camera lens. "In case you only watch this one video and then throw the tablet in the trash—which, *entirely* fair—then I must tell you something. I just… *Putain.*" They shift, wriggling low in the frame. "I… You said you wanted me out of your life. And I took you back to *before* you said that, in that other timeline…and…I understand now what that means. What that…makes me."

They grind the heels of their hands against their eyes. "*Merde*. I'm… I don't expect this will make a difference to you, but I'm sorry. Even *telling* you that I'm sorry is for *me*, not… *Ugh*. Fuck, fuck, fuck. The fact that I am sorry doesn't obligate you to forgive me in any way, I know that. So." They breathe out, as if relieved to have that out of the way. "Plus, there's that whole helping a demon unleash Hell on Earth thing. That wasn't *great*, granted, but I'm less sorry about that."

Cayenne tips their head to one side, a new, thoughtful wrinkle appearing between their brows. "You know why I think there are so few of us chronomages? Not because we die from accidentally poofing into walls or whatever. I think we go mad from all the folded-up time we cause. From trying to fix our mistakes. I— *Putain*, this was *not* supposed to be me talking about myself. If there's anything you want to say to me, any questions I can answer, *anything* I can do for you…" Cayenne raises a palm up, an offering. "Hit record."

The video ends.

Ravi inhales a long breath of crisp air, and hits record.

"You're the one who's been helping us. Our mysterious benefactor. You in the future sabotaging yourself in the past." He hits stop, scrolls down to the next video and hits play.

"Aha," Cayenne says with a wan smile, "yes, *c'est moi.*

A maddeningly tricky needle to thread, you wouldn't believe. It's been a full-time job figuring out how to undo what I did back then without destroying everything altogether. Some of it wasn't actually *helping* you, *per se*, like luring Val away from the Gala, but it was the only way to work out the right sequence of events. Yes, *me*, doing work." They scoff a bit, lips twisted into something almost resembling a smile. "Good thing past-me is—what's that American expression? It's such a good one. Ah, yes—like a monkey fucking a football," they say with double-edged, self-effacing relish.

"I've always been the worst kind of fool, and after we met…Well. I never had anything to lose, before you. It's the most dangerous I've ever been. That's saying something, considering I used to be a time assassin."

The video plays on and Cayenne keeps talking. Ravi heaves a sigh, head tipping back. What's the point of this? Five seconds of a half-hearted apology before five minutes of self-absorbed monologuing?

"James has been a big help," Cayenne says grudgingly, rolling their eyes. "He's the fucking worst, and I hate him, but he's also kind of the only friend I have. *Si dépriment*, oof."

"What do you want?" Ravi bluntly asks in the next video. "A thanks?"

"No, *mon ch*— Sorry. Habit." They clear their throat. "I

want you to know that I'm not going to bother you again. No version of me will. I've made sure. No…no drunken phone calls, or…or any more schemes, or tricks or…" Cayenne presses their hands over their eyes for a long moment. "I told you that I am not a good person. I did that a lot. I figured, well, they've been warned. I've been honest from the start, and if I'm not believed? That's not on me. Because it's so much easier to just admit I'm awful and say there's no point in trying to be anything else."

Ravi hits record. "You *really* do like talking about yourself. So, let's do that." He props the tablet on his knees and crosses his arms over his chest. "Let's talk about you, Cayenne.

"Île du Diable, a French penal colony, opened off the South American coast by the city of Cayenne in the early 1850s. Some years later, an illegitimate redhead was born to a half-Lokono woman and one of the wardens. Sixteen years go by with no further mention. Then there's some kind of accident. Something bad. A lot of people die. Accounts get rocky. Accounts from Paris, over fifty years later, are even worse. Kind of hard to track crimes that never *technically* happened. Though your disposal of Marquette was pretty public."

Ravi isn't entirely sure what to expect when he plays the next video, but it's definitely not the soft, warm smile

Cayenne wears. "You have good investigators, my—" They swallow the endearment unsaid. "I thought I erased everything from Guyane."

Good investigators. Ravi huffs a mirthless laugh. Cayenne always did seem surprised when he figured something out for himself.

Cayenne stares off into the distance for several heartbeats. "I thought if you knew, I'd be… I don't know. Unsettled. Angry. But as it turns out, it's nice to be known. Cayenne isn't entirely a *nomme de guerre*. My grandmother took care of me, when I was very young. She would call me Aji, her little red pepper. Everyone else in the village called me Ghost, for obvious reasons." Cayenne holds their hands up in frame, waggling their fingers. "But she got sick. They had doctors, of course, but not for the natives. Not for the whores." They shrug, picking at their fingernails. "When my father took me in, it was quite a noble act of Christian charity, he was always sure to remind me."

Ravi curses under his breath as he hits record. "What do you *want*, Cayenne? Why did you send this tablet to me? Were you hoping for my *sympathy*?"

Cayenne sags. "*Non*, though I'm sure you feel some anyway. Can't help yourself, you poor thing. You're a good person, Ravi. The best person. I've never met anyone better, and don't think I ever will. I did this because I want you to be *happy*. And you won't ever be, if you are always expecting me to jump out of the bushes, or something."

Cayenne sits up very straight, lifting their chin. "After this, you won't ever see or hear from me again. I've broken every other promise I've made you, but this one I'll keep, I swear it, Ravi. You can… You can have your Trust to guide as you see fit. Your legacy secured. Your team, your friends, your work, your family, your…lover. Everything you wanted, all out in the open. No more hiding yourself away, my darling." They swallow hard. "Sorry. That one slipped out."

Ravi quells an angry growl. "How *generous* of you."

Cayenne groans, covering their face. "I'm not saying this right. All of that? All of those things? *You* chose them, Ravi, you worked for it. I'm not *letting* you have it, fuck, that's not… I'm not very good at this."

"Did you send the urumi to Harry?" Ravi demands, stabbing the play icon the instant his video stops recording.

Cayenne has slightly shifted in the next video, different trees as their backdrop. Their hair is now tied back in a low tail. "No," they say, with a sly smile. "You did."

Ravi just sends back a two second clip of him staring flatly, unimpressed.

"No sense of stagecraft," they mutter, then begin to speak with expressive twists of their hands. "Past-me—

airport-era-me—tucked the urumi far in the future, almost to the limits I can travel. It's been sitting there in that Moscow safe untouched since then. Bear with me, this gets a little loopy." They swoop their fingers in a crisscrossing X. "So current-me, me *now*, can go and get it, box it up, and have it sent back to *your* present time in a safety deposit box. As a gift."

Ravi massages his temples. "That… Cayenne, that makes no *fucking* sense, why would I want that?"

"I said bear with me! So, you'll have the urumi, plus one more thing I can also put in that safety deposit box." They hold up a silver pocket watch and give it a wiggle. "For one hour in 2016 you are *actually* in 2015, battling that ice monster thing in Chicago! Remember? The first time you met me. One hour where you won't be in two places at once, where you can't overlap yourself. Once I calibrate the watch with chronal energy, you can take the urumi to the post office, zap back to that moment in time, and mail it to Harry. You click the watch again, and you're back!"

They grin, bright and expectant, as the video ends.

The tablet tumbles to the grass as Ravi pushes to his feet. He paces back and forth in front of the bench half a dozen times, raking his nails into deep furrows through his hair. He regrets ever hitting play.

"What the *fuck*, Cayenne? Is this…is this how it always

happened? Am I stuck in some *fucking* time travel bullshit *loop*? This is…" He grinds his teeth. "Do I have any free will at all?"

"Oh, no, no, darling, of course you do. This is *completely* up to you. That's the whole *point*. Don't do it if you don't want to." Cayenne gives a careless shrug. "Your timeline will change, and something different will happen. Pick it up and maybe the urumi will go to you, maybe it'll find Harry anyway, maybe it'll go to someone else, maybe you can just throw it away. *I* don't fucking know. And the free will thing? That's probably the main reason why everyone from seers to otherworldly beings to the gods themselves hate chronomancers. We make things…sticky."

"*Sticky*," Ravi reels. "Yeah."

Cayenne's lips trace an amused curve. "You've gotten very adept at sarcasm, *mon tig*— *Désolé*, sorry, I'll stop doing that. The pet names. I'm told it's 'emotional manipulation.'" They hook their fingers into air quotes and roll their eyes.

"Can the urumi stay there in that future safe without sending it to me? Harry already has it now, so…"

Cayenne's next video starts with them rocking a hand side to side, their expression uncertain. "Maybe? More likely it'll overlap itself someday, or even shift its tether. Like *you* did at…at the Gala. If it does, that's bad news. *Things* don't usually work like *people* with time travel, but I don't know if a divinely forged, wisdom-granting, memory-carrying weapon might be an exception. You can roll the dice if you like. It's totally up to you." They move as if to end the video, then stiffen in alarm. "*Obviously* don't try to bring both swords into the same place at the same time, that would be *catastrophically* bad."

Ravi glares narrowly. "Can I just say what absolute fucking horseshit it is that you've dumped this insane choice in my lap? This is supposed to be a gift? An apology? How is this *burden* supposed to make me happy?"

Cayenne throws both hands up high. "Look, I don't know what to tell you. This is how Harry gets the fucking thing. I'm sorry. I can't unsteal it. The best I can do is return it to you, the rightful owner. After that, what you do with it is your decision. *Your* choice."

Ravi pauses, finger hovering over the record icon. There's a fair point in there somewhere, he's loath to admit. He sets the tablet aside and laces his fingers together behind his neck, elbows out, and leans back, face tipped up to the sky. He stays like that for a long time.

"Tell me what my future is like," he says when he finally starts another clip. "Right now. Keeping on the path I'm already on."

Cayenne is leaned far over, holding the tablet between their knees. They shake their head in flat refusal. "You wouldn't thank me for that. Seers have it worse, but the Cassandra problem exists with time travel too. What if I say something that puts you in jeopardy? Even little things can have big consequences. Maybe you go left when you would have gone right. Zig when you should have zagged." They trace a vague shape into the air. "What if I influence you so that you don't…fuck if I know, buy the right kind of car and you *crash*, or don't pack the right weapons and end up short of bullets when you need them most? Or if your timeline is off by just a *little* bit, and you don't cross the street at the right time, or if you have one kid instead of twins, or if you miss a vital warning that would have helped in a fight? It's too risky, I can't tell you. I'm sorry."

"Twins?"

When the video starts, Cayenne's head is cocked in puzzlement. "Who said anyt—" Their eyes widen with alarm. "*Putain de bordel de merde!* Fuck, I've already started this video, I can't delete the last one. Oh, fuck." Cayenne drops their head into their hands with a heavy groan until the only thing on-screen is the part of their hair. "Unbelievable. *Very* nicely done, *je suis une stupide mousson.*" They pull their face up out of their hands, wearing a strained smile. "Just kidding. Forget I said that. Another classic Cayenne lie."

"Send me the urumi," Ravi says firmly.

"Ravi, *je jure devant Dieu*, I didn't mean to say that."

"Cayenne, as with every shitty thing you have ever done to me, your intention doesn't matter as much as the result. Send it. The watch too."

Cayenn's eyes are considerably redder at the start of the next video. "Okay. You're right. I never listened then, but I am now. Whatever you want, Ravi."

"*What I want*," Ravi grates. "I want this to be the last time I ever deal with you *or* time travel for the rest of my days. I want to close this chapter of my life and move on."

"The last time. Ravi. I…" Cayenne bites their lip nearly bloodless. "*Mon Dieu*, I hate goodbyes."

As the video records, Ravi turns to watch the sky for a moment, sparrows wheeling around the spreading oaks. "There's a custom in India. To never really say goodbye. Because if you do, it implies you're never going to see each other again."

Ravi faces the screen head-on, and through unknown quantities of time and space, by some alchemy of technology and magic, his gaze meets Cayenne's. One deep, measured breath, then he lets it go.

"Goodbye, Cayenne."

A rueful smile. "Goodbye, Ravi."

It's the last file on the tablet.

Epilogue

FESTIVITY PREPARATIONS ARE well underway by the afternoon. Every eave and window frame of the lake house is liberally adorned with white lights, enough to light up the whole street when daylight fades. Constance lent her artistic skills to help lay out *rangolis* in colored sand and spices at every entrance and had even taken off her boots without complaint to join Ravi and Val indoors, placing candles and diya lamps on every available surface. The lamps won't be lit until sundown, but even so, Ravi is delighted with the results, the space transformed into a proper holiday display. Bright flowers and the aroma of spices tug at a thread of nostalgia Ravi hadn't even realized was stitched in him.

Harry and Nate arrive about the same time. After admiring the rangoli mandalas, they both toe off their shoes and carefully step over them into the house. Nate came straight from work, messenger bag slung over his shoulder, whereas Harry juggles a loose assortment of bottles weighing down each arm.

"Did I ever tell you I was a bartender for a brick when I was nineteen?" Harry says by way of greeting, bumping her shoulder into Ravi's as she heads toward the dining room. "I'm gonna be the party mixologist, it'll be great. Might as well leave all this here, I figure." She shrugs the bottles up, glass clinking. "Don't really need it at my place, so I might as well stock the bar here. What the fuck am I gonna make with green chartreuse and Aperol and all that fancy shit, anyway?" She disappears behind the door frame, then pokes her head back out to say, "The house looks awesome, by the way. We're still doing poker later, right?" Not waiting for his answer, she vanishes again, only for two other distant female voices to ring out in welcome.

Ravi smiles at Nate. "Hi."

"Hey there, handsome." Nate grins back, hanging up his bag and cardigan before rolling up his sleeves to the elbows. "Ready to get cookin'?"

"I'll give it a shot, but you should probably keep your expectations low." Ravi steps close to kiss Nate, a flutter rising in his breast. "Though if you need takeout reheated, I'm your guy."

Nate leans into the kiss with a pleased hum. "That you are. You'll be fine. You can be on slicing and dicing duty. You're great with knives." As he looks Ravi over, he tilts his head to the side, the warmth in his smile gathering a mischievous edge. "Whoa, how did Milan ship you another bespoke T-shirt so quickly?"

Despite himself, Ravi laughs. "You know what, Doc? You're a real comedian."

*

BY THE TIME the sun hits the treetops, Ravi's hard at work on the second of Harry's well-made Tequila sunrises. A multicultural array of snacks and desserts covers the kitchen island. Nate's gluten-free poutine hits the exact middle mark between delightful and disgusting, in Ravi's opinion and to Nate's great amusement. However, his replica of Ravi's favorite coconut shrimp is so spot-on that Val teleports out to bring back a plate from Kerala itself for a taste-test comparison. While the original is spicier, Ravi declares Nate's version as more flavorful. Nate flushes all the way to his hairline, grinning happily. He pushes his reading glasses up the bridge of his nose and busies himself with the recipes, offering suggestions and helpful techniques as Ravi takes a stab at a few simple dishes.

To Ravi's complete shock, the micchar turns out okay. The curry leaves got a little over-crispy in the fryer, but he'd learned the trick of it for the gulab jamun. The dish won't win any beauty contests, but all the right flavors and textures are present and accounted for. Constance proclaims herself a big fan of the saffron syrup, at times bypassing the sweet fried dumplings in favor of spooning up the sauce alone.

"A king's ransom in saffron," she chirps with delight. "'Tis like cooking with gold."

"Some people do that," Nate mentions, biting into a dumpling while aiming a thumbs-up at Ravi. Ravi's ears warm as he finds an unexpectedly deep well of satisfaction that he was actually able to *make* something, to do something useful off the battlefield. "Gold flakes in fancy desserts and such."

Harry's socked feet swing from her perch on the counter. "I brought Goldschläger. I can throw saffron, black pepper, and penicillin in it to create the ultimate blow-your-medieval-mind cocktail."

"Every day in this land is a revelry of obscene decadence," Constance laughs. "Hot showers 'blow my mind' well enough without wasting fine spices. I've only heard of saffron before I came here, though we called it something else. 'Blood of the crocus,' or near enough. How do you say saffron in your native tongue, my friend?"

"Which one, Hindi?" Ravi leans a hip on the counter and takes another sip of his Tequila sunrise. Harry fixed it strong, and his head is a little light and floaty. "*Kesara.*"

Constance repeats it, but Val shakes her head and suggests, "More emphasis on the first syllable."

This time Constance puts on a terrible, exaggerated Indian twist that makes Ravi laugh out loud, coughing into his drink.

Harry's eyes go very round. "Okay, definitely not like that. New rule, none of that. No drama club dialect work."

"Aw," Ravi complains. "I have a really good generic white guy impression."

"You do? Never mind what I said, I have to hear this *immediately.*"

"Seconded," Nate is quick to add, hastily swallowing a gravy-laden fry.

Ravi sets down his drink. He props both fists on his hips, glances imperiously around at the spread of food, and bellows, "You fellas got any ranch dressing?"

Val catches Harry before she slides off the counter and hits the floor, laughing fit to burst. When Nate can speak again, clutching at his sides, he wipes moisture from the corner of his eyes.

"Oh, *fuck*, that's uncanny."

Ravi grins.

Constance pats him on the arm. "I do believe I'm missing some cultural keystone here, but 'tis quite a thing to see you in such jovial spirits, nephew-to-be."

She squeaks in surprise as Ravi pulls her into a brief hug. "Yeah. Thanks, Constance." He steps back with a bright smile for his team. "Who's ready for some poker before we light up the fireworks?"

*

IN THE BACKYARD, lights strung overhead and the air still redolent of smoke and powder from sparklers and ground fountains, a thin sliver of the rising moon reflects off the rippling surface of the lake.

Val sits cross-legged on the grass, Constance braiding her hair into complicated plaits while the angel relates a tale to Nate; the story of the first time she ever beheld fireworks, long ago in China. Rapt, Nate absorbs the story with obvious delight, occasionally interjecting with clarifying questions, jotting notes in a Moleskine journal. Vibrating with loud purrs, Griswold rolls over in Val's lap, paws in the air while he graciously accepts belly pets.

Ravi smiles, stealthily extricating himself from the group. Out past the warm glow cast by the lights, Harry sits by herself on the lakeside bench. As he pads over the grass, she lobs a cucumber into the lake. It hits the water with a fair bit of force, more of a *bloop* than a splash.

"You trying to feed the kappa or knock it out, *qaatil?*" He settles in next to her, both arms spread across the back of the bench.

"Little of column A, little of column B. What's *qaatil?* Sweet apple of my eye? Loveliest of betrotheds?" She bats her lashes with exaggerated sweetness.

He grins. "Killer."

Harry slaps a hand over her mouth to cover a loud guffaw. "Oh, fuck you, man," she says through laughter. "Kill a guy *once* and he never lets you hear the end of it."

Ravi chuckles, stretching out his legs in the grass.

Harry sighs, looking up at the moon. "Still can't believe how bad Val kicked our asses. You could barely see her over that pile of chips."

"She slow-played us. Nate's right, we should take her to Vegas."

"Casino-based monsters, beware." Harry gives him a sideways glance. "You gonna tell me what's been on your mind all evening?"

He makes a face before he can pull up a mask of impassivity. "*Detectives.* No fair. You've been plying me with alcohol all night."

"If it makes you feel better, I'm sure no one else noticed. Your super-spy game remains strong." Harry kicks her feet out, mirroring his body language. "Trust stuff bothering you? Somebody's arm you need me to twist?"

"No, that's all progressing better than expected." Ravi tips his head back for a moment to enjoy the night air. As usual with mission debriefs, he starts with the most salient point and works his way out. "Cayenne from the future got in touch." Harry sits up very straight, and he waves a hand to allay her concerns. "Not in person. I'm fine, really. They assured me that their past self will never bother us again. I'm actually inclined to believe it."

Harry gives Ravi a long, slow blink. "Kind of a lot to absorb there, champ. The fuck." She pinches the bridge of her nose and crosses her legs underneath her. He gives her a few moments. After a bit she sighs, twisting the pearl on her finger. "Okay, so, future Cayenne *is* our mysterious helper. That sucks *so fucking hard*."

Owing any measure of their success to any version of Cayenne does, indeed, suck extremely fucking hard. But Ravi's hard-pressed to muster up any indignation or out-rage. It is what it is, and Ravi's made his choices to be on the path he's now on. He regrets none of them, and *that* is an incredibly freeing feeling.

"Yeah. Hence why I wanted to keep this to myself until

later. I wanted to…have a nice time, just for us. For the team."

"And it's been a genuine delight, seriously you've gone above and beyond, but did you just *hence* me? Hence! You've been banging too many dishy professors, dude. Next it'll be *therefores*."

"Just the right amount of dishy professors, I think." Ravi's grin fades. "There's one more thing."

"Uh-oh. Is this another bandage off moment?"

"Cayenne sent me the urumi as a gift, and the choice whether or not to send it to you in the past."

In the ensuing silence, a distant whip-poor-will calls out, perhaps a final farewell to autumn before it flies off for more southern climes.

"Wow, okay," Harry huffs, holding her hands palms out, "shittiest gift ever."

Ravi barks out a laugh. "Right?" Unable to tamp down his misgivings, he looks at her askance. "I'm sorry, Harry."

"Dude, do nooooot apologize," Harry groans, lolling her head to the back of the bench. "Because I totally get the whole, like, kaleidoscopic implications of your decision backwards and forwards. And yeah, sure, it's a *lot*, and it's not all roses for either of us, but… There's *no* telling what our lives would have been like if events would have gone differently. And I'm kinda coming around on the whole…

you know. Being Chosen thing. I don't know. Work in progress. So, I'm not going to ask why you decided to send me the urumi. I know that's a layered thing. Like a complicated lasagna." She stacks her hands on top of one another. "Nice work on sidestepping forensics, by the way. Clean work."

Her tone goes unexpectedly tentative. "I do have a question though. I've... You've never been salty with me about it. Me being Chosen instead of you. Not even once. You spent your life preparing and training for it, expecting it, counting on it, and...nobody would blame you for being royally pissed off that the noodle sword would even give me the time of day, much less bond to me. But you've been in my corner from the word go. *Why?*"

All Ravi can do is give her the honest truth. "Because you'll be a better Chosen than I would have been. I wouldn't have pulled together a team like you have. I wouldn't have made friends, and allies, and improved the lives of everyone around me the way you have. I'd have tried to lone wolf it, been thoroughly miserable, and probably already be dead. Permanently, I mean." He smiles, bumping his shoulder into hers. "*Therefore,* I'm glad I got assigned to you, Harry McAllister."

She sways with the contact, and when she rocks back into place, she lets herself rest against his side. They sit in companionable silence for a few minutes, listening to the others laugh and talk.

Eventually Harry clears her throat and speaks. "If you think the Pepper was telling the truth—*it's a Diwali miracle!*—about leaving us alone, then that's a big fucking relief. Because we've got a job."

"Oh?"

"I also didn't wanna spoil the vibe, kept it under my hat. But Bobby dropped me a line. He thinks something fishy is going on in Boston. Possible haunting, or maybe something worse." She levels a toothy smile his way. "Whaddya say to a good old-fashioned monster hunt?"

"Hell, yeah," he says, returning the grin. "I'll back your play."

*

AFTER THE OTHERS have gone home, Ravi gets to work extinguishing the dozens of candles still burning. He's halfway through with the living room when Nate appears in the doorway, drying his hands on a kitchen towel.

"Now *this* is some mood lighting," he remarks, tossing the towel back into the kitchen. "That was really nice, babe. Looks like we can add party planning to your list of marketable skills."

"It's surprising how many battlefield tactics can be applied to social gatherings." If Nate likes the ambiance, Ravi decides to leave a few diya lamps still burning.

"I think Sun Tzu said that once," Nate chuckles, and as he moves into the room, Ravi can see what he means by mood lighting. The lamplight paints Nate's handsome features in stark relief, warm light gilding the cut of his jawline and cheekbones, the clever arch of his brow. Breath catches in Ravi's throat.

"Have a seat," Nate says. "Got something for you."

Remembering Nate's earlier offer, Ravi raises his brows. He arranges himself with arms stretched out over the back of the couch, knees wide, and looks up with a sly curve of his lips.

"You minx," Nate husks, eyes roving. "Sorry to disappoint, it's just a present." He digs into his messenger bag and extracts a neatly wrapped package. He holds it up with a little *ta-da!* and takes a seat next to Ravi, setting the present on his lap.

Ravi pulls his limbs back in from their suggestive sprawl to pick up the gift. About the size of a loaf of bread, and almost light enough to be one. The wrapping paper is vibrant marigold yellow.

"What is… You didn't have to get me anything, Nate."

"Said I would, didn't I?"

"You said you'd get me a *sword,* but I thought you were kidding. And this isn't exactly sword sized."

"You're right, I did say that. Maybe I did *and* I did not get you a sword," Nate says enigmatically. He looks enormously pleased with himself.

Ravi peels back the tape and uncovers a plain pinewood box with a sliding top. Inside, nestled in a bed of shredded excelsior, rests a *bichuwa*. The small dagger looks finely made, with a recurved blade in the shape of a scorpion's sting. The hilt is one solid piece that loops into a highly decorated knuckle guard, etched designs reminiscent of medieval Indian artwork.

"Nate," Ravi breathes, "this is...*really* nice. It looks maybe Mughal era?" He picks it up. Surprisingly well-balanced. Though it looks primarily decorative, the blade has obviously been expertly made. "Where did you get this?"

Nate's grin widens. "I had Val drop me off at the Everglades the other day so I could make a stop at the liminal market."

Astonished, Ravi blinks at Nate. "You went to the Floating Bazaar?"

"I did! I've only ever been to the Snowblind Fete before, up in Iqaluit. Much smaller." An excited glow spreads over Nate's face, a boyish glint in his eyes. "Ravi, the bazaar was *so* cool. All the shops were set up on rafts or boats, and of course it was twilight, so everything was lit by these glowing fish in the water, or by jars of fireflies hanging everywhere. And there was this Baba Yaga-looking lady cooking up kettle corn, and this guy who was a talking tree, and this green elf girl selling human artifacts, it was *amazing.*"

Ravi's jaw drops. "What? That's awesome!"

"I know! You ever been to a liminal market before? I feel like that's gotta be a Trust thing, right? Like a border patrol? Neutral territory or no, I bet anywhere that dimensional planes rub up against each other warrants a little extra scrutiny."

"It is, yeah. There's a Florida branch disguised as a park ranger station, and just about all they do there is keep an eye on the market gate. I've been to a liminal market in Britain. Just a small seasonal one, only open on equinoxes and solstices. A warlock we were after tried to avoid apprehension by running through it."

Nate stretches an arm across Ravi's shoulder, pulling him into a relaxed embrace. The ease with which he does it, the casual intimacy, still takes Ravi's breath away, makes him feel like every time is the first time.

"Did you catch him?"

"Mm-hm. It was actually a lot of fun. I got to knock over a fruit stand, slide across a counter. Classic foot chase stuff."

Nate laughs. "How are you the coolest? Did you have to buy all the fruit?"

"The shop guy tried to make me pay for it with my shadow. I didn't really have time to sightsee, then. All these years stationed so close, and I've never been to the Floating Bazaar."

"I'll take you. I made a few friends I'd love to introduce you to, including this amazing tattoo artist. *Pretty* sure she's related to a Mayan tattoo god. Hardcore. Her linework was incredible. I didn't have time for new ink, or I totally would have gotten something." He presses a kiss to Ravi's temple. "Thought she'd be great for that tiger tatt you've been talking about."

"Of course, you made friends with a tattooist demigod. How are *you* the coolest?"

Nate goes a little pinker. "Also used some of that diamond money and picked up a magical quiver that replenishes any arrows I fire."

"Now *that's* excellent." Anything that keeps Nate a little safer is better than any present. Ravi angles the box on his lap to admire the *bichuwa*. "Thanks for this, *jaan*. It's beautiful." It's a nice dagger. Not exactly easily concealable, or practical to carry into fights, but Nate's not a weapons guy. Ravi can appreciate the gesture regardless.

Nate's smile goes a little sly. "It's got a name and everything."

"Yeah?"

"Uh-huh." Slyness goes downright tricksy, dimples flashing. "Varunastra."

Ravi stares at Nate for a solid fifteen seconds. Then he looks at the *bichuwa*. Then back at Nate. "No, it's not," he whispers, more breath than speech.

"Only one way to find out." Nate gestures encouragingly at the dagger.

"What the… You're telling me that this is Varunastra. From the legends. *The* Varunastra." Ravi blinks, feeling very slow on the uptake. "Varunastra, that the god Varuna created from water and storms. Varunastra, that can assume the shape of any weapon the wielder is familiar with."

"That's the one."

"…*Baap re*." Speaking in hushed tones, Ravi picks the blade up, this time gingerly. "More warriors in history have wielded this than I can count. Karna. Bhishma. *Rama*." Heartstrings twanging sharp, Ravi swallows thickly and looks up. "*Nathaniel*. This is… How did you… I can't—"

"I'm pretty good at giving gifts. It's a talent."

"I… This is *priceless*. How did you…" No amount of diamonds in the world would be enough to pay for a treasure like this. He turns it over in his hands, wondering how it works, how he could ever possibly prove worthy enough to wield it.

"It wasn't cheap," Nate admits with a cluck of his

tongue. "I had to pay in stories."

"*What?*"

"No lie. Like five straight hours of storytelling. I felt like Scheherazade." He slides a hand over Ravi's wrist, angling Varunastra up higher. "So, the myths say that the weapon's abilities can be triggered by meditation and mantras, but the seller said that a strong will could achieve the same thing. *Your* will can pretty much bench press an elephant, so I think you can just want it to be something else, and it will."

"That's… It'll probably take a lot of practice to get ri—" The blade shivers in Ravi's hand and flows like liquid into a long, wickedly curved talwar. He gasps, turning the gleaming scimitar over in his hands. It's beautiful; a pattern of marbled steel, gold, and ivory worked into the hilt. Better yet, it's perfectly balanced, and as light as a fencing épée.

Ravi feels utterly poleaxed. Fuck, he could *have* a poleaxe right now if he wanted.

"What the fuck. *Muhje vishwas nahi ho raha!* This is unbelievable," he quickly translates. "Can it… I've heard it can be any weapon the wielder is familiar with. Can it…?"

It's an ancient legendary weapon, there's no way it can possibly—

The sword shivers again and shifts into a thick-barreled, magnum Desert Eagle hand cannon with muzzle brake and adjustable sights, all in ivory and marbled

Damascus steel. Ravi sucks in a shocked breath. Another thought, and the handgun expands into a fully assembled replica of Ravi's trusty M24 SWS, long-range scope and all, albeit the surface now impossibly tooled in that same intricate Damascus pattern.

"Stylish," Nate remarks cheerfully. "That tracks. Little like you, sunshine."

"Nathaniel *fucking* Corbin," Ravi barks. He phases the sniper rifle into a small rondel dagger and drives it point-down into the surface of the coffee table, heedless of damaging the wood. Nate jumps a little in surprise, but Ravi clambers into his lap, knots his fingers in Nate's hair, and yanks him into a fierce, bruising kiss.

His heart is suddenly too big for his chest to contain, a savage thing full of wildness, ready to break its tether and gallop free.

Ravi slips down off the couch between Nate's knees and shoves them wide. "Let's see how fast I can make *you* come." He flicks up a steely gaze, running his tongue over his lips. "Objections?"

Eyes wide, pupils already blown, Nate swallows hard and shakes his head, legs falling further open in clear invitation.

"Good."

Not wasting any time, Ravi opens Nate's fly and jerks

his pants down his hips, growling with impatience. His mouth already waters, pulse thrumming steady in his veins. Nate's twitching cock fills quickly in Ravi's hand, sending his own arousal climbing. Nate hisses a shocked curse, his hands flying back to grab the couch cushions, a flush claiming his throat. In no time at all, Ravi has Nate exactly where he wants him, hard and heavy in his hands, and gusts a hot breath across sensitive skin before dragging his tongue up in broad, leonine swathes.

Nate gasps, a whimper catching in his chest. "Ravi, fuck—" His head falls back, but his eyes stay locked on Ravi's face, glazed and awestruck.

Ravi's pretty sure that Nate has had more sexual partners than he has, but when Ravi learns a skill, whether it's firing a gun or sucking cock, he dedicates himself wholeheartedly to perfecting it. And right now, he aims to impress. So, he pulls out all the stops, sliding his mouth down around Nate's length, down and further down, giving him the tight squeeze of his throat without hesitation, so deep he has no further to go, nose brushing blond curls.

Nate's hands fist so hard in the couch the fabric creaks. A string of heartfelt, unselfconscious praise trips from his lips, each word stoking Ravi's desire higher.

"Holy *shit*, Ravi, that's… *Nngh*, fuck, you're good with your mouth. Jesus. Perfect, incredible, yeah, babe…"

This amazing, *unbelievable* man went to another dimension, spent hours and hours of effort, and not to mention what must have been days of research, just to buy a gift for him. For Ravi. That alone would be enough to make Ravi's head spin, but Varunastra itself? He can't even conceive of anything more perfect.

Ravi has never felt confident with words, always finding them insufficient when compared to action. How can mere language fully illustrate the depth of his feelings, the way he feels like he's made of molten gold, held in cupped hands and brimming over?

Instead, he casts a hungry look up through his lashes and slings Nate's thigh over his shoulder, yanking Nate bodily down the couch and burying him impossibly deeper down the vise of his throat. He welcomes the stretch, throwing himself into every eager backstroke of his tongue and every rippling swallow.

Nate doesn't last much longer, spilling hot down Ravi's throat while white-knuckling couch cushions, keening and gasping, his curses shattering into nonsense. Grinning, Ravi pulls back, impressed despite himself. A new personal record. Definitely way under two minutes.

"*Guh,*" Nate attempts, his temples damp with sweat. "Wow. Words. I can do those. *Fuck.* So, I uh. I guess y'like your present?" He smiles, voice breathy, and swipes a hand through Ravi's hair, pushing it off his forehead. His eyes crease at the corners, warm and admiring.

Dropping his face to Nate's thigh, Ravi tries to get his expression under control, certain his wild, incautious heart is blindingly obvious. A reckless thing, his heart; unwise as any newborn, but Ravi still wants to give it, to hold it out in his hand like an offering. *Please take this. Please be patient with it, it's new minted.*

"Best present I've ever gotten in my life," he manages against denim, voice thick and mangled. "And I once got a yacht for my birthday."

Nate snorts a laugh and pulls Ravi up onto his lap. He thumbs over Ravi's jaw, nails rasping pleasantly through facial hair.

"You have a yacht?"

"Not anymore. I don't even like sailing. Plus, they're too much upkeep."

"Tell me about it," Nate murmurs against Ravi's lips, mirth tangible in the relaxed sprawl of his limbs. "My family has a canoe up at the lake, and we have to replace the oars every *decade*. Boats, man. Such a hassle." He slides a palm between their bodies, cups Ravi's straining cock through his common-man jeans, and licks into his mouth with a soft moan.

"Fuck, sunshine, I can taste myself on your tongue."

Ravi gasps sharply, bucking into the touch, so hard it's painful. "Nathaniel," he hisses, then demands, "tell me what you want." He pours his yearning into a claiming kiss, more teeth and tongue than anything else.

Nate goes slack under him, heartbeat visible in his throat. He cups Ravi's cheek in his hand, whispering into the kiss, "You," as his tongue swipes over the seam of their joined lips, "just you."

Ravi's heart swoops like an eagle in flight, rising high where the air is thin, lightheaded from altitude. He snakes a hand into Nate's hair and pulls, scraping the edge of his teeth up that bared throat. "Tell me," he insists, or pleads. "Want to hear it. Want to give you what you need, *jaan*. Anything."

Nate shivers. "*Christ*. Need you inside me. Is that okay?"

"Yeah. Need that too."

Nate groans, "Ravi, please, *ruko mat*." The borrowed Hindi sounds lovely with the exotic angularity of Nate's accent. Figures he'd have picked up how to say *don't stop*, having heard it often enough from Ravi. "Did I get that right?"

"*Haan*," Ravi whispers, "perfect."

Nate scrambles for the hem of Ravi's shirt and pulls it off over his head. He surges forward to run the hot brand of his tongue over Ravi's chest, tracing scars. Ravi arches into it, back bowing, the frantic edge to Nate's touch shooting fresh desire straight through him. Ravi eats up every little shudder, each gasp from Nate's lips. He *aches*, pleasantly dizzy with anticipation.

It takes far too long to peel off their clothes, years to crowd themselves together on the narrow couch, another age to retrieve foil packets from their wallets, a millennium before Ravi finally, *finally*, guides Nate up on his knees over Ravi's hips, pressing himself up into that eager heat. The slick velvet slide is enough to make Ravi's eyes roll back in his head, self-control fraying at the edges.

"*Yeah.*" Nate rocks his head back, easing himself down onto Ravi's cock. His sheen of sweat picks up glints from the lamplight and paints him glowing. "Oh, fuck, that's perfect. That's… You feel—" More pupil than iris, Nate's eyes slide shut as words fail him.

"You feel amazing," Ravi rasps, a vast understatement. He looks up, reverent. How had he earned this kind of luck? "*Sundar.*" Beautiful.

Nate grins in a blinding, joyful flash, leaning forward to pin Ravi's wrists above his head, riding him mercilessly. Ravi shudders, every muscle going molten. It'd be the simplest thing to twist out of the restraint, but he can't think of anything he'd rather do less.

The pitch of Nate's voice goes rougher and deeper with

every greedy snap of his hips. Ravi works one hand free to wrap around Nate's cock, hard again so soon, slick with arousal.

"You close?"

Nate nods enthusiastically, teeth grooving a line in his red-bitten bottom lip.

"Good." With a wicked grin, Ravi releases his grip.

Nate lets out a distressed whine. "Oh, you're *mean*."

"You think?"

Still smiling, Ravi takes two handfuls of Nate's ass and grinds up into him for a few slow, languorous strokes, before easing all the way out. Nate barely manages one little noise of complaint before Ravi braces a foot on the floor and flips him over, sending Nate bouncing to his hands and knees while Ravi shifts to kneel behind him.

Nate quickly changes his tune, arms braced on the cushioned armrest, back arched. "Jesus *fuck*, that's hot. Pleasepleaseplease—"

Ravi joins them back together with a glad hiss. "Still think I'm mean?"

"*Absolutely*." Nate shoves himself back, starting up a fast, demanding rhythm Ravi is quick to match. "Don't stop."

Ravi's not going to last, hurtling too close to the edge. He releases tensed, toned thighs to rest a palm over Nate's breastbone, right over his stuttering pulse. Nate clasps Ravi's hand and presses it tight, cleaving so close over his sprinting heart that it feels as if Ravi is holding it bare in his palm.

"Yes," Nate says, and somehow that's the best part.

It hits in a sudden, scorching flood. Ravi drags Nate upright with him, tattooed back pressed to scarred chest as he comes in a sweet, golden rush that rolls up his body in warm, slow waves, honey in his veins. He twines his arms tight around Nate's middle, holding him close as possible to bury his face in the soft fall of cornsilk hair, unable and unwilling to keep a broken-throated shout locked behind his teeth.

Shivering, he presses open-mouthed kisses to the back of Nate's neck, the salt of his skin thick on Ravi's tongue, and strokes Nate through another peak, flushed and shaking, the slick drag of his body fever-hot around Ravi, impossibly good.

Afterwards he drags in breath after breath, head sent weightless and spinning in a way the earlier cocktails hadn't managed to achieve. Ravi swallows hard and clings tighter, separating an unimaginable concept. Nate settles back against him, strong arms up overhead to card his fingers gently through Ravi's sweat-damp hair.

"I…I really like you, Ravi," Nate whispers.

"I really like you too, Nate," he says with quiet certainty. He drags a line of kisses across Nathaniel's shoulders, over the intricate inked branches of his tree. A sturdy, growing thing with deep roots, nourished into an enduring, flourishing profusion of leaves.

"Stay with me here tonight?" Nate asks, voice hoarse, chest hitching. "It's Friday. We can…we can stay together the whole weekend, if you want."

A smile breaks like dawn across Ravi's face. "A weekend is a good start."

Acknowledgements

Thanks to the Quills, to the Loft, to Nirmal, Ritika, and of course to Team Glamour. And a heartfelt thanks to the first-draft readers for getting into a heated argument about Cayenne that let me know I'd really nailed the narcissistic personality disorder.

About the Author

Fox Beckman is an author with a penchant for spicy stories about swords, sorcery, and smooching. A member of both the Loft Literary Center and the Author's Guild, Fox lives in the Twin Cities with too many hobbies and a very patient spouse.

Email

fox@foxbeckman.com

Twitter

@foxbeckman

Website

www.foxbeckman.com

OTHER NINESTAR BOOKS BY THIS AUTHOR

Trust Trilogy

Stolen From Tomorrow

Shards of Trust